THE
CRIMSON
MOTH

ALSO BY
KRISTEN CICCARELLI

Edgewood

THE ISKARI SERIES
The Last Namsara
The Caged Queen
The Sky Weaver

THE
CRIMSON
MOTH

KRISTEN
CICCARELLI

MAGPIE

Magpie an imprint of
HarperCollins*Publishers* Ltd
1 London Bridge Street
London SE1 9GF

www.harpercollins.co.uk

HarperCollins*Publishers*
Macken House,
39/40 Mayor Street Upper,
Dublin 1
D01 C9W8
Ireland

First published by HarperCollins*Publishers* Ltd 2024

3

A catalogue record for this book is available from the British Library.

ISBN: 978-0-00-865056-8 (HB)
ISBN: 978-0-00-865057-5 (TPB)

Printed and bound in the UK using 100% Renewable Electricity by CPI Group (UK) Ltd

FOR THOSE AFRAID TO BE
WHO THEY ARE

Comrades! Only through the death of the old world can we prevent the return of evil. We must destroy these witches and snuff out their magic. Everything is permitted for the sake of this higher aim: freedom from their oppression.

Let their blood stain the streets forever.

—NICOLAS CREED, YOUR GOOD COMMANDER

GIDEON

THE CROSSROADS

THE CAPITAL

MINISTRY OF PUBLIC SAFETY

OLD TOWN

OUTER WARDS

THE DOCKYARDS

THE NEW REPUBLIC

VAST NORTHERN WATERS

SHALLOW BAY

WINTERSEA

THE
ROSEBLOOD
PALACE

SELDOM
HARBOR

OPERA
HOUSE

OAKHAVEN
PARK

TOWN
SQUARE

THE
HARBORFRONT

THORNWOOD
HALL

THE BARROW
STRAIT

RUNE

OVERTURE

WHEN THE BLOOD GUARD suspects a girl of being a witch, they strip off her clothes and search her body for scars.

During the Sister Queens' rule, witches wore their casting scars with pride, putting their power on display like jeweled rings and silk garments. Scars signaled wealth and rank, and most of all, *magic*.

Now they marked the hunted.

The last time Rune laid eyes on a witch's scars was two years ago, after the witch queens were murdered in their beds and the blood of their council flowed in the streets. The Blood Guard seized control of the city, and the purgings began.

It was sunset when a surging crowd gathered at the center of the fog-soaked city. Rune stood among them, unable to unsee the thirsty, fevered looks around her. The people wanted vengeance. Wanted to gulp it down like a rich red wine.

The gulls shrieked overhead as the old witch stumbled up the steps to the purging platform. Unlike those who came after her, the crone neither wept nor begged for mercy, but met her fate with a stoic glare. The Blood Guard ripped one sleeve from her shirt, revealing the evidence of her crimes: patterned scars flowing down her left arm, etched like delicate white lacework against her golden skin.

Rune couldn't help but find them beautiful. Once a sign of superior status, the scars were now impossible to hide, making the old woman easy prey for witch hunters.

It was why Rune never cut herself.

She couldn't afford to let them find the scars.

ONE

RUNE

MIRAGE: (n.) the lowest and most basic category of spell.

Mirage Spells are simple illusions held for short periods that require little blood. The fresher the blood, the stronger the magic, and the easier casting will be.

—*From* Rules of Magic *by Queen Callidora the Valiant*

*L*IGHTNING SNAKED ACROSS THE sky as Rune Winters made her way through the wet forest, barely sheltered from the rain by the pine canopy overhead. Her lantern's glow lit the path before her, its surface broken by twisted roots and pools of rainwater.

It was a terrible night for casting. The rain seeped through her cloak, the dampness loosening the spellmarks she'd drawn on her wrist in blood. She needed to redraw the symbols before the rain washed them away entirely, taking her magic with them.

The illusion disguising Rune had to hold until she knew for certain Seraphine wouldn't kill her.

As a former advisor to the Sister Queens, Seraphine Oakes was a powerful witch. And after two years of searching, Rune had finally tracked her down. Now that she had, what would she find at the top of this wooded headland—friend or foe?

Rune worried her lip with her teeth as she remembered her grandmother's last words to her, two years ago.

Promise me you'll find Seraphine Oakes, my darling. She'll tell you everything I couldn't.

After the Blood Guard arrested Nan and dragged her from the house, they smeared a bloody X across the front door, declaring to everyone that an enemy of the Republic had been found within and was on her way to be purged.

The memory of that day stabbed like a knife.

An anxious hum buzzed in Rune's blood as she continued onward. Like an overture, growing louder and faster. If Seraphine saw through the illusion cloaking Rune before hearing her out, she might expel Rune from her house—or worse, strike her dead.

Because wherever Rune Winters went, her carefully crafted reputation came with her.

She was an informer. A witch hater. A darling of the New Republic.

Rune was the girl who betrayed her grandmother.

It's why she'd disguised herself as an old peddler tonight, leading a mule laden with goods. The smell of wet donkey hung in the air, and her load of pots and pans clattered with the beast's every step—each detail summoned into being by the magic in Rune's blood and held together by the symbols drawn on her wrist, binding the spell to her.

It was a Mirage—the most basic of spell classifications—and yet it had taken all of Rune's mental energy to cast. The resulting headache still roared in her temples.

The branches shook with rain. Lightning flashed overhead, illuminating the tiny cottage perched at the cliff's edge where the forest ended. The windows glowed warmly with lamplight, and Rune could smell the woodsmoke pluming from the chimney.

With her spellmarks fading fast, the illusion flickered around her. She needed the spell to hold for a little longer.

Setting down her lantern, Rune withdrew the glass vial hidden in her pocket and uncorked the lid. Dabbing the blood inside the vial onto her fingertip, she held her wrist to the lamplight and retraced the symbols, reinforcing them. One altered her appearance—graying her hair, wrinkling her skin, hunching her shoulders—while the other summoned the manifestation of the mule beside her.

The second she finished, the spell roared in her ears and the taste of salt bloomed on her tongue. The illusion snapped back into place, its bindings to Rune strengthened, and the pain in her temples throbbed harder. Swallowing the briny tang of magic, she pulled her hood over her hair, gritting her teeth against the worsening headache, then picked up her lantern and stepped out of the woods, continuing down the path toward the house.

Mud sucked at her boots. Rain pelted her face.

Her heart felt like it was going to thump right out of her chest.

Whatever happened when that door opened was now in the hands of the Ancients. If Seraphine saw through her magic and cursed her dead, it would be no less than Rune deserved. And if she showed mercy . . .

Rune bit her lip, trying not to hope.

Moving through the yard, she heard the anxious whinny of a horse from the silhouetted stable. Probably frightened by the storm. When she reached the house, she found the front door already open and a triangle of golden light spilling into the yard.

Her stiff fingers curled against the brass ring of her lantern's handle. Was Seraphine expecting her?

Some witches foresaw snatches of the future—though these

days it was a rare, often fickle ability. Nothing like the clear-sighted prophecies of the powerful sibyls of old. Perhaps Seraphine was one of these.

The thought made Rune straighten her shoulders and force herself onward. If Seraphine had foreseen this meeting, she knew who Rune was and that she was coming.

All the more reason to get this over with.

Leaving the mule illusion behind in the yard, she stepped across the threshold of the house. No one stood waiting for her. A fire lay dying in the hearth, the embers flickering red, and a plate of food sat on the table, the gravy congealed as if it had been sitting for a while. The rain spitting in through the open door dampened the stone floor beneath her feet.

Rune frowned. "Hello?"

Silence answered her.

"Seraphine?"

The house moaned at the sound of its owner's name: the beams creaking overhead and walls shifting in the wind. Rune glanced around, looking for any sign of the woman who lived here. The tiny house contained only a single room, with a kitchen in one corner and a small study in the opposite.

"You must be here somewhere . . ."

A roughly hewn ladder in the center of the room led to a loft. Stepping onto its rungs, Rune climbed to the top, where she found an unmade bed and three lit candles dribbling honey-colored wax onto the floorboards. She climbed down and checked the only other door at the back of the house, which led into an empty garden.

There was no sign of Seraphine.

Rune's skin prickled from unease.

Where is she?

The horse whinnied again in the distance.

The stable. Of course. If the creature had spooked, Seraphine would have gone to calm it.

With her lantern in hand and her headache still pulsing in her skull, Rune stepped back across the threshold and into the rain, leaving the door ajar, collecting her mule illusion as she went. Rain splattered her wrist, and the spell lurched around her, trying to hold. Hurrying, she was halfway to the stable when something squished beneath her boot. It was difficult to see in the dark and the storm, so she crouched low and set her lamp in the muck.

It was a garment.

Rune reached for the sodden fabric. Rising to her feet, she studied her findings in the lamplight: a plain, woolen work dress. The kind a servant might wear while scrubbing floors.

Except someone had sliced the back open.

Why would . . .

She glanced at the path and saw a second piece of clothing. Stooping, she discovered a cotton shift, brown with mud. Also sliced down the back. *No,* thought Rune, her rain-bitten fingers tracing the frayed edges. *Not cut.*

Torn.

Her stomach tightened.

With her wrist so exposed to the elements, the rain smudged out her spellmarks completely, and the illusion sloughed off. Her headache vanished with it. Before she could fix the marks, a sudden wind rose, growling like an angry wolf.

SLAM!

The door to Seraphine's house banged shut.

Rune dropped the woolen dress and spun to face the door, her breath catching in her throat. Closed, the door gave her a full view of the bloody X smeared from corner to corner across its wooden surface.

The mark of the Blood Guard.

Seraphine wasn't in the stable calming her horse. Soldiers had found her, stripped her, and taken her with them.

Nan's oldest friend was in the hands of the Blood Guard—the most dangerous place for a witch to be.

TWO

RUNE

*R*UNE RACED NAN'S TIRED horse, Lady, through the fog-laden streets of the capital.

Electric lamps lit the way, their white light buzzing as they illuminated the closed shops flanking her on both sides. Lady's galloping hoofbeats on the cobbles contrasted sharply with the surrounding quiet.

Two years had passed since these streets ran with the blood of witches and the Republic of the Red Peace was born. Rune had spent those two years searching for Seraphine Oakes, determined to fulfill her grandmother's last request.

The regime had executed all of Nan's witch friends, seizing their holdings and inheritances. The sole friend who'd escaped the purge was Seraphine, but only because she'd been sent by the former queen into exile nearly two decades ago and no one had seen her since.

Now, on the night Rune finally found her, witch hunters had gotten there first.

Was it a coincidence? Or was someone onto Rune? She supposed it was bound to happen. But now she would need to be especially careful. If someone within the Blood Guard suspected her, she needed to throw them off her scent.

Rune tried not to think about the bloody X on the door or

the torn clothes left in the mud. She knew exactly what had happened to Seraphine. She'd seen it firsthand the day the Blood Guard came for Nan.

It had been Rune who invited them.

Immediately after the uprising, soldiers rounded up every known witch and purged them. The New Republic's army had taken control of the harbors, ensuring no one could leave the island.

They seized Nan's ships, and it was only a matter of time before witch hunters came to Wintersea House to arrest her.

But Nan had a plan. Her old business partner had a fishing boat and was smuggling witches off-island. The boat left from his private cove at midnight, and there was room for both Nan and Rune aboard the small craft if they could get there in time.

Back then, Rune was only sixteen and hadn't yet come into her magic. It had never crossed her mind that she would, since her birth parents hadn't been witches, and only witches begat witches—though magic sometimes skipped children, and even generations, making it hard to predict. Rune's parents had drowned in a terrible shipwreck when she was a baby, leaving her an orphan with no family to take her in. So Nan had adopted her.

But it didn't matter that Rune wasn't a witch or related to Nan by blood. Under the Red Peace, it mattered that Rune hadn't turned Nan in. When the Blood Guard came for her grandmother, they would declare Rune a sympathizer and execute her alongside Kestrel Winters for the crime of not turning in a witch.

This was their only chance to escape.

Rune was hurriedly packing her things when a message arrived from Alexander Sharpe, her oldest friend.

Someone's betrayed you, it read. *The Blood Guard know your plans. Soldiers seized the fisherman earlier this evening and are waiting for you in his cove.*

But the news in Alex's message got even worse: *The roads leading out of town are closed off and they're arresting anyone who doesn't have permission to be traveling.*

There was nowhere to run; they were trapped in Wintersea House. They could hide, but for how long?

You need to report her, Rune. Before it's too late.

The message was clear: if Rune didn't turn Nan in immediately, they were both going to be executed.

Refusing would earn Rune a brutal death. But Nan was her *grandmother.* The person Rune loved most in the world. Turning her in would be like carving out her own heart and handing it over. So she brought the note to Nan, trusting her grandmother would know how to get them out of this.

She remembered the look of steel in Nan's eyes as she read the note. But instead of coming up with a new escape plan, she said: *He's right. You must report me immediately.*

Horrified, Rune shook her head. *No. There must be some other way.*

Nan pulled Rune into her arms, holding her close. Rune could still remember the smell of the lavender oil dabbed behind Nan's ears. *My darling: they'll kill you if you don't.*

Rune wept and ran to her room, locking herself in.

If you truly love me, said Nan from the other side of the door, *you will spare me the agony of watching them kill you.*

Rune's eyes burned with tears; her throat choked on sobs.

Please, darling. Do this for me.

Rune squeezed her eyes shut, wanting to wake from this nightmare. But it wasn't a nightmare. These were her choices: turn her grandmother in or die a grisly death at her side.

Hot tears spilled down her cheeks.

Finally, Rune opened the door and came out.

Nan squeezed her in a fierce hug. She stroked Rune's hair, the way she used to do when Rune was a child. *You must be very clever now, my love. Clever and brave.*

With Lizbeth's help, Nan put Rune on a horse and sent her galloping into the night.

Rune remembered the biting wind and pelting rain. Remembered the way her body trembled. The night was freezing cold, but the fear in her heart was colder.

She could have refused to do it. Could have marched straight up to the soldiers and handed herself in instead of Nan.

But she didn't.

Because deep down, Rune didn't want to die.

Deep down, she was a coward.

Drenched and shivering, Rune stumbled into Blood Guard headquarters and spoke the words that would doom her grandmother.

Kestrel Winters is a witch planning to escape, she told them, forsaking the person she loved most in the world. *I can take you to her. But we must hurry, before she gets away.*

She led the Blood Guard straight back to Wintersea, where they arrested Nan, dragging the old woman out of the house while Rune watched, silent and still. Holding everything in.

It was only after the soldiers were safely away that she collapsed to the floor and wept.

Rune had spent the past two years trying to make amends for that night.

But Nan was right: turning her in had proven Rune to be as loyal to the New Republic as the rest of them. *More* loyal, even. After all, what kind of person betrayed their own grandmother? A person who hated witches above all else.

It was a ruse the lives of countless witches now depended on.

Rune's trembling hands squeezed Lady's reins, and the leather strips bit through her deerskin gloves as she scanned the foggy streets of the capital. If she was lucky, the Blood Guard would detain Seraphine at a holding location. The Guard would wait until they hunted down a few more witches before transferring them to the palace prison together.

If Rune was unlucky . . .

The thought of the alternative—Seraphine already imprisoned beneath the palace, waiting to be purged—made a sick feeling surge in her stomach.

Rune pushed her horse harder, trying to outrun it.

That's what she needed to learn tonight: whether Seraphine was still alive, and if so, where the Blood Guard was keeping her.

As she and Lady arrived in the city center, a massive domed structure arose out of the gloom, rivaling the palace in magnitude.

The opera house.

There would be witch hunters within, not to mention Tribunal members. Some of them were bound to know where the new holding location was.

The opera house's copper-domed pavilion, where carriages dropped off patrons, came into view first. Five massive columns, each one rising to five stories in height, bordered the pavilion.

It always surprised Rune that the Good Commander allowed it to remain open. Shortly after the revolution, patriots ransacked the opera house, stripping it of much of its previous splendor. Paintings, statues, and other decor hearkening back to the Reign of Witches were smashed, burned, or thrown into the sea. But the interior, with its gold leaf and red velvet seating, remained—a stark reminder of the decadence of the witch queens.

As they entered the pavilion, Lady slowed to a trot and an elderly stable hand stepped forward from the entrance arch, dressed in a trim black uniform.

Rune dismounted. As her silk flats hit the stone walkway, her legs nearly buckled beneath her. Every bone in her body hurt from riding so hard to get here tonight.

"Citizen Winters. You're mighty late this evening."

Rune winced internally at the familiar voice. She preferred the younger stable hands to this old patriot. The young ones stood in awe of not only Rune's wealth and connections, but her reputation as a hero of the revolution.

Carson Mercer, however, remained unimpressed by Rune, and his low regard unsettled her. Did he suspect her, or was he just a miserable old man?

"The opera's half over."

At the disapproving tone of his voice, Rune stepped into her role. Pushing back the hood of her fine wool cloak, she shook out her hair, letting it fall in a sea of rust-gold waves. "I prefer to miss the first act, Mister Mercer. It's so tedious, otherwise. All you really need to know is how it ends. Who cares about the rest?"

"Indeed," Carson said, narrowing his eyes. "One wonders why you go at all." He turned to lead her horse toward the opera stables.

Not liking the edge in his voice, she called after him: "For the gossip, of course!"

The moment he was out of view, Rune anxiously tapped the secret pocket sewn into her gown, where her vial of blood lay hidden. Comforted, she forced the curmudgeonly stable hand out of her mind and entered the opera house—where members of the Blood Guard would be gloating about their recent capture. All Rune had to do tonight was keep her ears open and ask the right questions, and by the time the curtain fell, she'd have the information she needed to save Seraphine.

She passed several children begging for coins or food on the way in. By the marks carved into their foreheads, she could tell they were Penitents. The descendants of witch sympathizers. Meaning someone in their family had refused to inform on a witch, or had hidden one from witch hunters.

Instead of executing or imprisoning the descendants of witch sympathizers, the Good Commander carved the Penitent symbol into their foreheads, letting everyone know what they'd done. It was a warning. A way of dissuading others from helping witches.

Rune's fingers itched to dig into her money pouch and drop several coins, but it was illegal to directly aid a Penitent. And with Carson nearby, she didn't dare. So she only smiled a little. The children's echoing smiles twisted her heart with guilt as she passed them by.

Inside, Rune discovered Carson was correct: the opera *was* half over. Before her, the ceremonial staircase—divided into two divergent and interwoven flights of steps—was mostly empty. But the cacophony of voices coming from the grand foyer far above was an unmistakable sign that intermission was well underway.

Pressing her hand to the cool marble balustrade, Rune pushed the Penitent children out of her mind and started upward. She felt aware of the men around her as she ascended the stairs, their attentive gazes lingering on her long after she passed, reminding her of a recent conversation she'd had with her friend Verity.

Don't you think it's time you picked one?

A suitor, she'd meant. One of the many eligible young men

who lined up to take Rune's dancing ribbons at balls, invited her out on romantic dinners, and took her on long carriage rides. It wasn't *Rune* who tempted them. Sure, a few might genuinely be interested in the pretty face she presented to the world. Most, though, were after Nan's fortune, her profitable shipping business, and her vast estate. All of it "gifted" to Rune by the New Republic for her heroism during the revolution.

Rune had been stringing the useful ones along for over a year—all from well-connected families with access to secrets she needed. Secrets she could often get them to spill in dark corners and shadowed alcoves.

But she couldn't keep doing it forever. Their patience was limited, and Rune couldn't afford to make enemies of them.

Verity had made a list of the most valuable suitors and left it on Rune's pillow the morning after their talk.

She would need to choose one, and she'd need to do it soon.

But not tonight, she thought, hurrying up the steps. Tonight, she would mingle with the sons and daughters of the revolution, stealing whatever secrets she could.

When Rune arrived at the top of the interwoven staircase, the grand foyer stretched out before her, full of opera patrons dressed in muted silks and frothy lace, with cream-colored pearls strung through their hair, all of them illuminated by a dozen pairs of winking chandeliers hanging down the massive hall.

"Rune Winters," came a voice that stopped her in her tracks. "Sneaking in late, I see. Out on a tryst with one of your lovers?"

Several scandalized giggles followed.

The voice belonged to Verity de Wilde—Rune's best friend.

Verity stood beneath the lights with her hands on both hips and a playful smile tugging at her mouth. Wispy brown ringlets framed her white face, and her eyes were dark behind her spectacles. She wore a dress the color of sunflowers, with white lace sleeves and a low-cut back—one of Rune's hand-me-downs from last season. It had originally been sleeveless, but since sleeveless dresses were out of fashion now, Rune had enlisted her seamstress to add them before gifting it to Verity.

Flanking Verity was a group of their fashionable friends. Young men and women who'd dined at Rune's table and danced in her ballroom hundreds of times—and would do so again tonight, at her after-party.

Friends was perhaps too generous a term, since not one of them would think twice about turning her in if they knew what she was.

"Or perhaps," came another voice, causing everyone to turn, "Rune has been out rescuing witches all night. They say the Crimson Moth only works beneath the cover of darkness."

The words chilled Rune, who looked directly into the piercing eyes of Laila Creed. Laila was several inches taller—which always made it seem like she was looking down her nose at Rune—and a member of the Blood Guard.

She was also beautiful, with prominent cheekbones and raven-black hair crowned high on her head. Rune recognized the design of the high-waisted peacock blue dress. It was the work of Sebastian Khan, a popular dressmaker from the mainland whose wait list was almost a year long and whose dresses were the envy of the season. It was impossible to acquire one unless you had considerable wealth and connections.

Rune had two in her closet.

That fact that Laila wore the rare dress and not her uniform meant she was off duty tonight. She likely hadn't been one of the witch hunters who'd brought Seraphine in.

Rune's blood ran cold at the memory of Seraphine's empty house. Of how the Blood Guard soldiers found the witch right before Rune showed up. If she was being spied on, that spy could very well be Laila, who had never liked Rune, for reasons she could only guess at.

Donning her mask—the one she hid the true Rune Winters behind—Rune threw back her head and laughed.

"Ha! Can you imagine it? *Me*, spending my nights gallivanting across this damned island, with its ghastly weather and endless mud and rain? Think of what it would do to my *Minews*!"

She pulled up the hem of her skirt to show off the silk shoes, custom-made by Evelyn Minew, a couture artist halfway across the world whose designs were one of a kind and never replicated. It had taken half a year for Rune to get in touch with her, and another year for the shoes to arrive.

Take that, Laila Creed.

At the looks of astonishment and envy, Rune dropped her hem and, smiling, entered the circle forming around her, stepping a little in front of Laila to edge her out. Lowering her voice, a little conspiratorially, she said, "Did you hear? The vigilante smuggled her last batch of witches out through the sewers. The *sewers*! Just think!"

Their noses wrinkled with disgust.

Rune didn't need to fake her reaction. Her stomach twisted at the memory of it: the putrid odor of raw sewage filling the dark tunnel, sloshing around her knees as she and the twin sisters she'd rescued—they were barely thirteen—walked through the stench for miles beneath the city. A servant had found their bedsheets hidden beneath the floorboards and informed on the girls. The bloodstains weren't red, but black—the telltale sign of a witch who'd come into her powers at the onset of her first bleeding.

That night, Alexander Sharpe—the same friend who had tipped Rune off to the Blood Guard closing in on Nan—had been waiting on the other end with fresh clothes and a horse that would take the girls directly to the docks, where one of Rune's loaded cargo ships was ready to set sail. Alex was always waiting on the other end. Sometimes with horses or carriage; other times with boats. He was the getaway man in their heists, and he never let Rune down.

The cargo ship arrived in port two days ago, and the twins had sent a coded message saying they were safe on the mainland.

"Anyone who prefers wading through poo to sleeping soundly in a soft, clean bed is, well, *revolting*." Growing warm beneath her cloak, Rune untied the tassels at her throat.

The surrounding party murmured their agreement. Except for one person—Laila.

"But isn't that precisely what the Crimson Moth would say?"

Rune's fingers stiffened as the tassels of the cloak came undone. The garment slipped from her bare shoulders, and before she could grab it, someone stepped behind her, catching the fine wool and folding it over his arm.

"Come now," said a comforting voice near her ear. "If Rune was the Moth, would she have delivered her grandmother to be purged?"

As the owner of the voice stepped beside Rune, she glanced up. Alex Sharpe. In the presence of her oldest friend—a genuine friend, like Verity—every muscle in her body relaxed.

He looked like a lion tonight, with his golden hair shining beneath the light of the chandeliers. His gaze was warm and steady on her face, but his forehead creased ever so slightly, saying he knew where she'd been, and he'd worried about her.

Noah Creed—Laila's brother and a young man who'd made Verity's short list of *Suitors Rune Needs to Consider*—cut in.

"The Crimson Moth hasn't struck in weeks," Noah said,

also defending Rune. To support this theory, he added: "I heard they brought in another witch tonight, completely unhindered. The Moth didn't even *try* to rescue her."

Rune's attention homed in on Noah.

Where did you hear that, I wonder?

Noah shared his sister's deep brown eyes, high cheekbones, and ocher skin tone. Not only was he handsome in his black overcoat with sloping shoulders and silk lapel, but he was also the son of the Good Commander. That position put him *very* close to a firsthand source of the most classified intel, making him a fine option indeed.

But will he notice his wife slipping out of bed in the night? Or coming home exhausted after dawn . . . sometimes with bruises?

Rune turned her smile on Noah. "A witch? Brought in *tonight*? Don't tease us, Noah. Tell us more."

Noah's eyes widened at finding himself the subject of her attention. But he lifted his hands in protest. "Gideon Sharpe brought her in. That's all I know."

Gideon Sharpe.

Rune's lip nearly curled at the name of Alex's older brother. Devoutly loyal to the New Republic, Gideon was a ruthless, bloodthirsty witch hunter who'd sent more of Rune's kind to the purge than any other member of the Guard.

He'd also famously helped assassinate the Sister Queens, sparking the revolution into a blaze.

Rune hated him.

The two Sharpe brothers couldn't be more different.

Catching Rune's gaze, Verity raised a dark eyebrow, asking a silent question. In answer, Rune tucked a strand of hair behind her ear, showing off her grandmother's ruby earrings. She'd put them on earlier tonight, and they dripped from her ears like beads of blood. The earrings were her answer—*failure*—telling her partner in crime everything she needed to know about how tonight went. *Seraphine is in enemy hands.* Either Verity would figure out the rest herself or Rune would fill her in before the after-party she was hosting later tonight.

At the sight of the rubies, Verity's mouth pinched. Turning away from Rune, she quickly cleared her throat.

"Well, *I've* always thought Missus Blackwater is the Moth," she said, commanding the group's attention as she glanced across the loud, brightly lit hall toward an old woman with frizzy hair and a neck strung with too many pearls. Missus Blackwater sat alone on the opera café's terrace, murmuring to herself. "Can you imagine the old biddy leading the Blood Guard on a wild goose chase? What a perfect disguise!"

At that, everyone burst out laughing.

As more guesses were made, Rune took the chance Verity gave her and slipped silently into the crowd, armed with a new purpose: tracking down Gideon Sharpe.

THREE

GIDEON

*A*NOTHER NIGHT, ANOTHER WITCH.
Gideon Sharpe pressed his fists against the shower
tiles. Letting the hot water scald his back, he stared blankly at the
blood running like ink down his skin and swirling around the
drain.

He couldn't tell if the blood was real or imagined. The nightmares were no longer confined to his sleeping hours; they often
struck in the middle of his waking ones now.

But this was no nightmare. He knew whose blood this was.
It was as real as he was.

You shouldn't have left them alone with her.

The Tasker brothers had a lust for disobeying orders. And
though Gideon himself had no love for witches, he didn't tolerate unnecessary cruelty. He'd wanted to discharge the brothers
the last time they'd bludgeoned a witch half to death, but had
been told by his betters that beating a witch senseless was no
different from beating a disease-ridden rat.

So the abuse continued. Tonight was just one more occur-
rence.

And what are you going to do about it?

Gideon closed his eyes and turned his face into the steaming
hot water.

A problem for tomorrow.

Right now, he was too tired to think. Too tired to move from this spot. It had taken him nearly a year to track down the high-profile witch he'd brought in tonight, and he'd ridden hard to get her.

He'd prefer not to see a saddle for another week at least.

But he'd agreed to meet Harrow, one of his sources, at the opera tonight. It was Harrow who'd tipped him off to Seraphine's whereabouts, and she had news of the Crimson Moth—that perpetual thorn in Gideon's side. Gideon was desperate to hear it.

The thought gave him renewed motivation. Rubbing the bar of soap between his hands, he scrubbed his weary body with suds, washing all over until he came to the brand seared into his left pectoral: a rose with knifelike thorns half enclosed inside a crescent moon.

Her brand.

Despite the heat of the shower, Gideon shivered.

The youngest Sister Queen might be dead, but she'd marked him forever.

Gideon often thought about cutting it out, just to be rid of every last fucking trace of her. But digging the brand out of his skin wouldn't carve the memories from his mind. Or rid him of the flashbacks. Or soften the nightmares.

It didn't matter. Every time he got out the knife and put the honed edge to his skin, his hands shook too much to do the job right. So, for now, it stayed.

The thought of her made him wonder if the spirits of particularly evil witches could live on past their deaths, returning to haunt those they'd tormented while alive. He immediately wished he could unthink it. Gideon turned off the water, eying the steamy room around him as the cold air rushed in, raising the hairs on his arms and legs.

She's dead, you fool. And there's no such thing as ghosts.

Cressida might be dead, but there were equally dangerous witches out there. Three nights ago, another mutilated body had been found dragged under a bridge. Chest ripped open. Blood drained out. Gideon wasn't surprised when he learned it belonged to a Blood Guard officer. They always did. It was the third one this month.

Gideon couldn't prove the Crimson Moth was committing the heinous acts, but he had a strong hunch. The murders usually took place right before she struck, breaking his charges out of their prison cells and escaping his ever-tightening security. To do that, the Moth needed spells, and spells required blood. *Fresh* blood.

Which of us is next?

Running his hands over his face, Gideon shook the water from his hair, grabbed a towel, and dried himself off, directing his thoughts somewhere else. Anywhere else.

The opera.

Yes. Good. He would go over tonight in his mind, and the preparation would banish the eerie chill in his bathroom.

First, Gideon would button his tired body into a uniform and drag himself to the opera house. There, while some useless story played itself out across the stage, Harrow would tell him what she'd learned about the Moth. And finally, Gideon would come home, devise a plan while falling into bed, sleep dreamlessly—or so he hoped—and resume his hunt for the fiend upon waking, armed with new information.

And this time, he would catch her.

But first Gideon needed to get through a night at the opera. An activity even *less* tolerable than trudging through mud and rain on horseback, hunting down a witch.

The only good news was, he was going to miss the first half.

FOUR

RUNE

*H*ERE IN THE FOYER, the Blood Guard stood out like red poppies in a meadow. Their uniforms were impossible to miss, even in the brightly dressed crowd. But not a single one was Gideon.

Maybe he's not here tonight.

If Alex's elder brother had indeed brought Seraphine in, he might still be processing her. Or possibly taking the rest of the night off.

Rune couldn't stop herself from wondering if it was Gideon who'd ripped the dress off Seraphine and forced her to stand naked in the rain while he and his soldiers raked their eyes over her body, searching it for scars.

Her teeth clenched at the thought.

Gideon Sharpe.

She loathed him.

As Rune's rage simmered like a red-hot coal, she moved skillfully through the crowd, presenting a smiling, happy face, commenting on new fashions and hairstyles, or the *delightful* dinners of the New Republic's well-to-do that she'd attended last week, never lingering long, all while constantly looking for the next scarlet uniform.

She passed her usual marks: Blood Guard affiliates, daughters and sons of Tribunal members, people who not only were well connected, but enjoyed flaunting those connections and, in doing so, unwittingly giving information away. Their conversations droned in the air like bees drunk on pollen.

The chandeliers overhead lit the ceiling, which was painted with a blue-black sky full of stars—a rendering that had been allowed to remain untouched in the revolution's aftermath. There were two salons on either side of the foyer and along the wall, behind the columns lining the room, were several small alcoves for more . . . illicit meetings.

Rune was headed toward the salon, where Blood Guard members often gathered, when a hand grabbed her wrist, pulling her out of the crowd and into one of the shadowed alcoves.

Spinning to face her accoster, she found golden-brown eyes peering at her from beneath tawny brows.

The tension bled out of her.

It was only Alex.

"Rune." His fingertips pressed against the sensitive skin of her wrist as he drew her deeper into the darkness. "You look like you're prepared to walk into hell itself."

Rune had the sudden urge to rest here with him awhile, where it was safe, before throwing herself back into danger.

"What happened tonight?" he coaxed.

Rune shook off the urge, remembering her mission.

"Did you hear Noah? *Your brother* happened tonight," she said, annoyed at the thought. "Gideon got to Seraphine before I did."

Alex frowned. "So you—"

A chorus of voices—one of them Laila Creed's—echoed nearby. On instinct, Rune drew Alex deeper into the shadows, until they were nearly chest to chest. She wasn't worried about someone seeing them in here together. They'd simply assume it was exactly what Verity had pretended to accuse Rune of having earlier: a tryst.

What she worried about was being overheard.

They both fell silent, waiting for the voices to pass. The tip of Rune's nose was less than an inch from Alex's chin, and the smell of him—like leather and oak—filled the air. The small space seemed to shrink around them, and for a moment, Rune remembered the night she turned Nan in. Alex had raced to Wintersea, then held her through the night while she wept.

"You worry me," he whispered, close to her ear.

His voice was careful, soft. As if Rune were made of glass and he needed to handle her with caution.

"You spend your days looking out for everyone else, but who's looking out for you?"

"You're looking out for me," she whispered to his double-breasted lapel. "Not to mention Verity. And Lady."

"Lady is a horse," he countered. "And Verity throws herself into as much danger as you do."

He seemed about to say something else when the bells signaling the end of intermission chimed throughout the foyer. Rune stepped away from his familiar, steady frame and glanced out of the alcove. A column blocked most of her view, but she could see Laila's black hair, braided into that fashionable crown, heading toward the doors of the auditorium. The drone of conversation was already dwindling. In a few minutes, the foyer would be empty and silent.

And Rune had yet to find Gideon.

She refused to let tonight be a waste. She *needed* Seraphine's whereabouts.

"Is your brother here?" she whispered, scanning the emptying foyer like a hawk searching for the plumpest field mouse.

"I don't know. I haven't spoken to him all week. Why?"

She didn't answer. She didn't need to. Alex knew the thoughts in her head.

"Rune, no. My brother is a danger." He gently gripped her bare shoulder, turning her to face him. "To you especially."

"Your brother is a danger to every witch in the New Republic." She tugged herself free of his hand. "*Seraphine* especially. If I don't find out where he's put her . . ."

Didn't he understand? She didn't know where Seraphine was or when they planned to transfer her. For all Rune knew, she might already be en route to the palace prison. And if she was . . .

I'll never get her out. They'll kill her like they killed Nan.

Once the Blood Guard brought a witch inside the prison, Rune couldn't save them. The prison was impregnable.

And if I don't save her, I'll fail to do the last thing Nan asked of me.

It was unacceptable.

"Rune."

"What other choice do I have?" she said, coming back to him. "*You* won't do it."

As loyal as Alex was to the Crimson Moth, to *her*, he drew a line at his brother. Under no circumstances would he ever manipulate Gideon the way he, Rune, and Verity manipulated the rest of their peers. Rune had asked him once, and watched his bright gold eyes dim. His uncharacteristically sharp answer—*Absolutely not.*—stopped her from asking again.

Rune knew Alex had helped kill the youngest Sister Queen, Cressida Roseblood. He never spoke of it, except to say that he had done it for Gideon. At which point, he turned the conversation to other things. Rune didn't know what that meant. Had Gideon asked him to kill Cressida? Had he *forced* him to? Or had Alex done it to save his brother, somehow? The latter, if true, struck Rune as odd, since Gideon was the violent one; a natural predator. Unlike his brother, Alex was warm and kind and scorned the killing of witches. Not to mention, he was devoutly loyal to Rune.

The problem was, he was equally loyal to Gideon. Sometimes Rune suspected he was *more* loyal. But for some strange reason, it didn't make her trust him less. She knew, in her heart, Alex would never betray her.

He would just never betray his brother, either.

Which often put them at odds with each other.

Once, Rune might have understood Alex's devotion to his brother. Years before the revolution, Rune had wanted to earn Gideon's approval. Alex was her closest friend back then, and though Rune hadn't met Gideon yet, she'd heard stories about him. Biased stories, she now knew, told by Alex. Who worshiped his older brother.

Young, naive Rune had believed the stories. And the more of them Alex told her, the more she felt like she knew Gideon. She soon developed what some might call a crush. It was important, therefore, that she make a good impression the first time they met.

In retrospect, the whole thing was childish and absurd.

When they did meet, Rune was thirteen and Gideon fifteen. He not only refused to shake her hand, he outright insulted the outfit she was wearing: a dress she'd selected for the sole aim of impressing him. When Alex asked Gideon to apologize, he refused.

Alex's stories were wrong. So wrong. She learned that day it was the one thing he couldn't be relied upon for: accurate judgment of his brother.

Gideon was a beast of a boy, and Rune never cared to win his esteem again.

"I'll cast an illusion," she told Alex now, her fingers tapping the corked vial of blood concealed in her dress. Blood she'd collected from last month's bleeding. "He won't know it's me."

Except Rune only had one full vial left after this one. Once it was gone, she would have nothing until the start of her next monthly cycle. And she needed as much blood as possible to save Seraphine.

Alex shook his head. "He'll smell the magic on you. Gideon's not one of your moony-eyed suitors, Rune. He's—"

"So I'll invite him to my after-party." Where she would keep his cup full of enchanted wine and probe him with innocent questions that would lead to the answers she needed.

"He hates parties."

Rune threw up her hands and hissed: "Then I'll think of something else!"

She turned her back on Alex and was about to walk away when his strained voice said, "I'm sick of watching you walk into danger."

She paused, sighing as she stared out into the empty foyer. "Then don't watch."

Rune didn't wait for him to respond. She stepped out of the alcove—

And straight into a Blood Guard uniform.

FIVE

RUNE

HER FOREHEAD COLLIDED HARD with a chest as solid as concrete. The force of the soldier's stride would have barreled her over had he not grabbed her elbow, steadying them both.

"Forgive me . . ."

Rune looked up. Straight into eyes as black and cold as a bottomless sea.

Gideon Sharpe.

His penetrating gaze seemed to cut her open, peeling back the layers of the girl she pretended to be. Like a knife carving off the protective skin of an apple to get at the soft, vulnerable flesh beneath.

Rune's stomach tumbled over itself. She yanked her elbow out of his grip and staggered back, her heart beating fast. The Blood Guard captain before her—responsible for sending more witches to their executions than any other soldier—straightened, his features shifting from startled surprise to something dark and unreadable.

Rune cursed herself. The Crimson Moth might have reason to cower from this monster. But Rune Winters—the silly, shallow heiress she pretended to be—wouldn't think twice about it.

Before she could find her courage, Gideon's gaze ran sharply down her. The force of his attention was like a rifle aimed at her heart. It made her pulse race and her breath stick in her throat. Rune was a deer, and he was a hunter. Taking her measure, noting every detail and flaw, trying to decide if she would be worth the hunt.

A second later, he frowned and looked away.

Evidently, she wasn't.

"Citizen Winters. My apologies, I—"

Gideon's incisive gaze flicked over her shoulder, drawn to the sudden movement of his younger brother emerging from the alcove. At the sight of Alex, his rigid form relaxed.

Gideon stepped around Rune as if she were not only disappointing but entirely forgettable. "Alex. What's the matter? You look perturbed."

"What? Oh." Alex shook his head. "Nothing at all. Must be the terrible lighting." He motioned to the gaslights glowing on the walls.

Gideon cocked his head, unconvinced.

Alex quickly changed the subject. "When did you get back?"

"This evening."

The two brothers were inverse mirrors of each other. They had the same tall frames and handsome features: firm jaws, prominent brows. But where Alex was golden and warm as a summer day, Gideon was closed and dark as a locked, windowless room.

The two brothers were also the sons of the Sharpe Duet—a pair of lovers who started as humble tailors during the Reign of Witches. When their work caught the eye of the Sister Queens, Alex and Gideon's parents were recruited by the Roseblood family to become the royal dressmakers, launching them to short-lived fame. Both died that same year, right before the revolution.

Anyone in fashionable circles still fell reverently quiet whenever someone spoke the dressmakers' names.

"And?" Alex was saying, his voice a little strained. "Was your hunt successful?"

Gideon sighed and ran a hand roughly through his damp hair. "Despite an unfortunate incident, yes. We have the witch in custody."

He's speaking of Seraphine.

Rune felt her mask slip further as she remembered the torn clothes discarded in the mud. Had he and the others laughed as they stripped the garments off of the woman's back? She thought of the red X smeared across Seraphine's door, knowing whose blood he spilled to mark it.

Like a deer shaking off the paralyzing fear of its hunter, Rune reached for her voice, ironing out the hatred before speaking.

"What kind of unfortunate incident?"

Gideon glanced over, as if surprised she was still standing there.

He paused, reconsidering her.

This time, Rune studied him back, letting her gaze roam over him. The fit of his red uniform hinted at a hard, efficient form beneath. No softness. No warmth. Just unyielding muscle and strength, like an impenetrable fortress.

He had a strong, cruel mouth, and his black hair was still wet from the rain, or possibly a shower. And though he must have run himself as ragged as she had hunting down Seraphine, he stood before her polished and clean, from the pistol at his hip to the brass buckles on his boots, making Rune wonder if he had scrubbed off the blood with the same precision as his parents once sewed their elaborate garments for the queens.

The only disorderly thing about him were the knuckles on

his right hand. They were red and raw, as if from pummeling something.

Or someone.

Rune's blood burned beneath her skin. Afraid he would see the fury in her eyes, she peered up through her eyelashes, knowing the effect it had on other young men.

"I dearly hope you weren't harmed in this . . . incident?"

He seemed about to answer her when the sudden, final chime of the intermission bells cut him off.

All three of them looked to find the grand foyer transformed around them. Without the socializing crowds, its emptiness loomed large. The chandeliers overhead suddenly seemed too big and too bright, and the painted ceiling more magnanimous than their insignificant selves deserved.

The ushers began turning out the gaslights, casting annoyed looks in their direction. Beyond the auditorium doors, the orchestra started to play.

Taking the hint, Gideon began backing away from his brother. "I have the ring booked for tomorrow night. Want to go a few rounds?"

Alex nodded. "Sure. That would be nice."

Before turning, Gideon glanced from Alex to Rune to the alcove they'd both come out of. His lips parted ever so slightly, and something dawned in his eyes. Whatever it was, he kept it to himself and strode off.

Alex blew out a breath.

Rune swore quietly. She had let him intimidate her and found her courage too late, botching her chance to get the information she needed.

Her hands curled into fists. She needed to remedy this, and fast. She only had so much time before they transferred Seraphine to the palace prison.

Smoothing down her gown, she replaced the snarl on her face with a sweet smile, preparing to slip into the role she'd grown so good at playing these past two years. Seeing it, Alex reached for her. "Rune, don't . . ."

She stepped out of his grasp.

"Rune."

He didn't follow as she stalked after his brother. Her silk shoes barely made a sound on the mosaicked floor of the foyer, giving Gideon no inkling that he was being tracked. For now, their roles had reversed. Rune was the predator; he was the prey. And she was closing in on him.

At the far end of the hall, where the arches of the loggia framed the foggy city outside, Gideon turned and headed up a staircase. One that led to the box reserved for Blood Guard members.

A moment later, Rune followed.

Hitching her skirts, she ran up the steps, shoved aside the velvet curtains at the top, and stepped out onto the darkened balcony and into a sea of red.

It was teeming with witch hunters.

Rune hesitated.

She was the Crimson Moth—a wanted criminal, not to mention a witch, hiding in plain sight. But this wouldn't be the first time she had walked into a space full of the people who hunted her kind. She'd done it hundreds of times before without batting an eye.

So why was there a tiny seed of fear sprouting inside her?

Because Alex is right.

In a war room full of weapons, Gideon was the deadliest, and Rune was heading straight toward that honed edge, her throat bared.

He doesn't suspect you, she told herself, trying to calm the buzz in her blood. *All these stupid brutes see when they look at you is exactly what you want them to see: a silly little socialite. Gideon Sharp is no different.*

Armed with this reminder, Rune headed toward the empty seat at the front of the box. Beside it, Gideon reclined, elbow resting across the backrest. Perfectly relaxed. As if Seraphine's impending execution didn't plague him at all.

Rune gathered her courage the way she gathered her dress. Sitting down beside him, she said, "Mind if I join you?"

SIX

RUNE

GIDEON IMMEDIATELY WITHDREW HIS arm from
the seat back, startled by her presence. As the orchestra's
hum rose to a crescendo, the lights around the horseshoe auditorium dimmed. The second act was about to start.

"Actually, that seat—"

"I've never watched an opera from up here before," she
said, cutting him off. The exhilarating rush of danger coursed
through her as she peered down to the floor seats, which were
packed full, except for a few stragglers climbing over others to
get to their spots. "It's quite the view."

In the near-dark, she could feel the weight of his inscrutable
gaze. "Quite. Is Alex with you?"

"No. He . . ." Rune glanced up and their eyes locked. An
electric hum made the hair on her arms rise. Like being caught
in a storm right before lightning strikes.

"Miss Winters? Is everything all right?"

The question grounded her.

You are an actor, she reminded herself. *And this is a play.*

But which character was she—the heroine, the villain, or
the fool?

The fool.

"Everything is *wonderful*," she said, rallying. "I just love the opera, don't you?"

The stage lights flared, illuminating the satin gowns and colorful sequins of the actors positioned onstage. Illuminating Gideon, who watched her in the darkness.

"It's all so *pretty*," she continued, spinning the image of herself that she wanted him to see. "The costumes and the sets and the singing . . ." She flashed him the brightest smile she could manage. "Though the stories could be shorter. A lot shorter, don't you agree? I find them a little, well, boring, you know? And so hard to follow! By the time they're over, I'm always a little confused."

She laughed to solidify the part she was playing. But deep down, her soul wilted.

Before Nan died, they attended the opera every Saturday. It was Rune's favorite day of the week. Nan did Rune's makeup and hair and let her borrow whatever jewelry she liked. Rune loved waltzing up the steps to the foyer in a frothy new skirt, loved being included in the conversations with her grandmother's sophisticated friends, loved being transported to a different world inside the auditorium. But she loved the *afterward* best, when, on the way home, she and Nan fell into heated discussions about the stories that had played out across the stage.

That was before the Red Peace outlawed the old operas. The travesties that played here now were all preapproved by the Ministry of Public Safety. They weren't stories—not good ones, anyway. They were thinly veiled lessons about how to behave under the new regime. Reminders of who the enemy was and why you should despise them. The villains were always witches or witch sympathizers; those who ratted them out or hunted them down were the heroes.

It was all so nauseatingly predictable.

Nan would have hated them.

She stole a glance at Gideon. *He probably thinks they're high art.*

"Intermission is my favorite part," Rune continued. "And the after-parties, of course." She leaned in toward him, as if to spill a secret, and the smell of gunpowder wafted off his coat. "That's why I'm here. To invite you to my party."

Annoyance tugged his stern mouth into a harsh line. "I wish I had the patience for silly gossip and shallow company," he said. "Alas, I do not."

At the insult, a bloom of heat rushed up her neck, reminding Rune of the first time they met and the dismissive remarks he'd made. She was suddenly grateful for the darkness. Fisting her hands in the smooth silk of her dress, Rune nodded sympathetically. "I understand *completely*. Someone like you obviously prefers the company of stupid brutes with terrible style."

He glanced at her.

Rune mentally pinched herself. *What am I doing?* She needed to pretend his verbal jabs went over her head, not jab him with sharper ones. *Let him insult you. Remember why you're here.*

Wrestling her pride into a cage, she smiled innocently up at him.

He studied her, a bit warily. Seeming to decide he'd misheard her, he returned his attention to the opera.

This is going to be harder than I thought.

Clearly Gideon considered her not only worthy of insulting, but too stupid to realize she'd even been insulted. Ordinarily, she would use this to her advantage. But as he turned away, crossing his arms and staring hard at the stage, she realized he was closing himself off from her, not opening himself up.

Her presence was vexing him. Like it had the first day they met.

He hates parties, Alex had warned her. But it was the best move in Rune's playbook. The most effective way to lower a man's defenses was to ply him with her enchanted wine, get him alone, and flirt until the spell loosened his tongue enough to spill the secrets she needed.

Rune tapped her knee with her fingertips, trying to think.

She'd seen the way Gideon lit up at the sight of his brother. Rune had ceased to exist the moment Alex stepped out of that alcove. The Sharpe brothers might be opposites who disagreed on everything important, but something nameless and deep bound the two boys to each other. It wasn't the first time Rune had seen it.

"Alex would love it if you came."

Gideon tensed beside her. "You must not know my brother well if you think my presence in your home would cheer him."

Rune frowned, trying to untangle the words. What did he mean?

"And as I said, some of us have better things to do with our time."

Before she could try again from another angle, a shadow fell across them. Gideon looked up and shot to his feet. "Harrow. Finally. I thought I was going to have to watch this damned thing to the end."

"It might have done you some good," responded a feminine voice. "Isn't that the point of art—to tame the monsters in us?"

Rune's attention snagged on the question. It was a line from one of her favorite operas.

Squinting through the darkness, Rune tried to make out the identity of the speaker, but the ushers had snuffed all the lights on this level. She could see neither this girl's face nor her clothes. Nothing that might give her away.

"You've been reading too many fairy tales," said Gideon, stepping over Rune with his long legs. "You'll have to excuse me, Citizen Winters. Have fun at your . . . party." There was no mistaking the sneer in his voice.

Rune turned her head, watching the two of them walk out of the box, speaking in low voices. The moment they were gone, she squeezed her hand into a fist.

Failed again.

Leaning her head back against the velvet headrest, she ran both palms down her cheeks. She was losing valuable time. Rune needed to find Seraphine's location—preferably tonight. And she couldn't keep stalking Gideon Sharp, or he was bound to get suspicious. *Which is the last thing I need.* Gideon had gotten to Seraphine first on the night Rune was due to arrive at the home of his prey.

It might be a coincidence. Or it might not.

Gideon had seemed convinced by her performance, though. If someone was spying on Rune, she doubted it was him. But she remembered the suspicion in Laila Creed's questions earlier and had to consider the possibility that her enemies were closing in on her.

Rune sank further into her seat, trying not to think about the witch hunters currently surrounding her in this opera box.

If they are closing in, how can I throw them off my scent?

Her mind was a murky bog of exhaustion, tugging her thoughts down into the muck. Whenever she felt like this, she found Verity, whose sharp questions always sparked Rune's imagination, like a poker stoking a dying fire. Verity was the Crimson Moth's second-in-command. She came up with as many plans as Rune did and helped implement them.

So, when the actress onstage finished her aria, Rune hauled herself to her feet, pushed aside the balcony curtain, and went to find her friend.

SEVEN

GIDEON

R *UNE WINTERS.*

Every time Gideon looked at the young heiress, she reminded him of the sea: steal-your-breath beautiful on the surface, with the promise of untold depths beneath.

Whenever she opened her mouth, however, and he listened to the ridiculous things pouring out—at dinner tables, in parlor rooms, in the halls of the wealthy and popular—he remembered anew how deceptive looks could be.

There were no hidden depths to Rune Winters. Only surface, surface, and more surface.

Tonight was a reminder of that.

"Hello? Gideon?" Harrow snapped her brown fingers in front of his face. "I said: what do you want to drink? It's on me."

The raucous noise of the Crow's Nest came rushing in. The pine table was sticky beneath his elbows, and the air smelled like sour ale.

Gideon shook his head. "Nothing for me."

Harrow clucked her disapproval. She turned her head toward the bar, and Gideon tried not to stare at the place where her left ear should have been. She kept the hair on that side cropped almost to the scalp, where it shone like dark fuzz. As if she took pride in the disfigurement and wanted to show it off.

He guessed she was close to him in age, but didn't know for sure, and he'd never asked how she came by the loss of her ear. A family of witches had indentured Harrow before the revolution. Gideon could piece together the rest.

They'd been lucky to grab this table just as its last occupants left. Harrow refused to order at the bar in case someone snatched her stool while she was gone. So while she shouted her request to the barkeep, Gideon's mind wandered back to Rune.

He couldn't make sense of her sudden appearance on the balcony tonight. She'd barely spoken a handful of words to him in five years, and suddenly, she was . . . inviting him to her house? Why?

He tried to shake off the strangeness of it. But try as he might, he couldn't shake off the memory of her next to him in the opera box. Her strawberry blonde hair was a little wilder than usual, and her stylish gown put her elegant clavicles on display. The rust-colored fabric contrasted with her gray eyes and pale complexion, pulling his gaze toward her more times than he'd like to admit.

She might have been the shallowest girl in the opera house, but he couldn't deny that she was also the prettiest.

A waste of a pretty face, he told himself.

A better person would feel guilty for insulting her. Gideon didn't. He hoped he'd made his feelings clear, so she'd avoid him in the future. In fact, he thought he'd made his feelings clear years ago, when they first met.

He'd often observed the way his brother looked at her, noticed how his voice softened on her name, and while he had no idea what Alex saw in Rune, other than the obvious—which wasn't enough to tempt *him*—Gideon had no intentions of going anywhere near her. That was as true now as it had been when they were kids.

Back then, Rune Winters was the aristo his little brother wouldn't stop talking about. Alex found ways of inserting her into every conversation. *Rune thinks this. Rune loves that.* It would have annoyed Gideon if he hadn't been so goddamned curious.

But then he saw her. *Met* her. And he knew at once they'd never be friends.

"Those twin girls who escaped three weeks ago?"

Harrow's voice dragged him back to the table in time to see her creamy ale slosh over the side of her glass as she set it down. When the foam dribbled over her fingers, she licked it off.

"The Crimson Moth stole the pair the night you were supposed to transfer them to the palace prison. Remember?"

How could Gideon forget? They were exactly his sister's age when she died. Skinny little things. He could picture them huddled behind the bars of the cell he'd locked them in: wide-eyed and trembling as they clung to each other. "I remember."

He also remembered when they disappeared from that same cell one night later. A casting signature had appeared over the cot where they'd slept. Gideon could recall the mark perfectly in his mind's eye: a delicate, blood-red moth fluttering in the air. He'd been so angry, he wanted to grab the thing and squeeze it. But it was only a signature—the mark left behind after a witch cast a spell, like an artist signing their name to a painting.

The moth faded less than an hour later.

Harrow sipped daintily at her beer. "A dockworker found signatures aboard a cargo ship three days ago, after it docked in Harbor Grace. The two witches must have illusioned themselves to look like cargo."

And when the illusion faded, the signatures would have remained behind.

Harbor Grace was a busy port on the mainland. Everything

this island didn't make, grow, or mine was shipped over via that port.

Gideon frowned. "Were they recaptured?"

Harrow shook her head. "No. But . . ." She glanced around and leaned in toward him. He could smell the ale on her breath. "The cargo ship belongs to Rune Winters."

What?

The alehouse spun around them. Gideon flattened his hands on the beer-sticky table to steady himself.

That can't be right.

"Are you certain?"

Harrow leaned back, taking another sip. "My contact saw the signatures himself, in her ship's cargo hold."

"That doesn't mean she's involved," said Gideon, thinking it through. "Just because Rune owns the ships doesn't mean she knows everything that goes on with them. It could easily be one of the crew stowing witches away without her knowledge."

"But it makes her a suspect," Harrow pointed out. "And the best lead you've had in a long time."

For months now, Gideon had suspected the Crimson Moth was someone who traveled in elite circles. Someone with access to the most exclusive balls and private dinner parties. Someone who regularly rubbed shoulders with the powerful and well-connected.

Could that someone be Rune Winters?

Gideon remembered Rune at the opera, her conversation growing more and more irritating the longer she kept talking.

"It's not possible," he said. "There's not an intelligent thought in that girl's head."

And the Moth was intelligent. To go toe-to-toe with Gideon, to *outwit* him, she had to be. And if the mutilated bodies they kept finding across the city were her victims, she was also ruthless. Disturbed.

Evil.

It was difficult to reconcile those things with the ridiculous girl in the opera box.

If he needed more proof of Rune's innocence, all Gideon had to do was go back two years. He'd been at the Winters' estate when the Blood Guard arrested Kestrel Winters in her home. His orders? To watch Kestrel's adopted granddaughter, Rune, while the other soldiers seized the witch from her chambers.

Gideon hadn't taken his eyes off the girl—not an arduous task, to be sure. Rune was just as beautiful then. Like those marble sculptures adorning the lavish mansions of the aristocracy, existing solely to impress the guests. When a Blood Guard officer smashed his pistol into Kestrel's face, her granddaughter hadn't even flinched. Only watched, coldly and calmly, as they stripped the old woman down, found her scars, and dragged her off to be executed.

Rune had shown no hint of remorse.

If Rune had been Kestrel's blood relative, Gideon might consider her more carefully. But the girl's birth parents had been nothing more than fancy merchant folk. There were no witches in her bloodline—Gideon had checked—making it impossible that she was a witch.

"Rune sent her grandmother to the purge," Gideon told Harrow. "She's no witch sympathizer. Just an empty-headed patriot."

"Maybe that's what she wants you to think," Harrow countered.

Gideon shook his head. It made no sense. "Why would she risk her life to save other witches now when she heartlessly betrayed her grandmother two years ago?"

"It could be a deception."

Gideon was about to shrug this off, except that kind of

deception was exactly what he'd learned to expect from the Crimson Moth.

What if Harrow's right?

His comrade picked up her glass and slowly swirled the ale inside, watching Gideon chew on his thoughts.

He'd dismissed it, but there had been a moment in the opera box when Rune's mindless prattling had suddenly turned biting. *Someone like you obviously prefers the company of stupid brutes with terrible style.*

It didn't prove anything. Aristocrats like Rune Winters had always looked down on Gideon. The Blood Guard paid well, but good pay didn't elevate a man's station. Gideon might not be dirt-poor anymore, but he was far from her equal.

In Rune Winters' eyes, people like him—soldiers, sons of tailors, members of the working class—would always be *less than*.

But they'd found signatures on her ship. Gideon couldn't rule out the possibility that Rune might be the Moth—or at least in league with her.

"I'll keep my eyes on the docks," said Harrow.

He glanced up to find a thoughtful expression on her face. "I'll pay for whatever information you find."

The light in her golden eyes winked out. She stopped swirling her drink. "No."

Gideon sighed. Over a year ago, Harrow had approached him, offering her services. The Crimson Moth had stolen yet another witch from him the day before, and Gideon was desperate to outmaneuver her. He accepted Harrow's offer, expecting her to gouge him with her fees. Instead, she refused payment. When he asked her why, Harrow had simply pointed to her missing ear and walked away.

"Doesn't your little brother run in Rune's circles? Get him to spy for you."

Gideon tensed. This had always been a sore spot between him and Alex. His brother wanted nothing to do with the hunting and purging of witches. He'd made that clear these past two years, and Gideon no longer pressed him on it.

Their shared past haunted them both in different ways. Alex wanted to forget; Gideon couldn't afford to.

"Alex isn't interested in spy work."

"Mmm. I guess you'll have to do it yourself, then."

Gideon glanced up. "Do what myself?"

"*I* can't walk among them. Me in one of those fancy gowns, jewels dripping from my fingers?" Harrow turned her face to give him a perfect view of the side of her head where an ear should be but wasn't, making it perfectly obvious why she didn't belong in marble ballrooms, eating off gold-rimmed plates. "But you can."

"What are you proposing? That I *befriend* Rune Winters?"

"More than that, Comrade." Harrow's grin widened, and there was mischief in it. "You should woo her."

He nearly choked. "You're not serious."

The idea made him break out in a sweat.

Harrow leaned in. "You don't make friends, Gideon. Not easily, anyway. Certainly not with people like Rune. You do, however, collect admirers. Whether or not you notice them."

"She called me a stupid brute."

Harrow's mouth snagged in a crooked smile, as if this delighted her. "Sounds like a girl after my own heart."

"I'm serious. I have nothing to offer her. When girls like Rune pick out their future husbands, people like me don't make their lists."

"You might be surprised."

A cold horror crept over Gideon as he forced himself to consider it.

If Rune was the Crimson Moth, she was a master of disguise, and the only way to catch her was to play the same game she was playing.

There was only one problem.

Alex.

If Gideon did as Harrow suggested, presenting himself as one of Rune's many suitors, he'd be moving in on his little brother's crush. That's how it would look, at least.

All of Gideon's instincts rebelled against it.

But if Rune *was* the Moth, not only did he have a duty to take her down, he had a duty to protect his brother from her. If he hurt Alex in this process, so be it. It was a price he'd have to live with.

He hadn't saved Alex from one witch only to let him fall prey to another.

It was *this*—his brother, in danger—that forced his hand.

Gideon ran calloused fingers roughly through his hair, thinking back to the opera box, wincing at the cruel way he'd spoken to Rune. "There's another problem."

Harrow placed her elbow on the table and settled her cheek on her fist. "Tell me."

"I insulted her tonight. She invited me to her party, and I snubbed her."

The corner of Harrow's mouth twitched, as if she found Gideon squirming like a bug in a sticky web the funniest thing she'd seen all day.

She tapped her fingertips against the fuzzed brown hair of her undercut. "There's an obvious solution, but you won't like it."

Gideon nodded for her to go on.

"You need to get yourself to that party and back into her good graces."

"I need to grovel, you mean."

"Yes. But you can't just walk in there and say you're sorry. You need to prove that you mean it. If you're going to be a genuine contender for Rune Winters' heart, you need to beat out the competition."

He gritted his teeth at the thought.

Harrow leaned in. Even her eyes were laughing at him.

"The question is, Comrade: how are you going to do that?"

EIGHT

RUNE

MINORA: (n.) a category of small to medium spells.

Minora Spells require a witch's fresh blood. Old blood will typically not work and may cause painful consequences for the witch. Exceptions can be made when using the blood of another. Examples of Minora Spells include: closing a door from across the room or lighting a candle without a match.

—From Rules of Magic *by Queen Callidora the Valiant*

HER GRANDMOTHER'S SPELL BOOKS stared down from the musty old shelves of the casting room.

"Your supply is low," said Verity, running her fingers along the corked glass vials that hung on the opposite wall. Of the six vials, four were empty and two were full; one contained Rune's blood, the other Verity's.

"I know," said Rune from her casting desk, where she was tracing the mark for a spell called *Truth Teller* onto the bottom of a ceramic cup. Her guests would be here within the hour, and she needed to be ready. "But my cycle doesn't start for another two weeks."

Rune had developed her blood storage system shortly after learning she was a witch, using vials Verity stole from chemistry labs at the university. It was how Rune kept her body free of casting scars: by collecting her blood at every monthly cycle, she could usually get enough to see her through the month—*if* she used it sparingly and mainly cast simple Mirage spells. The more complicated a spell was, the more spellmarks it required, and the more blood needed to keep it alive.

A few months after her grandmother's purging, Rune bled for the first time. All of her friends had started their monthly cycles years before, around the age of thirteen. But Rune's first bleeding arrived late, at sixteen, after the revolution. Bringing with it the knowledge that she was, in fact, a witch.

She still remembered the painful cramping in her lower abdomen. She'd been at a party when it started, and had to excuse herself. In the bathroom, she'd found the black stain in her underwear, shining like ink.

Rune had stared at it, disbelieving.

It was the initial sign of a witch: at the onset of your first bleeding, you didn't bleed red, but black.

Rune had seen Nan cast, and had gleaned some of the fundamentals from her. But everything else she'd learned from Verity, whose two eldest sisters had been witches and had let their younger sister help them with their spells. It was Verity who started collecting her own blood and giving it to Rune in order to help her cast stronger spells.

Like this enchantment. *Truth Teller* was a Minora spell and therefore more advanced than Rune's usual Mirages. So she was using Verity's blood instead of her own.

Verity turned away from the vials, moving toward the center of the room, where Rune sat at the desk. A spell book lay open beside her. On the yellowed pages in red ink was the symbol for the truth-telling spell. It was what Rune was using to enchant the wine cup.

"I'll worry about my supply later," said Rune, still drawing the mark in blood. The taste of salt stung her throat, and the roar of magic was loud in her ears. "Tonight, we need to find out where they're holding Seraphine."

The moment the spellmark was complete, magic swelled inside Rune like a wave. She swallowed back the briny taste in her mouth and waited for the roar in her ears to recede.

As the blood dried and the spell solidified, Verity pushed her spectacles further up her nose. Rune couldn't help but notice the shadows under her friend's eyes. Likely from too many late nights helping the Crimson Moth, then staying up until morning to finish her biology homework.

Verity was a scholarship student at the university in the capital.

"We've been trying to find the new holding location for weeks and have nothing to show for it," Verity pointed out. "What makes you think tonight will be any different?"

"Because it has to be?" said Rune, desperate.

Pushing herself onto the desk, Verity seated herself next to the spell book, and her lavender perfume invaded Rune's senses. Floral scents were in fashion these days, and the one Verity doused herself in had been a gift from her sisters.

"Rubbing elbows with patriots and witch hunters worked a year ago," said Verity. "But the Blood Guard have gotten smarter. If we want to rescue Seraphine in time—if the Crimson Moth intends to stay one step ahead of the witch hunters—we'll need a better tactic. Have you given any more thought to my idea?"

"The one where I say goodbye to my freedom by marrying some smug suitor?"

Verity rolled her eyes. "Don't be dramatic. You say goodbye to *running yourself ragged* by strategically marrying someone who will unwittingly help you save witches." She started casually turning the thin pages of the book, absently skimming through the spells. "Did you see Charlotte Gong tonight? She was wearing a gold ring on a chain around her neck."

"So?" said Rune, setting the enchanted cup down now that the bloody spellmark on the bottom was dry. No one ever thought to check the bottom of their beverage for evidence of magic. Especially not in a witch hater's house.

"So: she's engaged. To Elias Creed." Elias was Laila and Noah's eldest brother. "He works for the Ministry of Public Safety. I put him at the top of your list of suitors, remember?"

"Pity," said Rune, without a hint of disappointment. She was happy for Charlotte, who had a sweet temperament and once told her the witch purgings gave her a stomachache.

"Pity indeed. Elias would have been perfect for you. Boring. Not too intelligent. Close to a source of valuable intel. Soon all the good ones will be taken, and you'll be out of options."

"Perhaps *you* could marry instead and give me all the intel you extract."

Verity gave a small smile. "I would if I could. But no one useful wants the poor little charity case."

This was, unfortunately, true.

Verity's mother had hated witches so deeply, she'd outed her eldest daughters to the Blood Guard, resulting in their deaths. Because of this, Verity had cut all ties with her parents, and in doing so, cut herself off from their monetary support. Rune suspected the story was even darker than her friend let on, from the way Verity went icy quiet when people brought it up, her eyes blackening like thunderclouds.

Verity's position at the university was now dependent on scholarships. Scholarships she could keep only if she attained top grades. Otherwise, she'd be stripped of her room and board and forced out onto the street.

Rising from the desk, Rune crossed to the window of the annex and looked out. Her grandmother's garden labyrinth sprawled out below, illuminated by the waxing moon. The sea was a black mirror in the distance.

She didn't feel ready to marry. It wasn't a matter of not being in love with any of her suitors; Rune had never expected love. In fact, in her grandmother's absence, sometimes Rune felt half-alive. Like her heart was a withered thing in her chest.

Rune was no longer capable of love, nor did she need it. What she needed was to make the most strategic choice.

It was more the *finality* of yoking herself to someone for the rest of her life that made her balk, especially when that someone could never know who she really was.

But Verity's right: it's time.

For a plan like this to be most effective, the person would have to be someone with intimate knowledge of the Blood Guard's secrets. Maybe she was being too picky, but when Rune looked at the list of suitors Verity had drawn up for her, when she considered the ones who were the most well connected, she suspected she could do better.

That she *must* do better.

Like there was a name missing from her list.

"Noah Creed is a good choice. They say his father is grooming him to become the next Good Commander. But he's clever," said Verity, still skimming the spells in the book on Rune's desk. "Bartholomew Wentholt is a better option. He's not that bright, and his mother is a celebrated witch hunter."

"Bart is obsessed with himself," said Rune, still staring out the window.

"Yes, but that could benefit you. He can't pay much attention to your comings and goings if he's checking his reflection every ten minutes."

Rune sighed and walked back to the desk, where Verity had

the book open to two spells Rune had been trying to master for weeks now: *Deadbolt* and *Picklock*. They were for locking and unlocking cell doors.

"Fine," said Rune, pressing her fists to her hips. "Here's the plan. I'll woo Bart. Invite him to my room. Ply him with wine." She glanced at the cup, now enchanted with *Truth Teller*. "If the information he gives me is valuable, I'll choose him. If not, I'll try again with Noah."

If a suitor didn't have access to good information, or wasn't capable of retaining that information, he wasn't worth her time.

A knock interrupted them. Rune's blood spiked at the sound. The false wall of her bedroom hid this room, and she always shut it when she came here—she didn't want the servants catching her red-handed in her grandmother's casting room.

"Miss Winters?" called a muffled voice.

Rune blew out a breath through her lips. It was only Lizbeth.

After Nan's arrest, the staff of Wintersea House all fled in the night, not wanting to serve in the house of a known witch. Or not wanting to serve in the house of an informer. Possibly both.

Only Lizbeth had stayed.

"Your guests are arriving."

"Thank you. We'll be right down."

Rune lifted the enchanted cup from the desk. She would leave it in the kitchen for Lizbeth, who would fill it with wine and await Rune's summons. They'd done this so often, with so many suitors, it was rote.

Rune glanced over to find Verity shrugging. "Noah or Bart— either will get you what you want, I think. And while you're making your decision tonight, Alex and I will find out where they're keeping Seraphine."

She jumped down off the desk.

Rune opened the latch in the false wall and pushed it open.

She waited for Verity to exit the casting room before stepping out after her.

"I was thinking yesterday, while feeding Henry . . ."

Henry was a spider. A *mimic* spider, Verity liked to remind her. Rune shivered, remembering the collection of arachnids Verity kept in jars on the shelf of her dormitory room. It was for a research project she was working on.

"Remember how I told you the mimic spider preys on small mammals?"

Rune preferred to not remember, actually. She hated spiders, and was now recalling the last time she'd visited her friend's dormitory, when Verity handed her a massive jar containing a sleek, long-legged creature that stared at Rune while it feasted on a fuzzy lump twice its size. Possibly a mouse.

"Their webs need to be strong enough to catch and hold much bigger food," Verity continued, oblivious to Rune's squirming. "They feign weakness, and their cries summon rodents looking for an easy meal. But once the predator stumbles into the mimic spider's web, they quickly become the prey. And once they're caught, the spider devours them slowly over days. Eating them alive."

Verity glanced pointedly back at Rune.

"Be like the mimic spider."

Rune wrinkled her nose. "That's . . . disgusting."

But the image stuck in her mind as she shut the door behind them.

"I NEVER WALK ANYWHERE if I can help it. Why walk when I have three carriages at the ready to take me wherever I want?"

Bart Wentholt was boring Rune out of her mind. She

swallowed a yawn as the two of them strolled the perimeter of her ballroom, which was alive with dancing guests.

"You should join me for a ride in my newest one. Maybe this Sunday? It would have to be in the afternoon, of course. I never get out of bed before noon."

How convenient, thought Rune. *I only fall into bed at noon.*

Bart glanced toward the windows, where his reflection smiled back at him. Rune wanted to catch Verity's gaze and roll her eyes, but there were too many others watching her. Alex, who was half engaged in a conversation a few feet away. Noah, who was dancing with a girl across the room. And several other young men on Verity's short list of *Suitors Rune Needs to Consider,* all waiting to pounce the moment Bart left her side.

Instead, Rune fiddled with an ice-blue ribbon tied around her wrist, its silky surface embroidered with the Winters' crest. She'd already given out the rest of her dancing ribbons to young men who'd asked at the beginning of the night. Rune had saved this one for Alex, as she always did. It was not only a way of passing on information to each other without looking suspicious, but a welcome respite.

"Will your mother be home?" Rune hoped that wasn't too forward. "I so enjoy her witch-hunting stories. Or does her work for the Blood Guard keep her very busy these days?"

"Oh, you haven't heard the dreadful news?" Bart was still looking at his reflection. Rune watched him brush his copper hair off his forehead so that it fell more stylishly to the side. As if the news he was about to relay didn't disturb him at all. "They honorably discharged her last week. One of the little beasts she was hunting slashed the tendon in her ankle with a knife. She'll never walk straight again."

What? "That's terrible!"

Terribly *inconvenient.* Rune made a face. His mother's position as a witch hunter was the sole reason she was considering Bart. She mentally struck him from the number one spot on Verity's list, already turning her attention to the young man who held second place: Noah Creed.

As the song played by the hired quartet ended, Noah's gaze fixed on her. She fiddled with the last remaining ribbon on her wrist, marked for the next song, and looked to where Alex danced with Charlotte Gong, who was indeed wearing a gold ring on a chain around her neck.

People considered it bad luck to wear a wedding ring on your finger before your wedding day. So girls hung engagement rings around their necks to show them off.

Her gaze moved from Charlotte's ring to Alex.

Rune had considered Alex as the solution to her suitor problem, of course. He was her oldest friend, and like a brother to her. Things between them might not be romantic, but good marriages were built on a lot less.

The problem was, Alex wasn't the most strategic choice. If Rune's prime directive was getting access to a source of regular, valuable intelligence, choosing Alex was impractical. Any information he gleaned, he gave to her freely.

Rune tore her gaze away from her friend, fixing it on Noah instead.

If she disentangled herself from Bart—who was currently using his reflection to adjust his cravat—she could give the ribbon she'd saved to Noah before the next dance began.

It seems I've made my choice, she thought, swallowing her disappointment.

Noah was perfectly acceptable. He was the son of the Good Commander—arguably the most powerful man in the republic. And his sister, Laila, was a witch hunter. So, as the hum of instruments faded into silence, signaling the end of this dance,

Rune abandoned Bart to his reflection. It would likely be several minutes before he even realized she'd left his side.

As dancers moved off the floor, she started across the ballroom toward Noah, whose face brightened at her approach.

Untying the ribbon from around her wrist, Rune fastened on a smile. She was preparing to continue her tiresome charade a little longer, when someone stepped into her path, cutting her off from her mark.

"Citizen Winters."

Rune halted at the voice. Her mind clanged like the bells of a firehouse, raising the alarm.

She knew that voice.

Gideon Sharpe.

What was he doing here in her ballroom?

Her brain was in the middle of shutting down, preparing her body to fight or flee, when she suddenly saw the flower he held out.

"I owe you an apology."

A what?

His palm cupped the rose, its stem hanging down between a gap in his fingers. If there were a more perfect rose, Rune had never encountered it. Crimson petals spiraled out from the center, bending back in mid-bloom.

"I was unthinking earlier," said Gideon, holding it out to her. "And unkind."

Knowing that every set of eyes was on them, Rune reluctantly took the rose. She found the stem not full of thorns, or even living; it was soft and sheer. Looking closer, she discovered jade-green silk wrapped tightly around some kind of wire. The petals, too, were fabric. Someone had delicately stitched the edges of each one.

Rune's gaze skimmed the front of Gideon's gray suit. It was rare for her to see a garment and not be able to place the designer. Fashion was her specialty. But this style of suit was wholly unfamiliar to her. *Vintage?* she wondered, impressed despite herself at how perfectly it fit his frame.

He seemed even bigger and broader out of uniform than in one.

"I was returning from a tiring witch hunt tonight," he explained. "It's no excuse, but the fatigue made me short-tempered. I was not myself."

She lifted her eyes to his face.

As their gazes clashed, the ballroom went quiet. The lights, the voices, and the fashions of her guests faded to nothing as an unexpected thought struck Rune.

Gideon Sharpe is the missing name on my list.

It both terrified and tempted her.

But it was one thing to spend her nights as the Crimson Moth, outwitting the Blood Guard and rescuing witches from execution—that kind of danger was familiar. It was something very different to seduce the deadliest witch hunter of all: a cold, brutal soldier who wanted nothing more than to put the Crimson Moth to death.

I'd have to pretend more than ever.

Continuously pulling the wool over his eyes would be Rune's biggest challenge yet. She would be in constant danger.

But it would be worth the risk . . .

Because Gideon Sharpe was by far the most tactical choice. If she and Gideon were courting, Rune would have intimate access to all the information she needed to rescue every witch—now and in the future.

She cleared her throat. "You have impeccable timing." If he'd been fifteen seconds later, she would already be in Noah's arms, her decision made. "I'll gladly accept your apology . . ." Lifting the ribbon she'd untied from her wrist, Rune held it out to him. ". . . if you'll dance with me?"

NINE

GIDEON

NORMALLY, **GIDEON WENT OUT** of his way to avoid parties like this. So when Rune held her ribbon in the air between them, he didn't know what the hell he was supposed to do with it.

As it hung in the space between them, catching the light, every guest in the room fell quiet, their eyes moving to the bumbling idiot standing awkwardly before their hostess, reminding Gideon that he didn't belong here. How the revolution had changed so much, and also nothing at all.

He was still the poor son of a tailor. The outdated suit he wore declared that to everyone. Gideon had grown up playing on dirt floors, eating watered-down soup to last the bitter winters, feeling his clothes get tighter and more threadbare because there was no money to replace them. All while the people currently gawking at him ate off gold-rimmed plates, fed their leftovers to their fat hounds, and retired their wardrobes at the end of every season.

While Gideon led a desperate group of men through the rat-infested cellars of the palace to murder tyrants in their beds, the "revolutionaries" around him hadn't stooped to pick up a gun. Or gotten their hands dirty at all. Instead of losing their loved ones in the fighting on the eve of the New Dawn, many of these aristos had handed those loved ones over to be purged, betraying family and friends to keep their status in the New Republic after paying lip service to the Sister Queens for years. As if politics, for them, was not life or death, but simply a matter of swapping outdated gowns for whatever the newest trend was.

Gideon would rather ride his horse through a foot of mud, uphill, in a bloody hurricane than rub shoulders with the people here tonight.

And Rune Winters was the worst of them.

The brush of warm fingers on his wrist broke the spell in the room. Gideon looked down to find the hostess herself tying a blue dancing ribbon around his wrist.

His skin itched where she touched, and he fought the instinct to excuse himself, walk out the doors, and never look back. Gideon forced himself to hold still, thinking of Harrow's report. Of the casting mark found on Rune's cargo ship.

You're here for the Moth, and the sooner you catch her, the easier it will be to purge the world of every last witch.

Gideon studied the girl before him. Was this her?

It seemed absurd. This darling of the New Republic, picking the locks of his holding cells, making off with his prisoners in the night, slaughtering Blood Guard officers in the street. And yet, it could be the reason he'd failed to catch the Moth these past two years: because she'd hidden herself so skillfully in plain sight.

When Rune finished tying the ribbon, she lifted the silk rose, tucking it into her red-gold hair, which was now braided into a semi-crown at the back of her head.

He'd spent the last two hours making it for her, feeling slightly ill as he sewed every petal. Roses always brought the painful memories rushing back. But Harrow's advice—to woo Rune—kept ringing through his head, and his mother could never resist the silk roses his father used to make her after they argued.

That, of course, was before the Sister Queens broke his mother's mind.

"Oh dear. Clumsy me! I'm making a mess of it . . ."

Gideon looked down to find Rune struggling with the stem of the rose—which was snagged in her hair.

"Here, let me . . ."

Rune dropped her hands as Gideon worked to separate the strands of gold from the wire stem. They stood so close now that her fragrance filled the air. Gideon braced himself, remembering another girl, another scent. But there was no reek of magic on Rune. All he could smell was the salty sea air blowing in through the open windows.

Which means nothing.

After a long soak in the bath, Cressida hadn't smelled of magic either.

Cressida.

The name was a growl in his mind. Had Cressida ever dined beneath this roof? For all he knew, Cressida and Rune might have been friends.

He swallowed the sick feeling in his throat, carefully tucking the silk flower into the weave of Rune's hair until it sat snug and fashionably to one side. The way his mother used to wear the flowers his father made her.

Before he could step back, the music started. Gideon glanced up to find himself surrounded by pairs of dancers on all sides.

Rune's eyes sparkled as she reached out her gloved hand, positioning it high in the air. She stepped in closer, settling her other hand on his shoulder. "Ready, Captain Sharpe?"

Beneath the soft weight of her grip, Gideon tensed.

What am I doing?

He didn't know this song, never mind the steps of whatever dance it cued.

Unlike the couples already moving around him, mirroring each other as they glided and twirled along with the melody, Gideon stood frozen as a statue while Rune held herself gracefully poised, ready to dance.

Her eyebrows arched, as if to say, *What are you waiting for?*

His neck grew hot beneath his collar. "Miss Winters . . ."

She must have heard it in his voice, because she quickly lowered her hands and stepped back. "Oh. You . . . don't know how."

Most of her friends still watched them, some of them murmuring behind their hands. Were they laughing at him?

Was *she* laughing at him?

He thought again of another girl. Another party. One where he'd been paraded around and humiliated.

Gideon thought he'd extinguished that shame. But it flared now like glowing embers.

Harrow was mistaken. Gideon had no chance in hell of successfully courting a girl like Rune. He'd just arrived and was already embarrassing her. When she realized he had no wealth or grand estate—he'd given his spoils of war to Alex after the revolution—she would join in their laughing, if she hadn't already.

He needed to salvage this.

Remembering Harrow's advice, he closed the distance between them.

"If we were at a different type of party," he said, close to Rune's ear, "I could give you a different answer."

Another memory seeped up, filling his mind with the fast-paced melody of a fiddle. He could see his little sister in her cotton nightgown, still awake despite it being far past her bedtime.

The humidity of the kitchens made her hair curl and stick to her sweaty skin as she danced with the dishwashers, cotton towels tucked into their waistbands. The cook, cheeks pink from the ovens, stood in the corner slashing his bow across his fiddle as the palace staff clapped and stomped and passed around a skin of ale before joining in the dancing themselves.

Sweet memories were rare for Gideon.

This one almost made him smile.

But as the memory faded and the flickering lights of the room around him came back into focus, he remembered that Tessa wasn't here. He'd buried his little sister deep in the earth, where she'd never dance again.

Because of a witch.

Remembering where he was, and who stood before him—a girl who might be a witch in disguise, a girl who loved to be the center of attention—he said, "I seem to have scandalized your guests. I wonder if we should give them something more to discuss?"

Rune turned her face to his, clearly intrigued. "What did you have in mind?"

Getting you alone.

Alone, she would be vulnerable.

"Care to give me a private tour of your home?" It would provide him with the opportunity to search not only Rune for evidence of witchcraft, but also her house.

A smile curled her pretty mouth. "Of course. I should have offered."

Her hand slid into his, surprising him. She was smaller than he'd realized, her palm nearly half the size of his.

"Come with me."

Gideon let her plunge them through the murmuring guests, scattering their gossip like moths. For such a small thing, her grip was startlingly strong as she led him to the grand staircase on the other side of the room. Letting go of his hand, she started upward, leading them out of the noisy ballroom.

He was halfway up the steps behind her when a familiar voice called from below.

"Gideon?"

With one hand on the railing, Gideon froze, then turned to find his brother standing at the bottom of the stairs. Alex had discarded his suit jacket somewhere in the room, revealing brown suspenders over a crisp white shirt. His eyes flickered to Rune at the top of the steps, and back to Gideon, who stood between them, then lowered to the pale blue ribbon tied around Gideon's wrist.

"What are you doing here?" Alex demanded. "You hate parties."

"Not all parties," said Gideon, thinking again of the ones he and his sister used to attend after midnight in the palace kitchens.

"This kind, you do. Which means you're here hunting."

"Rune invited me," said Gideon, a little defensive.

"No doubt." Alex's eyes narrowed on Rune. To her, he said, "I'd like to claim my dance now."

Gideon glanced back to find Rune's eyes full of bullets, all directed at Alex.

Sweet Mercy. What had he walked into?

Rune clearly did not want to dance with Alex. And if she truly was the Moth, Gideon didn't want his brother anywhere near her.

"She's already promised me a tour of the estate," he said.

"*I'll* give you a tour," said Alex, moving up the steps. "After I dance with Rune."

His brother wasn't even looking at him; his icy glare locked with Rune's.

This was not a battle he wanted to be in the middle of. But if Gideon hoped to convince Rune he was truly vying for her affection, he needed to stake his claim. Doing so would drive a wedge between him and his brother, and there was already a sizable fissure in their bond, one cracked open years ago that had been growing wider ever since.

He thought of the casting signatures on Rune's cargo ship.

I couldn't protect Tessa, he thought, watching Alex. *But I can still protect you.*

He was about to cut his brother off when Rune herself stepped between them. Alex stood on the stair below hers, peering down at her.

"The song is already over, Alex. You'll have to wait until next time."

Before he could argue with her, Rune turned and left both brothers behind, her rust-colored gown shimmering as she went. At the top of the stairs, she glanced over her shoulder, eyes glittering in the gaslight. It was darker there, and the shadows sharpened her edges.

"Coming, Gideon?"

He paused, shooting an apologetic glance back at Alex.

I'm doing this for you.

But his brother didn't look wounded. He looked worried.

Exactly who Alex was worried about, Rune or Gideon, was hard to decipher. And he didn't have time to figure it out. Fixing his attention on the task at hand—unmasking the Crimson Moth—Gideon quickly caught up to Rune. Together they left the party, and Alex, behind.

TEN

RUNE

*R*UNE'S FINGERTIPS PRICKLED WITH annoyance.

Yes, Alex had warned her away from his brother. Yes, Rune had flat-out disregarded his warning. But she had expected a scolding from him, not a direct attempt at sabotage.

She would have to nip his meddling right in the bud—as soon as she'd won over Gideon.

How am I going to do that?

She'd been expecting to leave the party with Bart or Noah tonight. Gideon was a very different type of suitor. Not only did he hunt witches for a living, there was also a good chance he suspected Rune of being one. It might even be why he was here tonight.

She wondered about his change of heart—was his irritation in the opera box actually due to fatigue? Or had something come to light about Rune that he needed to investigate himself?

She simply couldn't trust him.

Rune thought about Verity's mimic spider, Henry, pretending to be weak in order to catch predators in its web.

Verity's right. She needed to be like Henry.

Rune had invited her greatest predator into the heart of her home. Now she had to ensnare him here so she could finish him the way she'd finished so many others before: by plying him with wine from the cup she had enchanted. *Truth Teller* would compel him to tell the truth without realizing he was being compelled.

As Gideon Sharpe's long-legged stride caught up to Rune, she remembered the scene from the ballroom. It surprised her that he didn't know how to dance, since Alex was such a proficient dancer.

But that's because I taught him, thought Rune. Clearly no one had taught Gideon.

She wouldn't have asked him to dance if she'd known he didn't know how. Humiliating him like that, in front of all her friends, would not win him over. And from the rigid line of his shoulders and the stiffness in his step beside her, she could tell his guard was still up.

If she was going to ensnare him, she needed to first put him at ease.

"I apologize for my guests. You're a novelty here, you must know that. They couldn't help but stare."

He scanned their surroundings, taking in everything from the pale blue floor tiles to the white marble columns lining this hall. "Is that a nice way of saying I lack pedigree?"

"Not at all!" She forced a laugh, settling into her persona. "Just look at your suit."

"It was my father's," he said, defensive.

Rune frowned, her footsteps slowing. *He thinks I'm making fun of him.*

How was she botching this so badly?

"Wait . . ." She frowned, realizing what he'd said. "It was your father's suit, or your father made it?"

"Both."

Rune stopped walking altogether. Gideon was several yards

ahead. Realizing she was no longer at his side, he turned to face her.

"Gideon. You're wearing a vintage suit made by the Sharpe Duet, and you think my guests are laughing at your pedigree?"

He cocked his head. "Yes?"

She stared at him. *He really doesn't know.*

Nan and her friends owned nothing made by the Sharpe Duet, but not for lack of trying. Until now, Rune had never even seen one of their garments up close.

"A collector would pay tens of thousands of dollars for that jacket alone," she told him. "Because it's so rare."

"Because my parents are dead, you mean."

Rune winced. Technically, yes. That they were no longer alive to make more garments increased the value of those currently in existence. But the Sharpes' designs had been rare *before* they died. Once the Sister Queens employed them, Sun and Levi Sharpe tailored for the Rosebloods alone, ensuring few originals were ever made.

Surely he knew this?

"What I'm trying to say is, if my guests are staring at you, it's because you're Gideon Sharpe, a living legend. A hero who risked his life leading revolutionaries into the palace and single-handedly killing two witch queens."

She didn't fake the awe in her voice. Rune might despise him for what he'd done, but that didn't mean she wasn't impressed by the courage it had required.

"They're staring at you because you're at the same party they are. You're not exactly known for accepting invitations."

"I lack basic manners, you mean." He nodded, as if understanding. "I don't see how that's different from lacking in pedigree, though."

She growled a little. He seemed to be intentionally misunderstanding her.

To her surprise, Gideon smiled. If you could call the slight twitch at the corner of his mouth a smile.

Is he . . . teasing me?

A furious heat rushed up her neck. *Has he been teasing me this whole time?*

Seeing her blush, the corner of Gideon's mouth *did* curve upward, staying that way for several seconds.

Rune looked away, trying to focus. *Remember the plan. Lure him in.*

"If you attended more of my parties," she said, continuing forward to rejoin him, "I could ensure you knew how to dance to any song when a girl asks you."

"Are you offering to give me lessons?"

The question caught her off guard.

Am I?

Rune had taught his brother. Alex was an eager pupil, happy to let her lead. She doubted Gideon would subject himself to such a thing.

"I . . ."

"A girl like you has better things to do with her time, surely."

She didn't. Not during the day, which was full of dreary social calls: picnics and luncheons and carriage rides, all so she could wring gossip from her friends like drops of water from a wet towel, desperately hoping it might help her save one more witch.

But he didn't really seem interested.

"You don't have to deflect," she said. "You can simply say you don't want to dance with me."

He glanced sharply toward her. "That's not . . ."

This time, *he* stopped walking. When Rune turned to face him, she found his jaw clenched. He rubbed a hand over it.

"I have a counteroffer: you could accompany me to an *actual* party." He glanced back in the ballroom's direction. "There will be no ball gowns. No hired musicians. No songs with ridiculous steps . . ."

He trailed off, studying Rune in the flickering light of the gas lamps throughout the hall. Remembering himself, he shook his head. "A girl like you wouldn't be caught dead dancing with riffraff in disreputable locales."

The idea of it thrilled her, actually.

Though it definitely shouldn't.

"Who says I'll get caught? Name the date, and I'll be there."

The frown creasing his forehead deepened. "Careful, Miss Winters, or I might call your bluff."

"Are you so sure I'm bluffing?"

Again, his mouth twitched. As if he wanted to smile.

It felt like victory.

Rune let the subject drop and led him up another grand staircase to the third floor, where two double doors led into the second-largest room of the house.

"This is Alex's favorite room."

Gideon followed her into the dark expanse, which carried the faint smell of stale tea and old books. In front of them, windows stretched from the floor to the ceiling three stories above. The panes faced Nan's gardens and, beyond that, the cliffs leading down to the sea. In the distant water, the moon's reflection was a white candle flame flickering in and out of the waves.

Rune lit the gaslights, illuminating the room, and watched Gideon walk a slow circle, taking in the walls of shelves lined with books, the balconies on the second and third level, the spiral staircase rising to the top of it all.

"Any spell books in here?" he asked.

Rune's heart tumbled over itself.

After the New Dawn, the Good Commander declared all objects used for witchcraft to be contraband. Finding a spell book in a citizen's possession was enough to accuse them of sympathizing with witches.

"Feel free to look," she said, hiding her panic behind a smile. She'd hidden all of her spell books in the casting room. "I won't stop you."

Gideon seemed about to say more when a large silhouette near the window caught his eye.

"Is that . . . ?"

It was a grand piano. Alex had his own piano now, but he still preferred this one. He often spent all day here, practicing on it.

"No wonder Alex spent so much time here."

Alex had been coming to Wintersea House nearly every day since he was eleven years old to play piano. Rune had *hated* her lessons, hated practicing, hated even the sight of those black and white keys. But Nan refused to let her quit. Alex was not only desperate to play, he was actually good at it. It was a shame that his family couldn't afford to give him lessons. So Rune blackmailed her tutor into giving Alex hers, and by the time Nan found out, months had already passed.

Gideon strode over to the instrument, walking around it before coming to stand on the other side of the bench, facing the keys.

"Do you play?" she asked.

"Not at all." He pressed down on a single ivory key. The E note rang, smooth and clear, through the room. "My brother is the musical one."

Rune nodded. No one played as beautifully as Alex. Even Nan had come round to him in the end, wooed by his raw talent.

"The day his acceptance letter came from the Royal Conservatory, he hid it from our parents." Gideon pressed down on another key—A this time—and the note hummed from deep in the piano's heart.

Rune frowned. Alex had never told her that. "Why?"

"Our family could barely afford rent, never mind that kind of tuition. He didn't want them to feel ashamed."

If Alex had come to Rune, she would have convinced Nan to lend him the money—or figured out a way to pay it herself. The Royal Conservatory was a prestigious school on the mainland. Their music program was so competitive, the school accepted only a handful of students each year.

But Alex *had* studied at the Conservatory. For a few years, anyway. When the revolution struck, he left the program and never went back.

Intrigued, she sat down on the bench next to where Gideon stood behind it. "If your family couldn't pay the tuition, where did he get the money?"

Gideon pressed down on the next key—the middle C—moving further down the keyboard, closer to Rune. The progression of notes he'd chosen formed a minor triad, resulting in a melancholic sound. It was a sadness Rune felt in her chest.

"We got lucky." His voice hardened on that word: *lucky*. "My parents' fashions began catching the attention of the aristocracy."

Another key; another sorrowful note. This one was so close to Rune, his sleeve brushed her bare shoulder as he reached to play it.

"The eldest witch queens, Analise and Elowyn, were so taken by my mother's designs, they wanted them for themselves."

Gideon stepped directly behind Rune and the shadow of him spread up her back. Startled by the move, she froze, her pulse thrumming. With one hand still on the key to her left,

Gideon reached around Rune with his free hand, pressing down on the keys to her right—F, then F-sharp—caging her in.

The hair on her nape rose. There couldn't be more than an inch of space between them now. Rune's senses heightened as she wondered if the mimic spider ever underestimated its much larger prey and was sometimes caught in its own web instead.

If she survived this encounter unscathed, she'd ask Verity.

Gideon's voice was beside her ear. When he spoke, his breath rushed against her cheek. "Analise offered my mother a position as royal seamstress, with my father and me assisting. The yearly stipend was more than enough to send Alex away to school."

Swallowing, Rune kept her voice light as she said, "That's when your family went to live at the palace?"

"All of us except Alex, yes." He fell silent for a long moment. Beneath his breath, he said: "He escaped what the rest of us could not."

What does that mean?

Alex rarely spoke about his family. What Rune knew, she knew from other people's gossip: shortly before the revolution, a terrible sickness stole his little sister's life. Not long after, his parents drowned in an unfortunate swimming accident, orphaning him and Gideon.

But several pieces of the story were missing. It started when the queens employed the Sharpes. Somewhere in the middle, three members of their family died. And by the end, Gideon and Alex had slain all three queens in their sleep.

What connected these things?

Rune had met the youngest queen, Cressida, only once, at one of her seasonal parties. The witch queen had reminded Rune of an elegant swan, poised and aloof. She had porcelain skin, the bluest eyes, and hair like ivory. She spoke only half a dozen words to Rune before floating off to join her sisters.

Cressida had a reputation for being shy, and she rarely left Thornwood Hall, her summer home. Some people attributed this to pride, saying Cressida thought herself better than everyone else.

She's a queen, Rune had thought at the time. *She is better than us.*

One of the more vicious rumors, Rune remembered now, had been about Cressida's lowborn lover. She never brought him with her to public gatherings or appearances, as if she were ashamed of the dalliance. Rune would hear it whispered about at parties, but few people knew the young man's name, never mind what he looked like. So it could have easily been a lie intended to undermine the girl.

And now, two years after Cressida and her sisters were slain, along with the witches on their council, the boy who led those revolutionaries into the palace stood directly behind Rune, his breath in her hair, his fingers on the keys of her piano.

Why did you kill them? she wanted to ask. *Why do you hate us?*

But Rune already knew the answer. Gideon hated witches for the same reason everyone else did. Rune was well versed in her society's hatred. They made no secret of it.

We are vermin to them, Nan told her right before the revolution, when things were already turning. Even before they murdered the queens, riots spilled through the streets. Witches were dragged from their houses and beaten—or worse. The Roseblood sisters sent their army to put the perpetrators down like dogs, but it only made things worse. *They see us as a contamination of what is natural and good. They fear our magic the way they fear disease.*

The queens were never given a proper burial, and to this day, no one knew where the bodies lay. People had different theories, of course: they'd been burned in a pit, or dumped in the sea, or chopped into pieces to prevent resurrection.

No one knew for sure.

Since their deaths, and the birth of the New Republic, the Good Commander had been stripping the magic from every captured witch by purging her of its source: stringing them by the ankles like animals, slitting their throats, and leaving them to hang until every drop of blood drained from their bodies.

Rune shuddered.

As if sensing it, Gideon withdrew his hands from the piano keys and stepped back. The absence of him was like a too-heavy coat slipping from her shoulders, allowing her to breathe. He turned toward the thousands of book spines filling the walls, illuminated by the incandescent lighting.

"Do you mind if I look around?"

Relieved by the distance between them, she waved her hand. "Go ahead."

If he had lived at the palace, he'd lived among witches, which meant he knew how to spot the signs of her kind. Spell books were an obvious giveaway, but there were none in the library. Casting marks were another tell, but the only spell cast recently enough to leave marks was in Nan's casting room, where Rune had enchanted the cup she'd given to Lizbeth.

There's nothing to find, she thought, watching the witch hunter.

Perhaps she should use the cup now. Gideon appeared at ease, and the sooner she learned where the Blood Guard were keeping Seraphine, the sooner she could rescue the woman before they transferred her.

After several moments of watching him browse, she said, "Reading can be so tedious, don't you think? Sometimes I get exhausted just looking at all these books."

Gideon, who was currently perusing her collection of operas and plays, either didn't hear her or was ignoring her. The light illuminated his fingers as he traced the titles on the weathered spines. When he arrived at Rune's favorite play—about a mysterious hero who risks his own life to rescue aristocrats in danger—Gideon slid the book off the shelf and opened it to the first page.

Rune clenched her jaw, annoyed that he'd chosen it. She didn't want him holding something she loved in his hands. They were the same hands he used to strip witches out of their clothes. To search them for scars. To give them over to be purged.

"For a girl who hates reading, you own a lot of books."

"They were my grandmother's. Nan was obsessed with books." Rune tapped her fingertips against the piano bench, itching to tell him to put her book back and never touch it again. She counted to ten, lost her patience, and said instead, "Would you like to see a witch's bedroom, Citizen Sharpe?"

To her great relief, he closed the book and returned it to the shelf. When he turned to face her, his eyes were deep wells.

"I'd like nothing more, Miss Winters."

Rising from the bench, Rune tugged the bellpull, letting Lizbeth know she was ready to put the last part of her plan into action.

ELEVEN

RUNE

*I*N HER BEDROOM, THE lamps were already lit. Their flames burned dimly, as if the room had been patiently waiting for its mistress.

Rune turned to Gideon, who looked like a wolf stepping into unfamiliar territory: wary, aloof, ready to bare his teeth at the first sign of danger.

His stony gaze scanned the room, taking in the lavender walls and the loft ceiling made of glass. Other than the four-poster bed, there were only a few furnishings, all of them tasteful and understated. Just the way Rune—the real Rune—liked things.

The sea breeze blowing in through the windows ruffled Gideon's hair. "This is your bedroom."

She clasped her hands in front of her. "That's right."

This was her favorite place. Her *safest* place. And she had invited a dangerous enemy straight into it.

"You said it belongs to a witch." He stalked slowly toward her, his gaze pinning her in place.

"It belonged to my grandmother, yes,"

Gideon halted.

Did you think it would be that easy?

She frowned, staring at him. He wasn't very good at this game.

Sudden footsteps made them turn toward the doorway, where Lizbeth stood. On the tray gripped in her hands sat two cups and a decanter of red wine. "Your refreshments, Miss Winters."

Rune nodded her thanks.

Lizbeth, who'd played her part in this charade dozens of times, brought the tray to the low table in front of the love seat. "A telegram arrived for you earlier. I'll leave it with your drinks."

A telegram? It must have been from someone important, otherwise Lizbeth would have waited until tomorrow.

"Oh, and . . ." She paused at the door. "Verity was looking for you."

"You can tell her where I am. And that I'll return to the party soon."

Rune waited for Lizbeth to leave before sinking into the plush cushions of the love seat. Lifting the decanter, she poured wine into both cups. The one she'd enchanted earlier buzzed beneath her fingertips. As Gideon sat down next to her, she held it out to him.

He shook his head. "No, thank you."

Rune's outstretched hand remained between them, holding out the wine. "Oh, you simply *must* try some." She forced a smile. "It's from my vintage collection. This bottle came all the way from the Umbrian mountains on the Continent. Lizbeth uncorked it for us. Here." She pressed it toward him.

Gideon still didn't take it. "I don't drink."

What? Cold sweat beaded down her back.

Why hadn't Alex ever mentioned this important fact?

She swallowed, the cup hovering between them. "Are you sure?"

"Very sure."

Rune's mind went strangely blank. This had always been the way: pick a suitor, lure him away from the party, then ply him with truth-telling wine. Sometimes she got the information she needed, sometimes she didn't, but it was never because they refused her.

"Please," said Gideon, his eyes narrowing as he studied her. "Don't abstain on my account."

Oh, I won't. A sip would relax her and help her reassess before forging a fresh path. Setting down the enchanted cup, she reached for the other.

"Something wrong with that one?"

Rune froze like a rabbit in a snare.

"Wh-what?"

"The wine you offered me. After I refused it, you set it down and took the other."

Shoot.

"D-did I?"

Shoot. Shoot. Shoot.

He stretched his arm across the back of the sofa, his hand gripping the smooth mahogany frame behind Rune. "You wouldn't be trying to drug me, would you?" His mouth quirked, as if he were flirting. But his eyes were dark, and the look in them dangerous.

He knows.

What had Alex told her earlier this evening? That if she tried a spell in Gideon's presence, he would smell the magic on her.

Rune tried not to panic. Every witch's magic smelled different. Rune was only capable of minor spells and illusions—weak castings—making her magic's scent hard to detect. In fact, the only person who'd ever recognized the scent of Rune's magic was Verity. A few months after the revolution, Rune had cast her very first illusion before attending a ball. Verity—who didn't know Rune then—should have reported her the moment she smelled the magic. Instead, she took Rune aside and told her to be more careful.

They'd been friends ever since.

Even if Gideon suspects me, he has no proof.

She put her cup down and lifted the enchanted one. Cupping the bottom of it with two hands—hiding the spellmark drawn there—she locked eyes with him, pressed the cup to her lips, and took a long swallow.

"If it's drugged," she said, coming up for air, "you'll know in a few minutes."

Releasing his grip on the polished wood, he bent his elbow and leaned his temple against his fist. "Looking forward to it."

As the alcohol flooded her, warming her down to her legs, something rushed along with it.

Magic.

Like unruly ivy pushing at the windows of a house, forcing open the locks and letting itself in, she could feel *Truth Teller* breaking down her defenses, loosening her inhibitions, allowing someone to reach in and easily pluck what was inside.

Rune clung to the cup, wondering what the hell she was going to do.

It's your spell. Work around it.

She had no idea if it was possible. She'd never tested *Truth Teller* on herself.

But the enchantment wouldn't force its victim to offer the truth unprompted; if Gideon wanted to get something out of her, he needed to ask a question. And Gideon didn't know Rune had enchanted the cup, never mind enchanted it with a spell for telling the truth. So, theoretically, he had no reason to interrogate her.

This will be fine. Stay calm.

Hard to do when she felt like a cornered animal.

Gideon sat inches from Rune, making it easy to see how much bigger and stronger than her he was. She couldn't help but notice the warmth rolling off him. With it came a heady scent, not only of gunpowder, but something stronger, like freshly cut cedar. It was so pleasant, she wanted to lean into it.

Alarmed by the instinct, she immediately leaned away instead. Trying to appear unbothered by everything spinning out of her control, she reached for the folded telegram Lizbeth left on the tray and started to unfold it.

"Is there a reason you abstain?" If she could keep him talking, it might prevent him from asking her questions.

"I don't like not being in control of myself."

"But isn't that half the fun?" she asked, glancing at him.

He looked away, but not before his eyes darkened. "I might have agreed with you once."

Rune lowered the telegram, curious. "Oh?"

"There was a time when I needed it to survive. Along with other, stronger substances." His lip curled. "Or that's what I told myself."

Stronger substances? Rune wondered what those might be. Years ago, when the Sister Queens ruled, laudanum had been popular among Nan and her friends. *Is that what he means?*

"Alex could tell you all about it, I'm sure."

Frustrated that she couldn't enchant the truth out of him, she asked, "What if I want *you* to tell me about it?"

When he looked at her, his eyes were full of shadows.

He didn't answer her question. Instead, he nodded to her telegram. "A love poem from one of your admirers?"

"Uh, no." Rune glanced down, reading the subject line, and immediately frowned. "It's . . ."

```
MISS RUNE WINTERS
WINTERSEA HOUSE


THE MINISTRY OF PUBLIC SAFETY IS DELIGHTED
TO NAME YOU GUEST OF HONOR AT NEXT WEEK'S
LUMINARIES DINNER. PLEASE PREPARE A SPEECH
EXTOLLING THE NOBLE VIRTUES OF THE REPUB-
LIC. SEE YOU THURSDAY NEXT.


                         AILA WOODS
             PUBLIC SAFETY MINISTER
```

Rune felt her legs go numb.

The Luminaries Dinner was a monthly tribute to heroes of the revolution, intended to bolster loyalty to the regime. Rune had planned to skip it this time because the last one had been so hard to stomach.

As she read the telegram again, her heart sank.

If she declined to be their guest of honor, the Tribunal would see it as disloyalty.

She had to accept.

Not only did she have no time to prepare a speech, but the Luminaries Dinner always required the worst kind of pretending. She would have to act proud of what she'd done. Have to feign ambivalence about the violent loss of the person she loved most. Her speech would cheer on the Republic while calling for more purgings, and denounce the evil of witches in their midst.

She would spit on Nan's memory yet again.

In the beginning, pretending had been easier. Rune could

push down her anger and grief. But the more fealty she swore to the New Republic, the more witches she failed to save, the harder it became.

If there weren't a hundred other reasons to despise Gideon Sharpe, this would be sufficient: he didn't have to hide who he was. He didn't have to pretend to hate the things he truly loved.

If she didn't loathe him so much, she might envy him.

Rune fell back into the cushions. "Wasn't Lola Parsons supposed to be the guest of honor this month?"

Gideon's brow furrowed as he glanced from her to the telegram. "The Guard took Lola into custody last week." He gently took the paper from her, scanning its contents. "One of her servants reported a casting signature in her cellar. She denies it, but we believe she was harboring a witch."

Oh.

"They're asking you to be the guest of honor instead?"

Rune nodded, a little numbly.

His brow furrowed further. "And that's a bad thing?"

Rune could feel the answer—the real one—surge up her throat.

Yes. I can't stand it any longer. If I have to toast the villains who murdered my grandmother one more time, I'm going to set them all on fire.

Her answer—the absolute truth of the situation—swelled on her tongue, pushing at the roof of her mouth. She could feel it slipping past her teeth . . .

No no no no no.

Panicking, Rune tried to think of any other reason this invite should upset her. If she could push out a smaller truth before the more dangerous one escaped, she might subvert the spell.

"I don't have a dress to wear!"

Gideon drew back, startled by the outburst.

Rune clamped her mouth shut to prevent the real reason from escaping. But it subsided—for now, at least.

He raised one dark brow. "Is that all?"

Curse him.

The surge began again—because no; it was not all. *Truth Teller* was drawing the words from her depths, like water from a well.

I hate this horrible Republic. I would burn it to the ground if I could. But if I don't play along, girls like me will continue to die.

This time when the words threatened to burst out of her, Rune squeezed her hands into fists as she held them back, trying to think of something—anything—else to say instead. Something less damning, but still true.

"There's no time to have a dress made! My seamstress is booked until next month, but the dinner is next week."

Rune threw him a pitiful look that wasn't entirely false. She'd gone hot all over and her heart beat painfully fast.

"Hmm. That is unfortunate."

But the spell wasn't finished with her. It snaked up her throat, threatening to choke her.

Tell him, it prodded. *Tell him the rest.*

"And . . ." The words itched. She tried to swallow them but couldn't. "They'll want me to talk about Nan."

She had his full attention now.

He was staring at her, his gaze piercing. "And you don't want to."

She shook her head no, eyes burning with the tears that were building. She was terrified of blurting out the rest. Rune reached for her throat, prepared to squeeze if something worse tried to escape.

As a hot tear slipped down her cheek, Gideon visibly softened. "I'm sorry. It must have been hard to be raised by a witch."

It wasn't a question, so Rune didn't have to answer. Her chest still rose and fell with her rapid breaths.

He glanced over her shoulder. She followed his gaze. Between the translucent cerulean canopies of her bed, which were drawn back and tied to each of the four posts, an enormous portrait hung on the wall.

Kestrel Winters took up most of the picture's frame. She wore a black velvet dress with lace trim, and she'd pinned her curls back, allowing the artist to catch every ridge and crease of her solemn face. She was close to sixty in this rendering, and her beauty often reminded Rune of a mighty oak.

It was the child on Nan's lap, however, that drew the viewer's eye. She wore a crisp lace dress with pale blue ribbons—but that was where her elegance ended. Her cheeks were bright red from running, and her strawberry blonde hair, which had been painstaking combed not long before this sitting, was a messy tangle.

A grass stain spoiled the knee of one white stocking, and though Rune had been told to sit still, the artist couldn't paint over her fidgety energy. Her eyes were bright and full of mischief, as if she badly wanted to laugh, but held it in, for propriety's sake.

It was Rune's favorite painting. She always felt like it was trying to tell her a secret.

Keeping a portrait of a witch you'd betrayed wasn't illegal, but it might rouse Gideon's suspicions. "I almost got rid of it after they purged her," she said softly. "But I didn't want to forget that evil lurks where we least expect it. So I kept it, to remind me."

Gideon could interpret this to mean the evil of witches like

Nan. But for Rune, the evil was in her own actions, in what she had done to the person she loved most.

"You were very cute," he said, studying the child in the painting.

Rune glanced sharply up at him. The wine hadn't worked, but perhaps her tears had?

Is that your weakness? she wondered. *Girls who cry?*

Either way, she hadn't lost this game yet. She needed to retake control before the spell forced an even deadlier truth from her.

"I *was* cute?" she teased. "Am I not anymore?"

She couldn't coerce the truth out of him with wine. But there were other ways to get information. Methods she'd used on plenty of unsuspecting young men.

The thought of using those same tricks on Gideon snarled her stomach in knots, but she'd run out of options. If she wanted to save Seraphine, she needed to find out where the Blood Guard was keeping her. Wherever that was, Gideon had likely put Seraphine there himself.

He turned the full force of his attention on her, and she shivered beneath the weight of it.

"Cute? No." His eyes gleamed in the candlelight, taking her in. "No, I wouldn't say that."

She ran her fingers lightly down the edge of his lapel. "How would you describe me, then?"

Gideon stayed silent, watching her fingers.

Rune hated this part of the game. The flirtatious touching—which inevitably led to *kissing*—was always the last, most desperate step in obtaining information.

But it was a necessary evil. And Rune would do whatever was necessary to save more girls from sharing her grandmother's fate. A fate Rune had delivered her to.

Gideon still hadn't given her an answer.

"Well?" She pressed her hands to his chest, preparing to run them over his shoulders. "Surely, you—"

He reached for her wrist, stopping her. Rune looked up to find his attention fixed on the hand he'd captured.

Without speaking, his fingertips gently grazed her palm. Her heart climbed into her throat as he traced her fingers slowly, *slowly*, like he knew exactly what he was doing. Like he'd done it thousands of times before.

She swallowed, her skin sparking where he touched her.

Gideon leaned in, brushing his rough cheek against hers.

"Rune . . ." His breath was warm against her throat. "Do you want to go back?"

"Back?" she murmured.

"To the party." His fingers traced down her neck and across her collarbone. "Your guests will wonder where we are."

He was giving her an escape if she wanted it. *Like a gentleman.* The thought startled her.

She shook her head. "Let them wonder. Unless . . ."

Rune pulled back a little, peering into his face. She saw now that his eyes weren't black, but a deep, dark brown. "Do *you* want to go back?"

He gave her an incredulous look. "And do what? Make conversation with Bart Wentholt?" He scowled. "I have more stimulating conversations with my horse."

It was so unexpected—Gideon Sharpe, making a joke— that a laugh burst out of Rune.

He let go of her hand, falling quiet. When her giggling subsided, she looked over to find a thoughtful expression on his face.

"Your laugh is like a fuse," he said. "It lights you up."

Rune's heart thudded. No one had ever told her that before. *He doesn't mean it.*

Gideon Sharpe was a cold, heartless murderer. Not a soft-hearted suitor. He played the same game she did, and was more skilled at it than she'd thought.

Fear nipped at her.

Perhaps bringing him here had been a mistake.

Her gaze trailed over him: the broadness of his chest and shoulders, the corded muscles in his arms, the shadow of soon-to-be stubble darkening his cheeks. He was so much bigger than her. If he wanted to, he could easily lift her from this seat and carry her to the bed.

Rune froze.

Where had *that* thought come from?

She reached for the cup of wine, a little shaky, no longer caring about the spell it carried—she was already enchanted—and took another sip, careful to conceal the bottom with her cupped hands. She needed to calm her nerves. Their eyes locked over the lip of the cup, and Rune slowly lowered the wine into her lap.

As if knowing the effect he had on her, Gideon leaned in. Again, he lingered. Touching his temple to hers, running the backs of his fingers tenderly up her arm. Her skin blazed in his wake. His touch was stronger than the drink, pulling her under.

How is he so good at this?

Rune closed her eyes, trying to stay in control. "How much time do you have?"

"My next shift starts at dawn."

His witch-hunting shift, she told herself. Emphasis on the *witch-hunting.*

When his thumb stroked the line of her jaw, Rune had to bite down on a whimper. It was almost as if he were a weapon specifically designed to compromise her.

"Hunting anyone in particular?" she asked.

"Perhaps." His breath was hot on her neck.

"Who?"

He paused. "Why do you want to know?"

Rune swallowed. Was that suspicion in his voice, or flirtation?

Danger, danger, said her brain.

"What do you do with them, when you—"

Taking her chin gently in his fingers, Gideon turned her face toward his. His eyes were intense, his breathing shallow and uneven.

"Rune," he said, pupils dilating. He looked *hungry* suddenly. Like a man who hadn't eaten in years. "Less talking."

He's going to kiss me, she realized.

And the scariest thing was, Rune wanted him to. More than she wanted information, more than she wanted to rescue Seraphine . . . in this moment, she wanted to know how his mouth would feel against hers. If it would be soft or rough. If it would be as tender as his fingers, or if he'd give in to that ravenous hunger, taking his fill of her.

It shocked her out of her stupor.

Rune was no longer the mimic spider, luring her victim into a trap. She was inside her own trap . . . about to be devoured by her prey.

Desperate to extricate herself, Rune remembered the cup still in her hands.

Before Gideon completely overwhelmed her, she dumped her wine down the front of his suit.

TWELVE

RUNE

GIDEON SHOT LIKE LIGHTNING from the sofa. On his feet, he stumbled away from Rune, staring down at the dark stain seeping through his rare and expensive jacket.

Guilt pricked her like a pin.

"Oh, Gideon! I'm so sorry . . ." Rising from the love seat, Rune grabbed the wool shawl hanging off the back of her dresser chair. She felt shaky. Light-headed. "Clumsy me. Let me clean you up . . ."

He backed away from her, arms raised. "It's fine. Please— don't ruin your shawl." He unbuttoned the jacket, shrugged it off, and held it out to inspect the damage.

"I'll call for Lizbeth. Maybe if she soaks it—"

"What is going on here?" a voice exclaimed from the door-way.

Rune spun to find Verity entering the room, pearls gleaming from her neck and wrists. She looked windblown and out of breath, as if she'd heard Rune's startled cry and, expecting the worst, ran to her bedroom.

At the sight of Gideon, Verity abruptly halted, staring like she'd caught them in the middle of something scandalous. Her heart-shaped mouth formed a shocked O.

"This appears to be my cue to leave," said Gideon. Folding

his soggy jacket over one arm, he caught Rune's eye. "I'll see myself out, Miss Winters. Good night."

Before she could answer, he trod past a still-gaping Verity and disappeared into the hall.

When he was out of earshot, Verity hissed, "Are you *out of your mind?*"

She'd gone dark as a thundercloud.

"That"—Verity's index finger sliced the air in the direction Gideon had gone—"was *not* the plan. Gideon Sharpe is not on your list!"

Rune crept to the door and peered out, watching the Blood Guard captain's form recede down the hall. She was warm all over, her body humming with the memory of their close encounter. When Gideon was good and truly gone, she said, "That's because he's never shown interest."

Verity went quiet. "Has he shown interest?"

Rune's skin buzzed where Gideon had reached for her chin. She could still hear the hunger in him as he murmured her name.

Maybe?

Either that, or he was a cold, calculating master of seduction.

"I don't know." Rune closed the door and turned to her friend. "But he showed up tonight and gave me this." She tugged the silk rose from her hair, wincing as several strands came with it, and held it out for Verity to see. "Suddenly, none of the names on your list were good enough. I had to improvise."

Verity's mouth thinned to a hard line. She took the flower as if it were a living rose, full of thorns. "Something's amiss here," she said. "Gideon Sharpe doesn't court girls like Rune Winters."

Ouch.

For some reason, that stung.

"Gee, thanks, Verity."

Verity glanced up. "Oh, Rune. I didn't mean it like that."

Rune brushed off the comment. "Maybe he needs a rich wife. Maybe he gambles too much and is neck-deep in debt."

"Or maybe he's playing you," said Verity.

Rune looked away, thinking of the enchanted wine, of the way his tracing hands knew exactly how to disarm her. He was experienced in a way Rune wasn't. *That* had been clear.

Verity's right. I'm in way over my head.

Gideon had turned the tables on her tonight. First, with the wine. Then, on the love seat. And finally, by refusing to give up Blood Guard secrets despite passionate distraction. None of her tricks had worked on him. Courting him, therefore, would mean enduring a high level of danger, but for how much reward?

Sighing, Rune walked over to the bed and fell backward, letting the duvet catch her in its downy softness. Closing her tired eyes, she said, "It seemed like the perfect opportunity."

"It's too much of a risk." Verity sat down on the bed and took Rune's hand, gripping it tight. Quietly, she said, "I don't want to lose you, too."

Rune heard what her friend didn't say: *I lost my sisters. You're all I have left.*

It was true for them both. Rune and Verity had lost the people who mattered most and only had each other now. And Alex.

The bed's promise of blissful tranquility called to Rune. She'd ridden hard through terrible weather to get to Seraphine. Every bone in her body ached for rest. The longer she lay here, the more likely it was to drag her under.

"Promise me you'll reject him and choose someone safer," said Verity.

Rune knew she should heed her friend's wise advice. It only made sense to pursue someone easier and less dangerous than Gideon Shape. But if Gideon already suspected her, wasn't courting him the best way to put those suspicions to rest?

"Reject who?" interrupted a new voice.

Rune's eyes flew open. She raised herself to her elbows, groaning a little at the fight against gravity, and saw Alex enter the room.

"Your brother." Verity's hand was still clenched around the rose's wire stem. She held it out to him. "Maybe you can talk some sense into Rune."

Alex took the rose.

Sighing, Verity pushed herself from the bed. "I'll see you both back at the party."

If I can make it that far, thought Rune, falling into the covers once more.

Alex stared after Verity. "What's with her?"

Rune made an inarticulate noise, too tired to explain.

Claiming the spot Verity had vacated, Alex lay down beside her. Even with several inches between them, Rune felt the warmth of his body. Together, they lay on their backs, staring at the stucco ceiling.

"Where's Gideon?" Alex asked, voice tightening around his brother's name. He held up the silk flower, contemplating it.

Rune winced, remembering their thinly veiled argument on the stairs earlier.

She and Verity hadn't told him about the list of suitors, knowing he wouldn't approve. *Better to tell him once it's over and done,* Verity said when she first made the list. Remembering Alex's interference tonight, Rune found herself inclined to agree.

Alex was fiercely protective of his older brother.

"Gideon went home." Rune's eyes closed. The comforting

call of sleep lapped against her mind like waves against the shore.

A little voice inside Rune reminded her that her party wasn't over. That she needed to get up, go downstairs, and resume her role as hostess.

Just a little rest, she told the voice. *And then I'll go down.*

Silence filled the space between them as Alex went to that quiet place inside himself where he could collect his thoughts. Considering and arranging each one before showing them to the world.

There was a time when his long stretches of silence had unnerved Rune. She didn't know what they meant and tried to fill the space with her words. But nearly a decade of friendship had taught her to love his silence, and now it was as comforting as his music.

When he finally spoke, she was closer to asleep than awake.

"Rune?"

"Mmmm."

"Whatever you're doing with my brother needs to stop." The bed moved as he sat up, and Rune felt him reach down for her shoes, sliding one off, then the other. She wanted to tell him to keep them on, because she had to go back downstairs, but he continued before she could. "Hunting witches is Gideon's obsession. If he discovers what you are, he won't hesitate to kill you."

"Why does he hate me so much?" she asked, eyes still closed.

Rune felt him lie back down beside her, then turn his face toward her, his breath feathering her cheek. "My brother saw horrible things when he lived at the palace. Things that damage a person irreparably."

She thought of Gideon refusing the wine earlier. *There was a time when I needed it to survive.*

She wanted to know more, but it was wrong to pry one brother's secrets out of the other.

Alex hadn't really answered her question, though. Gideon had disapproved of Rune since the day they'd met five years ago, long before this damage Alex spoke of. It seemed there was something unique about Rune that Gideon couldn't abide.

It bothered her more than she cared to admit.

Alex stretched out his arm toward her. It roused Rune a little, and she lifted her head, letting him tuck his arm under her like a pillow.

"It's too late for Gideon," he said, turning her on her side and pulling her back against his chest. "You, on the other hand, can still be saved."

If her eyes were open, she would have rolled them.

We've known each other for seven years, she thought, remembering when she first met Alex. She'd been eleven, and accompanying Nan to the Royal Library, which was a glass building full of every spell book in existence—before the Blood Guard burned them all and converted the building into their headquarters. As she wandered the aisles of books, Rune heard music coming from somewhere in the library. The song brimmed with emotion, and she'd searched every floor until she found the boy playing it.

In all those years, how many times have I needed saving?

She must have asked aloud, because Alex said: "It's not the times you *don't* need saving that I'm worried about. It's the one time you'll need it, and there will be no one to do it."

If she hadn't been so tired, she might have pinched his arm. Instead, she shifted closer, nestling into him. Breathing in the clean smell of his freshly ironed shirt, Rune let herself relax for the first time all day.

Alex was familiar.

Alex was safe.

"Rune?"

But whatever he said next was lost in the sound of her snoring.

THIRTEEN

RUNE

TWO YEARS PRIOR

*T*HE DAY RUNE LEARNED *she was a witch, she was hosting Alex's sixteenth birthday. She'd spent months planning the event at Thornwood Hall—ordering the decorations, hiring the entertainment, and deciding on the menu weeks in advance.*

By the evening, Rune was tired and achy from being on her feet all day. But when the dancing began, there was a new ache in her body: an unfamiliar cramping low in her abdomen. It was so painful, she couldn't hold a conversation, never mind concentrate on the steps of a waltz. But Rune was the hostess; she was determined to see the evening through to the end.

It was only when a sudden wetness appeared between her legs that she excused herself and made for the bathroom. There, she hiked up her skirts, pulled down her underwear, and found . . .

Blood.

Black blood.

That couldn't be right.

It had soaked through the cotton. So she took the underwear off and ran the tap at the sink, shoving them under the water. Then she grabbed the soap and started to scrub.

And scrub.

And scrub.

The stain wouldn't come out. In fact, it was spreading unnaturally fast.

I'm not a witch, *she thought, as black water circled the drain.* I can't be a witch.

The cramping worsened. Rune wanted to curl up in a ball on the floor and rock until it went away. This will be fine, she told herself. I'll hide these in my purse and go straight home to Wintersea. No one will even know.

But when Rune glanced over her shoulder to check the back of her dress, she found the stain seeping through its yellow silk, too.

If anyone saw—or had already seen—it wouldn't only be humiliating, but incriminating.

Her breath sharpened. Desperation drove her now. She peeled off her dress and held it under the tap, scrubbing at the black blood. Scrubbing until her fingers felt raw and her arms hurt.

But the stain didn't lift, only spread across the yellow silk.

She couldn't deny it any longer.

The magic of her first bleeding was turning her dress black.

I'm a witch.

The realization turned her cold.

The doorknob rattled. Rune jerked her head toward it, found the door opening, and quickly threw herself against it.

"There's another bathroom on the second floor!" *called Rune, her heart beating in her throat.*

"Oh!" *Lola Parsons said from the other side.* "Sorry, Rune."

Naked now, Rune pressed herself against the painted wood, waiting until Lola was gone before locking the door.

This bathroom didn't have a window she could sneak out of, and the only door led to the hallway where Alex's guests walked back and forth. With her clothes not only wet, but growing blacker by the second, she couldn't leave.

She was trapped.

A knock on the door made her jump.

"Rune?" Alex called from the other side of the wood. "Everything all right? You've been gone for almost an hour."

Alex, help! *she wanted to say.*

But that would require admitting the truth. And if she did, he'd report her. He might be her oldest friend, but he'd also murdered a witch queen and been rewarded for it.

Rune's wet clothes slipped from her hands, landing on the floor with a splat.

"Rune?" Alex repeated.

"I'm n-not feeling well," she managed.

The handle turned. But when Alex pushed, the lock held it shut.

She stepped back, fear zipping down her spine.

"Rune, let me in."

"I'd really rather not," she whispered.

"You're scaring me," he said. "I have the key, Rune. I can open the door myself, but I'd prefer that you do it."

Knowing she couldn't stay in here forever, knowing she had no other choice—if she was a witch, Alex was going to find out, one way or another—Rune grabbed one of the bath towels and wrapped it around herself. She brushed the tears from her cheeks, unlocked the door, and stepped back.

Alex opened it and the door swung in. He nearly stepped inside when the sight of her in nothing but a towel made him halt. "Why are you . . . ?" Spots of pink appeared on his cheeks, and he seemed about to look away when he noticed her tear-streaked face—or perhaps her smudged makeup.

Finally, he entered, shutting the door behind him.

Rune backed up until her shoulders hit the wall, feeling like this was it, the end of everything—their friendship, her life. She sat down on the tiles, letting more tears fall.

"What is this really about?"

His attention snagged on her dress in a heap on the floor, then the underwear in the sink. The black stain still spreading across the fabric.

Rune saw the realization sink in.

His face fell. "Oh, Rune. No . . ."

He stood staring at the clothes, his hands curling into fists.

"I'm sorry," she whispered.

"Stay here," he said. "Don't leave this room."

Without another word, he opened the door and stepped out, locking her in.

He'll report me now, *she thought, lying down on the tiles, pulling her legs into her chest. She closed her eyes against the ache in her abdomen, weeping quietly, waiting for the Blood Guard to arrive.*

She could open the door and make a run for it, but what would be the point? And where would she go? The Blood Guard would only hunt her down.

When the door opened, it was Alex who stepped inside, locking it again behind him. A bundle of clothes was tucked under one arm, and in his hand was a mug of steaming tea.

Rune didn't bother sitting up.

"These are Emily's," he said, setting the clothes on the floor beside Rune. Emily was his cook. "This is also from her." He set down the mug. "She says it will help ease the pain."

She frowned, not understanding.

"I'm going to prepare a hot bath for you, all right?"

Rune pushed herself to a sitting position, watching him run the water in the tub. "Where's the Guard?"

He cocked his head at her. "What?"

She cleared her throat. "The Blood Guard. Wh-when will they arrive?"

Alex stared at her like she'd gone mad.

"Rune. Your secret is safe here." Letting the water run, he came back to her. Getting down on his knees, he touched her cheek. "You can sleep in the spare room tonight. And tomorrow morning, we'll figure out what to do."

She stared at him in disbelief. "If they find out, they'll kill you, too."

He smiled at her, tucking a loose strand of hair behind her ear. "They can go right ahead."

Rune flung her arms around him, clinging tightly. He pulled her close, holding her for a long time. It was there, in his arms, that Rune realized for the first time she could trust Alexander Sharpe with her life.

FOURTEEN

GIDEON

WHEN GIDEON FINALLY ARRIVED back in Old Town, with his father's wine-soaked jacket in hand, he'd gone over his evening at Wintersea House several times in his mind.

Had he made a mistake, moving so fast? He'd noticed the way Rune trembled beneath his touch and had a feeling she deliberately dumped that wine on him.

He'd come on too strong.

Gideon sighed, going over tonight's events one more time. Rune had certainly been a little awkward, if not downright odd. First, there was the weirdness with the wine. Then, her dismay over the telegram invitation. And last, her questions about his work while she tried to seduce him.

It wasn't enough to accuse her of anything. For that, he'd need some concrete evidence. Casting scars, for example. If she had them, he needed to find them.

And if she isn't the Moth?

If she wasn't, why invite him to her bedroom? Why flirt so shamelessly?

Unless she was actually interested in him.

Not possible, thought Gideon.

He trudged up the lamplit streets of Old Town, mulling

everything over. It was foggy tonight, and as he approached the street leading to his tenement, the soft sound of footsteps echoed behind him.

He glanced over his shoulder, but the fog was thick as smoke.

As the sudden smell of roses bloomed in the damp air, a chill skated over his skin.

She's dead, he told himself. *You're imagining it.*

Still, thinking of the body they'd found beneath the bridge three nights ago, he increased his pace.

The footsteps quickened in response.

Gideon's stomach knotted. He reached for the pistol holstered at his hip, only to remember he'd left it at home tonight. The opulent halls of Wintersea House were no place for a gun.

You're a Blood Guard captain. Footsteps in the fog do not scare you.

But it wasn't the footsteps so much as the smell.

Her smell.

He was coming upon a footpath that led into the back alley behind his tenement. It was difficult to find if you didn't live in this neighborhood and already know it was there. As the footsteps started closing the gap between them, Gideon arrived at the opening to the path. He sidestepped onto it and pushed his back against the wood fence.

If the pursuer knew about the path and followed him down it, at least he'd have the element of surprise.

The footsteps grew louder. Closer.

Gideon tensed, ready to defend himself, when the footsteps passed him by.

He remained where he was, holding his breath. The fence behind him sagged as he leaned against it. As the footsteps receded into the distance, the pounding of his heart soon drowned out the sound.

The smell of her was gone.

Had it ever really been there, or was it all in his head?

You're an idiot. It's probably a lamplighter heading home for the night.

Pushing away from the wall, Gideon remained on the footpath, taking it to the back of his tenement. The door there didn't lead to his apartment directly, but through the abandoned space below: the old tailor shop that once belonged to his parents.

Gideon boarded it up years ago and rarely had a reason to enter it. Earlier tonight, however, he'd gone inside looking for fabric and sewing needles to stitch Rune's flower.

The shop's interior door opened onto the stairwell leading to the apartments above. Gideon entered the shop and was halfway to the door when something made him stop.

I don't have a dress to wear, Rune had told him. *My seamstress is booked until next month.*

Gideon fumbled through the dark until he found the matches he'd left near the door earlier this evening. He lit a lamp and the flame's orange glow illuminated the room: walls lined with bolts of fabric; a large worktable for measuring, cutting, and sewing; a back room for taking customer measurements; and a front counter with a dusty old register.

Gideon stalked toward the fabrics, where a dozen leather-bound notebooks lay stacked on a shelf.

He hadn't touched these notebooks since his parents died. They were full of his father's notes and his mother's sketches, detailing her original designs.

Gideon lifted the only blank notebook from the shelf, grabbed a piece of charcoal from the jar next to it, and pulled a stool up to the worktable.

If his mother were designing a dress for Rune Winters, what kind of dress would it be?

He started sketching. The black charcoal burst across the white page as he thought of Rune on the love seat: her rose-gold hair flaming in the light of the lamps; her skin flushing as his fingers traced her; her pulse stumbling as he leaned in to kiss her.

Again, he scolded himself for intimidating her. But she was the one who'd invited him back to her room. She had summoned the wine.

She had made the first move.

Either way, he needed to keep up this charade. If she was the Moth *and* the one leaving corpses scattered across the city, the closer he got to her, the easier finding evidence of her crimes would be. And if she wasn't, someone close to her likely was, and it would still be in his best interest to infiltrate her inner circles by courting her.

If she'd let him, that is.

Gideon's plan was forming on the pages of his mother's sketchbook.

He kept drawing until he'd ripped out more pages than what remained in the book. He kept drawing until the side of his hand and wrist were black with charcoal and his spine hurt from bending over so long.

It was dawn by the time he had a design he didn't hate. One he could work with.

The question was: would she like it?

FIFTEEN

RUNE

*R*UNE'S RIDING BOOTS CRUNCHED the stone path cutting through the university's campus, where she was meeting Verity and Alex. The blustery wind eddied the dirt into the air and swirled the hem of her riding cape.

The pink granite face of Summer Hall greeted Rune, its studded wooden doors shut tight. Hoisting her satchel higher on her shoulder, Rune pulled open both doors and stepped inside. Purple wallpaper greeted her, patterned with giant dahlias, and the green tiles clicked beneath her boots. There were four dormitories on the university's campus. Summer Hall was known for its pastel colors and botanical patterns.

If the moment you walk in you're accosted by flowers on all sides, you've found the right place, Verity told her the first time she ever gave Rune directions.

She smiled to the girl at the front desk, who waved her past, used to Rune's frequent visits. The walls changed to blue irises, then yellow sunflowers as Rune turned down halls, making her way to Verity's room.

She knocked on the small door, and when it swung in, Verity looked out, squinting. Her dark brown curls were flat on one side, and her spectacles were missing.

She looked like she'd just woken up.

"Sorry I'm early," said Rune. "I need your help with a spell."

Verity blinked. "I completely forgot about our meeting."

"Oh! Do you want to reschedule?"

Verity shook her head. "No, no. Come in. Just . . . step over the mess."

Rune followed her friend into the tiny, closet-sized dorm room, shutting the door behind her. Clothes lay in heaps across the few feet of floor between the wall and the bed. Piles of books leaned against the walls and glass jars crammed the shelves. Some jars held living things within them—insects, small rodents—while others held dead things preserved in liquid.

Rune spotted Henry, the mimic spider, in the biggest jar. Already snacking on some winged thing he'd caught in his web.

Verity shoved the scattered clothes into one pile, making room for Rune on the floor.

"I'm sorry for last night," she said, kicking aside a stocking.

"Oh? What for?" Shrugging off her satchel, Rune pulled out a spell book.

"When I saw Gideon in your bedroom, I overreacted." Verity sat on her small bed, staring straight ahead at the white roses on her wallpaper. "I remembered the Blood Guard soldiers coming for my sisters, and I guess I panicked."

Verity rarely spoke about her mother's betrayal of her two eldest daughters—witches, both. All three de Wilde sisters had been extremely close.

With the heavy tome still in her arms, Rune sat down next to Verity and reached for her hand, which was ice-cold. Rune rubbed it between her warm ones. It was always so drafty in this room.

"What happened to your sisters was horrible," said Rune. "I'm sorry for scaring you."

Verity shook her head. "I just don't want anything bad to happen to you. You're the closest thing I have to family now."

Throwing her arm around Verity, Rune pulled her close, trying to comfort and warm her simultaneously, noticing how bony her shoulders were getting. Wasn't Verity's scholarship supposed to include meals along with boarding?

"You're the closest thing I have to family, too," said Rune, leaning her head against Verity's. "You and Alex."

Verity nodded to the spell book sitting on Rune's lap. "What did you need help with?"

Rune opened the book and turned to the spells she'd been practicing: *Picklock* and *Deadbolt*.

Across the page were two symbols, each one an inversion of the other.

"They're Minora spells, so I should be able to cast them using the blood you gave me, right? But when I try, it's like wading through sludge, and nothing happens."

Verity took the book and pulled it onto her lap. "These are more complicated Minoras. You probably need fresher blood. Can you show me?"

Nodding, Rune reached into the inner pocket of her riding cape and pulled out a glass vial, half-full of blood.

Verity waited, pulling her legs onto the mattress and crossing them beneath her. While Verity was not a witch herself, her sisters had always let her sit in on their spell castings. Verity had gleaned far more from her sisters than Rune had ever gleaned from Nan. So when Rune had trouble with a spell, Verity was the person she came to.

After pushing up her sleeves, Rune rose from the bed and approached the door to Verity's room. Verity was an expert at cleaning blood from any surface, so Rune didn't hesitate. After locking it manually, she pulled the cork stopper out of the glass vial, dabbed her index finger in the blood, lifted her hand, and began drawing the symbol for *Picklock* on the wood of the door: three interconnected lines—two straight, one curved.

Casting spells was like playing a musical instrument, or cooking a delicious meal. The more you studied and practiced your craft, the more skilled you became. Or that's how it was supposed to work under normal circumstances.

Because Rune used old blood, her spells were weaker than if she had a fresh source. Fresh blood, and a lot of it, was required for more powerful spells.

Making things more difficult was being restricted to the small amount of blood from each monthly bleeding, limiting the number of spells she could cast, as well as the type.

Mirages, for example, were illusions. They tampered with people's perceptions. Mirages were Rune's spells of choice because they were less complicated and required less blood.

Minoras, on the other hand, did things to change the material world—like locking and unlocking a door—and were more challenging. A Minora required the fresh blood of the witch casting it. Using Verity's borrowed blood was a way to cheat, because blood from someone else always boosted the power of a spell. But it only worked so well, and only some of the time.

It was like trying to cook a mouthwatering feast when the only ingredients on hand were some withered root vegetables, stale bread, and smelly fish. You could cook the food, but it would be neither mouthwatering nor a feast.

Rune dabbed blood onto the pads of her fingers and started to draw the symbol. As she dragged the mark across the door, the taste of salt bloomed in her mouth and a familiar roar echoed in her ears. Like the roar of the sea.

For Rune, casting spells always felt like swallowing the ocean. Like she was standing in the surf as the tide came in, only it was coming in faster and more forcefully than was natural, and it took all her strength to keep her feet planted and not get thrust over.

Rune shut her eyes as the magic swelled and her body trembled from the effort. The sea roared louder, its brackish taste stinging her throat.

She clenched her teeth and kept drawing, forcing more of the bloody symbol onto the door in front of her. Pain throbbed in her temples as that invisible wave started to crash. Rune felt its weight descending. She braced herself, trying to finish the mark as it came tumbling down on her. Her hand shook harder. She gripped her wrist, trying to steady it. There was only one line left to draw . . .

"Rune," Verity said. Her voice sounded muffled. Far away.

I can do it. It's almost done.

"Rune, stop. You going to—"

The next time the wave swelled, Rune lost her footing. The spell crashed down and her legs buckled. Rune collapsed beneath it, drowning in that thunderous roar.

SIXTEEN

RUNE

SOMEONE WAS SHAKING HER.

"Rune!"

Her head throbbed. In fact, her whole body throbbed, pain reverberating outward from one intense point at the back of her skull. *Ughhhh.*

"Alex . . . can you help me sit her up?"

Rune forced her eyes open. The room blurred and swayed above her. She saw a smudge of gold overhead, heard Alex murmur something to Verity, and closed her eyes again.

From the hard surface beneath her back, she knew she was on the floor.

"What happened?" she whispered.

Alex scooped her into his arms and set her on Verity's bed.

"You fainted," answered Verity.

It wasn't the first time. It happened whenever she pushed herself too hard on a spell that was too difficult for her.

If Nan were still alive to guide her, maybe this would be easier. But Rune's first bleeding came a few months after they'd purged her. She'd had to learn everything on her own, or with Verity's help. And after two years of being a witch, Rune could still only cast a handful of spells.

As the pounding in her head subsided, she forced her eyes open. The room spun.

"You overexerted yourself," said Verity. "It's like when too much electric current flows through a wire. The wire can't hold that much power and overheats, causing a fire or explosion."

Rune frowned at her friend. "I don't follow."

"Your power—the amount of magic you're capable of—is too much for your conductor, or the quality of blood you're using. So the spell short-circuits."

But Rune had no other blood to use.

Sighing, she waited for her vision to clear. Finally, Alex and Verity came into view, their brows furrowed as they stood over her. An uncorked vial lay on the floor, its contents spilling out in a glistening pool of bright red blood.

"No, no, no . . ." Rune scrambled toward it, but it was too late. Most of the blood had seeped into the cracks between floorboards and was already drying.

Rune touched her index finger to the precious, sticky blood. *What a waste.*

She only had one full vial left until her next cycle started.

Her hand fisted as she stared at the mess. "I wish I was better at this."

"You could be." Verity crouched down next to her. "This blood is old, Rune. No matter how much practicing you do or how perfect your marks are, some spells are going to be impossible or dangerous to cast without fresh blood. You might get away with a basic Minora spell and some Mirages, but if you want to cast more complex spells, you need fresh blood. Otherwise, this will keep happening."

"To do that, I'd have to cut myself," said Rune. Which would create casting scars, which she couldn't risk.

When a witch drew blood by cutting her skin, the magic used to cast a spell discolored the scar, turning it silver. It was why casting scars were considered beautiful during the Reign of Witches. Many witches made their cuts with care, intentionally creating elaborate designs across their bodies. Some employed skilled artists to do the cutting for them. Popular places were down the arms and back, and along the shoulders, collarbones, and wrists. But these were also highly visible, so after the revolution, witches with scars in these places had been the first to be identified and purged.

Rune's grandmother had kept her scars contained to her arms. If Rune closed her eyes, she could still see them. The delicate cuts began at the edge of Nan's collarbone and flowed down to her wrists in silvery designs depicting nautical scenes: a ship in a storm, half-swallowed by waves; sea monsters swimming in the deep.

"You wouldn't *have* to cut yourself," said Verity.

"What do you mean?" asked Alex from behind them.

Verity glanced back at him. "My sisters used to say that a witch's skill is a combination of study and practice. The more she learns and memorizes, and the more she consistently practices her spellmarks, the more she excels at her spells. But an equally vital component is the blood she has access to. An accomplished witch can master complex spells using her own fresh blood, or someone else's. Rune can't use her own, for obvious reasons, but she *could* use someone else's—if they were willing to bear the scars."

Nan had mentioned it to her once—that some witches used the blood of others to amplify their spells. This was necessary for immense magical workings, such as Majoras and Arcanas— the two highest categories of spellcraft. Majora spells required someone else's blood given with permission; Arcana spells required someone else's blood taken against their will.

Arcanas were the most powerful of all spells and had been outlawed for centuries. Not only were they considered wicked, they came with a considerable cost: if a witch took someone's blood against their will, the spell using that blood would corrupt the witch. She would crave the power it gave her, and resort to more coercive bloodletting, often killing her sources.

"You're saying Rune could, for example, use my blood to do magic?" asked Alex.

Verity nodded. "She's capable of powerful spells. She's simply working with a diminished resource. Basic spells like Mirages can be done using old blood, but the more powerful spells require the sacrifice of *fresh* blood."

Alex glanced at Rune, his eyes sparking.

"No," said Rune, seeing the thoughts in his head. "Absolutely not."

"Why? If it would help you—"

"*You* would bear the scars." If Rune were to take Alex's blood, even with his permission, silver casting scars would appear where she'd cut him. It would put him at too great a risk.

Verity looked like she was about to say something, when the sound of voices in the hall made them all twist toward the door—which shone with a bloody spellmark.

"I need to clean this," said Rune, realizing the danger she'd put her friend in. She started to rise. "Before someone sees . . ."

Verity put a hand on her shoulder, pressing lightly down. "Stay here and rest a minute. I'll clean up."

Verity left to fetch a bucket of soapy water and a mop, locking the door behind her. In the silence, Rune's stomach growled. Magic always made her ravenous.

Alex lifted the spell book lying open on the bed. "'*Picklock* and *Deadbolt*'?"

From the floor, Rune looked up to find him standing over her. The open spell book in his hands cloaked her in shadow.

"It's my backup plan," Rune explained. "In case we can't find Seraphine before they transfer her. *Picklock* will open the more complicated locks of the palace prison."

Or it would, if I could cast it.

Alex shut the book and frowned down at her.

"You've never been inside the palace prison," he pointed out. "How would you know which locks need picking?"

"Noah Creed took me on a tour of Oakhaven Park once." Oakhaven Park was the Creed family estate. "His mother is the prison warden. I saw a map on the wall of her study."

"And the Creeds are throwing a masked ball tomorrow night," murmured Alex, putting her plan together. "You're going to steal the map."

She shook her head. "Too suspicious. Stealing it would alert his mother, who would likely double the prison's security and put the Blood Guard on high alert."

Alex sat down beside her on the floor. Together, they took up all the space in Verity's tiny room that wasn't claimed by her bed and books. Handing the heavy tome back to Rune, he asked, "So what's your plan?"

"If I can remember where his mother's study is, I could trace the map."

The look on Alex's face suggested he didn't think this plan was any better than stealing it outright, but if that's what he thought, he kept it to himself. "I imagine it's a large map. Where exactly are you going to hide this tracing while you dance and flirt all night?"

She smirked at him. "Wouldn't you like to know."

To her surprise, his face flushed.

A prickling silence filled the space between them. They both glanced away.

"I'll cover for you," Alex said.

Before she could thank him, he qualified: "On one condition."

Rune narrowed her eyes. "What condition?"

"Once Seraphine is safe, you promise to lie low for a while."

Rune wrinkled her nose. "You know I can't do that."

"Then I'm afraid I can't help you. Which is unfortunate, seeing as I know exactly where Warden Creed's office is."

"You do?" Rune's eyes widened. "Wait. You're blackmailing me!"

"And *you* are fainting from overexertion. You need a break, Rune."

She hated the pitying look in his eyes and looked away, to the broken vial on the floor. So much wasted blood. Blood she might have used to break Seraphine out of her cell.

But Alex was right. She was wearing herself too thin.

It would be nice to rest.

There had been fewer and fewer purgings lately, mostly because of Rune—with Verity and Alex's help—stealing witches from Blood Guard holdings and smuggling them off the island. But that wasn't the only reason. Any witches who once hoped things would get better had realized by now things were getting worse. They'd fled—if they could—or were well hidden.

So maybe Rune could justify taking a day or two . . .

"A month."

"*What?* No."

"I'm going to Caelis for a month."

"WHAT?" Caelis was the capital city of Umbria, a peaceful country on the Continent, directly across the Barrow Strait.

I need you here! she almost said. "Why go so far?" *And for so long?*

"I've been corresponding with the Conservatory's dean about finishing my studies."

A storm of emotions whirled through Rune. Anger, that he'd leave the fate of innocent witches in Blood Guard hands. Annoyance, that he had a life and desires apart from their mission.

But it isn't his mission, Rune told herself. *It's mine.*

Alex helped her to the point of endangering himself because he was a good person who believed that what the New Republic had done—what it was still doing—was wrong. But he wasn't a witch. He would never know what it felt like to be hated and hunted. To watch people like you purged for the simple crime of being who they were.

This fight would never truly be his. And it was unfair to expect him to continually put himself at risk for her.

She was being selfish.

A too-familiar ache swelled beneath Rune's rib cage as she glanced down to the spell book gripped to her chest, thinking of Nan. Remembering a time when she'd felt whole and seen and understood. A time when she hadn't felt so utterly alone.

Stop feeling sorry for yourself. Nan is gone. You can't undo the past. You can only go forward and make things better in the future. That's what Nan would want you to do.

"If I go back to school, I'll need somewhere to live," said Alex, no longer looking at her, but staring toward the window. "There's a house for sale near the harbor, close enough to the school. If it seems like a good fit, I'm going to buy it."

Rune nodded, even though she didn't like the sound of this one bit.

"If I buy it, I want you to come with me."

"For an entire month?" She shook her head. There was no way. How many witches would die in that time? Even one was too many. "If you help me rescue Seraphine, I promise to go with you—but only for a week."

"Two weeks," he pressed, turning his attention to her and folding his arms over his chest, like that was his final offer.

Just then, someone rapped on the door.

They both froze.

"It's me," said Verity from the other side.

Rising to her feet, Rune shot Alex a look that said, *We can talk about this later*, and opened the door.

While Verity scrubbed the blood off her door and Alex mopped the floor, Rune picked up the pieces of her broken vial. Dropping the glass shards into a wastebasket, she glanced over at her childhood friend.

Alexander Sharpe was one of only two people in the world she could trust without a second thought. Imagining him in Caelis, so far away, filled her with a sadness so deep, she wanted to sink to the floor and cry.

What would she do without him?

⟢✦⟣

WHEN RUNE RETURNED TO Wintersea House, a telegram was waiting for her.

Expecting it to be a reminder for the Creeds' masked ball tomorrow night, she opened it intending to skim and set it aside when she noticed the sender had included their address: *Old Town*. It was an industrial part of the capital, full of tradespeople and day laborers and other working-class families.

None of her friends lived there.

Curious, she turned her full attention on the message.

```
MISS RUNE WINTERS
WINTERSEA HOUSE


I APOLOGIZE FOR MOVING SO QUICKLY LAST
NIGHT. IF YOU'RE NOT PUT OFF BY ME YET, I
MAY HAVE A SOLUTION TO YOUR PREDICAMENT
REGARDING THE LUMINARIES DINNER.
                                  GIDEON
```

A solution?

Verity's warnings clanged through Rune as she remembered how close she'd come to letting Gideon kiss her. How much further would he have gone if she'd let him?

With past suitors, Rune had always drawn a line at kissing. She never, under any circumstances, went further than that. Having this rule made her feel like she was still in control. Like she couldn't totally lose herself, no matter how desperate things got.

This is a second chance to find out where they're holding Seraphine, she told herself, silently apologizing to Verity. *I have to take it.*

She dictated her response to Lizbeth, who took it to the telegraph office.

```
GIDEON SHARPE
113 PRUDENCE ST, OLD TOWN

I'M INTRIGUED. TELL ME MORE.

                                    RUNE


P.S. IF ANYONE NEEDS TO APOLOGIZE FOR LAST
NIGHT, IT'S THE PERSON WHO RUINED YOUR
JACKET.
```

A reply arrived in the afternoon.

IT WILL BE EASIER TO SHOW YOU. ARE YOU FREE
TOMORROW AT 10 A.M.? IF SO, MEET ME AT THIS
ADDRESS.

GIDEON

P.S. I PROMISE TO GO SLOW THIS TIME.

SEVENTEEN

GIDEON

ON HIS WAY TO the boxing arena that evening, Gideon stopped by the telegraph office and retrieved Rune's reply.

LOOKING FORWARD TO GOING SLOW.

RUNE

He smiled as he read it. He felt better tonight. Rested and ready. If Rune was the Moth, he would find out tomorrow morning.

He was still smiling as he entered the boxing ring, stripped off his shirt, and slid on his gloves, preparing to warm up. He was so lost in his plans that he didn't notice when the doors of the arena burst open and his brother stormed in.

"What the hell are you up to?"

The tone of Alex's voice wiped the smile off Gideon's face. He turned to see his brother drop his boxing bag and tug off his shirt. Grabbing his gloves, Alex ducked under the ropes and stepped into the ring with him.

"Nice to see you, too, Alex."

"Coming to Rune's party last night? Going off alone with her?"

Out of the corner of his eye, Gideon noticed the other men in the arena glancing their way.

"I—"

"You can't stand Rune Winters." Alex dropped into a crouched stance directly across from Gideon without warming up.

He couldn't tell Alex the truth, because Alex would tell Rune everything. He wouldn't care that Gideon suspected she might be the Moth, or that he could be in danger. Alex assumed the best of people.

"Maybe I changed my mind," said Gideon, falling into his fighting stance.

Alex shook his head. "You're my brother. *I know you.* What are you up to?"

Gideon took a lazy swing. Alex easily ducked and swung back. Much harder. Gideon blocked it and stepped aside.

"She's a pretty girl with a nice inheritance. Everyone knows she's on the market for a husband. I thought I'd try my luck."

"You'd hate it."

Alex swung again, fast and furious. Gideon jumped back in the nick of time and the breeze of his brother's fist whooshed through his hair.

"Hate what?"

"Being married to her." Alex dropped his hands. "You'd have to attend her parties. Entertain and impress her guests. You despise these people."

Gideon mirrored his brother, lowering his fists. "Maybe I could learn to like it."

Some desperate emotion flashed across Alex's face, and guilt settled like a stone in Gideon's gut.

Alex's hands dropped to his sides. "People like Rune don't end up with people like you."

The guilt evaporated.

Gideon knew precisely what Alex meant. People like him were damaged. Dirty. People like him didn't belong in the ballrooms of people like Alex and Rune.

His fists coiled. "That so?"

"Yes." Alex's golden eyes flashed like electricity.

"Enlighten me. What type of people do girls like Rune end up with? Men like you?" Gideon raised his fists. "Men who stand on the sidelines, pining in the shadows, too afraid to go after what they want? Have you gotten so used to being handed everything in life that you think she'll hand herself over to you, too?"

Alex slugged him.

Pain exploded in Gideon's jaw.

He staggered back, hitting the ropes as the taste of blood burst through his mouth. His ears rang as he gripped the ropes tighter to keep from falling on his ass.

I deserved that, he thought, spitting blood. Shaking off the buzzing pain, he pulled himself upright to find Alex already ducking out of the ring, grabbing his shirt, and walking away.

"Alex," he called. "Alex, come on! I didn't—"

But the door of the ring was already swinging shut, with Alex on the other side of it.

"Damn it."

Gideon hadn't meant a word of that.

Mostly.

Alex had struck right where Gideon was softest. Weakest. So Gideon had struck back. Which was not how it was supposed to be.

Gideon was the older one. He was supposed to protect his little brother. To take punches, even when those punches came from Alex himself.

Disgusted with himself, standing alone in the middle of the ring, Gideon let his head fall back. Closing his eyes, he let out a rough sigh.

Alex was right.

"I'm a piece of shit."

EIGHTEEN

RUNE

*T*HE FOLLOWING DAY, A luncheon was being held in honor of Charlotte Gong's engagement. Rune had agreed to attend long before Gideon's telegram arrived, and therefore needed to make an appearance. The luncheon wasn't until noon, though, leaving her free to meet Gideon beforehand.

So, early that morning, Rune rode for the capital and told no one where she was going.

After stabling Lady in one of the Old Town stables—garnering several startled looks from the stable hands, who weren't accustomed to fancy show horses in their stalls—she set out for Prudence Street.

It was shortly after ten o'clock when she found it, and the street was bustling. Smoke plumed from chimneys and the smell of the factory coal fires hung in the air, clashing with the sounds of haggling food sellers. Passing workmen threw curious glances at Rune as she tried her best to stay out of the way. She stared up at the tired-looking tenement buildings, noticing the cracks running through the brown bricks and the facades in need of fresh paint.

The Good Commander had given Thornwood Hall, Cressida's summer home, to Alex as compensation for killing the youngest Roseblood sister. But Gideon had done far more than

Alex in service of the New Republic—leading the revolutionaries into the palace, disposing of Cressida's two older sisters, devoting his life to hunting down witches. Surely the Commander had offered his Blood Guard captain whatever he wanted, in gratitude. So why did Gideon still live *here*, of all places?

Rune spotted the number 113 on a street-level door next to a boarded-up shop window. As she approached, raising her fist to knock, the faded letters of the marquee overhead caught her eye.

THE SHARPE DUET: TAILORING AND DRESSMAKING.

"Oh," she whispered.

Suddenly, the door swung in. Gideon stood in the frame, towering over her.

Were you born massive? she wondered, staring up at him. *Or were you once as small and fragile as the rest of us?*

He wore plain trousers and a white shirt, sleeves rolled to his elbows. Over his shoulders hung a long strip of measuring tape.

"You're late."

Fashionably late, she thought as he stepped aside, inviting her in.

Instead of leading her up the steps to the apartment above, Gideon led her through a door to the left and into the darkened tailor shop that once belonged to two of the most famous designers in fashion history. Her entire body hummed with anticipation.

Despite her friendship with Alex, she'd never been to the Sharpe's home before. Nan forbade Rune from ever setting foot in the outer wards. *They're dangerous, dirty, and full of criminals,* Nan would say whenever Rune protested. *Not for the likes of us.*

Inside the shop, boards covered every window, letting in thin cracks of sunlight. As her eyes adjusted to the diminished light, she tried not to gape at the fabrics, the sewing kits, the patterns . . . all of it lying about as if it were no big deal.

Gideon must have inherited it all from his parents.

But why did he keep it?

Clearly, no one had touched any of this in years.

Sun and Levi Sharpe once stood right where I'm standing, thought Rune, imagining the seamstress and the tailor hunched over the long worktable, sketching ideas late into the night, stitching fabrics until their tired eyes wouldn't open anymore and they blew out their candles and went to bed.

"This," said Gideon, standing at a worktable, "is my solution to your problem."

She stepped up beside him, glancing down at the notebook lying open on the table. An oil lamp burned beside it, illuminating the pages. Her eyes widened, and she leaned in closer.

Someone had drawn her—*Rune Winters*—on the paper, clothing her in the most beautiful dress she'd ever seen. Tapered lace sleeves. Elegant scooping neckline. Fitted bodice with a subtle, embroidered pattern she couldn't make out. An A-line skirt trailed several inches behind her.

Rune's mouth opened. Then closed. Gideon reached down and turned the page, showing her more detailed sketches of each part: sleeves, bodice, lace-up back, even matching silk shoes.

"Is this . . ."

"What I'm going to make you. For the Luminaries Dinner."

Still, it wouldn't register.

This was a trick, right?

Her suitors had given her gifts in the past, but they were always flowers or jewelry or carriage rides. Nothing like . . . this. Not a dress *designed* for her.

Something fluttered and swooped inside Rune, like a flock of birds taking flight. She tried to bite down on the enormous smile spreading across her face.

"Gideon. Are you sure?"

"Entirely. I only need one thing."

She was prepared to give him anything he wanted for the garment splashed across the pages of that notebook.

"Your measurements."

"Oh." Her smile faltered. "Right. Of course."

The only person who'd ever taken her measurements was her seamstress.

"If you're not comfortable—"

"No! So comfortable!" She tried to smile, but it wobbled as she thought about what such a thing would entail: stripping down to her underwear in front of Gideon Sharpe. Rune swallowed, going hot all over. If she wanted the dress, she would have to allow this ruthless witch hunter to get close enough to see her every flaw; to measure the fleshy curves and dips she normally kept hidden—not because she had scars to hide, but because she was . . . well, *shy*.

Wait a minute, thought Rune, her eyes narrowing on the notebook's pages. *That's what this is.*

Not a kind gesture. Not a solution to her problem.

He wants to look for my casting scars.

She felt that dark gaze watching her. As her eyes lifted to his, she remembered who she was dealing with. This was no suitor—not really. And the dress design sitting in his sketchbook solved *his* problem. Not hers.

Or so he thinks.

A genuine smile replaced her wavering one.

Rune had no casting scars. And if he found no scars, he had no reason to continue suspecting her.

Oozing confidence now—this was a game she knew how to play, after all—Rune undid the buttons of her fitted wool jacket and slid it off her shoulders. "Where should we do this?"

For a moment, he hesitated. As if second-guessing his plan.

When Rune met his eye, silently daring him to back down, he seemed to find his resolve. With his notebook in hand, Gideon led her to the back of the shop, where a large, folded mirror displayed her reflection in three panels and a measuring block stood in the center of the space.

Thankful that she'd worn nice underwear, Rune undid the buttons of her blouse.

Gideon started to turn around. "If you need—oh."

Rune was already undressing. His gaze dropped to her lace bralette and remained there for a beat, before quickly shooting back to her face, his cheeks burning with color.

"This okay?" said Rune, trying not to smirk.

He nodded curtly and turned away. Setting the notebook down on a shelf piled with white tulle, he took a long time opening to a blank page.

Rune unlaced her riding boots and took her time wriggling out of her trousers, relishing Gideon's sudden bashfulness.

"Did you do this a lot, when you assisted your parents?"

As if he sensed that she now stood in nothing but her underwear, he didn't turn to look at her. Only cleared his throat. "Do what a lot?"

"Take people's measurements."

"I only ever took Cressida's measurements." This answer seemed to sober him. He dragged the measuring tape from his shoulders and turned to confront her, keeping his eyes on her face. Not letting them lower even an inch. "Ready?"

"Yep." Rune bounced on the balls of her feet, trying to stave off the chill in the air.

He stepped closer, bringing the lamp with him. "I'll start at the top and work my way down."

She knew what he meant, but the way he said it made her imagine him working his way down her in a . . . less vertical way. Apparently, she wasn't the only one. Gideon froze, opened his mouth to clarify what he meant, and coughed instead.

He lowered the lamp down to the measuring block, engulfing her in its warm glow—*To better see my scars,* thought Rune—and started measuring.

His hands made quick work of it, telling Rune how practiced he was. She couldn't help comparing those hands to his brother's. Alex had the hands of a musician: wide palms, slender fingers. Elegant and beautiful as a song.

Gideon's hands were strong and rough and calloused. Hands that could hold a gun as competently as they could haul a witch into a prison cell—or take a girl's measurements, evidently.

He never fumbled or brushed her skin. As if he were trying very hard not to touch her more than necessary.

To distract them both while he measured her bust, Rune said, "I wish Alex had told me you were an accomplished tailor. If your finished garments look anything like your sketches, I would have employed you years ago."

"Cress would never have let me work for you."

The way he said the young queen's name—*Cress,* not Cressida—made Rune feel funny.

"She wouldn't have let me *talk* to you." Gideon retreated to write the number in his notebook. "But I did serve you and your friends tea once," he said when he returned to Rune, looping the tape around the smallest part of her waist this time. "It was at Thornwood Hall, during one of Cress's parties."

Unable to recall it, she glanced up to find Gideon's face mere inches from hers, his attention fixed on the measuring tape. "If you were her tailor, why were you serving tea at her party?"

The tape went slack, but he didn't move on to the next measurement.

"I was living at Thornwood Hall by then. Cress moved me there from the palace to . . . better fulfill her needs. The night of that party, I was being punished." He ran a hand roughly through his hair. "For neglecting my duties."

Rune frowned harder, about to ask him what he meant, when he cut her off.

"Hips are next."

He didn't want to elaborate, clearly. While the tape encircled Rune's hips, pulling her closer into his warmth, she tried to remember it: a younger version of Gideon Sharpe, refilling her cup while she gossiped with her friends.

But she couldn't remember him, and the guilt of it twisted in her belly.

But why should I remember him?

Her mind wandered back to that nickname. *Cress.* Was he the only one who called the queen that?

When Gideon left to write Rune's hip measurement down, she asked, "I didn't know Cressida very well. What was she like?"

He stayed bent over that book, not writing or answering for a long time. "She was . . . beautiful," he finally said. "And alluring." He seemed half-lost in a dream. "And powerful."

Rune suddenly remembered the rumors about Cressida and her lowborn lover. Rumors she'd dismissed as silly gossip. She wondered now if there might be some truth to them.

Gideon had said he'd lived at Cressida's summer home, and he was certainly easy on the eyes.

If dark, brooding, and brutal are your type, she thought with a scowl.

The way Gideon talked about the youngest Roseblood sister was so informal. Not at all like someone who had served her. More like someone who'd known her well.

Or been intimate with her.

Rune shifted. An uncomfortable feeling snaked through her at the thought of him sharing Cressida's bed. If he'd been a witch queen's lover, Rune would need to be much more careful. He would pick up on the smallest of cues.

"Are you familiar with the pitcher plants that grow in the island's bogs?"

Though he'd turned around to face her, there were several paces between them. Rune stood in the lamp's glow, still in her lace underwear. Gideon was in the shadows outside it, fully clothed. And yet, in this moment, he seemed to be the vulnerable one.

"Those deep purple flowers that trap and eat bugs?" she asked.

He nodded.

"Cress was like that: pretty from a distance, tempting you closer. Like a fool, you were happy to approach." He was staring at the space over Rune's shoulder, his expression haunted. "It was only after she'd reeled you in that she revealed her true nature. But by then, it was too late."

He met Rune's gaze.

"She was already eating you alive."

NINETEEN

GIDEON

*I*N THE BEGINNING, THE attraction had been mutual. The first time he met Cressida Roseblood, he'd traveled to the palace with his mother to deliver a dress. While his mother spoke privately with the two eldest witch queens, Gideon waited in the hall, knowing how much rested on this moment. If the sisters liked his parents' work, Analise and Elowyn would employ the Sharpe Duet full-time to be their dressmakers.

It would give Sun and Levi an enviable salary.

It would change their family's fate.

Gideon had been standing against the wall when Cressida walked by with her handmaidens. Not realizing who she was, he'd done a double take, soaking up her ivory hair, bright blue eyes, and slender frame.

She had stopped and turned back. Smiling, she'd slowly approached and asked his name, then stayed to converse with him. He was completely taken in by her beauty, flattered by her flirting, and, most of all, surprised at being treated like her equal.

She only left his side when his mother returned, looking dazed, saying she'd signed the contract.

"I guess we'll be seeing more of each other."

Gideon still remembered the way his pulse had stumbled at

those words. At the look she had thrown him before disappearing down the hall.

It started out slow. Once his family moved into the palace, Cressida invited him on walks in the gardens, or horseback rides along the shore. He started joining her at breakfast on her terrace in the mornings.

They traded kisses in empty palace rooms, hands wandering over each other.

It seemed like a dream back then. Too good to be true.

And it was.

"Gideon?"

Rune's voice broke through the memories. For a moment, half-stuck in the past, Gideon saw not Rune Winters standing on the measuring block before him, but Cressida Roseblood. Watching him like a lioness. Contemplating whether to play with her food before she ate it, or go straight for the jugular.

His heart hammered; his palms sweated.

"Is everything all right?"

Rune's voice pulled him fully into the present. *Cressida is dead.* This was a different girl standing on his measuring block.

Rune stepped down, padding softly toward him.

On instinct, Gideon stepped back.

She froze, biting her lip, as if sensing his distress but not knowing how to ease it.

Snap out of it, Sharpe.

He cleared his throat. "Sorry. Yes. Everything's fine. I shouldn't have brought it up."

"I'm the one who brought it up," she said, her stormy gaze studying him. "If you want to talk about it—"

"I'd rather not."

What was he thinking? This was the absolute worst person

to tell his most shameful secrets to. The queen of gossip herself, who could ruin his reputation with a single whispered word.

Why had he said so much?

"Okay," said Rune, who hugged herself.

She was shivering, he realized. Of course she was. It was freezing in here and she was standing in her underwear.

You idiot. Grabbing one of the woolen blankets his mother had used to keep herself warm on late winter nights in the studio, Gideon returned and flung it over her shoulders.

"Just one more measurement and I'll be done."

She nodded. As he bent down, pressing the end of the tape to the floor next to her heel, his gaze slid over her smooth legs, checking for any silvery marks on the skin, just as he'd done with the rest of her body. But there was nothing. Her legs were so perfect, Gideon had trouble tearing his eyes away from them.

He'd found no hint of any casting scars. Frankly, that she would strip down and stand before him this whole time, for his perusal, seemed proof she had none.

Perhaps he'd been wrong. Maybe Rune Winters wasn't the Moth.

"Stand on this for a second."

When she stepped on the tape end, he pulled it straight to the top of her head, holding it taut, and noted her height. She was a whole foot shorter than him.

As he wrote the last measurement down in his notebook, he heard her move toward the shelves.

"Are these . . ."

He turned to find her cocooned in the woolen blanket, which fell to the top of her thighs. She seemed perfectly unbothered by his attention as she peered at his mother's old notebooks. As if standing half-naked in the same room as him was the most natural thing in the world.

Gideon swallowed, trying to stop his gaze from raking down her legs.

"My mother's sketchbooks," he said, loosening the collar of his shirt. "She kept all of her designs in them."

"Your mother's . . ." Rune jerked her face toward him, wild-eyed. "May I?"

"Go ahead."

The smile that bloomed across her face did something strange to his insides.

Rune scooped every book from the shelf and carried them to the worktable, where she dropped them in a pile and sat down on a stool.

Awe softened her face as she drank in the images, reverently turning the pages. She looked almost . . . innocent. Gideon brought the lamp over to the table so she could see better.

He'd been careful not to touch her today, remembering his brother's words in the boxing ring. Remembering who she was. Who *he* was.

You are beneath her.

Gideon picked up a stool and set it down on the other side of the table, where he planted himself.

He immediately realized his mistake.

From here, he had a perfect view of the low scoop of her bralette, the delicate lace leaving little to the imagination. He had just measured her bust, so why it suddenly mattered, he wasn't sure. He kept his gaze on the line of her throat instead.

If they were truly courting, though . . .

If they were *together* . . .

He shot his thoughts dead. *Didn't you learn your lesson from the first witch who drew you in?*

He and Rune would never be together. If Rune was the Moth, this courtship—if he could even call it that—ended with

Gideon arresting her and Rune going to the purge. And if she wasn't the Moth, he'd step aside and hope his brother finally worked up the courage to go after what he wanted.

And that was the way it should be.

When she caught him staring, Gideon looked away too late. Their gazes snagged.

Slowly, Rune closed the sketchbook she was hunched over and rose from the stool.

"I guess I should return this." Walking around the table, she let the blanket fall from her shoulders, holding it out to him. When he took it, she hoisted herself onto the table directly beside him, letting her lovely legs dangle over the edge.

Gideon fought to keep his eyes on her face, when all he wanted to do was let them drop.

Picking up the notebook with her measurements, Rune flipped to the dress he'd designed for her. Her fingers traced the lines of his sketch the same way her eyes had traced his mother's designs.

He'd pleased her. It was written clear across her face.

He didn't like what this knowledge did to him. Warming him through. Thawing his icy heart.

It shouldn't feel this good to make her happy.

"What are you doing this afternoon?" she said, touching her fingertip to the uppermost button of his shirt. "I have a luncheon at noon, but after that . . . There's a quiet beach near Wintersea House where I ride sometimes. Do you want to join me?"

"Can't," he managed, drawing the blanket into his lap. "I have to work today."

She ducked her chin, disappointed. Not wanting it to seem like he was rejecting her, he quickly added, "Depending on how this evening's transfer goes, I might get off early. I could meet you afterward."

Her attention shot back to his face. "This evening's transfer?"

He nodded. "Laila and I are transferring a witch to the palace prison."

Rune lowered her gaze. "Is it far? The place you have to bring her from, I mean." She slowly unfastened the button of his shirt. He had the urge to pull her down into his lap.

Focus, you idiot.

"Not too far. She's being held at the old mine near Seldom Harbor."

"I see." Rune's lips pressed into a pout as her fingers dropped to the next button. "There's a masked ball at the Creeds' tonight. You could meet me there afterward."

Gideon struggled to keep his hands to himself. The wool of the blanket itched against his palms.

"I'll try my best."

Her mouth curved to the side as she released the button without undoing it. Before pushing off the table, though, she leaned in toward him and the bridge of her nose grazed his cheekbone.

"Thank you for the dress, Gideon."

His name on her lips sent a tremor through him. His hands clenched. He wouldn't be able to hold out much longer.

"My pleasure," he murmured.

When she pulled away and turned to get dressed, he decided against watching her shimmy back into her trousers, choosing to tidy up instead.

TWENTY

RUNE

*A*FTER APPEARING BRIEFLY AT Charlotte's luncheon, Rune raced back to Wintersea House, grinning the entire way. Not even the gray clouds on the horizon could dampen her mood.

It had been so easy! Rune couldn't believe how quickly Gideon had given up Seraphine's whereabouts. She'd had to get nearly naked, but still.

Worth it.

Gideon, she decided, *was* the suitor she'd accept.

It was only as she burst through the doors of her bedroom and quickly started changing that she recalled what he'd said about the youngest witch queen.

Cressida would never have let me work for you.

Her fingers slowed on the laces of her riding trousers.

She had me serving that night to punish me.

He hadn't elaborated. And Rune had no way of knowing what the truth was. Perhaps he was being punished for some truly heinous deed. Or perhaps he was lying.

But Rune remembered the harrowed look in his eyes. The way he'd stepped sharply away at her approach, as if he thought, for a moment, that she was Cressida herself. And he was afraid.

Cress was like that: pretty from a distance, tempting you

closer . . . It was only after she'd reeled you in that she revealed her true nature. But by then, it was too late. She was already eating you alive.

Rune shivered.

But there were two sides to every story. And since Cressida was dead and couldn't tell hers, it was unfair to take Gideon at his word.

She banished all thought of him and finished dressing.

Pulling on a hooded sweater, she wondered if she should send a message to Verity. One of her ships was due to leave at dawn, and if she was successful tonight, she intended to put Seraphine on it. It would mean she wouldn't make it to the Creeds' party tonight. And if she didn't, she would need Verity and Alex to come up with an alibi for her.

But to put that in a message risked the information falling into the wrong hands. So, she decided against it and rode straight for Seldom Harbor.

TWENTY-ONE

GIDEON

"RUNE WINTERS HAS NO casting scars," Gideon told Harrow as they climbed the marble steps together.

Harrow arched a thin brow. "You certainly move fast."

"It's not like that," he said quickly. "I needed her measurements for a dress I'm making her."

Harrow's brow arched higher. "You, my brawny friend, are cleverer than I gave you credit for."

They passed under the columned entrance and into Blood Guard headquarters. When it was still the Royal Library, this building preserved witch propaganda, histories full of lies, and entire floors of spell books. Gideon remembered the marble busts of notable witches that once lined the wings, as well as the gilt-framed paintings depicting the golden age of witches. All of it was gone, destroyed in the early days of the New Republic.

"If she doesn't have scars, I can't accuse her."

"How closely did you look?"

Gideon thought back to the dark, boarded-up shop. To Rune's nearly naked form, standing in the glow of his lamp.

"The lighting was poor, but trust me, I looked."

His memory was like a faucet. Once he opened the valve even a little, he couldn't stop everything from rushing out. The memory of her soft, white curves. The delicate lace of her bra. The scent of her skin . . .

Gideon had gotten very close to a nearly naked Rune. And he had *looked*. There was nothing to find.

"She's flawless."

"She was completely nude?" asked Harrow.

"What? No. You don't do measurements in the nude."

"Well, there's your problem. The Crimson Moth won't have casting scars where someone like you could find them. How do you think she's escaped detection the past two years? You'll need to get her good and naked."

The words were a lightning strike. But Harrow was right. Rune *hadn't* been entirely unclothed. And he'd inspected her quickly, in dim lighting.

Gideon ran a hand over his face.

How was he supposed to get Rune Winters naked?

"Maybe I won't have to."

Harrow rolled her eyes. "You have some other plan?"

They entered the atrium, which was encircled by a massive staircase spiraling to the top floor. Overhead, the glass-domed ceiling revealed a sky full of clouds. Holding up the dome were statues of the seven Ancients, chiseled out of marble. Liberty, with her gun held high. Mercy, with her arc of doves flying toward the glass. Wisdom, with an owl on her shoulder and an open book in her hands . . .

"Do you remember it?" asked Harrow, halting halfway to the stairs, standing now in the center of the atrium. Gideon turned to find her staring at a spot in the middle of the floor, where the tiles didn't match.

"There used to be a tree that grew right here," she said, going quiet. "It reached all the way to the fourth floor."

Gideon nodded. Rioters had destroyed it, too, after the

revolution. Hacking it apart, uprooting the stump, and burning it all.

"Every spring, it blossomed for a month straight. My mistress, Juniper, loved to come when the blossoms dropped. They would carpet the floor in a sea of white." Harrow swallowed, lost in the memory. "She said that Amity herself planted it here and centuries later, people built the library around it."

Gideon had never heard Harrow speak about the witch who'd indentured her.

"Was she purged?" he asked.

This snapped Harrow out of the memory. Her footsteps started again, hastening toward the stairs.

"No."

A heavy silence hung between them. It meant this Juniper was still out there, somewhere. He wondered if her memory haunted Harrow the way Cressida's memory haunted him.

"Is she the one who . . . ?" Gideon pointed to his ear.

Harrow reached to touch the place where her ear used to be, before a witch had cut it off.

"No. But neither did she stop it."

What other kinds of cruelty had Harrow suffered at the hands of witches? And how could she not know—or care—if her former mistress was dead or alive?

But Harrow clearly didn't want to discuss it further, because she changed the subject.

"You were talking about your plan to entrap Rune Winters." Together, they started for the stairs. "The one that doesn't involve getting her naked. How is that going to work?"

Their footsteps echoed in unison as they climbed to the second floor, where Gideon's office lay.

"I gave Rune bad information this morning."

Harrow glanced over at him. "Oh?"

"I told her the location of a holding cell for witches near Seldom Harbor."

"And that's bad?"

"There's no holding cell near Seldom Harbor. Just a trap waiting for the Crimson Moth."

Harrow's golden eyes widened. As this sank in, she smiled, impressed.

"And you think Rune will show up there."

"I don't know. If she does, I'll have my fugitive. But even if someone else shows up instead, I'll know Rune is in league with the Moth—since she's the only person I gave the location to."

"And if no one shows up?"

Gideon sighed. "Then I abandon this false trail, break things off with Rune . . ."

And hope my little brother finds his balls.

TWENTY-TWO

RUNE

*T*HE OLD MINE NEAR Seldom Harbor stood on a small clifftop a hundred meters above sea level, sagging beneath the weight of a century.

Rune came prepared with an invisibility spell already drawn on her forearm in blood. She called it *Ghost Walker,* and it was her most-used spell on nights like this, one she'd created herself using a combination of two symbols she'd found in one of Nan's books. The symbols for *emptiness* and *evasion.* It didn't make her disappear so much as nudge a person's attention away from her.

She dismounted Lady a quarter mile up the dirt road. Leaving the horse to graze in a small copse of trees, Rune headed toward the mine, which was silhouetted by the light of a silver moon.

The wind and sea salt stung Rune's eyes—the only part of her face left uncovered. Dressed entirely in black, she'd hidden her hair beneath a hood, and covered her mouth and nose with a snug cowl. A fitted black shirt and leggings concealed the rest of her, along with calf-high leather boots.

The lantern hanging in the entryway swung in the gusty wind, scattering its light across the Blood Guard standing sentry. As Rune drew nearer to the stone building, she saw that the guard on duty was none other than Laila Creed.

With her spell cloaking her, Rune pulled out a slender silver whistle no wider than a fountain pen from the hidden pocket in her clothes. The same pocket contained her last full vial of blood.

Drawing closer to Laila, she put the cold metal to her lips and blew three short, hard notes. The notes were too high-pitched for Laila's ears, but Lady heard them immediately.

Lady had once been Nan's favorite show horse. Nan trained her to respond to different whistled commands, and her obedience had won them dozens of ribbons over the years.

In the darkness, sounding closer than she was, Lady whinnied.

Hearing it, Laila grabbed the pistol at her hip, eyes narrowing. Her gaze bounced off the space where Rune stood and turned toward the sound.

That's right, thought Rune. *Go check. Better to be safe.*

Glancing back to the mine's entryway—a sun-bleached door speckled with lichen—Laila strode hesitantly into the dark.

Rune opened the door and stepped inside.

The entrance to the mine was a small room with wood-paneled walls and two small windows—one of which was broken. The old floorboards shifted beneath her footsteps, and in the center of the floor was a hole big enough for two burly men to drop into. A ladder protruded out of it.

When she peered in, all she could see was darkness below.

Rune frowned, her skin prickling. The Blood Guard had been getting more and more creative with their holding locations, which made it more difficult for Rune to guess where they were keeping captured witches. Normally, though, there were more guards than this.

Crouching, she tried to see down into the first level of the mine and caught a shimmer of light in the distance.

Someone's there.

Still, Rune hesitated, unable to shake the feeling that something was off. But if Seraphine was down there and Rune walked away right now, they would transfer her to the palace tonight, and Rune might never get another chance to save her.

And if they'd already transferred her . . .

I'll just go down and look around.

Rune touched the small knife she'd strapped onto her thigh, drawing courage from its freshly honed steel. With her feet on the rungs, still cloaked by her *Ghost Walker* spell, she lowered herself into the darkness.

It got colder and damper the lower she went, and the ladder rungs were slick beneath her hands. As soon as her feet touched the ground, she let go and turned into the pitch, her gaze seeking the warm glow in the distance.

There was a rush of air. Movement in the dark.

The hair on her nape rose. *Trap,* said her brain, seconds before her body caught up.

Rune spun to grab the ladder and haul herself up, when a hand seized her wrist and clamped down with viselike strength.

"Gotcha."

Rune swung with her fist, but the darkness made her assailant as invisible as she was, and she missed his face.

Before she could try again, he seized her other wrist and forced her to her knees. Rune quailed at the strength in him as he easily wrestled her to the ground, pressing her cheek into the cold rock and pinning her there with his knees on either side of her hips.

Immobilizing her.

The smell of fresh-cut cedar and gunpowder overwhelmed her.

"You have no idea how long I've waited for this day."

The voice was unmistakable.

Gideon.

White-hot anger burned in her breast. He'd set her up. Baited the trap and waited for her to step into it.

I am such a fool.

And now he had her pinned. Defenseless. Exactly where he wanted her.

But how did he see her?

He doesn't, she realized. This level was so dark, he couldn't see anything. Neither of them could. He must have heard Rune coming down the ladder.

If she survived this, she would need to tweak her spell to muffle her sound.

"Your friend isn't here."

I gathered that, yes, thought Rune, crushed beneath his weight. He'd planted both palms on her shoulder blades, immobilizing her. Her hands were still free, but because of the way he pinned her, she couldn't use them to reach for her knife.

"Someone got your tongue, little Moth?"

No way was Rune talking. If it was too dark for him to see her, she might still have a chance of keeping her identity intact. She'd have to wait for him to let her up before she tried anything. He couldn't keep her pinned forever.

And if he has a lamp?

Ghost Walker kept Rune shielded so long as someone didn't know she was there, by nudging their attention away from her. The spell could try its hardest to force Gideon's gaze away, but he was sitting on top of Rune. He knew *exactly* where she was. Her spell could no longer deceive him.

And if Gideon had a lamp, the moment he lit it, all he'd have to do was yank her cowl down and pull back her . . .

There was the soft hiss of a flare. Then a red glow, like an ember, behind her.

No.

Panic zipped through her.

As the flare sizzled and the glow brightened, he reached for her hood. The moment he pulled it back and set free her hair—a red-gold shade he would instantly recognize—it would mean the end for Rune.

In order to hold the flare *and* pull back her hood, though, Gideon had to remove his hands from her. With the weight of him gone, Rune was free to reach for the knife strapped to her thigh. So she did.

Her fingers wrapped around the hilt.

He tugged at her hood, sliding it back from her forehead.

Rune drew the knife from its sheath and stabbed *hard*, not caring where the blade went in, so long as it went in deep.

Gideon howled and rolled off her.

Free, Rune stumbled to her feet and ran.

She'd never been inside a mine. She knew nothing about them. One thing Rune was pretty sure of, though: there was only one way in and out. And she was running in the opposite direction of it.

Rune quickly found the source of the light she'd seen from above: a lamp hanging midway down a narrow tunnel. The ceiling was so low, Rune had to duck to keep from hitting her head on it.

She thought of Verity and Alex. She should have taken their advice. Avoided the Blood Guard captain at all costs.

He hasn't won yet.

She heard Gideon stumbling behind her, cursing as he closed in. So long as he didn't catch her, she could still make it out of this.

But if he caught her, she'd go straight to the purge.

That thought made her run faster.

At the end of the illuminated tunnel was another ladder, this one leading to the level below. She didn't want to go further down, wading deeper into his trap, but as she glanced over her shoulder and sighted a limping Gideon in the distance, neither could she go back.

So down she went.

It was even colder on the level below, and the floor was slick with water. Rune slipped multiple times and had to grope the wall to keep from falling. Without the lamp on the first level, she couldn't see a thing. Several times she found the way blocked by cave-ins and had to double back.

The water deepened, too, the further in she went.

When Gideon's boots thudded on the ladder behind her, adrenaline zipped through Rune. Stumbling through the water, she lurched down another tunnel, feeling along the walls, trying to put as much space as possible between herself and the witch hunter.

She stepped into a pool of water and nearly fell straight in. At the last second, she scrambled, throwing her weight back and slamming into the rock wall behind her.

This mine isn't just caving in on itself, she thought, breathing hard as the damp seeped through her clothes. *It's being swallowed by the sea.*

Water flooded this whole level.

In the dark, Rune tried to follow the walls around the flooded hole . . . and nearly fell in again. There was no lip or ledge. Just a watery, seemingly bottomless, pit. Behind her lay the tunnel she'd come down.

A dead end.

Light flashed, and Rune turned to see Gideon in the tunnel, headed straight for her. He had that flare in his hand, and the closer he came, the more the small cavern she stood in brightened.

Rune glanced around her, trying to think. Her spell was still intact, and since Gideon didn't know for sure that she was in here, the spellmarks on her wrist would keep working their magic, pushing his attention away from her. Or so she hoped.

But even if it *did* hold, all Gideon had to do was continue walking and he'd bump right into Rune. There was nowhere for her to go. It was too cramped to dart around him.

Unless . . .

She eyed the dark pool. The top of a ladder poked up a few inches above the surface, suggesting this hole had once been the entrance to the mine's third level.

The water was murky, the color of mud. Rune couldn't see three feet down, never mind the bottom, even with Gideon's light growing stronger.

Pulling her hood down toward her eyes, Rune stared at the water. It would be cold. Freezing cold. Could she hold her breath long enough to stay hidden? She didn't know. But if she didn't want Gideon to catch her, she only had one option. And it was this one.

Reaching down, she grabbed the slippery sides of the ladder and slowly lowered herself in, gasping at the icy temperature.

She descended slowly, not wanting to make too many ripples. As she did, her eyes locked with Gideon's—or they would have, if he could see her. He glanced right past Rune, scanning the cavern's shadows.

Relieved, Rune let out a breath.

Ghost Walker was still doing its job. Convincing him she wasn't here.

He'll be able to see me as soon as I come up for air, she realized, glancing at the bloody marks on her wrist, knowing the water would wash them away in moments. But what other choice did she have?

Before Gideon closed the gap, Rune sucked in a lungful of air and went under, using the ladder to pull herself as far down as she dared, out of his reach and into the murky water.

She felt the spell weaken the further down she went, then fade entirely.

Rune opened her eyes and looked up, half expecting to be confronted by Gideon's dark and deadly gaze. Instead, she saw nothing but murk, and the dim glow of his flare in the cavern above.

Rune held herself still.

The cold water slowed her pulse. Soon, her lungs pinched, wanting air. But the glow overhead didn't recede. He was still in this cavern with her.

Her lungs burned. Rune squeezed her eyes shut, trying to hold on a little longer, knowing she only had seconds until her time ran out. When it felt like her chest would burst, she opened her eyes and looked up to find only blackness. Darkness everywhere.

Gideon had taken his flare and left.

She let go of the ladder and surged upward, gasping for breath when she hit the surface.

The moment she did, two firm hands grabbed her and dragged her out.

TWENTY-THREE

RUNE

*R*UNE BUCKED AGAINST GIDEON, whose arms were locked tight around her, keeping her back pinned to his chest.

"If I didn't want you dead," he said, his voice low in her ear, "I'd be tempted to admire your cunning."

Rune gritted her teeth. *I'm flattered.*

His flare had died. With no light, she couldn't see a thing—but she could feel quite a lot.

He was all hard, menacing muscle. There wasn't an inch of softness in him. With him pressed against her, Rune *felt* their size difference. One of his hands wrapped easily around her bicep.

His strength, combined with his size, would beat her every time in a physical struggle. So Rune stopped struggling.

She fell still in his arms, catching her breath and trying to regroup.

He was warm as a furnace, and Rune's body temperature was dropping rapidly. The chill of the water had seeped into her skin, and her wet clothes locked in the cold. But the heat of him staved off the worst of it.

"I'm happy to drag you out of here like this." Even his breath was hot against her cheek. "But if you'd prefer to walk yourself out, I'll put on the restraints."

No way was she letting him put those on her. The restraints the Blood Guard used on witches trapped their entire hands in iron, preventing them from casting spells.

But neither was she letting him drag her out of here.

If Rune knew where her knife had gone in, she could dig the heel of her boot into the wound. That would hurt enough that he might let her go. But without a light, it would be a mere guess, and if she missed the first time, she doubted he'd give her the opportunity for another.

"No preference, then?"

Rune kept her mouth clamped shut, still thinking. She knew the pool of water was directly behind them, and the tunnel directly ahead.

"Suit yourself . . ."

The moment she felt his grip loosen slightly, Rune planted her feet, bent her knees, and pushed backward with all her might. She heard a huff of surprise. Felt his weight shift as he lost his balance. He staggered back.

Rune had hoped he'd throw his arms wide in his struggle to regain his balance.

Instead, he dragged her down with him.

They fell into the water together.

But Rune was ready for the icy shock. The moment the water closed over her head and Gideon let go, Rune pushed away from him. Her hands patted the walls of the pool until she found the ladder. Grabbing the rungs, she heaved herself out.

Gideon cursed from behind her. She heard the water splash as he swam for the sides of the pool. In seconds, he'd be on her again.

Using the walls to guide her, she ran through the dark tunnel, taking it to the first floor. Far behind her, she heard Gideon's loud swearing.

Back on the first level, she dashed for the mine's entrance, following the lamplight. Swinging herself onto the last ladder, she scaled the rungs, climbing upward. She paused at the top, listening for Laila, and heard the girl's footsteps pacing the ground outside, beyond the door in the room above.

Pulling herself into the small room, Rune approached the broken window and peered out. Beneath the swinging lantern out front, Laila stood in uniform, her pistol cocked on one shoulder as she stared into the darkness beyond.

Rune adjusted her cowl and hood, hiding her face and hair once more, as Gideon's voice roared from below.

"Laila!"

He sounded much too close.

Laila spun, her footsteps approaching the door.

"She's in here!"

Gideon was already climbing the ladder. With Laila just outside, Rune was trapped between them.

Rune pressed herself against the wall beside the door, listening to his boots thud against every rung. Getting closer. She squeezed the vial in her hand. She had seconds. If she could quickly redraw the spellmarks for *Ghost Walker* . . .

The door swung in and Laila stepped inside.

Rune froze.

Before Laila could realize someone was in the room with her, pressed against the wall, Rune realized this was her one and only chance.

She lunged outside.

Laila spun to face her.

Rune slammed the door shut and wedged herself against it,

pushing all of her weight into the wood. Laila pushed from the other side.

The door shuddered.

Gideon would arrive any moment. Rune needed some way to seal it shut long enough to get away. The last time she'd tried *Picklock,* she'd fainted from the effort. And its sister spell, *Deadbolt,* would be just as difficult to cast.

If you want to cast more complex spells, Verity's voice rang through her mind, *you need fresh blood.*

Rune drew the knife at her thigh. Its sheath had kept it semi-dry, and while some water had leaked in, the blade was still coated in Gideon's blood. The blood was diluted, but *fresh.*

She knew it was dangerous—she hadn't asked his permission to use it, nor would she get permission if she had. But she hadn't stabbed him intending to use his blood. So maybe it would be okay.

But what if it isn't?

Laila fired her pistol. Rune winced as the shots cracked through the air and the bullets lodged in the rickety door. A few more shots, and those bullets would break through.

If Rune didn't cast the spell *now,* she was done for.

Hoping she wasn't about to corrupt herself, Rune swiped her fingers through Gideon's blood, lifted them to the door, and drew the mark for *Deadbolt.*

Salt prickled her tongue. That roaring sea swelled inside her. But this time, Rune wasn't standing in the waves, fighting to stay upright while the magic pummeled her back. This time, the waves were beneath her, and she was sailing swiftly through them on a craft of her own making.

Is this what it's supposed to feel like?

Rune immediately understood why witches used fresh blood; it was so *easy.*

Beneath the roar of magic, something clicked into place.

This time, it was Gideon who threw himself against the door. She heard him grunt; felt the force of his weight. But the door barely trembled. *Deadbolt* kept it locked, trapping both Blood Guard soldiers inside.

Rune stumbled back, smiling in triumph.

More shots rang out. Bullets splintered the wood.

Her smile died on her lips.

Rune turned and bolted.

She slid the whistle from her pocket as she ran. Pressing it to her lips, she blew one hard, fierce note. Lady barreled out of the copse and up the dirt road, heading straight for her.

Another shot rang out, and this one whizzed past Rune's head, rustling her hair. She glanced over her shoulder to find Laila aiming the barrel of her pistol through the broken window.

Lady arrived, slowing a little, and Rune launched herself at the horse's back, struggling to mount as she trotted beneath her. Finally in the saddle, Rune's boots in the stirrups, she dug in her heels, letting Lady know this was one of those urgent situations she frequently got them into that Lady needed to now get them out of.

But it was a few seconds before the massive horse could pick up enough speed to carry them out of range.

A third shot rang out. This time, Rune felt the sharp sting of a bullet as it sliced her forearm. Warm, sticky blood seeped out.

She couldn't afford to stop and check how bad it was. Right now, she needed to steer Lady away from Laila and her stinging bullets.

After that . . .

Rune stared at the lights of Seldom Harbor on the horizon, trying to think.

Two Blood Guard soldiers had seen the Crimson Moth at the old mine tonight. Rune Winters, therefore, needed to be seen somewhere else. Preferably far away.

She needed to get to the Creeds' masked ball, and fast.

TWENTY-FOUR

GIDEON

GIDEON WAS HAULING HIMSELF up the last three rungs of the ladder when he heard Laila's pistol go off. He glanced up to find his hunting partner desperately pulling on the door, her black ponytail swishing with every yank.

"Damn it!" Laila snarled. "She locked us in!"

Gideon pulled himself into the room. His wounded leg protested every step as Laila moved aside to let him try.

"Gideon, you're bleeding . . ."

The Moth's knife had missed the major arteries and tendons, but his thigh still hurt like hell. What annoyed him most, though, was not getting a look at her face before she plunged the blade in.

"It looks worse than it is," he said, taking the tarnished metal latch in both hands and yanking on it.

The door didn't budge.

I had her, he thought, throwing himself at the door. *She was in my hands.*

But why hadn't she gone for his neck with that knife? The Moth was a coldhearted killer. Gideon had seen the corpses she'd abandoned in the city streets, ruthlessly bled dry.

So why aim for his leg?

Laila moved to the window. The pane was smashed. Lifting

her gun, Laila aimed through the broken glass and fired three times.

"I think that last shot might have hit her," she said, peering out.

The idea of Laila hitting her mark made Gideon stiffen.

If it was Rune . . .

Gideon scowled. Who cared if it was Rune? Rune or not, the Crimson Moth wouldn't think twice if their situation was reversed—the proof was in his throbbing, bleeding leg.

And if it was Rune, he told himself, *she's a traitor to the Republic.*

Whoever she was, the Moth had been in his grasp tonight. It was as close as he'd ever come. If he and Rune had been courting longer, he'd be able to tell if that slight frame pressed against him in the darkness belonged to her. He'd know how Rune felt beneath him and would have been able to compare it to the girl he'd pinned down tonight. But as close as he'd come to Rune Winters, it wasn't nearly close enough to know the difference.

Gideon's shoulder hurt from throwing himself at the door. He had just lifted his good leg to kick it down when Laila said, "It won't work."

She motioned to something out the window.

Striding over, Gideon glanced through the pane. A blood-red moth fluttered below the hanging lantern outside, its delicate wings thin as residue. Like a fingerprint he could almost see through.

"It's a spell."

Gideon sighed. It would likely be hours before it faded and the door unlocked.

He turned to Laila. "Did you get a look at her?"

Laila shook her head. "She kept her face covered and moved too quickly. We should have brought the hounds with us. And the Taskers."

Gideon had intentionally left the Tasker brothers behind after they'd defied his orders and abused the last witch. Clearly that had been a mistake. Two more soldiers would have made the difference. Not to mention the witch-hunting hounds.

If Gideon were being honest, he hadn't brought the hounds because the thought of siccing them on Rune made his stomach turn. He'd remembered her trembling beneath his touch in her bedroom; shivering in nothing but her underwear as he took her measurements.

Gideon had gone soft on a murderous witch—or at the very least, a witch sympathizer.

Fool.

He'd let her dupe him into thinking she was an innocent girl. Someone vulnerable and in need of protection.

He admitted none of this to Laila, who was smashing the rest of the broken pane out of the window frame with the butt of her pistol.

"This is what we know," he said, giving up on the enchanted door, which wouldn't open until the signature faded. "The Crimson Moth showed up at that wrong location tonight. A location I gave to only one person: Rune Winters. Even if she isn't the Moth, she's obviously in league with her."

It was enough to arrest her.

"If it was Rune, she'll know you set a trap for her," said Laila, using the scarlet sleeve of her coat to clear glass shards out of the pane. "She'll know we're coming for her. I'd be on the first ship off the island if I were her."

It was a desperate move. And though it was undoubtedly what any criminal should do if they wanted to escape him, the Crimson Moth didn't strike Gideon as someone who made desperate moves.

There's a masked ball at the Creeds' tonight, Rune had told him that morning. *You could meet me there.*

When the window was free of glass, Laila pulled herself through and out the other side. "We should ride for the docks."

"I have a better idea." Gideon winced as he limped to the window, trying not to put weight on his wounded leg. "You head back to headquarters, assemble a hunting party, then go to the docks and make sure no ship leaves port tonight."

From outside, Laila frowned at him. The lantern hanging above her head illuminated her face. "You're not coming?"

"I'm going to your parents' ball."

Laila frowned harder.

"Rune invited me," he explained. "If she wasn't here tonight and the Moth is someone else, Rune won't yet know this was a trap. She'll be at Oakhaven Park."

Grabbing hold of the window sill, he glanced out at the moth still fluttering over the door.

"And if she is there?" Laila asked, stepping away from the window.

Gideon pulled himself through with a grimace. "I'll arrest her for treason."

TWENTY-FIVE

RUNE

*T*HE GROUNDS OF OAKHAVEN Park backed onto a forest that spanned hundreds of acres. The home itself was modest compared to Wintersea House and had belonged to Seraphine Oakes before the queen sent her into exile.

Once a close friend to the Rosebloods, Seraphine fell out of favor with the previous queen—the mother of Elowyn, Analise, and Cressida. Nan never spoke of it, because it distressed her, but some believed that Seraphine's power surpassed the royal family's. So out of fear, or jealousy, or both, the witch queen banished her.

Oakhaven Park sat empty until the revolution, when the Good Commander gave it to his wife, Octavia Creed, as a spoil of war.

Some couples keep separate bedrooms, Alex joked once, *others keep separate estates.*

Though the wind had turned her clothes from sopping wet to damp, Rune still shivered as she rode Lady as far as she dared into the woods surrounding the property. Octavia kept a patrol, Rune knew, and she had no desire to run into it. Once she was inside the forest, shrouded by jack pines and balsam firs, her icy, trembling fingers unbuckled the saddlebag concealing her evening outfit.

Rune was happy to strip the damp clothes off her body. Standing naked in the breeze but for the sheathed knife strapped to her thigh, she tightly braided her wind-dried hair into an effortless style she'd watched Nan employ whenever they were running late to some function. It was still a little damp, but not obviously *wet*.

Next, she inspected the gash from Laila's shot, which was still bleeding. Rune had been lucky. If Laila's shot had been an inch closer, she'd have a bullet in her arm that would require digging out.

This was a flesh wound: bloody, but not deep. She withdrew one of the cotton strips she kept in Lady's saddlebag for emergencies, bound it around the wound, and tucked the ends underneath. Thankful she'd had the foresight to bring gloves, Rune pulled them on, concealing the bandage, and donned her dress and shoes.

Last, she put on her mask for the evening: a white fox face with pointed ears.

Fully dressed, Rune opened one more saddlebag and pulled out four sheets of tracing paper and a fountain pen. After folding the sheets and rolling them tightly around the pen, she tucked them down the front of her bodice.

Taking her whistle out for the third time tonight, she blew two long notes into the thin metal cylinder, telling Lady to go straight home. The moment the horse trotted away, Rune followed the footpath through the trees, allowing the house lights in the distance to guide her.

Normally, it would be exactly Rune's style to arrive fashionably late, waltzing in through the front doors and announcing herself to everyone. Tonight, though, she didn't want people to notice her delayed arrival. She wanted people to think she'd been here the whole time.

Drawing nearer to the house, Rune contemplated going in through the kitchens, pretending to have gotten lost, but that would only make the servants talk. As she drew nearer still, she eyed the windows. They were close enough to the ground for her to open and climb through without soiling her dress. She'd decided on the latter when voices nearby caught her attention.

"All that's left to do is sell Thornwood Hall."

Alex? Rune was so relieved by the sound of his familiar timbre, she almost missed the words he had spoken.

Sell Thornwood Hall?

She tucked her questions away for later. Adjusting her mask, she donned a more tedious costume, one that was second nature by now: the guise of a superficial girl who cared only for designer dresses, extravagant parties, and juicy gossip. Rune stepped out of the woods, heading toward the ring of young men circling a fire that blazed in an ornate iron fire pit.

Despite their masked faces, her eyes found Alex in an instant. Through his lion mask, he gazed into the fire. As if pondering a problem that was plaguing him and searching for the answer in the flames.

Unlike his brother, who was built like a soldier, Alex had a slender frame. As a devoted musician who spent his days practicing and composing, he often forgot to eat.

At her approach, Alex's attention snapped toward her.

"Rune?"

Seeing him was like a drowning woman sighting a buoy. She wanted to throw herself in his direction, loop her arms around his neck, and hold on for dear life.

She did none of these things.

"The darkness sure turns you about!" Still shivering, she stepped toward the delicious warmth of the fire. "I came outside for some air, and the next thing I knew, I was lost in that jungle." She motioned to the woods behind her.

The gentleman wearing a wolf mask said: "I didn't realize you were here, Rune." The voice belonged to Noah Creed. "Did you just arrive?"

Before she could spin the story that she'd prepared, Alex unbuttoned his coat and dropped it over her shoulders.

"Your teeth are chattering. Let's go inside before you freeze."

The warmth of his body was still in the fabric, and Rune soaked it up. Wanting to thaw herself out further—and give Noah an answer—she put her hands to the fire. "Oh, but—"

"I insist." Alex pressed his palm to the small of her back, turning her away from the heat.

The tone of his words, which sounded friendly, had a sharpness beneath for Rune alone. She glanced up to find his golden-brown eyes sapped of warmth. From the way his lips thinned, he wasn't only worried, but angry, too.

Angry at me?

Too tired to resist, she let him lead her toward the house. Glancing over her shoulder, she waved goodbye to Noah and the boy in the frog mask—Bart Wentholt, she guessed, from the red hair.

She'd implemented the first part of her plan: to be seen at this party. All she needed now was Alex and Verity's cooperation to make it seem like she'd been here the whole time.

In the fire's absence, she pulled Alex's wool jacket firmly around herself. He silently led her out of the gardens, past the cherubic statues, and up the stone steps to the house. Servants bustled past them, some carrying empty trays from the ballroom bursting with music and chatter, while others rushed toward it with trays full of drinks and desserts.

Rune had turned to follow them when Alex grabbed her

hand. Sliding his fingers through hers, he pulled her in the opposite direction.

"There's no need to manhandle me," she said, getting irritable. The less irritable half of her was surprised at the fingers interlaced with hers. They'd never held hands before.

Alex ignored her. "Where have you been?" he said, his jaw clenched as he tugged her down a long, empty corridor. The gold foil of patterned ferns glittered against the dark green wallpaper. "I've been thinking the worst."

"There was no time to tell you." Rune glanced over her shoulder while keeping her voice down. "And it was too risky to send a telegram. Promise me something? If I start acting strange—scary-strange, like saying or doing mean things for the pleasure of it—you must tell Verity, okay?"

What Verity would do, Rune didn't know. But once a witch started corrupting herself with bad magic, she began to crave its power like a drug. After that first hit, it was difficult to resist coming back for more.

Rune did not want to go down that path.

"What are you talking about?" said Alex.

She didn't feel any different. But maybe no one did. Maybe a witch had no idea what was happening to her until it was too late.

Before the hall turned, Alex opened a door, his hand still gripping Rune's as he pulled her into the room.

It smelled like books and burning wood inside. Bookshelves lined three of the four walls. Letting go of Alex's hand, Rune trod across the woven carpet, drawn to the light of a crackling fire in the hearth, and passed a massive oak desk.

I've been here before.

Her gaze shot to the wall over the fireplace, and there it was: the map of the palace prison.

A map she needed if she had any hope of saving Seraphine.

Alex had remembered and brought her straight to it. The realization warmed her more deeply than the fire. "Alex, you're—"

"You still haven't told me where you were tonight."

Alex stood behind her, the friendliness stripped from his voice, leaving only the sharpness as he removed the coat from her shoulders. Still shivering and not ready to part with its warmth, Rune almost seized it, then realized he was peeling it away to look at her arm.

Her silk glove had blood seeping through it.

Oh no.

Was that the real reason he'd draped the coat over her?

Did Noah and Bart notice?

More gentle than his tone, Alex turned her toward him and started tugging the glove off her fingers, one by one. The thin silver ring on his smallest finger glinted in the firelight. "How did this happen?"

"Laila shot me," she said, watching the silk slide down her arm to reveal the makeshift bandage, which was good and soiled. "Or shot *at* me. I was lucky; she mostly missed."

Alex went quiet. It was so rare for him to get angry. But she could feel the anger in him now, coiled tight like a spring.

"And why was Laila shooting at you?"

"I was at the old Seldom mine, looking for Seraphine. Your brother set me up."

Alex's gaze narrowed behind his lion mask. "What do you mean, he set you up?"

Taking the ruined glove, Rune threw it onto the fire, destroying the evidence. She slid off the second one and burned it too. Hopefully Verity had worn gloves tonight that she could borrow. Otherwise, she'd need Alex to escort her home with his coat over her shoulders—and *that* would certainly make people talk.

Boys who let girls wear their coats home were making their intentions known.

But if they're busy talking about Alex and me, thought Rune, *they won't be wondering about when I arrived.*

Rune told him everything that had happened in the mine, leaving out the part beforehand, where she went alone to Gideon's tenement building, stripped down to her underwear, and let him take her measurements. That was irrelevant information, she decided.

As she filled him in, Alex crouched down and lifted the hem of her dress, reaching for the knife he knew she kept strapped to her thigh. They'd been in this situation so many times, working like cogs in a clock that had run smoothly for years, that Alex knew exactly where the knife was sheathed.

"Gideon intentionally misled me," she said as Alex drew the knife from under her dress and used its sharp edge to cut a long strip off her cotton shift. "If he didn't suspect me before, he does now."

If he noticed blood on the blade, he didn't remark on it.

When he rose to face her, Alex handed her the makeshift bandage to hold while he untied the bloody one from around her arm.

While he focused on his task, Rune studied him. Alex's golden mask ended at the tip of his nose, cutting across his cheeks and revealing lips that were pressed tight at the sight of the gash in Rune's pale skin. The wound wasn't deep, but it was still bleeding freely.

"I asked you to end this thing with Gideon," he said, throwing the soiled bandage into the flames, then wrapping the fresh cotton strip around the wound.

"*He* contacted *me*," she said, defensive. "*He* wanted to meet."

Alex's elegant fingers secured the bandage and tucked the ends underneath. "And you had no choice but to obey?"

"He's my best chance of finding Seraphine."

Alex breathed in deep. As if Rune were a child testing his patience.

"I need an alibi," she said, changing the subject. "Can we say I came to this party with you tonight?"

Her wound freshly bandaged, she turned her focus to the map over the mantel. From here, it looked like a series of circles within circles.

Before Alex could answer her, she moved to Octavia Creed's massive desk in the center of the room, piled high with records. Grabbing the heavy desk chair, Rune dragged it back to the fireplace, climbed onto it, and pulled out the tracing paper and pen from inside her bodice. She set both down on the mantel.

"We *could* say you came with me tonight," said Alex, watching her. "*If* you've agreed to my offer."

Rune, standing on her tiptoes, was about to cover the upper left-hand corner of the map with the first piece of tracing paper.

"What offer?" she said, glancing over her shoulder. Her fox mask obscured her view of him. She would have pushed it back off her face, except both her hands were occupied.

"My offer to help you rescue Seraphine," he said from where he leaned against the prison warden's desk, looking at her. "I said I would help, *if* you agreed to come with me to Caelis for a month."

Rune bristled, gripping the fountain pen hard in her hand. "Two weeks, we said."

"It will take us three days to sail there, and three days to sail back. So: no. You'll have to come for the full month."

Why is he so adamant about this?

It wasn't like him.

Rune returned to the map, pressing a little too hard on the tracing paper as she followed the lines showing through from behind. "You know I can't leave. I have—"

"What happens when you succeed, Rune?"

"What do you mean?" she said, still tracing. There were seven concentric circles, each depicting a section of the prison. She was on the second section.

"What happens after you rescue every last witch from the purge?"

If Rune were honest with herself, deep down, she didn't believe she could save them all. She hoped to save Seraphine, and more witches after that. But eventually, Rune expected to be caught. She was only one girl. And there were hundreds of witch hunters.

"I can't rescue them all," she admitted, staring at the untraced lines showing faintly through the translucent paper.

"For this exercise, let's say you can. When it's over, will you still hide yourself in plain sight, pretending to be what you despise? Resenting everyone around you? They will never change their minds about you, Rune. Don't you want to be free of them? Of all of it?"

Rune lowered her pen. She didn't want to think about this.

Because Alex was right.

Once, this island had been her home. It had been exactly where she belonged. But unless witches somehow seized power, it would never be that way again. And even if a new Reign of Witches were possible, there was no going back to her old life with Nan. That life ceased to exist the day they dragged her away to be purged.

Rune lifted her pen to the paper and kept tracing. She had three prison sections left to copy.

I'll never succeed—not completely. Witches would always be in danger in the New Republic. So this little game of *What if?* was a waste of time.

When her tracing was complete, Rune lowered the last piece of paper. It was then that she remembered what Alex had said around the bonfire outside.

All that's left to do is sell Thornwood Hall.

"You're leaving for good," she realized aloud, turning to face him. "Not for a month, and not just to study. You're going away forever."

It felt like someone had pulled the chair out from under her.

She struggled to find words. "Does Gideon know?"

"I haven't told him." Alex glanced away. "I doubt he'll care. In fact, I'm sure he'll be relieved."

Rune frowned. That made no sense.

Alex pushed away from the desk, walking toward her. He stopped in front of the chair she stood on, his masked face tilted to hers. "I want you to come with me."

"For a month, yes. You said that."

"Not for a month. I want you to leave with me and never come back. I want you to be free of this, Rune. You shouldn't have to live in constant fear for your life." He reached for her fingers again, sliding them gently through his. "But I'll settle for only a month. For now. If I must."

For now. As if he were being patient with her. As if he'd wait for as long as it took Rune to come to her senses.

"In Caelis, we'll go to the opera house every day of the week. Where they show real operas, not that propaganda you despise."

She looked away from him, afraid he'd see how much she

wanted that—to watch a real opera again. To talk about the in-
tricacies of the characters and themes on the carriage ride home.
It would never be Nan sitting next to her. But that would be
okay, if Alex was beside her instead.

"We'll go to the ballet and the symphony. We'll spend week-
ends in the Umbrian mountains."

His words tempted her. *Caelis*, where people didn't care if
you were a witch, and certainly didn't report you to the police.
And *Alex*, the boy she trusted most in the world.

She closed her eyes. This fragile feeling in her chest felt like
hope.

No.

She shut the feeling down. She pulled her hand free.

"What you're describing is a happy ending. A *fantasy*." She
used his shoulders to steady herself as she hopped down from the
chair. "And that's great—for you. Not everyone gets to have that."

Countless witches had their happy endings stolen from
them. Witches like Nan. And Verity's sisters. Seraphine's would
be stolen, too, if Rune couldn't save her in time.

Tucking the tracings under her arm and the fountain pen
between her teeth, she dragged the chair back to the desk.

"You're right. Some people are determined to live out their
own personal tragedies."

She stopped, her hands still gripping the back of the chair.
Her whole body prickled with anger. "What's that supposed to
mean?"

"How many of the witches you save turn around and try to
save you, Rune?"

"I've told you before, I don't need saving."

"And you'll be telling me that the day they string you up to
die while the city cheers. You'll be saying it while they cut your
throat and bleed you dry."

Why was he doing this? Alex was the one steady rock in her life. Always there to lean on.

They didn't fight. Not ever.

"Maybe that's what I deserve," she said, setting the small stack of tracing paper on the desk, each piece containing one quarter of the prison's map.

"*What?*" The word tore out of Alex like thunder from the sky.

Putting the pen down, Rune rolled the pieces tightly around it and slid them all back down her bodice.

"Look at me, Rune."

He stood behind her now. But instead of turning, she stared down at a dark knot in the desk's wood.

"I betrayed my grandmother. I led the Blood Guard straight to our house." She fisted her hands as a wave of self-loathing crashed through her. "The day they killed her, I stood there and watched it happen. I let them all believe I hated her." She was glad for the mask over the upper part of her face, which would help hide the tears forming in her eyes as she turned around to face him. "Innocent people don't do things like that."

She should have stormed that platform and denounced them all. She should have yelled the truth to the sky: that she loved Kestrel Winters, and they were demons for wanting her dead.

"You did what you had to do to survive." He pushed back his mask. "Kestrel wanted you to live, Rune. Don't throw away the gift she gave you."

She glanced sharply away from him. *You're wrong.*

It was no gift, being allowed to live while the one you loved most was dead—because of you.

Rune remembered the day they killed her. Kestrel Winters didn't cower and beg like a criminal. She stood before her killers with the dignity and poise of a queen. When Rune went to the purge, she wanted to go exactly like that. Knowing she'd done everything she could to deliver other witches from Nan's fate.

"Sometimes it feels like you're afraid to look at me," said Alex. Placing his warm hands on her cheeks, below her mask, he tilted her face back to his. "Is it because I don't want to hurt you? Or hunt you? Or watch you die?"

His grip was firm. Resolved.

"Do you believe you deserve those things, Rune?"

Looking at him was like watching an opera she didn't like. One of those ridiculous comedies where the character gets everything she ever dreamed of and lives happily ever after. Those operas were so unrealistic, they always made Rune want to cry. Or stand up and leave.

Sometimes, she got the same feeling looking at Alex.

He gently let go of her face and pushed back her mask. As if he wanted her to look at him.

"Rune . . ."

A sudden rattling at the door made him step sharply away from her. Alex grabbed his jacket to drop over Rune's shoulders, to hide her bandaged arm, but it was too late.

Verity burst in.

"*Here* you are." Their friend's brown curls were loose around her shoulders, and the scarlet dress she wore made her white skin paler than usual. "If I have to listen to Bart Wentholt wax poetic about his shoe collection again, I'm going to scream. Does it never occur to him that *nobody cares*?"

She halted, glancing from Alex to Rune.

"What happened to your arm?"

TWENTY-SIX

GIDEON

GIDEON LEFT HIS HORSE with the stable hand and strode through the gilt doors of Oakhaven Park. A small chandelier winked overhead, sending fractured light over the guests in the front foyer, all of them waiting for staff to pull up their carriages. On either side of Gideon were twin marble staircases, both leading to the second floor of Octavia Creed's home.

Gideon had fought alongside her husband, the Good Commander, at the New Dawn. The Commander was only Nicolas Creed then. A simple soldier in the palace guard.

They'd met years ago, in a boxing club, when Gideon was getting the shit kicked out of him nightly. Those matches always ended the same way: with Gideon hauling his bruised body from the floor of the ring, dragging himself to a table at the bar in the back, and pretending not to notice the sneering men around him. All of them disgusted by his presence. *Witch's whore*, they'd called him. They didn't want Gideon in their ring. But neither would they throw him out, fearing Cressida's wrath.

Since they couldn't get rid of him, the men took turns beating Gideon to a pulp night after night. Taking out their anger and hate on a target Gideon was happy to provide them.

Really, they were doing him a favor.

Gideon never told Cressida how he came by the bruises, and she either didn't care, or pretended not to.

One night, after crawling out of her bed like the insect he was, Gideon noticed a man old enough to be his father watching from across the bar as Gideon drank himself into oblivion before a match.

While the other men spat on Gideon when they walked by, this man only stared. He assumed the guy would wait for Gideon to leave, follow him out to the alley, and finish whatever the boys didn't finish in the ring. Sometimes, they did that. These men who hated him.

He caught the man's eye, welcoming it.

When Gideon's match started, he was already high from the laudanum in his blood. His vision blurred and his body swayed, but he could still feel the man's gaze on him. When he lay on the floor afterward—numb despite the punches he'd taken, feeling none of the welts coming up on his skin, unable to taste the blood in his mouth—it was this man who stopped them from dumping Gideon next to the refuse out back, where they usually put him.

Instead, he helped Gideon over to a private table and ordered him food. As the room spun, Gideon lay his bloody head down on the sticky tabletop, wishing his opponent had broken a bone this time, because maybe then he would feel something.

"If one day you wake up and decide you want to hit back," said the man across from him, "come find me." He wrote an address down, pressed it into Gideon's open palm, and folded his limp fingers over the paper.

That man was Nicolas Creed.

He'd been the only person in that club to see Gideon as something more than a witch's whore. He'd looked beneath the bruises, to the boy with nothing left to live for.

It was Nicolas who taught Gideon how to box, showing him he didn't have to take punches—he could throw them, harder and more skillfully than his opponent.

It was Nicolas who'd believed in Gideon when Gideon didn't believe in himself.

It felt like a lifetime ago.

Now, as he stood in Nicolas's wife's foyer nearly three years later, Gideon buried the memory before he limped up the staircase, following the contented buzz of chattering guests. People stared as he passed, surprised by the captain's presence. He scanned their masked faces, looking for Rune, and moved on when he didn't see her.

Gideon wore no mask. While Laila and the others had headed for the docks, he'd gone home to clean and dress the knife wound in his leg, then changed into another one of his father's suits—Gideon didn't own any of his own—and rode straight here.

"I hope things went smoothly for you, Gideon." The voice belonged to Charlotte Gong, and it stopped him in his tracks. He turned to find her face half-hidden by a rabbit mask. A gold engagement ring gleamed at her neck.

Smoothly? He considered asking what she meant, except time was of the essence. He needed to find Rune and arrest her.

The moment he stepped into the ballroom, Gideon realized the magnitude of the task before him. There had to be a hundred people in here, likely more wandering the grounds, and all of their faces were hidden behind masks.

Sighing roughly, Gideon began a sweep, starting from the eastern side of the ballroom, keeping to the edges to avoid the dancing. He looked for a certain shade of strawberry blonde hair, and when he came up short, he widened his search to include her friend Verity (brown curls) and Alex (tawny hair). They were often at Rune's side, and if he could spot one, the other two would likely be nearby.

At the thought of his brother, Gideon paused.

If he arrested Rune tonight, he needed to do it without his brother knowing. In private would be best. To do that, he'd have to get Rune away from this crowd.

He could break the bad news to Alex once it was over.

Gideon had started his second sweep of the room when someone called his name.

"Citizen Sharpe! You made it! I feared you wouldn't."

He spun to face the owner of the voice and found a girl in a glittering fox mask staring at him. Someone's suit jacket hung from her shoulders.

Rune?

Her lips were bright red and smiling beneath the cut of the mask, and she'd braided her hair into a tight knot at the back of her head. It looked darker than its usual red-gold hue. As if she'd gotten caught in the rain, and it was still damp.

Or perhaps fell into a small body of water.

His eyes narrowed.

Remembering Laila's words from earlier—*I think my last shot hit her*—Gideon's attention moved from Rune's face downward, checking her quickly for signs of a wound. His gaze skimmed the fitted bodice of her gray dress and the silk gloves covering her arms, but she appeared to be in fine form. Not at all like a criminal who'd raced desperately to get here tonight.

Stepping in closer, she laid her hand on his arm.

"How did the transfer go?"

He frowned. Was she going to pretend tonight hadn't happened?

"It went exactly as planned." Technically true. He'd transferred

Seraphine Oakes earlier today, after meeting with Harrow. The witch was locked in a cell deep in the palace prison.

Gideon glanced around to see if Alex lurked about—or any of Rune's suitors. He needed to get her alone, as soon as possible, and make the arrest.

"I was telling the girls at Charlotte's luncheon about it," she said, tucking her hand into his elbow and leading him deeper into the room. As if she truly didn't realize he was about to arrest her. "Naturally, I'll need to give them an update."

She smiled up at him, waiting for details.

Gideon blinked. "You . . . did what?"

If Rune had gossiped away the information he gave her, it meant other people had the same information.

Gideon suddenly remembered Charlotte on the stairs. *I hope things went smoothly for you.*

Seeing his reaction, Rune's hand fell from his elbow. "Oh. Was it supposed to be a secret?" She worried one red lip between her teeth. "I should have realized. *Drat.*"

His thoughts spun.

Rune had told him about the luncheon earlier, before he'd given her the false lead. Knowing how much Rune and her friends loved gossip, he was certain she *had* spilled the information at her little gathering.

"How could I be so senseless?" she cried. "I feel awful!"

Feeling overly warm, he unbuttoned the collar of his shirt. "How many guests were at this luncheon?"

"Hmm. Hard to say." She twisted her lips. "A few dozen, maybe?"

Knowing the way gossip spread in Rune's social circles, that number had likely ballooned long before tonight. And if dozens of people knew the location he'd given Rune as of noon today, any one of them might be the Moth, or in league with her.

Anyone could have been at the mine tonight.

He stared at Rune, unsure if she was obtuse, or a master of deception. She had drastically widened his net of suspects—but intentionally or unintentionally?

Is she actively sabotaging me? Or is she innocent?

He didn't know. And either way, he could no longer arrest her. Not without further evidence.

Gideon ground his teeth together. He was back to square one.

"Rune, we're leaving now. Are you ready?"

They turned to find Alex standing several paces away in a crisp white shirt with his usual brown suspenders. It made Gideon realize whose coat hung from Rune's shoulders.

"Verity has an exam tomorrow morning," Alex explained to Gideon. He pushed back his lion mask from his face and locked eyes with his brother.

The girl in question—Verity de Wilde—stood next to Alex, her face half-hidden behind a raven mask. She crossed her arms tightly over the bodice of her scarlet dress as she stared down Gideon, like she did not approve of how close he stood to Rune.

"What does Verity's exam have to do with you?" Gideon asked Rune.

Verity's clipped voice answered for her. "Rune and I came with Alex tonight. He's taking us both home."

Oh.

Gideon stepped back, away from them all. If Rune had come to this masked ball with his brother, she couldn't have *also* been in Seldom Harbor.

It was another strike against him.

Rune might lie, but Alex wouldn't. His brother would never knowingly sabotage him by aiding a dangerous witch. Not after everything their family had been through.

As the three friends turned to leave, Gideon watched Alex press his hand to the small of Rune's back.

At least he's taking my advice.

For some strange reason, this didn't make Gideon feel better. It made him feel much worse.

TWENTY-SEVEN

RUNE

*T*HE CARRIAGE BUMPED AND jostled Rune as Alex's driver took them down the cobbled lanes of the city. Verity and Alex sat facing Rune, who sat alone on the opposite bench.

She should have felt victorious at the look on Gideon's face when he realized she'd turned the tables on him. Instead, she felt . . . drained. Like she could sleep for a month straight if given the chance.

Maybe that's what I'll do in Caelis, she thought. Then caught herself. She still hadn't decided if she was going with Alex, never mind going for a month.

An unfamiliar tension radiated between them since leaving the warden's study, and she could feel his eyes on her from the other side of the carriage. What had he been about to say before Verity barged into the room?

"Let's get a look at this map."

Right. The map.

Outside, the moon was almost full. It cast just enough light through the windows to see. Sinking down to the floor of the carriage, Rune pulled out the tracings and unrolled them, piecing them together.

Verity and Alex leaned forward to get a better look.

"There are seven sections," said Rune, squinting at the circles she'd traced. A gate marked the entrance to the first and biggest section, the outermost circle. In each concentric circle after it, moving toward the center, were more gates. Seven in total. And each entry was named after one of the seven Ancients.

Mercy, Liberty, Wisdom, Justice, Amity, Patience, Fortitude.

Rune remembered when the opera house columns still bore the painted likenesses of the Ancients. The images were destroyed by fire when patriots ransacked the building during the revolution. The columns had since been painted over, but Rune could still picture the renderings of the witches in her mind: Amity, mid-laugh and her hair a wild tangle; Wisdom, with her secretive smile; Justice, turning her face toward the sky . . .

"Do you know which section they're keeping Seraphine in?" asked Alex.

Rune shook her head. Not only did she not know what section or cell Seraphine was in, Rune didn't know how many guards she'd need to evade. Or how one passed through the gates, which would be locked. Who held the keys? Once she was on the other side of all the gates, how would she get back out?

"This feels impossible," said Rune, her shoulders slumping.

"There's a reason they call it impregnable," said Alex.

"Unhelpful," said Verity, shooting him a look. She joined Rune on the floor, crossing her legs beneath her dress and leaning over the map as the carriage jolted beneath them. Rune's nose prickled. One of these days, she would gently suggest to her friend not to dab so much perfume on . . .

But not tonight. Tonight, if Rune felt exhausted, Verity *looked* it. There were dark circles under her eyes, and every few minutes, her loud yawns broke the silence in the carriage. Not for the first time, Rune felt guilty stealing Verity away from her studies, certain her friend's grades were suffering for it.

Verity would scold her if she knew what Rune was thinking. She and Rune were in this together. In it in a way Alex never would be. Rune had lost her grandmother to the purge; Verity had lost her sisters. Both wanted to rescue as many witches as they could—to make up for the ones they hadn't been able to save.

"I wish I had a spell for walking through walls," said Rune, leaning her head back against the carriage seat and staring at Alex.

"Is there such a thing?"

She shrugged. "I've never come across one."

Verity pushed her spectacles up the bridge of her nose. "I'm sure there's a spell for *blasting* through walls. But you'll need a lot more blood to pull off that kind of thing. Blood you don't have."

She pulled a pencil and notepad from her pocket and started writing. The edge of her tongue popped out of the corner of her mouth as she dutifully made a list.

"We'll need to know: where Seraphine is located; how the gates work; roughly how many guards . . ."

"How Rune will get *out* after she gets *in*," Alex added, sounding displeased but taking part.

"What day they're planning to purge her," said Rune.

This was her last chance. If she arrived too late this time, she wouldn't get another.

When she finished her list, Verity lowered her notepad to her knee and started tapping the paper with her pen. "That's a lot of information."

"Laila will know some of these answers," offered Alex. "Her mother's the warden, and she's a witch hunter. She'll have been inside that prison more than once."

"The girl who shot me tonight?" Rune arched her brows, remembering the opera house, and Laila's less-than-playful guesses about why she'd been late.

Verity seemed to remember the same thing. She shook her head. "I don't like the way Laila looks at Rune these days. Best to avoid her. However . . ." Mischief danced in her eyes. "Her brother might be helpful."

"Noah's not a witch hunter," Alex pointed out.

"But his sister is, and his mother is a warden. Noah's smart. He pays attention. And . . ." Verity spoke to Rune now. ". . . he's at the top of your list of eligible suitors. If you got him alone—"

"Eligible what?" interrupted Alex. He looked to Rune. "What is she talking about?"

Rune winced, remembering how they'd excluded Alex from this plan. Deciding it was well past time to fill him in, she said, "Verity made me a list of eligible men to—"

"*No.*"

The ferocity of the word surprised them both.

"*I'll* talk to Noah," said Alex, his voice like quiet thunder. "I've invited him and Bart over for cards this week."

Rune glanced up to find him glowering at her.

"What are you going to do, casually ask him how to get past the gates of his mother's prison?" She shook her head. "The likelihood of Noah knowing any of these answers, never mind all of them, is so slim. It's not worth the risk of raising his suspicions."

Alex opened his mouth to argue, but Rune didn't let him.

"I already have a better solution."

It had been burning inside her this whole time, like a quiet candle flame. She hadn't mentioned it because she knew what they'd say.

Verity looked up from her list. "Let's hear it."

"Gideon knows every single one of these answers. If I use my truth-telling spell—"

"You tried that already," Verity pointed out. "It didn't work."

"You *tried* that already?" Alex dragged his hands through his hair.

Rune ignored him.

"It didn't work because he refused the wine," she argued with Verity. "But I can fuse the spell to anything. A coat. A shoe. A watch. I could enchant a thimble and slip it into his pocket. He wouldn't even know it's there."

"He'll know," said Alex. "He's well acquainted with magic."

"Not *my* magic," countered Rune. "Every witch's essence is unique."

After the trap he'd laid for her—a trap she'd stupidly walked straight into—Rune wanted nothing more than to end things with Gideon. He was altogether too clever. But to cut him loose now, when he suspected her most, would be akin to an admission of guilt.

Rune couldn't retreat. She needed to go on the offensive. She had to appear smitten. Like she'd never encountered him at that mine tonight.

"As a Blood Guard captain, Gideon has brought witches through those gates hundreds of times. He'll know where Seraphine is, as well as her purging date."

"He already suspects you, Rune!"

"He didn't arrest me tonight," she pointed out. She'd bought herself more time with that luncheon. How much time, she didn't know.

This didn't seem to soothe them. Rune couldn't exactly blame her friends. She might have outwitted Gideon temporarily, but she hadn't thrown him off her scent for good.

"All I need is something to enchant. Something he'd wear on his person."

"And the spellmark?" challenged Verity. "He'll see it and realize what you are."

"Then I need to enchant something where I can easily hide a spellmark. I'll figure it out, okay? The Luminaries Dinner is in four days. I'll ask him to accompany me. And afterward, I'll use the spell to get the answers I need from him."

"*Afterward,*" said Alex, darkly.

Verity said nothing. She'd gone utterly quiet.

They suddenly both annoyed Rune. Couldn't they see this was their best option?

"If either of you come up with a better solution, I'll call the whole thing off. Until then, this is the plan."

Alex turned sharply to the carriage window, his fingers twisting that silver ring around and around his smallest finger. Verity merely scowled.

AFTER ALEX DROPPED HER off at Wintersea House with barely a word of goodbye, Rune dictated a telegram for Lizbeth to handle:

GIDEON SHARPE
113 PRUDENCE ST, OLD TOWN

COME WITH ME TO THE LUMINARIES DINNER?
                                        RUNE

Afterward, she promptly fell into bed, trying not to think about Alex's anger, or his tempting invitation to Caelis, or the tension between them tonight. Fighting with Alex made her feel unbalanced. Like a ship they'd been sailing smoothly on for years had suddenly plunged into stormy waters.

Alex never blurred the line between his loyalty to Rune and his love for Gideon. He liked to keep them separate. In courting Gideon, Rune was shrinking the gap between those parts of his life, and it was making him anxious. That's all this was. That's why he was being so protective.

Rune shook her head. She couldn't afford to be distracted right now. So she put her oldest friend out of her mind and fell asleep.

TWENTY-EIGHT

RUNE

*I*T WAS A FULL day and a half before she received a response from Gideon. Rune was in her casting room, working on her Luminaries speech, when Lizbeth interrupted.

"A package arrived for you."

Rune, who was in the middle of spewing extravagant lies onto the page with her pen, asked her to leave it on the desk. Only when she came to the end of the paragraph did she look up.

It was a plain white box tied with pale blue ribbons.

Wintersea blue, she thought.

Eyeing the box, Rune rose to her feet. Stretching the kink in her neck, she rolled her shoulders and shoved aside the speech she was writing, pulling the package closer. Loosening the ribbon, she removed the lid, pushed back the brown paper, and discovered a folded mint green garment inside. Resting on top of it was a note written in black ink.

Are you asking me to be your date?

—Gideon

Rune read and reread those words before flipping the paper over and looking for more. But that was all he'd written.

Is that a yes? she wondered.

Glancing at the pale green fabric, she set the note aside and pulled out the dress. Something flickered inside her as it unraveled. Her pulse sped up as she took in the tapered lace sleeves and the delicately embroidered bodice.

After loosening the laces, Rune stripped out of her clothes and stepped into the elegant dress. The silk was smooth as water against her skin and the lace sleeves fit her arms like gloves. Without someone to do the laces up, she left the back open, stepped into the matching silk shoes the dress had arrived with, and walked into her bedroom to stand before the full-length mirror.

Her heart nearly lodged in her throat.

The mint green and white lace complemented her pale complexion and brought out the shades of red in her hair. As her fingers traced the almost imperceptible pattern of waves across the bodice, Rune tried to remind herself how much she loathed the boy who'd made it.

But it was the most beautiful dress she'd ever seen, never mind worn, and Rune couldn't stop the startling warmth rippling through her. She wished she'd asked Lizbeth to stay, to tie the laces so it would fit properly.

Wading back to her desk in the casting room, tulle swishing around her legs, Rune sank into the chair, grabbed a pen and pad of paper, and jotted down a response.

Gideon Sharpe
113 Prudence St, Old Town

Yes, Gideon. I'm asking you to be my date.

Rune

P.S. My plan is to win you over so you'll keep making me dresses forever.

P.P.S. Let me know when it's working.

She found it hard to concentrate after that and was almost relieved when Lizbeth interrupted again. Rune had moved from writing her speech at her desk to reciting it as she paced the room.

"Miss Rune . . ." Lizbeth glanced over her shoulder and stepped into the casting room. "There's a visitor here to see you. He's in the foyer."

Rune, who wasn't expecting any callers, looked up from the page she was reading. "Who is it?"

Lizbeth lowered her voice. "That Blood Guard captain."

Gideon? Rune's eyes widened. *What could he want?*

"Tell him . . ." She was still wearing the dress he'd made her, the laces down the back undone. "Tell him I'll be right down. And maybe offer some refreshments?"

Lizbeth nodded, then disappeared.

Darn. She'd purchased a suit jacket for Gideon in town yesterday—to enchant with *Truth Teller*, and to atone for the one she'd ruined with wine. Not that she could ever truly atone for ruining a Sharpe Duet jacket. Even now, the memory stabbed her with guilt. To fit him, though, the seamstress needed to make a few adjustments, so Rune didn't yet have the jacket in her hands, and therefore couldn't use it to get information.

It's fine, she told herself, shrugging off the dress. *Just make yourself presentable and go down there.*

Rune reached for the clothes she'd cast off earlier, only to find them wrinkled from lying in a heap.

Needing something else to wear, Rune ran to her wardrobe and pulled on the first thing she found: a simple cotton sundress that fell to her knees. She hurried barefoot down the stairs and immediately slowed upon seeing the young man in her foyer.

Gideon faced away from her, clasping his hands behind his back as he eyed his surroundings. He wore plain brown trousers and had rolled his shirtsleeves to his elbows, showing off his forearms.

Rune's heart stumbled at the sight of him. This was the same boy who had her pinned beneath him two nights ago. The same boy she'd stabbed in the leg with a knife.

"Gideon," she said, recovering. "What a pleasant surprise."

He spun to face her, and Rune quailed a little beneath his penetrating gaze. How much did he remember from the mine? It had been so dark down there. Even when he lit the flare, he hadn't removed her hood in time to see her. But could he still *know*, somehow, that it was her?

Her legs felt like jelly. Rune gripped the railing a little too hard and kept descending the stairs. "What brings you to Wintersea?"

"I came to ask if you'd like to take a walk with me."

"A . . . walk?"

"You said there's a beach near here." He seemed uncertain, suddenly, and unclasped his hands. "If you're busy—"

"Oh! Yes. I mean, no, not busy. Yes, there is a beach." She reached the bottom of the steps, weirdly out of breath. "A walk would be lovely."

"Great," he said.

Why are you really here? she wondered.

She tried a smile, then glanced toward Lizbeth, who'd entered the foyer with a knit shawl in her hands. Taking it, Rune flung it over her shoulders.

Rune and Gideon stood awkwardly for a moment before she realized he didn't know the way to a beach he'd never been to.

"Right." Her cheeks reddened. "Follow me."

She led him through the house, and only once they'd entered the gardens did she wonder if she should have strapped on her knife.

TWENTY-NINE

GIDEON

GIDEON SLOWED HIS STRIDE to match Rune's as she led him through the labyrinthine hedges. She carried a lantern in one hand as they walked through her gardens, while her other hand clasped her shawl closed at her throat.

Her hair was loose, and the breeze kept tugging strands across her face, giving him the infuriating urge to drag it back with his fingers.

No paint adorned her lips tonight. No rouge reddened her cheeks. Even her feet were bare. She looked wild and raw and exposed out here. Not the girl he was used to seeing all done up at parties.

It threw him off guard. He'd come here to win back her trust because she was his best lead. But he found himself . . . faltering. Unsure of himself. The silence between them rose like a crescendo.

He glanced down at the angry gash on her forearm. How did a girl who spent her days planning parties and spreading gossip come by such a deep wound?

"Did you hurt yourself?"

Rune startled. "Oh! Yes, I . . . took a tumble while riding yesterday. Sliced my arm on a rock. I can be *so* clumsy." She smiled up at him, tucking the arm under her shawl and changing the subject. "Have you given more thought to my invitation?"

"To the Luminaries Dinner? I thought my answer was obvious."

She glanced at him, her lips parting.

Apparently, it was not.

He almost laughed. "Rune. Of course I'll accompany you. You expected me to turn you down?"

Her eyes held his. "I don't know what to expect with you."

The words hung in the air between them.

Was that Rune Winters talking? Or the Crimson Moth?

Gideon had no proof that she and the Moth were the same. Rune had a solid alibi last night, and yet she was freshly injured—much like the Moth might be after Laila shot at her. He couldn't arrest her, but neither was he convinced of her innocence.

It was why he was here. If Rune *was* the Moth, no way would she trust him after the stunt he'd pulled at the Seldom mine. He needed to patch the hole he'd made, because the only way to unmask her was to get closer to her. And the only way to do *that* was to convince her to trust him again. If that was even possible.

What would I do if this were a real courtship?

Gideon recoiled at the thought. He didn't know how to fall for someone as superficial as Rune Winters.

Maybe that was the wrong way to think about it.

How would he fall for a girl *pretending* to be superficial—in order to outwit him?

That was easier.

Gideon cleared his throat. "Your gardens are beautiful."

He winced, imagining Harrow rolling her eyes. *Is that the best you can do, lover boy?*

"Are they?" Rune murmured, taking in her surroundings. "I try to keep them well tended, but I lack my grandmother's . . . devotion. She loved these flowers like they were her children."

At the mention of Kestrel, Rune's face softened. She continued, unprompted, as her gaze roamed the hedges.

"Sometimes, if I squint, I can almost see her still trimming her roses. Or sipping tea in the greenhouse, with her box of seed packets beside her, planning out next season's garden . . ."

She quickly glanced at Gideon, her face blanching. As if she'd said more than she meant to. "I—"

"We never had a garden," he said, to put her at ease. "But my mother grew herbs in a box on the windowsill."

He immediately wished he'd thought of something else to say. His family's lack of land was an obvious reminder of the gap between them: their stations, their upbringings, their lives. It was a gap that had narrowed since the revolution, but it would never close.

Proving him exactly right, she said: "You could have a garden now, if you wanted. You could live somewhere far grander than even Wintersea House, with gardens more well kept, as a reward for everything you did for the Republic. I'm sure the Good Commander would grant it all to you, if you asked."

"I'm happy in Old Town."

"Are you?"

Gideon flinched at her question, remembering the day he took her measurements in his parents' shop. He wondered what she'd been thinking as she walked the sooty streets of his neighborhood. Breathing in the smoggy air. Listening to the rattle and hiss of the factories nearby.

"Old Town didn't impress you, I take it."

She stiffened beside him. "I only meant—"

"Was that your first time there?"

She didn't need to answer; he could easily guess.

In all the years Rune and Alex had been friends, she'd never set foot in their tenement. Alex had always gone to Wintersea House. Either his brother had been too ashamed to invite her into their home, or he'd invited her, and Rune had declined to come.

"When my parents died, the shop and apartment passed to me," he explained.

"But why choose to live there? Why not sell it and ask the Commander for an estate of your own? Thornwood Hall, for example, could have been yours."

Thornwood Hall.

Gideon shivered.

A dark shadow hung over that house. He could still feel Cressida there. Still smell the stench of her magic in the air. The few times he'd gone back, he'd been plagued by living night-mares.

"I would rather sleep beneath a bridge than sleep in Thorn-wood Hall," he said, more to himself than to her. "If you found Old Town beneath you, I certainly won't admit to the neighbor-hood we lived in before that."

"I never said Old Town was beneath me."

Her voice came from several paces behind him, making him realize she'd stopped walking. Turning to face her, he found her edges lit up by the red-gold light of the setting sun and her white sundress whipping around her knees in the wind. They were at the edge of the gardens here. The hedges were lower and less manicured. Wild, like her.

"Your neighborhood is . . . quaint."

"*Quaint* is a word polite people use when they don't want to be insulting."

Her cheeks reddened and her hair blew across her face. "Are you so determined to misunderstand me?"

Gideon paused, studying her. If he and Rune Winters were truly courting—which would never happen—this is exactly the argument he would have with her.

"Is it *quaint* that the residents of Old Town scrape their pennies together to keep the lights on? *Quaint* that parents spend half the year starving, so their children don't have to? When Penitent children beg in Old Town streets? Or the old and infirm freeze to death in their beds because they can't afford to heat their apartments?"

These things were regular occurrences in Old Town.

Rune stared in horror at Gideon. Of course she didn't know about these things. She lived in a different world. One that was only an hour's ride on horseback but might as well be as far as the moon.

Gideon turned and kept walking, annoyed with himself for bringing it up. Annoyed at her for being . . . well, her.

"I'm not sure why you're angry at me," she said to his back. "If Penitent children are begging in the street, it's the Republic you should blame. The Good Commander made their families outcasts for aiding witches."

Gideon stopped.

"Or don't you remember that the Commander promised us a better world?" she continued before he could respond. "One where no one lives in squalor."

Despite his anger, she was right. Gideon remembered the rallies. The speeches. The pamphlets hidden in pockets and shoes or between the pages of books passed under the noses of the aristocracy. Nicolas Creed *had* promised to usher in a better world. But that world had yet to fully arrive.

"If people live in poverty," she said, "you should direct your anger at *him*."

He whirled on her.

"You think we weren't impoverished before? You have no idea what the real world is like, Rune. You live a pampered, privileged existence and always have. I'm not saying that's your fault. I'm simply stating facts. If you don't want to look at ugly things, you don't have to. You can pretend they don't exist."

A bright flush of red swept up her neck.

"People like you and your grandmother flourished under the Reign of Witches, when things were worse than they are now. So don't pretend you care. You didn't then, and you don't now. The Sister Queens or the Good Commander . . . it's all the same to you."

She winced, as if he'd struck her.

Seeing it, the fight went out of him.

Fuck. That was too far.

"Rune . . ." He ran his hands roughly through his hair. "I'm sorry."

Did he have to be so brutally honest? She seemed so small, suddenly. He wanted to close the space between them but was afraid she might recoil.

"I agree with you: the revolution was supposed to make things better, for all of us, but there's a long way to go."

She stayed silent, watching him as the wind whipped through her hair.

I've ruined it, he thought. *She's going to turn around, go back, and never speak to me again.*

But instead of trying to salvage this—his last fraying thread to his only lead on the Crimson Moth—he gave her that out. He felt sick with himself for insulting her, and the right thing to do was suggest they return to the house.

Before he could, she stepped toward him, stopping only inches away.

"If I thought you were beneath me . . ." Her eyes were hard as pewter, searching his. ". . . why would I be out on a walk with you?"

He searched hers back.

Why indeed?

Lifting his hands, he gathered the wild tangle of hair blowing across her face. It surprised him when she didn't flinch away, when she let him scrape it back instead. She seemed to soften as he held it, allowing him to see her clearly.

He shouldn't have liked it so much—the feel of her hair against his palms, the way she relaxed beneath his fingers.

"Beautiful heiresses might court common soldiers," he said. "But they don't marry them."

Her mouth quirked a little. "Did you just call me beautiful, Gideon?"

"I'm stating the obvious. Don't change the subject."

She looked away.

"You know it's true, Rune. People of your station don't marry down."

In Gideon's experience, those born into wealth and privilege wanted more of it, not less. Like the first hit of a drug, the moment people tasted power, they needed more to quench the craving.

"I don't know how to dance to your songs," he said. "I don't have the esteem of your friends. I don't use seventeen pieces of silverware at dinner." He let go of her hair, and it billowed out, catching in the wind once more. "I have no means of expanding your inheritance."

He knew he was walking a fine line, reminding her of the reasons they made no sense. That this charade they were playing was a weak one. But if the goal was to be vulnerable, to entice her to be vulnerable, too, he needed to speak the truth.

"People like *you* are impossible," she said. "I don't care about those things."

He almost rolled his eyes. "Of course you do."

"Then why are we here? If I'm so shallow—all trappings and no substance—what are you doing with me? Why would someone like *you* want someone like *me*?"

Gideon opened his mouth to respond, only he didn't know the answer.

He studied her, hair ablaze in the setting sun. Gray eyes like molten steel.

In his silence, Rune came to her own conclusions.

"Maybe you're right." She stepped around him, lantern in hand, and unlatched the white gate at the garden's edge, stepping into the meadow beyond. "One of us thinks ourself too good for the other. But it's not me."

The gate swung closed behind her.

Gideon stared after her.

What?

From this side of the gate, he watched her follow the footpath through the tall grass, heading toward the woods in the distance. For some strange reason, his thoughts trickled to Cressida.

He'd learned very quickly not to challenge Cress. Arguments with her came with consequences. When he disagreed or disobeyed, she would punish him—and sometimes others. Until he stopped resisting her altogether.

Rune, on the other hand, seemed rattled by his insults, but unfazed by his defiance.

It was uncharted territory. And without a map to guide him, Gideon stood motionless, watching her get farther away. Not even Harrow's voice in his head was any help.

If you genuinely liked this girl, he told himself, *you would go after her.*

Hopping over the gate, Gideon jogged down the path after her, his pulse beating wildly. As a general rule, Gideon avoided situations that rendered him vulnerable. Yet here he was, running straight into one.

"If we're going to do this," he said when he caught up with her, "there are some things you need to know."

She glanced at him.

"So you can decide if this is what you want. If *I* am what you want."

The forest ahead obscured their view of the sea, but he could taste the brine on the breeze. They were getting close.

She studied him in the light shining from her lantern. "All right. Tell me."

This is a game, he reminded himself, his chest tight. *It means nothing.*

But if that were true, why did he feel like he was walking straight off a cliff, hoping he wouldn't fall?

THIRTY

GIDEON

"*T*HE LAST GIRL I fell in love with was a witch," he said.

Rune stiffened beside him.

"I met her the day my parents became royal dressmakers."

His mother's designs had been catching the eye of the aristocracy for nearly a year. Several months before, the money from their growing business had allowed them to move out of the Outer Wards—the poorest district in the capital—and into a tenement building in Old Town.

In a day, the queens had elevated them much further, moving their family into the palace. Suddenly, they could afford Alex's tuition. Suddenly, Gideon no longer needed to skip meals so his little sister, Tessa, could eat her fill.

"My parents could hardly keep up with the queens' demands, so they brought me in to help. Alex had left to study at the Conservatory, and Tessa was too young to do anything except get in the way. Cressida asked that I be assigned to her exclusively, so I went to live at Thornwood Hall."

His stomach churned as he tried to decide how much to unearth. He didn't want Rune to know every sordid detail of his past. But there were some things she deserved to know, before she entangled herself with him further.

"Cress didn't only want me for her tailor." He darted a glance at Rune, who walked beside him, staring straight ahead. "And I was happy to fulfill her . . . other needs."

"You two were intimate, you mean."

"Yes."

He wanted to block out the memories flooding in. Late nights in Cressida's gardens that somehow always ended in her bed, his fingers tracing the silvery casting scars she proudly displayed on her skin like the most exquisite art.

Each casting scar had been etched by Cressida or her sisters, the collection like a wild garden growing up her body. Scar lines formed roses and lilies, buttercups and irises, all tangled with leaves and thorns and stems. The silver flowers climbed her calves and thighs, covering the left side of her torso and breast, and flowed down her arms.

Gideon's favorites were the petal-shaped scars scattered across her collarbone.

She'd completely bewitched him.

He spared Rune all of this.

"It didn't take long before things went wrong."

"What do you mean?" Rune's voice pulled him out of the memory. They were in the woods now, and like in the meadow behind them, someone had cleared a path through the trees. The leaves glowed gold in the haze of the setting sun.

"My mother became . . . unwell." He remembered her bruised and bleeding fingers, her red-rimmed eyes, the way her bones poked out of her skin. "She started seeing things that weren't there and accused my father and me—even Tessa—of things we hadn't done. Stealing her notebooks. Ruining her fabrics. Sabotaging her in every way."

His muscles bunched at the memories. His mother accused them of worse things, too: her husband, of being unfaithful to her; Tessa, of poisoning her; Gideon, of abusing Tessa. Nightmarish things. Things that still kept him awake at night. And always, he could smell it on her: the coppery scent of a witch's spells.

"The Sister Queens were slowly torturing her."

"That makes no sense," said Rune. "If they wanted your mother as their dressmaker, why torment her?"

He threw Rune a look. "You obviously didn't know the Rosebloods. Witches are cruel by nature, but the Roseblood sisters were evil. They tortured and killed those who crossed them, then used the blood of their victims for their spells."

Rune shook her head in disbelief. "That's impossible."

"I saw it with my own eyes."

"No, I mean . . ." She shook her head. "What you're describing are Arcana spells, which are forbidden. Queen Raine outlawed them centuries ago."

He glanced at her, surprised that she knew this. But her grandmother had been a witch. Of course she would know things about witchcraft.

"An Arcana is the highest level of spell a witch can cast," she explained. "They require blood taken against someone's will. The magic that results is powerful and deadly, but it corrodes the witches who use it. If the Roseblood sisters were casting Arcanas, they would have knowingly corrupted themselves."

It reminded Gideon of something Cressida had said, years ago, when he walked in on her and her sisters standing over a body in a pool of blood. The sight of it, combined with the strong stench of magic, had almost made him vomit.

The more power we wield, Gideon, the more they want to see us fall. What are we to do? Let those who hate us plot our demise? To play by the rules when everyone else disregards them—that is foolishness. Once you've seized power for yourself and those you love, you must do everything to keep it. Even sacrifice your soul. If you don't, you'll watch your loved ones harmed by those wanting what you have.

Rune fell silent beside him. For several minutes, the only sounds in the woods were their footsteps crunching the pine needle path and the wind rustling the forest's canopy.

This next part would be the hardest to get through. Gideon glanced at Rune, trying to justify skipping it, but if this were a real courtship, he would want her to know.

One of us thinks ourself too good for the other. But it's not me.

He was about to put her words to the test. If they didn't hold true, he certainly wouldn't blame her.

"When I told Cressida we were done, that I wanted nothing more to do with her, she warned that if I refused her advances my little sister would suffer my mother's fate. I was terrified of her by then, and I desperately wanted to spare Tessa. So I did whatever she asked." He ran a hand roughly through his hair. "She killed Tessa anyway."

"I thought your sister died of the sweating sickness," said Rune.

It's what Alex must have told her.

"Do you remember the party where I poured you tea? Cress convinced herself that I was cheating on her with a handmaid and wanted to punish me. When she realized that serving tea wasn't humiliating for me, she changed tactics, telling me I had to prove my devotion by making her three dozen silk roses by sunrise—the kind my father used to make for my mother—and if I failed, something terrible would happen to my little sister."

He looked down at Rune, who drew her lips in a tight line. "The silk flower I made you took me two hours to sew."

Rune's eyes went dark, doing the math.

By the time the sun rose, Gideon had somehow sewn a

dozen roses. To Cress, this was further proof that he wasn't sorry enough. That same day, she used a spell to strike his little sister with the sweating sickness. Cress locked Tessa in her room and refused to let anyone tend to her.

Gideon threw himself at the door—which Cressida had enchanted to hold against all force—beating it with his fists, while Tessa wept and begged from the other side, delirious with fever, calling for their mother. He screamed at Cressida, who only smirked. So he lunged and pinned her down. He had his hands around her throat, prepared to stop squeezing only when she went limp beneath him, but the guards dragged him off and chained him to the floor of a cell.

By the time they let him out, Tessa was dead.

"My mother drowned herself a day later. My father hung himself a few days after that. And *still*, she wasn't satisfied." His hands fisted. "I knew there was one last person she could hurt, if I didn't do as she asked."

"Your brother," murmured Rune.

Gideon nodded. Alex had been the last unspoken threat hanging between him and the witch queen.

He'd started drinking after that. Every day. Sometimes as soon as waking up. It was the only way he could bear crawling back to her bed every night.

Sometimes, it felt like Cressida preferred Gideon unwilling. Like it brought her more pleasure to force him.

He recalled the night she branded him. She'd pinned him to the wall with a spell so he'd be helpless to stop her from searing his flesh. He remembered his body spasming beneath the glowing iron, every muscle tightening at the lightning-hot pain.

It's a curse, Gideon, she said, pressing harder as he tried not to scream. *One I will activate if you betray me again.*

"That's why Alex killed her," murmured Rune.

Gideon heard the hush of waves in the distance. The smell of the sea was strong here, and when the trees thinned, he saw the gentle roll of the dunes. As they emerged from the woods, he could see the entire shoreline stretched out before them. There was a causeway to the east, separating this shallow bay from the open sea beyond, where the water shimmered turquoise beneath a pink sky.

"I've spoiled a perfect evening," he said, awed by the view.

He wanted to dive in and let the sea wash over the stain he could never scrub clean. But as he started toward the water, Rune grabbed his hand to stop him.

"You've spoiled nothing."

He looked down to find their fingers entwined. When he glanced back, her eyes held a storm so fierce it took his breath away.

"You are not the things that happened to you, Gideon."

He wished that were true. "None of us can escape our pasts."

Gideon's past had shaped him. Haunted him. *Ruined* him. Everything he did on the eve of the New Dawn—helping Nicolas Creed and the other rebels take the palace, shooting Analise and Elowyn in their beds, hunting down Cressida only to be stopped by Alex, who had found and dealt with her so Gideon didn't have to—he did it all because of what the witch queens did to him and his family.

It was why he hunted witches still. Because so many had it as bad or worse than him. Harrow was only one example.

Witches were wicked to the core. If given enough power, they would abuse it. To stop them from rising again, to ensure no one was ever at their mercy, every witch needed to be eradicated.

At that thought, Gideon pulled his hand free of Rune's, remembering why he was here.

He suspected Rune Winters was a witch hiding in plain sight. To catch her, he needed proof. And there was one telltale sign every witch carried on them.

He remembered tracing Cressida's silvery scars in the dark while she slept.

Remembered Harrow's advice from two nights ago.

The sun was slipping below the horizon. Soon it would be gone, and the only light remaining would come from the small lantern in Rune's hand. Before the darkness descended, Gideon unbuttoned the top three buttons of his shirt.

Rune's forehead creased. "What are you doing?"

"Going for a swim."

"Now?"

"The water's calm. The night is warm. Perfect conditions for swimming." When the shirt was loose enough, he tugged it off and dropped it into the sand between them.

Whatever objection Rune was about to make died on her lips. At her startled expression, Gideon nearly laughed.

He cocked a brow at her. "You coming?"

THIRTY-ONE

RUNE

*T*HE SEA WAS FREEZING this time of year. Rune had opened her mouth to tell him so when Gideon shucked off his shirt.

The words died on her lips.

She pulled in a sharp breath, her blood running a little hotter at the sight of his muscled shoulders and arms. She coiled her fingers into her palms, pressing the nails into the skin, trying to stop herself from tracing him with her eyes: the rigid lines of his collarbones, abdomen, hips. His skin turning honey-gold in the setting sun.

Rune tried to look away, but something on the right side of his chest dragged her eyes back: the symbol of a thorny rose encircled by a crescent moon. Rune knew it on sight. The Sister Queens had their casting signatures turned into crests, and these crests were sewn into their garments. The queens wore them embroidered on the cuffs of their shirtsleeves, impressed into their jewelry, or emblazoned across their riding cloaks.

The rose and crescent belonged to Cressida.

A tattoo?

The sound of Gideon's pants dropping into the sand made the thought freeze in her head. She stared hard at that crest, knowing he stood almost naked before her, afraid to look anywhere else. The story he'd told still hummed through every fiber of her being. Rage and grief and shame—his voice had been full of it. And though Rune desperately wanted to believe there was another side to this story, that Gideon was twisting the truth, she couldn't ignore that crest.

It's not a tattoo, she realized, studying the red lines. *It's a brand.*

The youngest witch queen had branded Gideon the way a farmer burns his name into an animal, so that when he lets the beast out to pasture, everyone knows it's his and no one takes it home with them.

Cressida had permanently marked Gideon as her property.

The horror of it made Rune go cold.

"Gideon . . ."

Not seeing the realization dawning on her, he looped one finger into the seam of his underwear. "Last chance, Rune."

He dropped them next.

"Oh. My. Stars." Rune covered her eyes with her hands. "Gideon Sharpe!"

"Is that a blush coming up on your cheeks?"

The heat of his teasing chased out the cold.

"Why so bashful? Don't tell me you've never taken advantage of all those suitors lining up at your door."

Her skin burned hotter even as a smile crept across her lips. "You are *the worst.*"

Surprising them both, she laughed.

Rune wanted to drop her hands and look at him. Desperately. But she didn't want to take advantage, the way another girl had. So she stayed where she was, keeping her eyes covered.

His footsteps hissed in the sand. Instead of heading for the sea, though, they moved toward her. Rune took a step back and nearly tripped over a log. Gideon's hand grabbed her elbow, steadying her.

His breath hushed against her cheek. "Come with me." He stood inches away. All six gorgeous feet of him. She pressed her hands harder against her face. "Don't you want to feel the sea on your skin?"

"Absolutely not," she said from behind her hands. "That water is freezing."

"Suit yourself," he said, letting her go.

The water splashed as he walked into the sea. At the sound, Rune gave in to temptation, lowered her hands, and watched him wade naked into the waves.

She tried to remember the part she was playing. But the protective mask she wore was slipping fast. Rune couldn't pretend to be a shallow, gossipy girl after he'd bared his soul to her. She couldn't tell herself there were two sides to this story, or that Cressida and her sisters were the actual victims.

None of what had happened to him excused what he was doing now, of course: hunting witches down, one by one; propping up a violent regime. But it helped her understand him.

"Come on, Rune. The water's warm . . ."

Gideon had increased the stakes of their game tonight by telling her something deeply, painfully true. For Rune to match him, she needed to offer something equally so.

But she'd been living a lie for so long, she didn't know if there was anything true still in her.

If I didn't have to hide myself, she thought, *who would I be?*

Who was the real Rune Winters?

Not the socialite. Not the Crimson Moth. But the person deep down inside her.

Rune had been playing a part for so long, she couldn't remember.

Once, she'd been a girl who liked to wear ribbons and silks, lace and pearls. Someone who enjoyed dancing with cute boys and gossiping with fashionable friends. A girl who took tea with Nan on the terrace and went to the opera.

But what made that girl *Rune*?

She thought of the portrait hanging in her bedroom. Of a wild child in a white dress trying desperately to hold in her laugh.

If that girl were all grown up, what would she be like?

What would she do?

She would accept a challenge to swim naked in a frigid sea, thought Rune. That, she knew.

Slowly, she let her shawl drop. Reaching behind her, she tugged at the laces of her dress until they loosened, then pulled the cotton fabric over her skin and dropped it in the sand.

The warm breeze kissed her bare stomach and legs.

She took off her bralette next, then her underwear. Knowing all the while that he watched from the waves.

Standing naked beneath the dying sunlight, her hair whispered across her bare shoulders. Feeling mushy compared to Gideon's lean, muscled form, she fought the urge to cross her arms over herself as she walked down the sand toward the surf.

She *wanted* him to look. To search her body for scars so he could find none. Rune had plenty of ordinary scars. Everyday cuts and scrapes collected over the years. But none were the silvery kind he'd be looking for.

As she stepped into the sea, the water sent a shocking jolt of cold through her.

"You are such a liar." She hugged herself to fend off the chill. "I think a glacier melted in here."

Gideon laughed, splashing water in her direction. She flinched as the icy droplets scattered across her body. But she continued to wade in, taking sharp breaths as the cold crept to her knees, her thighs, her waist.

What is he thinking? she wondered, hugging her chest tighter. *Is he comparing me to other girls he's seen undressed?*

She wished she could wipe the questions from her mind. Because who cared what he was thinking? Not her.

When she finally reached him, the sea was as high as her throat and her feet arched to keep her toes on the bottom of the sandy bed.

"My grandmother used to bring me here as a child," she said, glancing at the silhouetted island in the distance, and the causeway connecting it to the shore. "She would stand on the sand and shout at me not to swim too far. She was always afraid the current would sweep me away."

Now would be the perfect moment to bare her soul. To tell him what being raised by a witch was like. After the secrets he'd entrusted her with, though, Rune didn't have the stomach to lie, or fake a hatred she didn't feel. But neither could she tell him the truth.

Like a true predator, Gideon sensed her weakness.

"Turning her in must have been very hard."

Not at all, she would have announced if they were in an opera box or a ballroom or surrounded by her friends.

But they weren't. They were alone, and playing a new game. One that was far more dangerous for Rune than for him.

Turning Nan in wasn't hard, she thought. *It was unbearable.*

Rune drew in a deep breath and risked one small, true thing.

"Nan was my best friend." Rune glanced away from him. "She was . . . the person I most aspired to be like."

The day the Republic killed her, a part of Rune died, too.

She remembered donning her finest dress that morning. Remembered brushing her hair until it shone like midsummer wheat. Nan had taught her to always look her best, no matter the occasion, and Rune had a feeling she didn't make exceptions for public executions. Not even her own.

After pushing to the front of the angry crowd, Rune had nearly buckled at the sight of Kestrel atop the purging platform. Her hair—normally coiffed and held in place by a jeweled pin—fell in untidy strands down her face. They'd bruised her regal cheek and snuffed the bright gleam from her eyes. Someone had even ripped the sleeves off her shirt so everyone could see her casting scars.

Kestrel's gaze was hawkish as she looked out over the sea of faces, as if she didn't notice the way they spit at her, didn't hear the vicious names they called her.

The moment her eyes found her granddaughter, the attention of the crowd followed.

Did you know? Rune could still hear them murmuring. *She informed on the old hag. Brave little thing.*

She'd schooled her features into exactly the girl they wanted to see: a young heiress so loyal to the Republic, she handed her beloved grandmother over to be executed. It was the role she needed to play now. Rune knew this was just the beginning.

But beneath the mask, her grief had cracked her heart in half.

As their gazes locked, Nan's parched lips moved, whispering three small words. Words Rune didn't deserve.

I love you.

The shriek of metal scraping metal had filled the air as the chains raised her grandmother skyward, by the ankles. There she dangled, upside down, with her hands enclosed in witch restraints, hair swinging.

One of the Blood Guard stepped forward with a knife and sliced her grandmother's throat. The blood splattered and gushed. Nan choked, gasping for a breath she couldn't take, her body writhing like a worm on a hook. All trace of poise and elegance vanished as she struggled against her fate. Rune dug her teeth into her lower lip, forcing herself not to scream. Not to weep. Telling herself to be stoic and still as the blood dripped like ribbons, thick and red, and Nan finally fell still.

Afterward, Rune watched them throw her corpse into a mass grave on the edge of the city. She couldn't take Nan home and bury her beneath the apple tree in the garden, where the blossoms would fall on her in the spring. She couldn't afford to show that kind of tenderness, in case someone suspected the truth rooted in her heart.

She told only the first part to Gideon. The part about watching Nan die.

He studied her as the sun slipped past the horizon, turning the sky dark purple and washing him in tones of blue and gold. As the waves lapped around them, a kittiwake called in the distance.

You told him too much, she thought, looking sharply away, afraid he'd see the tears in her eyes. *Now he has even more reason to suspect you.*

Her throat swelled and her eyes burned. She'd stripped off her mask, and without it, she was fumbling.

Suddenly, Gideon was moving through the water toward her. Before she could kick back through the waves and swim away, he reached her. Cradling her jaw in one hand, he tucked a strand of wet hair behind her ear with the other.

"It's not a crime to have loved a witch, Rune." He bent toward her until their foreheads touched and his breath tangled with hers. "If it were, you wouldn't be the only guilty one."

His gentleness snuck past her defenses, unlocking the deadbolts inside her.

Letting the enemy in.

She looked up as the tears fell down her cheeks. The sea hid their bodies, but it was clear on Gideon's face that he hadn't for a second forgotten what was under the waves. He seemed reluctant to close the distance between them, though, unsure if she would welcome it.

Rune tried to tell herself she *wouldn't* welcome it. Gideon had probably been in the crowd that day, cheering on Kestrel's death. She absolutely shouldn't want him any closer.

He was a witch hunter. He suspected her. He was closing in on her even now.

And yet.

She remembered him on top of her, down in the mine. How solid and heavy he was. She remembered him later, dragging her out of the water. The strength in his arms. The heat of him pouring into her.

What would it feel like to have his body flush against hers?

It was perverse, the way she wanted to find out.

Seeing the thoughts in her eyes, Gideon trembled with restraint. His throat swallowed and his pulse beat hungrily through the hand cupping her jaw.

So, this horrible wanting afflicted him, too.

This is a game, she told herself, nuzzling her face into his palm. *It's only pretend.*

It's how she justified dragging her fingers through his hair and pulling his mouth down to hers.

THIRTY-TWO

GIDEON

*I*F GIDEON WERE BEING honest, part of him secretly hoped it was Rune who'd escaped him down in that mine. Which should have disturbed him. It would make her his enemy, not to mention a murderous, evil witch. But a girl who could outwit him thrilled Gideon too much to deny.

Her kiss felt the same. Like the first taste of something forbidden. Heady and delicious. Awakening all his senses at once.

When her teeth grazed his bottom lip, a wicked heat surged through him and he reached for her waist. So soft. He wanted to sink into her softness. To bury himself in her.

As if she felt the same, Rune wrapped her arms around his neck and arched against him.

It wasn't supposed to feel like this. Nothing was supposed to feel this good. This *right*. As if there was nothing to be ashamed of. As if—just maybe—he could be worthy of a girl like her.

A voice that sounded like Alex hissed from deep inside him: *People like Rune don't end up with people like you.*

It was like a bucket of ice water dumped on his head. Sucking in a sharp breath, Gideon wrenched himself away from her, stumbling back.

What the fuck am I doing?

Alex was right, of course.

More importantly: Alex was in love with Rune.

In Gideon's hasty retreat, Rune lost her balance, went under the waves, and came up spluttering.

His body buzzed at the lack of her. As if Rune in his arms was the only true thing in the world, and until she was there again, everything was wrong.

He shook his head, trying to shake off that feeling.

"Gideon . . . I'm so sorry. I thought—" Her wet hair stuck to her cheeks, her throat, her shoulders. She swallowed hard, wide-eyed and trembling. "I thought you wanted to."

What?

She shook her head fiercely. "I'm *such* an idiot."

Kicking away from him, she swam for shore, her strokes punching through the waves, propelling her away from him. But not before he recognized the humiliation in her voice.

I thought you wanted to.

She'd completely misunderstood.

"Rune!"

Either she didn't hear him, or she was ignoring him. Because she only swam faster.

Gideon started after her. He needed her to know that he'd very much wanted to.

Still wanted to.

He watched her reach the shore and stumble out of the water as the tide pulled at her legs. Rune's naked form gleamed in the lantern's light, which glowed on the sand. Even in his rush to stop her, he couldn't help but admire her.

Maybe she isn't a witch. He couldn't see a single casting scar marring her smooth skin. And damn, did he look.

It made him hesitate. He forced himself to remember Alex. The brother he'd betrayed by kissing Rune tonight. How could he go after the girl Alex loved and kiss her again?

But if she was a witch and Gideon *didn't* go after her—if he didn't make it clear that he definitely wanted to kiss her—Rune would end this charade of a courtship, and he would lose his best chance to catch the Crimson Moth.

Gideon needed to catch the Moth, for all their sakes.

If Rune was that Moth, and Alex was in love with her, he had to do it for Alex most of all. He needed to protect his little brother from yet another dangerous witch.

Rune pulled on her white dress as Gideon reached the beach. Leaving her undergarments, she grabbed the lantern and fled into the woods.

Gideon dragged himself from the sea, shook the water from his hair, and quickly pulled on his trousers. Seizing his shirt, he sprinted after Rune, following the glow of the lantern before he lost her completely.

THIRTY-THREE

RUNE

*R*UNE SHIVERED IN THE breeze as she half walked, half ran back up the path through the woods, trying to put distance between herself and that beach as quickly as possible. The sun was long gone, and the trees were dark silhouettes around her. Her dress clung to her damp legs and her sopping wet hair dripped down her back.

But despite the chill, she was burning up.

"Stupid, stupid, stupid!"

Witches are cruel by nature. If Gideon believed that, and he suspected Rune of being a witch, he would think her no different from Cressida.

Of course he'd pulled away when she kissed him. The girl she pretended to be—the shallow, gossipy socialite—annoyed Gideon. And the girl she really was . . . he wanted that girl dead.

Rune repulsed him.

How did I misread him?

She wished she knew a spell to disappear for a straight week.

"Rune!"

Her heart skipped. Gideon's voice was too close. She glanced over her shoulder, but the darkness cloaked everything beyond the glow of her lantern.

Turning toward the house, she quickened her pace.

Not quick enough.

"Stop running from me."

This time, his voice was right behind her. Rune was about to bolt when he grabbed her wrist, forcing her to stop.

"You did nothing wrong."

She shook her head, a fiery shame flaring through her. "I shouldn't have presumed . . ."

He stepped in front of her, cutting her off from the path leading to Wintersea House. She couldn't help but notice that, in his haste to chase her down, he hadn't put on his shirt.

"You presumed correctly."

Then why pull away?

He's lying to you. You caught him off guard with that kiss, and it cracked his facade. He doesn't want to kiss you. He never did. He just knows how to play this game better than you.

Rune was about to dart around him, when a sudden sound echoed through the woods.

Voices.

Gideon turned sharply toward it. Rune, still breathless, spotted the owners of the voices first. The flames of half a dozen torches bobbed like fireflies in the distance, coming down the path.

"Someone's coming," said Gideon.

"Obviously," said Rune, turning out her lamp. She grabbed Gideon's hand and pulled him off the path.

At the sight of the marks carved into their foreheads, he frowned. "Penitents? They're trespassing on your property."

"They're not trespassing." She kept her voice down, stepping lightly through the underbrush, taking him farther away from the path, where the thickening trees shielded them from view. "I allow them to use the footpaths."

Gideon was invisible beside her, his hand still in hers, as the torches flickered past them.

"You allow them?"

She was glad he couldn't see the truth on her face. *I do more than that.* Sometimes, if she knew no one would catch her, Rune left fresh bread and cheese out for them to take.

"They use the paths to get to the beach, where they fish after sundown." Technically, allowing Penitents to use the paths on her property wasn't giving them direct aid, and therefore wasn't illegal. "Are you going to report me?"

"No. It's just . . . surprising."

"There are children among them. As you pointed out earlier, I didn't choose to be born into my position, just as those children didn't choose to be born into theirs."

"I'm not accusing you, Rune. I think it's . . . admirable." His warm hand squeezed hers.

Oh.

A strange silence descended.

Rune had loathed this boy since the day Alex first introduced them, and here she was, holding his hand in the dark. *By choice.*

The thought made her tug her fingers free.

Because he'd loathed her, too. Still did. Wasn't that why he'd pushed away from her kiss?

She wanted to understand it. What, exactly, had he seen in her then that made him reject her so adamantly?

"Do you remember the day we first met?"

Rune had been thirteen. She and Alex had been friends for almost two years when, one hot summer day, he invited her to go cliff jumping in Nameless Cove. The cove, he'd told her, had the best cliffs for plunging into the sea. Rune had never done anything so daring, and the thought of it thrilled her. But it was on the wrong side of town. Nan had adamantly forbade Rune from visiting Alex's home, which was in an economically disadvantaged part of the city.

But she'd said nothing about Nameless Cove. So Rune didn't ask permission, or even tell Nan she was going.

When they arrived, she found a group of kids climbing the rocks and throwing themselves into the sea. One boy consistently climbed higher than the others and threw himself furthest.

The boy was Gideon, the brother Alex had told her so much about.

"How could I possibly forget," Gideon murmured, pulling her out of the memory. The leafy canopy overhead was thinning, and with the moon shining through, Rune could see the frown marring his brow. "Rich girl takes a tour of the Outer Wards to see how the dirty peasants live, and decides it's not for her."

"What?" Her cheeks burned beneath the accusation. She didn't notice when the forest disappeared behind them.

"Isn't that why you asked Alex to bring you?"

"Alex invited me," she said, defensive.

"Of course." His jaw clenched. "To show you off like a piece of treasure."

Rune looked sharply toward his silhouette. "What are you talking about?"

"Nothing. Never mind."

She shook her head as the long meadow grass swished around them, tilting in the wind and brushing her bare legs. "You were so rude that day. I thought you were the rudest boy I'd ever met."

"Me?" He coughed. "*I* was rude? You've got it backward."

"You insulted my clothes."

"I did not."

"You did! You called my dress *foppish*."

"Oh, that. Yes, I remember." He rubbed a hand stiffly over his jaw. "The lace alone would have put three meals on the table of every kid swimming that day."

Rune opened her mouth only to realize she didn't know what to say.

"I didn't know."

"You didn't know that wearing a designer dress to the Outer Wards was announcing just how out of reach you were to the rest of us?"

Out of reach?

"I was thirteen," she said. "I'd never been past the city center. Alex was the only person I knew from the Outer Wards."

They reached the wooden gate leading into the Wintersea gardens.

"I was so excited to meet you," she murmured. He glanced sharply at her. "But you wouldn't even shake my hand."

As she opened the latch and stepped through, Gideon fell behind.

"I had never done it before."

She turned back. "What do you mean?"

"Only aristos shake hands when they greet each other. I . . . didn't know what you were doing. It felt like you were condescending to me. Or trying to keep your distance."

Rune's mouth opened and shut like a fish.

"You didn't know," he said, as if plucking the words from her lips. "I see that now."

"You could have given me the benefit of the doubt."

He sighed roughly. "Sure."

"Sure?"

"What is it you want from me? An apology?" He threw out

his arms beneath the glittering night sky. "I'm sorry I was rude to you, Rune Winters. Even at fifteen, I was an intolerable ass." Lowering his arms, he studied her. "Will that suffice?"

"That's not . . . I didn't—"

"Then why is this important?"

"I don't know!" She balled her hands into fists. "I guess it hurt. I wanted you to *like* me."

Rune suddenly felt more naked now than she had on the beach.

Gideon fell quiet, considering her. Wishing she could put the words back in her mouth, knowing she was giving him too much ground, Rune quickly turned and made her way into the gardens. She heard the gate swing open and shut behind her. It took him no time at all to catch up, matching her pace.

He stayed quiet for a long time as they walked between the hedges.

"I remember the sound of your laugh," he said as the back door of the house came into view. "It pulled me like a magnet toward the beach, where I found the most beautiful girl in the world standing on the shore."

Rune's footsteps slowed as they approached the door.

His stopped altogether.

"When I saw Alex at your side, I knew exactly who you were: *Rune Winters*. The girl Alex never shut up about. A girl who was entirely off-limits, because my little brother found her first."

Rune frowned, irked by these words.

"That's not the way friendship works," she said, turning back to him. "Alex didn't *find* me. He doesn't own me."

Gideon's gaze dropped to her mouth. "I'm not talking about friendship, Rune."

A shiver rushed across her skin.

Lifting his thumb to her bottom lip, he dragged it slowly across. His touch was like a switch, turning on an electric current that flickered through her.

"What about you?" he asked.

His eyes were bottomless pools. If she stared long enough, she might fall into them and never climb out.

"What about me?"

"You thought me the rudest boy you'd ever met." His voice was low. Rough. "Is that all you thought?"

Rune swallowed. No. No, it was not all.

She remembered watching Gideon jump from the cliffs that day. The way his body arced through the air like a shimmering fish. No crowing bravado, only the quiet self-assurance that came with competence.

"You were . . . impressive."

"Impressive," he murmured, the corner of his mouth approaching a smile. "Anything else?"

Rune bit down on her lip, not wanting to admit the rest. She remembered that same boy encouraging the younger kids who weren't brave enough to jump alone, climbing down from his heights to jump with them.

"Everyone admired you," she confessed. "It was impossible not to. But you weren't cocky about it, even though you could have been."

He drew back, as if her answer surprised him.

Is this still the game? she wondered. *Or is this real?*

That she couldn't tell unsettled her.

In the silence, Rune became intensely aware of him: the shadow of stubble on his jaw, the smell of the sea on his skin. He'd pulled his shirt on as they walked, and she stared at the buttons now.

"Do you still think I'm foppish?" she whispered.

Of all the questions she could have asked him . . . why had *that* one come out of her mouth?

His mouth quirked. "Yes." He reached for her ribs, cupping them with strong hands. "Do you still think I'm a brute?"

"Def—"

His mouth brushed the corner of her jaw, sending a rush of sensation across her skin and making her breath hitch. It wasn't a kiss, exactly. More of a caress. He moved lower, pressing his lips to a more sensitive place on her neck.

Rune's pulse skipped. She closed her eyes.

Gideon moved lower still, to the base of her throat. Kissing now. Tasting her. When his teeth grazed her collarbone, Rune inhaled sharply, fisting her hands. The soft insistence of his mouth was a dangerous undercurrent, threatening to drag her downward.

His kisses continued, increasing in urgency, trailing over her skin. Was this real, or were they still pretending? She pushed her hands into his hair, cradling his head, silently telling him not to stop.

Should she invite him in?

Invite him *up*?

If she could get away for a few minutes, she could cast *Truth Teller*, and this time she would draw the spellmark on something useful.

Rune tried to keep her wits intact as his hands slid into her hair. As he pressed her against the door. She felt magnetized. Unable to resist the pull of him.

Focus, she told herself.

There was one rule she didn't break in the games she played with her suitors. She might invite them back to her bedroom to coax out information, but she never brought them into her bed. It was a line she didn't cross.

Would that line hold with Gideon?

As he kissed along her jaw, the words tumbled out of her. "Do you want to come inside?"

"I . . ."

Rune glanced up, her body humming. His eyes were ink-dark and ravenous. This was happening. She was going to open the door and they were . . .

Gideon stepped back.

Cold air rushed into the space between them.

"Perhaps another night," he said.

Wait . . . what?

Rune straightened, trying to recover from her shock.

"It's getting late. I should go home."

"Right. Of course." The sting of rejection made Rune glance away. "I'll have one of the servants fetch your horse."

He shook his head. "There's no need. I know where your stable is. I can fetch my own horse."

She was about to insist—she would be a poor hostess otherwise—when he interrupted, catching her hand.

"Rune." His thumb brushed across her knuckles. "I *would* like to come in, but I promised to go slow with you." Lifting her hand, he kissed the sensitive part of her wrist, making her shiver. "And if I step through that door tonight, I'm afraid I won't keep my word."

A wild feeling swept through Rune. She didn't want him to keep his word. She wanted him to take her upstairs. This instant.

"Good night, Miss Winters."

Turning away, he headed for the stables. Rune watched him

disappear around the side of the house. Shakily, with her back to the wall, she sank to the terrace stones.

She could still taste him on her lips. Still feel the ghost of his hands on her ribs.

He doesn't actually want you.

Her skin tingled everywhere he'd touched her.

You're falling for his tricks.

Gideon was winning at this game. Because what they'd done tonight, Rune wanted to do again—for reasons that had nothing to do with rescuing witches.

"I loathe him," she told the shadows in the garden, trying to remember all the reasons this was true.

But her voice trembled as she said it.

THIRTY-FOUR

GIDEON

GIDEON STOOD BEFORE THE floor-to-ceiling window of his office listening to Harrow relay her most recent findings.

"The ship we found that casting mark on?" said Harrow. "An hour before it set sail, there was last-minute cargo brought on board: two barrels of wine delivered by an aristo."

Beyond the window, the scarlet sun set over the capital. Formerly the Royal Library, this antiquated building—now the Ministry of Public Safety—perched on a hill in the center of the capital, giving a view to the harbor.

Gideon wasn't admiring the view. He was using his reflection in the glass to adjust his new suit jacket while he listened to Harrow's report.

"Unfortunately, the man's hood concealed his face," Harrow continued. "And there was no moon that night. So the dockhands couldn't identify him."

"How do they know he was an aristo?" asked Gideon, doing up his cuff links.

The jacket was a gift from Rune, and had arrived less than an hour ago. *To replace the one I ruined,* said her accompanying note. He'd turned the note over, looking for the rest, but there was nothing more.

It had been three days since he'd left Rune in that garden. Leaving her there had been more difficult than he cared to admit.

"The dockhands said he had a sophisticated way of speaking, like someone with an education. He also wore a ring on his smallest finger."

"Is that all? It narrows down nothing." Gideon sighed. "Half the aristocracy bejewel their hands with rings."

"This one was plain and thin. Silver, maybe. They described it as a poor man's wedding band."

Gideon shook his head. "Perhaps he was a poor man. A man can be both poor and intelligent."

"I'm simply relaying information," said Harrow. "No need to get touchy. Both boys suspected he didn't share their station, despite his attempts to obscure it."

"He might have been nothing more than a merchant, late with his cargo."

Gideon wondered if Rune—or whoever she employed to oversee her shipping business—kept lists of inventories aboard each ship, and if such a list might still exist weeks after the ship delivered its cargo.

"I'll keep my eyes open for an aristo wearing a plain silver band," he said finally, returning to his reflection and eyeing the suit jacket. He'd never worn anything so fine. It was double-breasted, ocher in color, and made of satin. It fit him surprisingly well, and, judging from the shop name on the box, Rune had spent a small fortune on it.

When Gideon first opened the box, he could almost smell her. A delicate scent. Like the wind bringing him the essence of the sea. Beautiful and wild and . . . dangerous.

He frowned, shaking off the thought.

She clearly meant for him to wear the coat to the Luminaries

Dinner tonight. In fact, if he didn't leave soon, he was going to be late.

Turning away from the window, Gideon started for the door. "I—"

"There's something else," said Harrow.

Gideon halted, meeting her gaze. "What is it?"

"Rumors," she said. "Unverified."

No mocking smile tugged at her mouth, and no mischief gleamed in her eyes. He nodded for her to go on.

"Some of my contacts say there have been casting marks seen around town. In alleyways and attics. Often several signatures together. As if witches are gathering in small groups."

Like an alarm ringing through his body, all of Gideon's senses heightened at once. "Were any of these incidents reported to the Guard?"

Harrow shook her head. "People fear becoming suspects themselves. If soldiers find a witch's signature in someone's attic, they might be accused of sympathizing. Others secretly welcome the witches' return. Like those who suffered for their loyalty to the dead queens. Or those who were promised better lives under the Red Peace, only to find their conditions have worsened."

Gideon remembered the moth flickering over the door of the mine the other night in Seldom Harbor.

"Do any of these signatures belong to *her*?"

"No one has reported a crimson moth. But that doesn't mean she isn't among them. Or leading them." Harrow lowered her voice. "Gideon, Penitents are saying the witches are rising, coming to take back what's theirs. They think something big is about to happen. Something formidable enough to bring down the entire regime."

The thought of it turned Gideon's stomach.

Witches could not return to power. He'd devoted his life to ensuring it.

"The Good Commander needs to be told." If what Harrow said was true—that more people were secretly sympathizing with witches, letting them gather in their houses and factories—they might have to bring back the raids, like in the days following the New Dawn.

"Speaking of the Moth," said Harrow, "what happened to your trap? I expected Rune Winters to be imprisoned by now."

Gideon fisted his hand, remembering how close he'd come down in the mine. "My plan failed. I think we've gone down a false trail."

"Did you take my advice?"

His thoughts raced back to Rune in the garden. It had taken all of his willpower to walk away from her. On the ride home, he'd nearly turned back twice.

The thought of Alex had stopped him.

Gideon blew out a frustrated breath.

Did he regret kissing her? Yes. Absolutely. What kind of man kisses the girl of his little brother's dreams?

But he also *liked* it.

He thought of Rune on the beach, stripping off her clothes. Letting him look.

Heat flickered deep inside him.

Gideon ran a palm over his eyes, trying to chase the image out of his brain. "I took your stupid advice, yes."

"You got her naked."

He looked away as the blood rushed to his face.

Harrow whistled. "You *do* move fast. And?"

He shook his head. "There's nothing. No scars."

"But you were thorough?"

"As thorough as I could be."

"So, you slept with her?"

"What? No." The thought of it turned the flickering heat into a raging inferno. "*No.* We went swimming the other night."

Harrow raised a skeptical brow.

"I *looked*," Gideon growled. "I found nothing."

"You said you went at night. How well could you see?"

"Harrow."

"Gideon. This is a witch who's escaped detection for two years now. She won't keep her scars where anyone can find them. Did you look between her thighs?"

The thought of Rune's thighs made him grind his palms into his eyes. "Stop."

"Because if I were a witch hiding in plain sight, that's definitely where I'd keep mine."

Gideon groaned. "You're killing me, Harrow."

"You need to sleep with her."

"Absolutely not."

"Don't tell me you haven't thought about it."

Of course he'd thought about it. It had physically hurt to turn down Rune's invitation. The moment he got home, he'd gone straight into a cold shower, so he could stop thinking about it.

If they were truly courting, it's all he'd be thinking about.

But they weren't courting. Not really. So he needed to *not* think about it.

"It's the only way to know for certain."

"No," he said again.

It was too far. A crossed line.

"If you were committed, Comrade," said Harrow, crossing her arms, "if you truly want to catch your little Moth as badly as you say you do, you'd leave no stone unturned."

He ran both hands roughly over his face this time, then through his hair, tugging on it.

"Come on, Gideon. With a face like that, it won't be a chore."

Gideon felt too many things at once. His chest knotted with frustration. His body ached with desire. Worst of all, he suspected Harrow was right. It had been dark when they went swimming. He'd looked at Rune from a distance. And he hadn't truly inspected every inch of her.

The thought of doing so made him swallow hard.

If he wanted to know, without a doubt, whether Rune Winters was a witch, he would have to take this to the end of the line.

But could he live with himself afterward?

On the one hand, his brother might never speak to him again. On the other, if Rune *was* the Crimson Moth—and if the Moth was not only rescuing witches, but murdering Blood Guard soldiers and planning an uprising—Gideon had a responsibility to do whatever it took to find out. To stop her.

He growled low in his throat. "Fine."

He remembered Rune pulling off her dress. The fabric sliding up her legs, over her hips, along her torso. Thought of her dropping the dress in the sand and peeling off her undergarments.

Feeling strangely breathless, he said, "I'll do it."

Once he knew for certain if she was innocent, he could proceed accordingly. If Rune wasn't the Moth, nor in league with her, she posed no threat to Alex. In which case, Gideon would break off this courtship before things escalated further and point her toward the man who actually deserved her: his brother.

And if she is the Moth . . .

Flashes of memory shimmered like glass: Rune, wading naked through the water toward him. The soft give of her waist beneath his hand. The taste of her skin—like sea salt and soap.

But it wasn't only her physical attributes that had him spinning. It was her kindness. Her thoughtfulness. Her wildness. It was her willingness to argue with him.

If he wasn't careful, he might fall in love with her.

Gideon started toward the door.

"If you have nothing else to report, I'll take my leave."

He was already running late.

"Nothing else," said Harrow, falling into step behind him. "I'll walk you out."

The moment they walked out of his office and into the hallway, a soldier from his regiment strode toward them. Harrow leaned against the wall, keeping out of their way. At the sight of the young woman's blanched face, Gideon stayed where he was.

"Captain." The soldier halted before Gideon. "The Tasker brothers still haven't reported for duty."

"Still?" Gideon had thought it strange when he was first made aware of their absence earlier in the day. It wasn't like them. The Taskers' blood lust for witches made them devoted soldiers. Gideon might despise their tactics, but their work ethic was top-notch.

And it was evening now.

Tardiness was one thing. But missing an entire shift?

Gideon frowned, thinking of the mutilated bodies of Blood Guard soldiers found across the city these past few months. Like a trail of bloody bread crumbs.

An ominous feeling settled over him.

He glanced at his watch. "Can you send Laila to check their apartment?"

"Laila's at the prison tonight."

He could send another officer, but what if the brothers weren't there? Would another soldier know where else to look? Gideon would know. But he was already late for the Luminaries

Dinner. If he went to look himself, he might miss the dinner entirely.

Gideon ran his palm across his forehead.

"Fine," he said. "I'll go. But I need a telegram sent immediately."

"Of course, sir."

Walking back into his office, Gideon grabbed the fountain pen off his desk and scrawled a hasty note. Folding it, he wrote down the address, and handed it over. "Make sure this message gets to Wintersea within the hour."

THIRTY-FIVE

RUNE

MAJORA: (n.) the second-highest spell category.

Majora Spells are major spells requiring the fresh blood of someone else, either taken with permission or given freely. Examples of Majora Spells include: summoning a natural disaster or inflicting a deadly disease.

—From Rules of Magic *by Queen Callidora the Valiant*

"I ENCHANTED THE JACKET," SAID Rune, standing in her shift as Verity pinned up her hair.

"Gideon's jacket? That was bold." The words were mumbled around the pin clenched between Verity's teeth. "Where did you put the spellmark?"

"In one of the interior pockets."

Rune had drawn the bloody mark for *Truth Teller* inside the pocket a few hours ago and sent the package off. If it arrived on time, and Gideon wore it, Rune would pull the answers she needed from him like loose threads from a sweater.

Rune was determined to be more ruthless tonight. After three days of his silence—no telegrams, no flowers, no more requests for walks—Rune had to conclude he'd forgotten her. Normally after such an encounter, her suitors tried to secure her affection by sending extravagant bouquets or inviting her on intimate picnics in the countryside.

Not Gideon Sharpe. Clearly, he couldn't care less.

"There," said Verity, twisting up the last red-gold strand and putting one final pin in Rune's hair. "All done."

Rune glanced into the mirror. In a style that looked deceptively simple, her friend had braided several thin strands and weaved them into the loose waves, then pinned all of it up in an elegant bun at the back of Rune's head.

Having grown up with older sisters who'd taught her all their tricks, Verity always did Rune's hair better than she ever could.

"What are you going to wear?" asked Verity, who was still in the white blouse and pleated skirt of her school uniform. She'd come straight from class to get Rune ready for the Luminaries Dinner. Verity might be displeased with Rune courting Gideon, but she was still committed to helping her.

As Rune went to fetch her new dress, Lizbeth knocked at the door.

"A telegram for you, Miss Rune," said the housekeeper, setting it down on the dresser.

Rune picked it up, her pulse quickening. She broke the seal and unfolded it.

```
MISS RUNE WINTERS
WINTERSEA HOUSE


I WILL BE LATE TO DINNER TONIGHT. THERE IS
A MATTER THAT NEEDS MY IMMEDIATE ATTEN-
TION.
                                    GIDEON
```

Her shoulders fell, along with her hopes. This was the first she'd heard from him in three days, and there was neither an apology nor a promise to make it up to her.

Is there truly some urgent matter, or is he avoiding me?

"Who is it from?" asked Verity, peering over her shoulder.

Rune shook off the sting and held the telegram out to her friend.

"Gideon's going to be late."

Verity's eyes narrowed on the message. She glanced up. "Will your spell last long enough?"

"It should last until midnight." The magic would fade a little as the night wore on, but that wasn't what she was worried about.

What if he doesn't come at all? What if he's changed his mind about me?

Maybe their conversation had convinced him she was exactly as shallow as she pretended to be. Or her kissing wasn't up to his standards. Or maybe, upon seeing her fully undressed, Gideon had decided he was no longer interested.

Rune chewed at her thumbnail. She wasn't used to being rejected. She hated feeling like she wasn't good enough, smart enough, or pretty enough. Is this how a real courtship made you feel? Fragile and unsteady? Like the slightest breeze could knock you over?

Worse than all of this, if Gideon didn't come tonight, he'd ruin her plan before she could even put it into action. She needed him to come, to be *interested* in her, so she could get the information required to rescue Seraphine.

"I'm coming with you," said Verity, wrenching Rune from her thoughts.

"What? No. Don't ruin your evening." Rune sat on her bed. "You have homework to do, and tests to study for."

"And you have to give that dreadful speech. All alone. The least I can do is provide moral support. Who knows? Maybe I can do some poking around while I'm there. I could pretend to get lost, and when some helpful guard escorts me back, I'll ask a few innocent questions about the prison's security . . ."

In truth, if Gideon was going to jilt her, and so publicly, Rune wanted Verity close by. Looking her friend's uniform up and down, she said, "You'll have to borrow a dress."

"Obviously," said Verity, smiling as she moved toward Rune's closet full of clothes.

"Take whatever you like," said Rune. "Except for the green one hanging on the door."

It was the gown Gideon had made her.

She'd sewn a hidden pocket inside it. As her friend searched for something to wear, Rune opened the false wall of her casting room and stepped inside. As she went to retrieve her blood vial—in case she needed any extra spells tonight—a book on the desk caught her eye.

Rune rarely left spell books lying around, and she didn't immediately recognize this one. She stepped up to the desk, glancing down at its gilt edges and thick spine. Opening to the first page, she realized it was one of Nan's rarer spell books, full of powerful curses.

That's odd.

The spells in this book were too powerful for Rune to cast. So why was it on the desk? She didn't remember bringing it down from the shelves.

Maybe Verity did? Her friend liked to search these books for new spells that might be useful for Rune to learn.

The only other person who knew about this room was Alex.

And Lizbeth. Lizbeth sometimes came in uninvited to dust the shelves and sweep the floor.

Symbols graced the spell book's pages, along with stylized illustrations and detailed descriptions. As she flipped through it, the book fell open near the middle, to a spell called *Earth Sunderer*.

On the left page were seven golden spellmarks, each one more complicated than the last. Beneath them lay a description of what the curse did. The opposite page contained an illustration of a town carved in half. An earthquake had ruptured the city, breaking buildings and severing streets while the town's inhabitants screamed in fear.

"Don't even think about trying that one."

Rune glanced up to find Verity beside her, peering down at the page, a dress hanging over her arm.

"If an unlocking spell makes you faint, *this* spell will put you in a coma." Turning the book so she could see it better, Verity's gaze skimmed the description. "You need someone else's blood—and a lot of it—to cast this one."

The words reminded Rune of her conversation with Gideon in the woods, and the things he'd said about the Sister Queens. If anyone knew the truth, it would be Verity. Her sisters were friends with the Rosebloods, and they had often cast spells together.

"Verity? Do you think the Roseblood sisters used Arcana spells?"

Verity glanced up from the spell book's pages. "Why do you ask?"

"Gideon told me something strange the other night." A warm burn moved across Rune's cheeks as she thought of him on the beach. Of his clothes hitting the sand and the sea sluicing over his chest.

Of his mouth on hers.

She forged ahead. "He accused Cressida and her sisters of killing people and using the blood to cast spells. He said they were corrupted by bad magic."

"And you believe him?"

Rune thought of the brand on Gideon's chest: the raised, red skin in the shape of a rose and crescent. That scar alone seemed proof that Cressida, at least, was more than capable of extreme cruelty. "I don't know what to believe. It would explain why they were so powerful."

Verity's eyes grew clouded. "This is how my stepfather turned my mother against my sisters."

Rune drew back, startled. "What?"

"My sisters used each other's blood for their Majora spells. With permission, of course. But my stepfather walked in on them one day, in the middle of a casting. After, he declared their magic an abomination and convinced my mother the only way for my sisters to cleanse themselves and be *pure* again was to beat the wickedness out of them."

Rune stared in horror at Verity, who'd never told her any of this.

Seeing the way her friend trembled, Rune reached for her hand, lacing their fingers together. "That's awful."

Verity's grip tightened on Rune, her knuckles turning bone white. "He would lock them up for days. Beat their bare backs with belts. Force them to kneel for hours on broken glass." As if reliving the scenes, Verity dug her fingernails into Rune's skin.

"The worst of it was, my mother let him. She'd lost our baby sister in childbirth years before, and never recovered from her grief. My stepfather used her fragile state against her, convincing her that my sisters were wicked to their cores. So when she heard their screams, she did nothing. She sided with *him* over her own daughters."

And then she handed those daughters over to the Blood Guard, thought Rune.

No wonder Verity hated her parents. This was why she wore

herself down to keep her scholarship—so she'd never have to go home or be at their mercy.

But . . .

Ouch.

Rune glanced down to see her friend's fingernails about to break her skin. "Verity, you're hurting me."

For a moment, it seemed like Verity wouldn't stop. *Couldn't* stop. But she shook her head and let go. "S-sorry."

Rune pulled her hand toward her chest, studying the little half-moon marks in her skin. "It's all right. You're upset."

"My sisters weren't corrupt," said Verity, her eyes pleading with Rune to believe her. "They weren't abominations. Witches have been using each other's blood to amplify their spells for centuries. There's nothing wrong with what they did."

Verity nodded to the book on Rune's desk, lying open to *Earth Sunderer.*

"That spell, for example. No witch can cast something this powerful using solely her own blood. She'd seriously hurt herself."

Your sisters weren't using each other's blood against their will, though, Rune wanted to point out. Which was the accusation Gideon had made against the queens.

But Verity was distressed by the memory. And Rune couldn't blame her. So she let it go.

"Come on," said Rune, grabbing the blood vial she'd come in here to get, then eyeing the dress hanging over Verity's arm—one of last season's fashions. "Let's find you something better to wear."

THIRTY-SIX

GIDEON

*T*HE SUN HAD SET by the time Gideon arrived on Freshwater Street. Harrow rode atop a borrowed horse beside him.

After finding the Taskers' apartment empty, Gideon led them here, to the entertainment district of town, whose establishments the brothers liked to frequent. Gideon intended to ask around in the hopes that someone had seen them.

The entertainment district was the capital's underbelly, known for its brothels, gambling dens, and drunken brawls. Normally, the atmosphere lit up the street like a carnival, but now the district was eerily quiet. Up ahead, a hushed crowd gathered outside of an alleyway.

Harrow's gaze cut to Gideon, whose eyes narrowed on the sight.

Their horses fidgeted beneath them as they approached, smelling the stench of death before they did. Swinging down from the saddle, Gideon left his horse several yards away, and dispersed the gawking crowd as he strode through it.

Harrow followed him in.

The alley marked the space between two beer parlors and was lit dimly by only the streetlamps and a lantern on the ground. The latter seemed to belong to the elderly man standing over a blanket concealing two large shapes.

The smell of blood was thick in the air, making Gideon nauseous. Pulling the collar of his shirt over his nose, he approached.

"I was taking out the trash when I found them," said the man, his shoulders hunched like a crow. "It seemed wrong to let them lie here like this. So I . . ." He motioned to the blanket.

"Mind if I take a look?"

The man nodded for him to go ahead.

Gideon bent down and peeled back the blanket. Despite seeing dozens of scenes like this one in the past few months, he wasn't prepared for what lay beneath.

The face of one of his officers stared up at him, but the hollow eyes and bloodless skin were anything but familiar. James Tasker's mouth twisted in what appeared to be the state he'd died in: one of sheer terror.

Gideon forced himself to pull the blanket down further, his gaze descending to the Blood Guard's neck, which was hacked open like a second gaping mouth. White bone shone in the mess of torn skin, tendons, and congealed blood. James's spine appeared to be the only thing keeping his head attached to his body.

Bile rose in the back of Gideon's throat. He looked away, pulling the blanket back over the soldier's face.

"The second one is the same," said the elderly man, standing over Gideon. "Throat slashed open." He shook his silver head. "Poor souls."

"Indeed," said Gideon.

He had no love for the Tasker brothers, whose cruelty he hadn't been able to keep in check. He'd asked for them to be discharged several times, but he didn't want them *dead*.

Sighting Harrow farther down the alley, a borrowed lantern in her hand, Gideon stood up.

"Fetch the undertaker," he told the man, who nodded as Gideon stepped past him.

Gideon walked deeper into the alley, coming to join Harrow, who lifted her lantern into the air and nodded to the brick wall before them.

"Looks like she left you a message, Comrade."

Gideon glanced up. Blood glistened across the yellow brick. The Taskers' blood, he assumed. It took a moment before he realized the blood formed words, and those words formed a warning.

You're next, Gideon.

"What are you going to do?" asked Harrow.

"Report this to the Commander," he said, trying to ignore the icy dread spreading through his chest.

"And then what?"

"He'll want to reinstate a curfew. And resume the raids."

After the New Dawn, Gideon hadn't thought twice about infringing on the rights and freedoms of the New Republic's citizens. He did what had to be done to protect them, and if that meant entering and searching their homes without warning, if it meant locking them in their quarters after dark, if it meant hauling them into interrogation rooms if they so much as questioned whether the purgings went too far, so be it.

But that kind of power was easily abused. Gideon had seen soldiers take things way too far, and those kinds of measures now made him uneasy.

"And if the raids and curfews aren't enough?" asked Harrow.

They might not be. Curfews and raids had weeded out witches and their sympathizers early on, but they hadn't stopped the Crimson Moth. Gideon was dealing with a witch adept at hiding in plain sight.

"The only way to truly end this is to catch her."

Gideon thought of their earlier conversation about Rune, and what he had sworn to do. The idea that Rune was the Crimson Moth, a witch playing him like a fiddle—that she was capable of this kind of carnage—turned his stomach.

But he couldn't turn away simply because it made him uncomfortable. Nor could he let his feelings for Rune weaken his search for the truth. Gideon needed to keep his head about him more than ever.

She had seemed different under the moonlight the other night. Not at all the irritating girl who'd accosted him in the opera box. Gideon had been so enamored by the pensive, sensitive Rune that the discordance hadn't raised his suspicions.

Who *was* the real Rune Winters?

Gideon wondered if his initial theory was correct: that she was pretending to be something she wasn't to hide a darker truth about herself.

If so, he needed to find out what that dark truth was.

THIRTY-SEVEN

RUNE

*T*HE GLIMMER OF A hundred candle flames blurred at the edges of Rune's vision while she tried to focus on the young woman before her.

"It sounds awful, being raised by a witch."

"Horrible," said Rune, whose face hurt from fake-smiling. "The worst." But if this pain was her penance for the lies that she'd spewed—was still spewing—she'd bear it.

Her speech had been a triumph, judging by the throng of patriots gathered round and waiting to speak with her. Rune had felt sick during all six courses of the meal and barely touched her food. Her stomach grumbled loudly now as admirers swarmed. They were drawn like insects to Rune's devotion to the New Republic, her embodiment of its virtues, and, of course, her disgust for all witchkind.

Rune scanned the sea of faces, searching for Gideon, but didn't see him.

He's not coming, she thought, trying to squash the disappointed feeling burning behind her breastbone.

Am I really so forgettable?

With dinner over, all that was left was the music, mingling, and dessert. The staff cleared tables out of the center of the room and were now assembling some kind of stage, getting ready for the evening's entertainment.

From across the courtyard, Rune caught sight of Verity. Her friend wore a cream, off-the-shoulder gown with gold beading. One of her hands held a matching gold clutch while the other beckoned to Rune, finger crooked. As if she had some secret to relay.

"Excuse me," said Rune to the girls before her. "I'll be right back."

Rune cut through the fawning patriots and strode past the staff setting up a stage. As she wove through the maze of long tables set with crisp white tablecloths, the chilly evening air made her shiver.

Traditionally, the Luminaries Dinner occurred in the palace's grand ballroom. But this year, the organizers had moved it to the courtyard. The spring nights were still cool, though, making Rune wonder about the choice.

The moment she arrived at her friend's side, Verity linked their arms and led Rune toward an empty corner of the courtyard. When there was enough space between them and the other guests, Verity lowered her voice to a whisper. "Witches are kept in the seventh circle of the prison—past Fortitude Gate."

Fortitude was the seventh Ancient.

And the farthest gate from the entrance, Rune thought, recalling the prison map.

Keeping her face carefully blank, in case they were being watched, she asked: "How did you learn this?"

Her friend's mouth quirked to the side. "I used some of your tricks on a prison guard who was getting off his shift." Verity's eyes sparkled with mischief, making Rune wonder what tricks she'd used, exactly. "He also said that everyone who works in the prison carries an access coin corresponding to the section they work in. The coins are like keys, getting you where you're authorized to be, but no further."

Interesting.

"So in order to rescue Seraphine," murmured Rune, thinking aloud, "I'll need to find a guard authorized to go beyond the seventh gate." *And steal his access coin.*

"A guard," said Verity. "Or a witch hunter."

Rune shot her a curious look. "A witch hunter?"

"He said that all Blood Guard officers of a certain rank—usually the captains or their seconds—carry an access coin, allowing them to bring witches straight through to Fortitude Gate."

If every Blood Guard captain carried an access coin, Gideon surely had one.

Rune wondered where he kept it.

The cogs of Rune's mind were turning. If she stole Gideon's coin, and perhaps a Blood Guard uniform—though how she'd do that, she didn't yet know—would she be able to walk straight through the last gate?

A sudden commotion interrupted her thoughts.

Rune glanced toward the doors to find someone she recognized entering the courtyard. Someone who'd recently *shot* her.

Laila Creed.

Dressed in her scarlet Blood Guard uniform, Laila strode through the guests while gripping the arm of a prisoner. A black bag covered the prisoner's head, and from the iron restraints encasing her hands, Rune knew the prisoner was a witch.

While staff filled cups with hot coffee or chilled wine and handed out plates with sugar-dusted pastries, Laila marched her charge through the courtyard. The lights of a thousand candles flickered down the lengths of tables as guests murmured excitedly, their attention on the stage now assembled in the middle of the space.

No, thought Rune. *It's not a stage.*

Thick chains hung from a solid beam erected over the platform. Chains Laila was connecting to the ankles of the witch.

It's a purging platform.

Rune didn't think, just started forward.

Verity grabbed her wrist to stop her. "There's nothing you can do," she whispered, her face going whiter than snow. "Not here."

Rune's hands clenched and unclenched, knowing she was right. "Who—"

Before she could finish the question, Laila tugged the black hood off the witch.

They both sucked in a breath.

The face beneath the hood was shockingly familiar to Rune. She knew it from the gold locket Nan used to wear around her neck. It was a locket her grandmother rarely took off.

As a child, Rune liked to open the locket and peer in at the two young women painted on the two panels. On one side was Kestrel's face, rendered when she was about nineteen; on the other was Seraphine's, not much older.

The two women had grown up together, Rune knew. They'd been best friends since childhood.

Which was why the sight before her didn't make any sense.

The witch on the platform bore the *exact same face* as the one inside Nan's locket—sparkling brown eyes, sharp birdlike features, black curls that haloed her head like a cloud. As if Seraphine Oakes hadn't aged a single day.

Why is she so young?

Nan had been over seventy the day she died, and the woman on the platform—*Seraphine*—looked no older than twenty-three.

Rune's mind spun with confusion. As she tried to make sense of it, the Good Commander ascended the steps of the platform, causing a hush to fall over the entire courtyard.

The Blood Guard soldiers retreated. Nicolas Creed stepped toward Seraphine, whose hands were manacled at her sides. The witch restraints clasped her hands entirely in iron, so that her wrists ended in two black metal stubs, preventing use.

"Good evening," said Nicolas, dressed in his usual black. "We have a surprise in store for you tonight. We're simply waiting for . . ." His piercing gaze scanned the room before landing directly on Rune. "Ah. There she is. Citizen Winters, will you join me up here for a moment?"

Is this another trap?

Rune glanced into the sea faces, but the guests looked as surprised as she was. Verity's hand tightened on her wrist. But Rune couldn't refuse the Commander, and Verity knew it.

Reluctantly, she let go.

With no other choice, Rune started toward the platform. Drawing nearer, she could see the split in Seraphine's lip and the bruise ringing her eye, blackening her brown skin.

"Our guest of honor is a model patriot. Miss Winters' bravery, loyalty, and refusal to tolerate witchcraft is an example to us all."

At the name *Winters*, Seraphine's head whipped sharply toward Rune, her dark brown eyes narrowing.

With hate, Rune thought.

She swallowed, making her way toward the platform, realizing with increasing horror what was happening.

They were going to kill Seraphine. Right here, in the middle of this courtyard.

This was tonight's entertainment: a private witch purging for Luminaries guests.

Rune's pulse thudded loudly in her ears. Everywhere around her, faint whispers buzzed in the air. She glanced around, looking for Gideon. Had he known? Was this another one of his traps?

But Gideon was nowhere to be seen.

As she stepped up beside the Good Commander, who placed a heavy hand on her shoulder, Laila opened a black box and drew out the purging knife. She cradled it, almost lovingly, in a piece of red velvet. Then held it out to Rune.

A smile ghosted across her lips as she said, "Rune Winters, I grant you the privilege of purging Seraphine Oakes tonight."

THIRTY-EIGHT

RUNE

SILENCE RANG THROUGH THE courtyard as the lethal curve of the purging knife glinted in the space between them. A knife that had stolen not only Nan's life, but hundreds of others.

Rune expected it to burn her when she took it. But as Laila placed it in her hands, both the hilt and the steel were cold to the touch. Rune hoped her trembling didn't give her away.

What am I going to do?

If she refused to kill the witch before her, she'd reveal the truth to every single one of her enemies. Rune was surrounded. There weren't only Laila and the other Blood Guard soldiers to contend with. There was the Good Commander himself, not to mention the hundreds of patriots seated at tables, and the thousands of guards beyond, patrolling the halls of the palace.

Cold panic hummed in Rune's blood.

She was trapped.

The Commander signaled to the musicians to begin. This was the sickest part of private purgings: the music. As if slitting the throat of a girl and watching her bleed out over the floor weren't butchery or murder, but refined art.

Rune's fingers tightened around the knife hilt.

Laila retreated, moving toward the levers. In a moment, she'd pull them, and the chains would snap, yanking Seraphine's feet out from under her and drawing her toward the sky, to hang upside down. Like a cow to be slaughtered.

Rune and Seraphine were momentarily alone on the platform.

She could cast a spell. But to do that, she'd have to pull the blood vial from her pocket, uncork it, and draw the spellmarks. Someone would realize what she was doing and stop her before she could finish.

I could nick my finger with this knife, she thought. *Just the fingertip. And use the blood to draw a spellmark on my palm.*

But what spell would be quick enough? What wouldn't require much blood or draw much attention?

And the silvery scar she'd be left with would damn her.

Maybe that was the price she needed to pay, to save Seraphine. To fulfill her grandmother's last request.

The music still played as Laila grabbed hold of the levers.

"You disgust me." Seraphine spat. The spittle hit Rune's cheek, startling her and drawing her attention back to the witch. "Kestrel would be ashamed of you."

Beneath the grime of too many nights spent in a disgusting cell, Seraphine was fine-boned and pretty. She reminded Rune of a sparrow.

"You don't deserve the Winters name." The witch's eyes burned like black fire. As if, were their positions reversed, Seraphine would have already cut Rune's throat.

I went to find you, Rune wanted to say. *I've been trying to save you.*

With so many people listening, she didn't dare.

"Do you have *nothing* to say to me?" Seraphine's voice shook— out of hatred for Rune, or grief over Kestrel, or possibly the knowledge that she was about to die.

What they needed was a distraction. Something to put the room into a panic.

A fire would be good. Rune could cause utter chaos with a fire. But summoning actual fire was a complex spell that required a lot of fresh blood, and not only did Rune not know the marks, she didn't have the blood.

But the *illusion* of a fire . . . that she might manage.

Laila pulled the lever. There was an awful clinking sound of metal straining against metal. Rune knew what came next. So did everyone else.

The chains yanked Seraphine's feet out from under her. She flipped in the air, and her body swung helplessly as she was hauled skyward.

With no other choice, Rune decided to risk the casting scar.

She was about to touch the knife's sharp steel to the tip of her finger and press down hard, when the acrid tang of smoke burned in the air.

"Fire!" someone yelled.

What? Rune hadn't even drawn blood yet.

"FIRE!" More people took up the call.

Rune lowered the knife and glanced up. Black smoke thickened the air, drawing her gaze to the column of fire rising on the far side of the courtyard. Instead of red flames, these were black. Just like Seraphine's eyes.

Spellfire.

This isn't my spell, she realized.

She remembered the murderous look in Seraphine's eyes.

Is it hers?

Suddenly, the column moved. *Fast.* Snaking toward the purging platform. Heading straight for Rune. Realizing it, she inhaled sharply, and the sting of smoke burned down her throat.

Rune erupted in a fit of coughing and her eyes burned with tears, making it hard to see.

Help Seraphine.

As she stumbled through the smoke, someone called Rune's name—Verity?—but she didn't glance toward the sound. She needed to get Seraphine down before the spellfire devoured them both.

Black fire crackled around them. Its fiery heat curled up Rune's back and singed her hair. The knife hilt grew hot in her hands, burning her skin. She dropped it.

Before she could lunge for Seraphine, the dark flames snaked between them. The witch vanished, leaving Rune alone, trapped in the spellfire.

On some invisible command, the fiery circle constricted, closing in on her.

As if it intended to burn her alive.

THIRTY-NINE

GIDEON

AFTER LEAVING THE GROTESQUE scene on Freshwater Street, Gideon rode for the palace, hoping he hadn't missed the Luminaries Dinner entirely. After stabling his horse and eyeing the carriages being pulled up in the rotunda, signaling that dinner was nearly at an end, Gideon trod up the steps and headed for the courtyard.

He was striding down the grand hallway, trying to push the image of James Tasker's corpse out of his mind, when several screams of "Fire!" made him nearly jump out of his skin.

They were all coming from the same direction.

As more voices echoed the frantic call, Gideon started to run. After living in this palace, he knew the quickest routes, and when he reached the courtyard, he found Luminaries guests pushing through the doors, tripping over each other to escape.

The smell of smoke rushed out with them. Gideon looked over the heads of the escapees in time to see Rune standing alone on a purging platform, with a pillar of black flames spinning toward her.

"No . . ."

Gideon surged straight into the crowd of panicked guests, pushing them back, not caring about their protests. He ignored their frantic elbows and fists as he forced himself through the doors, trying to get to Rune.

Stumbling into the courtyard, he glanced up and saw her disappear into the flames.

"Rune!"

Gideon tugged off his jacket—the expensive one she'd sent him earlier today—and pulled it over his head before diving into the thick smoke.

He tried not to breathe as he barreled forward, bumping into tables and tripping over chairs. He picked himself up and kept going, even as the smoke stung his eyes and the heat burned his skin. When he tripped again, it was on the steps of the platform. Gideon stumbled up them, pulled his jacket tighter over his head, and ran straight into the dark flames spinning around the spot where Rune had disappeared.

It smelled like a pyre. All burning wood and singed hair.

When he burst through the other side, into the eye of the spinning flames, Rune turned towards him. His chest tightened at the sight of her ashen face.

Gideon closed the space between them in a single stride and threw the jacket over her, tucking her into it. Her whole body trembled with shock.

"You came," she whispered.

He pulled Rune against him, trying to shield her from the heat. What would have happened if he'd arrived five minutes later? If he hadn't made it here at all?

Don't think about that. Just get her out of here.

"Ready to run?"

She nodded.

Scooping her into his arms, Gideon plunged through the flames. He didn't feel the searing heat on his skin. Only Rune's forehead pressed against his throat, and the lock of her arms around his neck. Bursting out the other side, Gideon choked on the thick smoke, lost sight of the stairs, and half stumbled down them, nearly dropping Rune.

At the bottom of the steps, he regained his balance and steadied them both, then kept running out of the smoke, toward the edge of the courtyard. Rune's arms tightened around him as she watched the column of fire give chase over his shoulder.

"It's coming for us."

He could feel the heat on his back. See the flickering black at the edge of his vision.

Get to the doors.

This fire was no natural fire. There was a witch in their midst. A powerful one. He hadn't seen magic this formidable in years. He only hoped that whoever it was, she didn't also decide to lock the doors and trap them inside the courtyard.

When the doors were ten paces away, Gideon pumped his legs. Willing them to go faster.

His shoulder hit the wood first and the door gave instantly, swinging open and depositing him and Rune onto the floor of the hall. As they fell, Gideon twisted his body so that his shoulder blade hit the marble first, wincing at the impact, but sparing Rune, who sprawled on top of him.

The guests were gone. The hall was empty.

With her palms pressed to the floor on either side of his head, Rune sat astride Gideon. His jacket hung from her shoulders, mostly burned, and her red-gold hair was a wild mess, filling his vision.

A bewildered expression lit up her face.

"Why did you do that?"

He frowned at her, his hands moving to her hips. "What?"

"Why . . . why risk your life for me?"

Gideon sat up so they were eye to eye. "Did you think I'd let you be burned alive?"

"Maybe? I don't know! What am I supposed to think?" She was still sitting on top of him, her dress hiked to her thighs. "I didn't hear from you for three days. You didn't even send flowers!"

Flowers?

What is she talking about?

Gideon stared up at her ash-streaked face. "Do you . . . want flowers?"

"What?" Rune fell off him, trying to untangle herself from his jacket. "*No.* Never mind."

Clearly she was in shock.

Before he could make sense of it, the smell of burning wood filled the air. They both looked to find that unearthly fire eating through the doors. As if it were ravenous, and only Rune would satiate.

As guards and palace staff arrived with buckets of water to put out the flames, Gideon scrambled to his feet. He pulled the remnants of his coat—which was all but singed to ash—off of Rune. Knowing water wouldn't put out this fire, Gideon grabbed her hand and tugged her away from the door.

They kept running.

Remembering the days he'd lived in this palace, Gideon led her through the servants' quarters and the kitchens. The cooking staff froze, gaping at the Blood Guard captain and the disheveled aristocrat rushing through their workspace.

He took Rune out through the back door used for deliveries. Not long after it swung shut behind them, and they were safe—at least for the moment—Rune pulled her hand from Gideon's and fell against the stone wall, her breath coming in quick gasps. She bent over, pressing her hands to her knees.

Gideon kept his eye on the kitchen door, half expecting it to catch fire, too.

It was quiet out here, and they were alone. The full moon rose overhead, moving in and out of the clouds.

"What the hell *was* that?"

"A spell," said Rune.

"I know it was a spell. Why was it targeting *you*?"

"I don't know. *I don't know.*" Rune slid down the wall to sit in the alley dirt. Black soot from the smoke smudged her face. "But if you had seen the look in Seraphine's eyes . . . she wanted me dead, Gideon."

"You think it was her?"

Gideon might not be a witch, but he'd spent the better part of two years in the constant presence of one. For Seraphine to cast such a powerful spell, she'd need a lot of blood and, more importantly, the use of her hands—which were encased in iron.

"It's not possible."

The back door to the kitchen swung open, and Gideon immediately reached for the pistol holstered at his hip. But it was only a wide-eyed child. Belonging to one of the kitchen staff, probably. The young girl held a glass of water in her hands and, after shooting a fearful look at Gideon, crouched down to give it to Rune.

"The spellfire's gone, Miss Winters."

After taking the glass with trembling fingers, Rune touched the girl's cheek—a gesture that, for some reason, made Gideon's chest tighten. "Thank you, sweetheart."

Gideon watched her gulp down the water, trying to make sense of it all.

A witch had tried to kill her tonight.

Witches didn't kill other witches.

Therefore, Rune couldn't be a witch.

Right?

When the child went back inside, and they were alone again, Gideon remembered Rune's strange words to him a few moments ago. "What did you mean in the hall? About the flowers."

Rune's cheeks reddened. "I have no idea why I said that." She quickly got to her feet.

"You were upset with me. Why?"

She looked away, fisting her hands. "Please, let's just forget it."

Gideon stepped toward her. Taking her face in his palms, he guided her eyes back to his. "Tell me." Her jaw was clenched, so he ran his thumb along its edge until she relaxed.

Standing this near to her was dangerous. Like the moon and the tide, the closer he got to her, the closer he wanted her. Wanted her softness to chase away the memory of James Tasker's bloodless face. Wanted her kiss to erase the ominous warning written on the alley wall.

Rune was a bright light burning in a long, dark night.

Except she's not for you.

"I kept waiting for a telegram," she said. "Or some other sign that maybe I'm not so easy to walk away from. But there was nothing until your note tonight—and that was only to say you'd be late." She looked up at him. "I thought you were jilting me."

"*Jilting* you?" Gideon's eyebrows arched. He almost laughed. "Rune, I haven't stopped thinking about you for three straight days."

Her forehead creased in confusion. He was about to prove it to her, when the sound of footsteps crunching pebbles interrupted them.

Gideon let her go just as someone appeared at the far end of the path, silhouetted against the lights of the street beyond.

This time, Gideon did draw his pistol.

"Show yourself," he called out, stepping in front of Rune to shield her.

"*Merciful Ancients*," came a feminine voice. "I've searched the whole palace looking for you! Are you all right?"

Rune squinted into the distance. "Verity?" Stepping around Gideon, she started toward the voice.

"Wait," he warned. "It could be an illusion."

But Rune was already running.

"Why don't you shoot me and see if I bleed?" said Verity, materializing out of the darkness. She slit her eyes at Gideon while pulling Rune into a hug.

"Tempting," he said, holstering his pistol.

Rune cut him a stern look, then turned back to her friend. "Are you all right?"

Verity nodded. "I'm fine. But we need to get out of here. They haven't caught the witch responsible for that fire. She could be anywhere."

Gideon didn't like the thought of Rune returning to Wintersea alone. Not after a witch tried to kill her. "Let me send soldiers to escort you."

"I appreciate your concern," said Rune. "But it's unnecessary."

"*You* were the target of that spell," he pressed. "If the witch who cast it comes for you again, you won't be able to stop her."

"And you will?" asked Verity.

Of course I will, Gideon wanted to say. Except he was no match for a powerful witch, and they all knew it.

"I'll be all right," said Rune. Walking back to Gideon, she pushed herself onto her toes and planted a quick kiss on his cheek. "Thank you for not letting me burn."

He felt Verity's eyes on him. She made no effort to conceal the fact that she thought him unworthy of Rune. Annoyed by her disdain and overcome by the sudden urge to prove her wrong, Gideon cupped Rune's neck with both hands and captured her mouth with his, stopping her from leaving. He kissed her slowly, deeply. Claiming her in front of Verity. At least, that's how it started. As Rune softened, and her hand slid up his chest, he forgot their audience entirely—just as Rune remembered it.

She pushed against him, halting the kiss, and stepped out of his reach.

"Buttercups are my favorite," she whispered, breathless and walking backward. "But daisies are also acceptable."

The corner of Gideon's mouth turned up. "Noted."

It went against all of his instincts, watching her walk away, not knowing what danger waited for her beyond this alley. But as Verity had pointed out, there was little he could do to protect Rune.

Except for catching the witch who'd attacked her tonight.

Behind him, the kitchen door swung open. Gideon turned to find Laila stepping out.

"There's something you should see. But we need to be quick. It's already fading."

Curious, he followed her inside.

Back in the courtyard, which reeked of smoke but was devoid of spellfire, Laila peeled a scorched tablecloth back from a long table. She pointed underneath.

Gideon crouched down, ducking his head to see.

Something glowed in the space between the chairs, moon-pale and delicate.

"It's a casting signature," Laila said, her voice floating down from overhead.

Gideon dropped to all fours, squinting in its direction, trying to get a better look. He crawled under the table, the pebbles shifting beneath his knees, until he knew exactly what he was looking at.

He saw it every night in his nightmares. Found it carved into his chest every time he looked in the mirror.

A thorny rose enclosed by a crescent moon.

The sight of it made him nauseous.

"A witch was hidden among the guests tonight."

The brand on his chest flared suddenly. Gideon rubbed at it, but the pain faded quickly, leaving him to wonder if it was just in his head.

Laila joined him beneath the table, sitting cross-legged on the other side of the signature. With her head bowed beneath the wood overhead, her gaze flicked between him and the floating mark. "Who does it belong to?"

The past rose up to bite Gideon, trying to drag him backward in its teeth.

He wished he could deny what was right in front of his eyes. That there was some other explanation. But he knew this signature like he knew his own name.

"It belongs to a witch who should be dead."

His eyes met Laila's.

"Cressida Roseblood."

FORTY

RUNE

"QUITE THE PERFORMANCE," SAID Verity as Rune's carriage left the palace, bumping along the cobblestone streets. "With acting skills like those, you could audition for the Royal Theater."

Beside her, Rune sighed. Verity was upset. She'd been worried sick about Rune, who she'd watched get engulfed by spellfire, and when she finally found her alive, Rune was flirting with an equally dangerous force: Gideon Sharpe.

"Truly. If I didn't know better, I'd believe you were smitten with a Blood Guard captain who hunts down your own kind."

Rune looked away, unable to escape the guilt flooding in. "I'm not smitten," she said, watching the city center roll by through the window. "And I'm perfectly aware that he hates my kind. That's why I'm letting him court me, remember? To steal his intel."

"And how much intel have you stolen, exactly?"

Rune opened her mouth to answer, except the only information Gideon had given her was bad information.

Is she right?

Was courting Gideon nothing more than a dangerous waste of her time?

"I need to wear down his defenses more," she said. "Once he trusts me completely, he'll be at my disposal."

Verity turned to the window. "Whatever you say."

Knowing that Verity wasn't really angry at Rune, but at the people trying to hurt her, she changed the subject. "Is Seraphine all right?"

Verity nodded, visibly relaxing. "They removed her back to her cell."

With the tension defused, they sat in silence until the carriage pulled up to Thornwood Hall.

Alex's home was nestled inside a forest. The old trees towered over them as they exited the carriage and started toward the stone house.

More of a small castle, thought Rune, staring up at it. A turret graced each of its four corners, and candles burned in most of the windows, giving Rune the impression of eyes. Like Cressida's former home was watching her approach.

She hurried to catch up with Verity, following her inside.

Now that Verity had obtained information regarding the prison, they needed a cogent plan for breaking Seraphine out of that prison—as soon as possible.

Upon entering Alex's home, piano music greeted her immediately, floating through the halls, soothing Rune a little. While Verity stalked toward the kitchens in search of refreshments for their meeting, Rune followed the song to the other end of the house, drawn to it like a distressed ship to a beacon.

With the smell of smoke lingering in her hair, Rune drew her shawl tighter around herself. She'd spent two years being hunted by the Blood Guard. She was used to people wanting her dead. But it had never occurred to her that a witch might want her dead, too. The realization rattled her.

The conservatory door hung open. Sighting the pianist, Rune paused to watch him play.

Alex's lean shoulders hunched as his hands moved like spiders over the keys. The sight of him was like coming home. Like wrapping herself in a warm blanket on a chilly day.

Alex was constant and safe. Gentle and kind.

Rune leaned against the lintel and let herself wonder, just for a moment, what it would be like to accept his offer. To leave everything behind and go to Caelis, where she could live a life without fear and finally be herself.

No. She had a purpose here in the New Republic. A *duty*.

Witches were still being hauled to prison and purged. Rune couldn't abandon them. They were innocent people, and she owed it to her grandmother. Saving girls from being murdered by the Republic was the only way to make Nan's death mean something.

It was the choice she'd made.

And no matter how she might dream of a different life, this was the one she belonged in.

Alex's right hand stumbled, hitting the wrong key, and the song halted.

"Rune." He brushed his golden hair out of his eyes to look at her. "You startled me."

"Sorry." She stepped out of the door frame and into the room, moving toward him. "I didn't want to interrupt."

He rose from the bench, his gaze sweeping over her. "What happened?"

Rune looked down at herself. Ashy soot streaked the beautiful gown Gideon had made her. It probably streaked her face, too. "I . . . it's a long story. I'll tell it once Verity gets back from the kitchen."

Alex made room for her on the bench, looking worried. Rune sat down, letting her shawl fall to the floor behind them.

She nodded toward the keys. "Don't stop on my account."

With his eyes still on her, Alex placed his fingers on the piano and resumed the song.

And like that, he was gone again. Soaring away from her.

"You play better than your brother, that's for sure," she said when he finished, remembering Gideon plunking piano keys in her library.

"Oh? Has he been serenading you?" The playfulness of the question couldn't hide the edge in his voice. Before she could answer, he closed the fallboard, and the keys disappeared. "I have something to show you."

He rose from the bench and walked to the far wall, where his writing desk stood between two windows. Picking up a large sheet of paper, he brought it back and handed it to her.

"It's the deed to the house in Caelis."

Rune stared at the deed. A strange numbness flooded her. "You bought it?" The realization gave her a stomachache. "So soon?"

"I'm putting Thornwood Hall up for sale tomorrow. Please don't look so unhappy."

"Of course I'm happy for you." Rune handed it back to him. "This is what you want."

It just wasn't what *she* wanted.

Alex was her safe place. She could be herself with him. Alex, along with Verity, had filled the gaping hole in her life after Nan died. He and Verity were always there—after every dangerous night of saving witches, after every ridiculous after-party where Rune's head ached from gossiping and flirting and pretending to be someone she wasn't, in the quiet moments and the loud ones.

And unlike Verity, who was a fire constantly spurring her on, Alex was a cool spring, giving her a place to rest and recover, reminding her that she was a girl with needs and weaknesses, not some invincible savior.

What will I do without you?

Maybe that was the problem. Rune needed Alex more than he needed her. He'd given her so much, and she'd given so little in return.

She was doing it now. Being selfish. The selfless thing to do was let him go.

Rune swallowed the bitter taste in her mouth and tried to be a better friend.

"I *want* you to finish your studies." She smiled, hoping it didn't look forced. "And then I want you to become a world-famous composer whose name I can flaunt at parties, telling everyone I knew you when you didn't know the difference between adagio and allegro."

He studied her for a long time, deliberating something.

"Will you come back to visit me?" she asked.

"If . . . you want me to."

It wasn't the answer Rune needed. She wanted him to *want* to come back. To need her the way she needed him.

Sinking back down to the piano bench, his eyes locked with hers. Alex had the most beautiful eyes. Chestnut brown flecked with gold.

"But it's easier for you to make a clean break," she said, putting voice to the thing he wouldn't. "To put this island behind you." More quietly, she said, "To put me behind you."

"No." His voice was soft but firm. His hands lifted to gently cup her face. "Rune, never. I want . . ."

Before he could finish, Verity flew into the room with a tray of tea and cookies. "Is anyone else *starving*?"

Alex's hands dropped and he turned sharply away from Rune. As she watched him slide off the bench and stand before the fireplace, quietly stoking the flames, she remembered Gideon's words from the garden.

When I saw Alex at your side, I knew exactly who you were . . . a girl who was entirely off-limits, because my little brother found her first.

Rune had thought he was talking about ruining her and Alex's friendship. Now she wondered if he'd meant something else.

"So? How did the dinner go?" Alex asked as Verity set down the tray and poured out three cups of tea.

Verity relayed everything she'd told to Rune already—about witches being kept beyond the seventh gate, and the access coin they needed to move through the prison—before telling him about the spellfire Seraphine used to nearly kill Rune.

Alex spat his tea back into his cup. "Seraphine did *what?*"

Rune, still on the piano bench, crossed the room and lowered herself into the love seat. "We don't know for sure that it was her. It shouldn't have been possible, with her hands in restraints."

"Who else would it be?"

Silence answered him.

With the fire roaring in the hearth, Alex set down the poker and joined Rune on the love seat.

"If they'd intended to purge her tonight," said Verity, "Seraphine's days are numbered. We have to break her out of that prison as soon as possible."

"If Seraphine is being kept in the prison's seventh circle," said Rune. "In order to get her out, I'll need a Blood Guard uniform and an access coin for Fortitude Gate."

The question was: How would they obtain them?

Verity withdrew her pad of paper and pen from the gold clutch.

"If I used my *Ghost Walker* spell to sneak into Blood Guard headquarters, I could steal a uniform and someone's access coin there. The problem is, I only have one blood vial left. I'd like to save it, if I can. In case something goes wrong inside the prison."

Verity tapped her pen against her chin, thinking. "I might be able to get you a uniform. There's a girl in my dormitory who's an intern at the Ministry of Public Safety. She wouldn't have an access coin, but they gave her a uniform as part of her training."

Verity looked Rune up and down. "You're about the same size. All I'd have to do is get into her room, which is easy enough. And the access coin—"

Alex cut in. "I can get the coin."

Rune and Verity glanced at him. "How?"

"You said every Blood Guard of high rank carries one." Alex spun the slender silver ring on the smallest finger of his left hand. "My brother is a Blood Guard captain, and he has only one weakness that I know of. If you give me a few days, I'll get you his coin."

For as long as she'd known Alex, he'd refused to choose a side. Or rather, refused to choose *Rune's* side over Gideon's.

What had changed his mind?

"Unless you think they'll purge Seraphine before then."

"I have a feeling they'll wait until Liberty Day," said Verity, eyes shadowed in the firelight.

Liberty Day marked two years since the New Dawn—the night revolutionaries overthrew the queens. There was always a citywide festival, with celebrations from dusk till dawn.

"I agree," said Rune. "It's a public event, and the Good Commander always wants as many eyes as he can get on a purging when it's a legendary witch he's slaughtering. With Liberty Day less than a week away, he won't have to wait much longer."

They were deprived of their entertainment tonight, and Liberty Day was the next best opportunity to make a spectacle of her.

Which meant they needed to be ready to set this plan in motion before then.

FORTY-ONE

RUNE

A CRASH OF THUNDER SHOOK the house, cutting their meeting short.

"Perhaps it would be best if you both stayed the night," said Alex as the rain came down harder, roaring against the roof.

Verity shook her head. "I have an exam first thing in the morning." She rose to her feet. "I need to go."

"Then take my carriage," said Rune, noticing how her friend drooped with exhaustion. "It'll keep you dry, at least."

Lightning flashed, and the windows in the conservatory all lit up at once. Rune went to look out. Already, water was pooling on the ground. She hoped the roads weren't too muddy. The last thing she wanted was her friend stuck on the street in the middle of a storm.

After giving instructions to her driver, Rune watched from the front doors of Thornwood Hall as the carriage drove off with Verity inside.

Alex stepped up beside her. "I'll have the servants make up a room for you."

⁂

RUNE HAD STAYED OVERNIGHT at Thornwood dozens of times. But that was before Gideon told her the terrible things that had happened in this house. She suspected there were things he hadn't told her, sparing her the worst of it. Thinking about them made her skin crawl.

As Rune lay in the guest bed, staring at the ceiling she'd slept beneath so many times before, she couldn't help wondering: Which room did Cressida lock their dying sister inside? Which bed did she coerce Gideon into, night after night?

Was it this one?

Rune sat up, her entire body prickling. This was a mistake. She should have gone with Verity. There was no way she'd be able to sleep in this house when all she could think about was Gideon and his sister here, at the mercy of a cruel witch.

Throwing back the covers, she trod barefoot to the windows and pulled back the curtain. The thunder had only grown louder in the hour since Verity left, and the rain hadn't stopped. If the roads were muddy before, they were swampy now. It would be foolish to ride home to Wintersea.

But neither was she going to get any sleep in this house.

The chill of the floor crept up her legs as she walked into the darkened hallway. The servants had turned down the lamps and gone to bed, making the house feel abandoned. She counted doors until she came to Alex's room, then went inside.

When the floorboards creaked beneath her weight, Rune heard him stir in the bed.

"Rune?" Alex sat up. His hair was mussed as he squinted through the dark.

"I couldn't sleep," she said, padding to the bedside. "Do you mind if . . . ?"

Alex shifted, making room for her. Rune crawled into the warm spot where his body had been and burrowed into it. The pillow smelled like him. A warm, masculine smell.

They lay side by side for several moments, silent and still.

"Do you know what happened in this house?" she finally whispered. "To your brother, I mean."

Alex turned toward her in the darkness.

"He never speaks to me about it, but I have my guesses."

He stretched, pulling both hands behind his head. "It was after Tessa's funeral that I noticed something was wrong. Gideon looked . . . like someone had turned out the light inside him. At first, I thought it was grief. We'd lost our mother, father, and baby sister in the span of a few months. Of course he wasn't himself.

"When I left for school, Gideon wrote me a letter every week. But after Tessa died, his letters stopped. And when our parents died, and I came home for the funeral, it was like Gideon couldn't bear to look at me. He threw himself into his tailoring work for Cressida, avoiding me even though I was only home for a short while and didn't know when I'd see him next.

"I went back to school and kept writing him letters, but they now went unanswered. I asked some of our old friends to check on him, but no one had seen or talked to Gideon in months. There was something he wasn't telling me, and I couldn't understand why. We'd always told each other everything.

"I didn't realize what he was doing was saving me. I didn't know it was *him* who needed saving."

Alex swallowed, rubbing a hand over his forehead. Rune kept silent, waiting for him to go on.

"Just before the start of spring term, I received a letter from a friend who'd seen my brother at a boxing match the night before. *Stoned out of his mind* were the words he'd written. *Gonna get himself killed.* That didn't sound like my brother. So the same day, I asked for a leave of absence and boarded a ship home."

"I went to the boxing arena, looking for him. I checked every seat in the building, and when I couldn't find him,

I asked the bartender if he'd seen someone by the name of Gideon Sharpe. The man nodded to the boxing ring. *The witch's whore? He's right there.* It took me a moment to realize what he was saying. That the young man getting beaten in the ring was Gideon. His face was so bruised and bloody, I didn't recognize him.

"*The whore comes here every night,* the man told me. *After she's done with him.* I could see the disgust in his eyes. In all of their eyes. When Gideon got hit for the last time, when he went down and didn't get up, I watched them throw his body into the alleyway with the rest of the trash. As if this were routine. Like he came there every night, drunk or high, and let them beat him half to death. Like he thought he deserved it."

The words pressed down on Rune's chest, heavy as a boulder. She closed her eyes against them.

Sensing it, Alex reached for her beneath the covers. His fingers found hers, knotting them tightly together.

"I didn't know what to do. My older brother was a stranger as he lay unconscious in that alley. Nicolas Creed helped me shake him awake, and we managed to carry him to our parents' old apartment. When Gideon sobered, he was not happy to see me."

"He asked why I wasn't in school. I told him I wasn't going back to school until he was better. Well, he didn't want to hear that. He said I had to go back. That I belonged in Caelis, not here. Not anywhere near him. It might have hurt, if he didn't look so terrified. I remember thinking, *He's driving me away to protect me from something.*"

"From Cressida," said Rune.

He nodded.

Letting go of her fingers, Alex looped his arm snugly around Rune's waist. He pulled her against him so that her back was to his chest, hugging her the way a child might hug a blanket for comfort.

"I started going to the boxing ring at night, waiting for Gideon to show up. He ignored me. He hated that I was bearing witness to his misery and self-hatred. But if there was anything left in him to save, I had to *try*.

"Every night, Nicolas and I picked him up out of the alley and brought him home. When Gideon sobered, he and I would argue, and then he would storm out. Always going back to her. I think he was afraid of what would happen if he didn't."

Alex's arms tightened around Rune.

"One night, Nicolas told me there was only one way to save my brother. He took me to a meeting in his friend's basement. People packed the room, and as Nicolas got up to speak in front of them, I quickly realized what the meeting was: treason. There had been riots for years, but this was different. These men and women were plotting *revolution*. A world where no witches ruled. A society without magic. Only then would we have a world where the poorest didn't have to go without food, or work for little pay in atrocious conditions, or sell themselves into servitude to save their families from starvation—or so they believed. The people there had heartbreaking stories, and reason to be angry. But their hatred, their lust for revenge . . . it scared me.

"When Gideon found out I'd attended the meeting, he was furious. Those caught plotting against the Sister Queens disappeared and never resurfaced, he told me. No one knew what happened to them. I told Gideon if he wanted to keep me safe, he'd have to come to the meetings with me. So, begrudgingly, he did.

"After a few weeks, he started drinking and fighting less. A few weeks after that, he volunteered to lead an armed resistance into the palace alongside Nicolas. I wanted to go with him, but he refused. He saw me as the little brother who needed to be spared from hard things. Not his equal. Not someone he could trust to shoulder his burdens or watch his back.

"We had a huge fight about it and parted on bad terms. As Gideon and Nicolas led the others into the palace, I went to Thornwood Hall with a loaded pistol. I knew Cressida rarely left her private residence. And this was one thing I could do for my brother. A way I could protect *him*, for once."

Alex fell into silence. As if this was as much of the story as he could tell. His arms were still around Rune, her body tucked against his. She could feel his heart drumming against her shoulder blade.

After several minutes, she said: "Don't you find it hard to sleep in this house, knowing what happened here?"

"Why do you think I'm selling it?" he said. "Gideon inherited Thornwood Hall after the fall of the Reign of Witches. He wanted nothing to do with this house, so he gave it to me. He never sets foot here, if he can help it. Not even to visit me." Alex sighed, and his breath rustled her hair. "I've spent two years living here, trying to bring my brother back. But the Gideon I knew and loved . . . he's gone, Rune. He's not coming back."

Seconds later, she felt him trembling behind her. Felt the hot splatter of a tear against her neck. Rune turned toward Alex, but it was too dark to see him.

It broke something in her, feeling him weep. She wrapped her arms around his neck and hugged him close.

At her touch, Alex shook harder.

Rune held on, letting him cry himself to sleep in her arms. When the thunder quieted and the rain stopped, the moon came out from behind the clouds, spilling silvery light across the bed. Rune watched her sleeping friend, tempted to stay—for his sake.

But she couldn't. Not in this house.

When she was sure Alex slept deeply and there was no danger of waking him, she carefully untangled herself from his arms. With the storm over, she quickly dressed, borrowed a cloak and a horse, and rode back to Wintersea before the sun rose.

FORTY-TWO

GIDEON

WE'LL REINSTATE A CURFEW," said Nicolas Creed, rising from his desk. "Put more Blood Guard soldiers on the streets. Recommence the raids and interrogate anyone who so much as *seems* suspicious, even if you have no proof. We must ensure people understand the severity of this situation. If they're fearful enough, they'll comply."

Gideon, who'd just delivered his report on Cressida, glanced up into the Good Commander's face. "Normally I'd agree, sir."

Nicolas raised a brow. "You don't?"

"The curfews and raids were unpopular during the Red Peace. Not only will these measures make witch sympathizers more supportive of Cressida's cause, they may turn more citizens against us. People don't like their rights infringed upon, sir."

Nicolas stepped out from behind his desk. For a moment, Gideon noticed how much the man had aged. The lines creasing his mentor's face weren't there two years ago; nor was the gray streaking his hair.

"Walk with me? I have a Tribunal meeting in a few minutes."

Gideon nodded, and fell in line beside him, remembering the Nicolas from two years ago: someone who'd gotten into the ring with Gideon long after the boxing club closed and stayed there until dawn, never letting him quit. Believing in him when he couldn't believe in himself.

Back then, Cressida had broken Gideon so completely, there was nothing good left. He was at the bottom of a well, with no way to climb out. And though Nicolas tried again and again to lower a rope, it never seemed long enough.

After a particularly bad night, when Gideon refused to get up from the floor of the ring, Nicolas got down next to him.

I'm not going to give up. Nicolas's eyes shone as they stared into Gideon's. *I'm not going to walk away. I'm going to stay right here for as long as it takes. Do you hear me?*

Why? he asked.

Nicolas Creed was a stranger. He didn't have to care about some dead tailor's son.

Get up and find out.

Gideon didn't believe he was worth saving—he was too far gone for that. But as he stared back at Nicolas, he wondered if it was possible to believe in *this* man. To trust whatever Nicolas saw when he peered beyond the broken mess other people couldn't see past as they looked at Gideon.

Maybe he could replace the voice in his head—the one that said he was *worthless, disgusting, better off dead*—with Nicolas's voice.

So that's what he did.

He used this man's belief in him like a crutch. It took months. But, little by little, Nicolas's faith in Gideon became indistinct from his own. Soon, Gideon stopped letting his opponents beat him into oblivion. He started getting back up and hitting back harder and better. He started believing that *just maybe* there was something worth fighting for.

"I take your point about infringing on their liberties," said

Nicolas, breaking through Gideon's thoughts as they strode through the west wing of the palace, down its gaslit halls, and toward the throne room. Soldiers strode ahead and behind them, guarding the Commander. "A good leader cares deeply about those he's responsible for. Again and again, you've shown yourself to be that kind of leader."

Surprised by the praise, Gideon's chest swelled.

"Sadly, though, people don't always know what's best for them. Sometimes they need us to step in and protect them from themselves."

Gideon couldn't exactly disagree with this. If Nicolas hadn't intervened in his own life two years ago, he'd still be lying on the floor of the boxing ring wishing he were dead.

Maybe he'd even *be* dead.

"A good leader is brave enough to make the hard choices others don't want to make," continued Nicolas. "He does it for the sake of the good. He does it to protect the innocent. This is his duty."

"I agree."

But Gideon also remembered Rune allowing Penitents to use her footpaths. In a choice between mercy and punishment, Rune chose mercy. What if Gideon could do the same? Perhaps there was a way to find and arrest Cressida without violating the rights of everyday citizens. Without making them live in fear of the Blood Guard.

Heading for the Commons, where the Tribunal met, Nicolas exited the hall and entered the throne room.

Gideon followed him in.

The throne room was darker than the lamplit halls, and their footsteps boomed through the empty space. Night darkened the stained-glass windows. The gilded pillars cast long shadows over the agate floors.

Three black thrones loomed in the distance. At the sight of them, a chill gripped the back of Gideon's neck, squeezing like an icy hand.

That they were empty should have relieved him. The sight should have felt like a triumph over evil. Instead, it felt more like an absence longing to be filled. As if this room—those thrones—were waiting for their queens to return.

Gideon wanted to quicken his pace, to put the feeling behind him. But Nicolas stopped before the three seats of power, staring directly at them.

"The curfews, the raids, the interrogations—these are emergency measures. In an emergency, individual rights must sometimes be set aside until the danger has passed. You need to balance both things on the scales, Gideon: on one side is the temporary violation of rights to keep people safe; on the other is the very permanent possibility that Cressida Roseblood retakes her throne and exacts her revenge on us all."

He turned to face Gideon. "Which is worse, in the long run?"

It wasn't a question. Of course Cressida was worse.

Gideon studied his mentor. They were roughly the same height, and though Nicolas had a leaner build than Gideon, he was muscular. A fighter. Gideon wasn't sure who would win in a boxing match these days.

Nicolas gripped Gideon's shoulder. "I'm proud of the man you've become, and I trust your judgment. The choice is yours to make. Just remember: a great leader weighs the consequences of every decision, and must bear the weight of those consequences. So ask yourself: which consequences can you live with?"

Letting go, Nicolas rolled his shoulders as he glanced back at the thrones. As if the same icy hand gripped him, too, and he wanted to shake it off.

"Think it through," he said, turning to leave. "Then let me know your decision."

Gideon stared at the empty thrones.

They were a stark reminder of all he had fought for. If he didn't act swiftly, if he couldn't find Cressida and put down her uprising before it grew wings, he would lose everything that mattered: his freedom, along with his ability to protect the vulnerable.

People would suffer worse than before, because Cressida was a vengeful creature, and her vengeance on the Republic would be ruthless. Laila and Harrow. Alex. Rune. They were all at risk.

Rune isn't bound by the same duty I am, he thought, remembering her kindness to the Penitents. *She can afford to show mercy.*

Gideon couldn't. Gideon needed to keep people safe from evil. He had to stop Cressida at all costs.

"I've already made my decision," he called out to Nicolas, who was halfway across the room. The Good Commander turned back. "We'll reinstate the curfew, and the raids. And we'll triple the Blood Guard presence on the streets."

Now was not the time for mercy.

AFTER BRINGING HIS NEW orders to Blood Guard headquarters, Gideon set out for Old Town. It was early evening when he arrived home and found a telegram slipped under his door. Thinking it was from Rune, he picked it up and tore it open.

But it was from Thornwood Hall.

```
GIDEON SHARPE
113 PRUDENCE ST, OLD TOWN

BROTHER: I LEAVE FOR CAELIS AT THE END OF
THE WEEK TO RESUME MY STUDIES. I'M SELLING
```

MY ESTATE AND WILL BE HOSTING A SMALL GOOD-
BYE PARTY TONIGHT. NOTHING FANCY. JUST CARDS
AMONG A FEW FRIENDS. I WOULD DEARLY LOVE FOR
YOU TO JOIN US.

                                    ALEX

It had been two years since Gideon had set foot in Thorn-
wood Hall, but his nightmares frequently brought him back.
He hated that house and the memories it held. The thought of
Alex selling it was a relief.

But Caelis was across the Barrow Strait. Gideon had little
reason to travel to the mainland, and he couldn't afford to take
time off—especially with Cressida on the prowl. When would
he ever see his brother?

Gideon rubbed his jaw, remembering the punch Alex had
thrown in the boxing ring.

If Alex was leaving, Gideon owed it to him to face his demons and go to this party. To patch things up between them as
much as he could. Especially if they might never see each other
again.

Most important of all: Alex needed to know that Cressida
was alive. That he *hadn't* killed her. He would have to watch his
back going forward.

Gideon grabbed his coat.

Thornwood Hall was only a house. And he was sick of cowering.

FORTY-THREE

GIDEON

G IDEON STOOD IN THE rain, staring at the arched doors flanked by two roaring lions made of stone. The rain soaked his hair and dampened his clothes, making him colder by the second. But a deeper cold lived in his bones.

He couldn't make his legs move. Couldn't order his body to carry him into the house.

I was wrong.

I can't do this.

He was about to turn around and leave, already planning the apologetic telegram he would send Alex tomorrow, when Rune's words seeped in through the chill. Like the first spring day after a harsh winter.

You are not the things that happened to you, Gideon.

Her voice summoned something from beneath the nightmares. Something stronger than the pull of the past. It was a kick of adrenaline, a shot of courage.

Gideon drew in a deep breath and walked into the damned house.

The same sapphire carpets lined the floor. The same floral wallpaper adorned the walls. The air still smelled faintly of Cress's magic, too. Like blood and roses. The scent was stale and cloying.

As Alex's manservant escorted him through the halls of Thornwood, Gideon felt like he was walking backward in time. His muscles tensed as scenes from the past rose like mist before his eyes. But all he had to do was think of Rune, and the awful things would fade.

When they arrived at the parlor, Gideon made his way to the round table near the fire, where half a dozen young men sat playing cards, coins piled in the middle. He saw Noah Creed and Bart Wentholt and several other familiar faces.

His brother's back was to him.

"Gideon Sharpe!" Bart's red hair shone in the firelight as he motioned Gideon over to an empty chair. "What exceptional timing. Alex, deal him in."

Gideon sat and he shrugged off his coat. Across the table, Alex smiled brightly as he shuffled and counted out cards, apparently happy to see him. Leaning back in his chair, Gideon couldn't help but notice all the ways he admired his little brother.

Alex was appropriately social, for one thing. He had friends whom he invited over, and whose invitations he accepted. He knew how to hold polite conversations with all sorts of people. He never growled or glared or got into fights . . . except for that one time he punched Gideon in the ring—but that had been Gideon's fault.

Alex dressed and danced well. He used the correct utensil for each course of a meal, served the kinds of wines that impressed his guests, and knew the meaning of devotion. Even upon dropping out of school—something Gideon wished he'd fought harder to prevent—Alex had never stopped practicing his music.

After the revolution, it was Alex who stayed by Gideon for weeks, helping him fight off his laudanum addiction. Alex didn't leave Gideon's side until he no longer shook with the cravings.

Gideon didn't know what he would do without his little brother.

If Rune Winters was truly in the market for a husband, she could do no better than Alexander Sharpe.

That thought put a sour taste in his mouth.

Before swallowing it down, he let himself wonder: *What if Alex weren't in love with her? Would I stop pretending, and court her in truth?*

For a second, he let himself imagine it. He'd have to attend her parties. Learn how to dance to her songs. Spend less time in Old Town, and more time at Wintersea.

He could do that. Those were small prices to pay for the luxury of going on long walks in the woods with her. Or the privilege of arguing with her. Or the rare gift of seeing that wild girl she kept hidden beneath the surface.

It doesn't matter. His knuckles bunched. *Because it will only ever be pretend—or not at all.*

"Gideon?" Bart slid three copper coins toward the center of the table. "You in?"

Torn out of his fantasy, Gideon nodded.

"I'm in." He pulled a money pouch from the pocket of his coat, grabbed three copper coins, and threw them into the center of the table.

As Alex dealt the cards, Gideon noticed a pale line of untanned skin at the base of his smallest finger, where a ring usually rested.

Our mother's ring, he remembered. Gideon had given it to Alex after their parents' funeral.

Something Harrow had said flashed in his mind.

An hour before it set sail, there was last-minute cargo brought on board: two barrels of wine delivered by an aristo.

The man had worn a ring on his smallest finger.

Plain and thin. Silver, maybe. A poor man's wedding band.

Gideon watched the cards move around the table, dealt by his brother's hand. Trying to remember what their mother's ring looked like.

He immediately caught himself.

Alex, abetting a criminal witch? After witches tore our family apart?

It was unthinkable. Alex wasn't capable of subterfuge. He knew how badly Gideon wanted to catch the Crimson Moth.

Alex would never sabotage me.

"Gideon? It's your turn."

He looked to find Noah nodding to the cards facedown beneath Gideon's hands. When he glanced around the table, he found everyone waiting for him.

Gideon quickly picked out a straight and threw it down.

"You sent a tidal wave through the entire aristocracy the other week," said Noah, putting down a flush and beating out Gideon.

"Did I? When?"

"When you showed up at Rune Winters' after-party."

"Ah," said Gideon, laying down two pairs when his turn came back around. "Well, aristos aren't difficult to shock. Just use the wrong spoon at dinner. Or wear a dress out of season."

Noah smiled, but his eyes were like ice chips. Of the two Creed siblings, Gideon had always preferred Laila, who kept her aggression like she kept her gun—out in the open, where he could see it. Noah was . . . less straightforward.

"Truly, though. What's come over you? Last week, it was Rune's afterparty. Tonight, you're here playing cards. Next thing we know, you'll be hosting your own charity ball."

"If I do," said Gideon, drawing more cards to replace the ones he'd laid down, "you'll be the first person I invite."

Noah smiled thinly. "Don't you have a reputation to uphold—the New Republic's most unavailable bachelor?"

"Gideon," interrupted Alex, as if sensing the storm brewing and needing to quell it. This was why it was always better for Gideon to stay home. "Tell us what happened last night, at the Luminaries Dinner. Is it true what the papers are saying?"

"Yes, tell us everything." A young man whose name Gideon didn't know leaned across the table, his eyes gleaming in the firelight. "Was there really a witch attack *inside* the palace?"

He nodded. "It's true."

"Do you have any leads?" asked his brother, watching Bart discard.

"Possibly. We're still investigating."

Alex laid his cards last—four of a kind. Upon seeing them, everyone else threw down their own in defeat.

"Rune seemed shaken by it," said Alex, pulling the winnings toward him while Noah gathered everyone's cards and shuffled. The young men around him placed new bets and threw more coins into the center.

When did you see Rune? Gideon wondered, watching his brother. It had barely been twenty-four hours since the event.

"The *New Herald* reported that Citizen Winters is only alive because of you," said the young man whose name Gideon didn't remember. "Said you ran straight into the spellfire and carried her out."

Gideon preferred not to relive the moment when Rune had disappeared inside the fire. The fear of not getting to her in time still hummed a little too loud in his blood.

"I hunt witches for a living," he said, trying to shrug it off. "I'm no stranger to their magic."

"Was it the Crimson Moth?"

They weren't going to stop poking at this until he surrendered. So Gideon yielded, giving them a full account of the night before. As Alex's friends soaked up the story like sponges, more cards were laid and the coins in Gideon's pouch slowly disappeared.

He had never been good at gambling.

"Well, *I* for one am glad we have people like Gideon doing the dirty work for us." This came from Bart as he won the current round with a full house. "Can you imagine it? Putting yourself in that kind of danger *every day*?" He shuddered. "No wonder the girls all fancy him."

Gideon almost laughed, wondering what Harrow or Laila would say to that.

"Speaking of girls who fancy Gideon," said Noah, sipping his drink. "How *is* Miss Winters? Does she live up to her reputation?"

If Gideon had hackles, Noah's tone would have raised them.

"I'm sure I don't know what you mean," he said, staring hard at his cards but not seeing any of them.

The last thing he wanted was to get into it with the Good Commander's son. So he let Noah's comments go.

"You know exactly what I mean," said Noah, sensing Gideon's restraint and wanting to test its limits. "Rune Winters is a merciless flirt. She has a new suitor every week."

Unable to help himself, Gideon rose to the bait. Just an inch. "If I didn't know better, I'd say you sound jealous."

"Jealous?" Noah scoffed. "What's there to be jealous of? If the rumors are true, she's as loose as a whore."

Before Gideon was halfway out of his seat, a fist slammed against the table, making them all jump.

Gideon looked up, his body buzzing with anger. Across the table, Alex stared down Noah the way a lion might stare down a hyena. "Insult her again, and I'll show you the door."

Noah scowled. "It was a joke, Alex."

"Joke or not, I won't tolerate disrespect toward Rune."

Noah set down his cards, his knuckles bunching. The entire table went quiet as the two boys continued their glaring game.

"Well, this has been fun." Gideon pushed his chair back from the table. He needed to get out of here before he accidentally put his fist through Noah's face. "But I'm out of funds."

Not wanting to spark panic among the gentlemen here, he decided to leave a message with Alex's manservant, warning him about Cressida's return.

"One more round," said Alex.

Gideon tipped his money pouch upside down to show he wasn't lying.

"Surely you have something else you can bet with."

"I once bet my silk handkerchief," offered Bart. Which might have been helpful, if Gideon owned a silk handkerchief.

He was about to say as much when Alex pressed him. "Empty your pockets."

Gideon raised his eyebrows but did as his brother requested. Reaching into both trouser pockets, he pulled out their contents: a folding knife; a crumpled message from Harrow about their meeting tomorrow night; and his prison access coin for bringing witches past the seventh gate.

"That," said Alex, pointing to the coin, "will do."

Gideon shook his head. "It's not currency." Not the kind that was valuable to these gentlemen. "It's worthless to you."

"It's silver, isn't it? Silver can be melted down."

"I need it to enter the prison," said Gideon, already returning everything to his pockets.

"You can get a new one, can't you? Besides, don't the prison staff know who you are by now?"

"Sure. Except—"

"Just one more round," said Alex. As if he truly wanted his brother to stay. "For me."

Gideon remembered their fight in the boxing ring. He remembered daring Rune to strip down naked and swim in the sea with him, even though he knew how Alex adored her. He remembered kissing her in the garden, his mouth and hands insistent. Then kissing her *again* in that alley.

The shame of it scorched him.

Gideon sat.

"One more game," he said, tossing the prison coin into the pile of money in the center of the table. "And *then* I'm out."

Fifteen minutes later, he lost that round, too. And with it, his prison clearance.

"I'll walk you out," said Alex, tossing the coin once and depositing it into his pocket.

IT WAS RAINING LIGHTLY by the time they left the parlor. Drops speckled the windows and plinked against the roof as the brothers strode side by side toward the front hall.

"There's something you should know," said Gideon, trying to ignore the lingering scent of roses in this hallway. "But until I have more information, I need you to keep it between us."

Alex shot him a look. "All right."

"Cressida Roseblood was at the Luminaries Dinner. It was her spell that came for Rune."

Alex's stride halted. Slowing, Gideon turned to find the color seeping from Alex's face, turning his skin white as parchment.

"You're certain?"

"We found her casting signature under a table."

"Does Rune know?"

Gideon shook his head. "I haven't told her yet."

"Shouldn't you? If Cressida—"

"I believe Rune is aware of the danger she's in, but yes: she should know. I haven't had the chance to—"

"I'll tell her." Alex ran long fingers through his hair, walking on, like he was still trying to make sense of what Gideon was saying. "I'll ride to Wintersea first thing in the morning."

"Fine," said Gideon.

As they arrived at the entrance to Thornwood, Alex pulled open the front doors while Gideon shrugged on his coat. Rain dripped from the lintel and splashed across the slabs of stone. The sun had set a long time ago, and darkness cloaked the woods beyond the doors.

A question was burning inside Gideon. Before he stepped out into the rain, he turned to ask it. "Alex? Is there any chance Cressida wasn't dead after you shot her?"

Alex stared at him. "I shot her three times."

Gideon nodded. Alex hated revisiting that night. His brother didn't have a violent urge in his body. It would have gone against everything he stood for to take a girl's life. He'd done it for Gideon's sake.

The bodies of all three sister queens had gone missing the next morning. Defiled, Gideon had always suspected. But if Cressida was truly alive, what had happened in her bedchamber that night? Had Alex unknowingly not finished the job, or was some dark magic at play? There were stories of witches in the past powerful enough to raise the dead, but Gideon had always assumed those were tales witches used to frighten people into obedience.

He wondered now if they were true.

"Never mind." He put a reassuring hand on his brother's shoulder. "It might not be her. It could be another witch impersonating Cressida. Either way, we'll catch her. And this time, I'll finish the job myself."

Alex only nodded, saying nothing. Feeling like he'd ruined his brother's night, Gideon dropped his hand and changed the subject.

"When do you leave for Caelis?"

"Four days from now."

So soon? thought Gideon, swallowing the lump in his throat.

"Will you come to see me off?"

"Of course." Gideon turned to leave, thought better of it, then pulled his little brother into a tight hug. "I'll miss you."

As hard as it was to say goodbye to Alex, there was something that was going to be a lot harder.

If Alex was leaving for good in a matter of days, and if Gideon had truly decided Rune wasn't a witch, now was the time to step aside. That way, his brother could make his feelings clear to her before he left.

It was the only decent thing to do. And it would make amends for his previous betrayal.

The next time I see her, thought Gideon, stepping miserably into the rain, *I'll tell her it's over between us.*

FORTY-FOUR

RUNE

A KNOCK ON THE FALSE wall broke Rune's con-
centration. She glanced up from the *Earth Sunderer*
spell, which lay open in front of her, and found Alex standing
a few feet from her desk. He wore a collared white shirt and
pinstripe trousers. His hair shone like spun gold.

"Am I interrupting?"

She shut the spell book. "Oh. No. Of course not." Glancing
down, she found herself still in her nightgown, and blushed.
"I . . . wasn't expecting any visitors this morning."

He stepped further into the room, leaving the passageway
open. Alex was always forgetting to shut it behind him. If anyone wandered into her bedroom and saw the wall opened, and
the spell books beyond . . . Rune would be finished.

Rising from the desk, she went to close it.

"I brought you something," he said as the wall snicked shut
beneath her hands.

When Rune turned to face him, he pressed a silver coin into
her palm. It was nearly as wide as the length of her thumb, and
still warm from his hand. A woman's image was imprinted on
the silver.

Fortitude.

The Ancient's hair was braided over one shoulder as she held her chin high, and across her chest was a bandolier.

"Gideon's access coin," Rune murmured, not believing it. "You stole it?"

"Won it," he said. "In a game of cards."

Rune marveled at the coin, then glanced up. "You hate pitting yourself against your brother."

"Actually." He held her gaze. "I no longer mind so much."

He was choosing her, she realized. This boy who saw exactly who she was—*what* she was—and didn't care. Or rather: cared so much, he wanted to give her back what the revolution had taken.

In Caelis, we'll go to the opera house every day of the week. Where they show real operas, not that propaganda you despise.

Again, Rune let herself imagine it: a life far away from the Republic. No more worrying about who was watching or listening. No more pretending to be something she wasn't.

Rune would be free.

But what kind of person would that make her? How could she live a safe, comfortable life full of good, beautiful things *knowing* the Blood Guard was hunting down witches? Knowing she could stop it—but didn't?

Rune wouldn't be able to live with herself.

"There's something else," he said, turning away and letting out a rough sigh.

Rune studied him. "What's wrong?"

"Cressida Roseblood is alive."

Rune frowned, certain she'd misheard him. "What?"

Alex turned briefly back to her. "The fire that almost killed you the other night? It was Cressida's spell, not Seraphine's. Gideon found her signature after the fire."

"That can't be true," said Rune, shaking her head. "Cressida's dead."

Alex strode to the window, his footsteps echoing on the floorboards. At the pane, he stopped and looked out.

"She couldn't have been at the Luminaries Dinner," Rune said, suddenly needing him to agree with her. "Because you killed her."

He was silent for a long time. The silence turned the room cold.

"You killed her," she said again, forceful this time. "*Right*, Alex?"

"That's the other thing I came to tell you. I never finished my story the other night." He stared out the window. "On the eve of the New Dawn, while my brother was murdering her sisters, I *did* go to Thornwood Hall to kill Cressida. I found her asleep in her bedroom. She woke to the barrel of my pistol pressed against her head." He drew in a ragged breath. "I told her to get out of the bed, and she fell to her knees on the floor, begging me to spare her life. She told me she loved my brother, and that was why she did the things she did—because Gideon belonged to her."

Rune heard the anger in his voice as he spoke the words.

"Before that moment, I'd never wanted to hurt anything in my whole life. But Rune: I wanted to hurt *her*. I wanted to squeeze the air out of her hateful lungs and watch her writhe. I had one of the most powerful witches in the world on her knees at my feet, with my gun pressed to her forehead. The girl who'd killed my little sister and damaged my older brother beyond repair. All I had to do was pull the trigger. And I relished it."

"And that's when you shot her," said Rune, gripping the edge of her desk, the color leaching from her knuckles. *Say it. Tell me you shot her.*

He shook his head, staring out the window as if staring into the past.

"It was like there were two of me: the Alex who wanted to destroy her, and the Alex who *knew* dead witches weren't the answer. Deep down, I didn't believe the bloodshed and vengeance my brother craved would bring about a better world. Murdering them would make us no better than them. And that was what scared me: that despite my convictions, it could be so easy to give in to the bloodlust.

"So I raised my gun to the roof and shot three rounds. And then I told her to run. I told her if I ever saw her, if she ever touched Gideon again, I'd make her wish she was dead. I watched her disappear into the woods behind Thornwood Hall."

Rune suddenly felt light-headed. Still gripping the desk, she lowered herself into the chair.

"You lied," she whispered, feeling the world crumble in on her.

If Alex had told her this a few weeks ago, before she'd known what monsters Cressida and her sisters truly were, she would have adored him for it. A girl as powerful as the youngest Roseblood queen could save so many more witches from the purge than the Crimson Moth ever could. This alone should have made Rune happy. Or at least relieved.

But now . . .

Rune thought of the brand on Gideon's chest. Of the things Cressida did to him. If the witch queen was alive, Gideon was in terrible danger.

It frightened her.

It *angered* her.

Her fists trembled. "Why would you *lie*?"

"I thought if Gideon believed Cressida was dead, he might move on. Maybe even heal."

A tremor was building deep within Rune, shaking every-thing loose. She looked up at her oldest friend, but it was as if a fog had descended, and she could no longer see him clearly through the gray.

Alex turned from the window and strode towards the hidden door. "I need to tell Gideon the truth. I should do it now, before I lose my nerve."

"No," she said, rising from her chair. She might be disap-pointed in Alex, but she wasn't going to let him admit to sparing Cressida's life. "You'll be convicted of sympathizing with witches."

He stopped to look down at her. Quietly, and a little sadly, he said, "I do sympathize with witches."

The words softened her. This was *Alex*, after all. The boy who, upon learning she was a witch, had drawn Rune a warm bath to ease her cramps instead of handing her over to be killed. Who else would have done that?

No one.

"If you tell the truth, they'll kill you." Rune reached for his arm, keeping him with her. "You can't speak a word of this to anyone. Especially not Gideon."

Gideon would be the first to hand him over.

Alex wouldn't look at her, ashamed of the lie. Ashamed of himself and the mercy he'd shown.

Rune wanted to stay angry at him, and yet she knew the qual-ities that made him spare Cressida were the same ones that made him spare *her*. His gentleness and compassion; his firm refusal to take part in cruelty; his willingness to risk his life in order to do what was right . . . These things allowed him to see who Rune was, not what she was, and love her despite the danger.

"Sparing the life of someone you hate doesn't make you weak," she said, perhaps more to herself than to Alex. "It makes you better than the rest of us."

It was the lie that was wrong.

She cupped his jaw in her hands and tilted his face to hers, holding his gaze. "If anything happened to you . . ." She shut her eyes against the thought of it. "*Please,* Alex. Promise me you won't tell a soul."

His breath trembled out of him. Finally, he said: "I promise."

FORTY-FIVE

GIDEON

GIDEON PRESSED HIS BACK to the wall, breathing in the smell of oiled metal and ink. He drew his pistol and glanced at Laila, who mirrored him on the other side of this door, her scarlet uniform a pop of color in the darkness.

At Gideon's request, the Ministry of Public Safety had instituted a curfew, decreeing a temporary postponement of citizens' rights and allowing the Blood Guard to conduct raids wherever a casting signature had been found—or was suspected to be found.

It was Harrow who'd tipped Gideon off to this print shop. Three casting signatures were seen in one of its storerooms last week. The tip had come from one of the shopworkers, and as a result, Harrow had several spies watching the shop. She'd notified him less than an hour ago that seven people had entered after hours, when no one should have been there, and they hadn't come out yet.

On my count, Laila mouthed, holding up three fingers. A printing press loomed at the bottom of the stairs behind her, where the darkness hid the rest of their raiding squad.

Three.

Two.

One.

They pushed off the wall. While Laila covered for him, Gideon kicked the door with all of his might.

It burst open.

They entered the shop's uppermost room, their guns held high, while the rest of their raiding squad rushed in behind them. From the center, back-to-back, Gideon and Laila scanned the room, turning in a circle, their pistols pointed at empty space.

"There's no one here."

Dozens of freshly lit candles ringed the perimeter. Inside the circle of flames, where Gideon and Laila stood, someone had drawn symbols in blood on the floor.

Gideon looked from the bloody marks to the rafters, which were also empty. The door he'd just kicked in was the only way out. So where were they?

He lowered his pistol, eyeing the shadows cast by the flickering flames. "Where the fuck did they go?"

"Maybe they're not gone," said Laila, glancing at him.

Her words cast a chill over the room.

Stepping into the circle of flames, he walked toward the center, where a white casting signature glimmered in the air. Strange, how much could change in so little time. Because as Gideon approached, he was hoping for a different one.

This signature was neither crimson, nor moth shaped. Its thorns and petals made Gideon's blood run cold.

"Gideon?"

He glanced at the three guards still standing beyond the flames, as if afraid to step inside the circle. Behind them, Laila was staring at something over Gideon's head.

"I know where they went."

Turning away from Cressida's signature, he looked to where Laila's attention was focused: the long horizontal windows roughly ten feet up the wall. One of them was open.

"You three." He nodded to the soldiers outside the circle. "Check the alleys." Moving for the window, he called to Laila: "Give me a leg up?"

She strode over and cupped her hands. As he stepped into them, Laila pushed him upward. Gideon grabbed the frame of the open window and pulled himself into it. Reaching down, he grabbed Laila's outstretched hand and hauled her up beside him.

Gideon climbed onto the slanted roof first. But the fog was so thick, he could only see a few feet in front of him.

The print shop was part of several blocks of continuous row houses. This, combined with the fog cover, gave Cressida and any witches with her ease of movement tonight. They could be halfway across the city by now.

"We'll cover more ground if we split up," said Laila, half crouching beside him. Her eyes narrowed, scanning the fog. "Wait . . . there's something there!"

"Where?"

Laila took off, scrambling up the sloped roof and disappearing into the gray, her gun drawn.

"Laila, wait . . ." Gideon followed her to the roofline. One misstep would send him sliding down the sloped shingles on either side.

Three quick pistol shots rang out from several yards ahead.

Fuck fuck fuck . . .

He picked up speed, running across the roofline, listening for the next shot. None came. When a silhouetted form appeared at the end of the row house roof, he drew his gun.

"Don't move!"

The silhouette jumped, disappearing into the gray.

Gideon reached the edge of the roof but saw no sign of Laila. It was too far to jump from one length of row houses to the next, so Gideon dropped to the fire escape instead and vaulted down the steps.

Back on the ground, the fog thickened, obscuring the alley.

Another shot rang out, closer this time.

He headed toward it. "Laila!"

"I'm here," she said, jogging into view. "I don't think I hit them . . . but I saw them." She bent over, hands on her knees, catching her breath. "They ran west."

"How many?"

"Three, I think."

Gideon glanced in the direction Laila had come from, trying to see. But the fog cloaked everything. It gave him a bad feeling.

"I think we should head back."

"What? No. I almost had her!"

He shook his head. Something felt wrong about this whole situation. "We're going back."

Laila looked like she was going to refuse, but Gideon out-ranked her. So she fell silently into step beside him and they headed for the main street, the glow of the streetlamps lighting their way.

"I almost had her," she said again.

When a sound came from behind them—like the swish of a cloak, or a careful footstep—the back of Gideon's neck prickled. Laila tensed, hearing it too.

He glanced at her, his hand hovering close to his holstered pistol. Catching his gaze, she nodded. They turned as one, their guns raised to the fog, gazes flicking from one side of the street to the other.

"Show yourself," growled Laila.

Movement in the shadows made the blood drum in Gideon's ears. At the sound of another footstep, he pressed the trigger as far as it would go before firing.

A dark form solidified against the gray, stepping out of the fog. The figure pushed back their hood, revealing a familiar face. "Jumpy much?"

"Harrow," they said in unison.

Gideon loosed a breath and lowered his weapon.

"You scared the shit out of us."

Harrow's hair was in its usual topknot, putting her missing ear on display. "I thought I'd see if you needed any backup."

An unnerving thought occurred to Gideon.

The witches had disappeared into the fog, while Harrow had appeared out of it. He thought of Cressida, hiding in plain sight. Gideon was well acquainted with the kinds of tricks and deceptions witches were capable of.

Could Harrow be Cressida in disguise?

He immediately shook off the thought. *Impossible.* The amount of magic it would take to alter her appearance so drastically . . .

Gideon paused, thinking it through.

It would be possible for a witch as powerful as Cressida, but it would drain her considerably.

And I'd be able to smell the stench of magic on her.

Harrow smelled like . . . well, *Harrow.*

Normal. Not a witch.

For two years, he'd been trying to hunt down and unmask the Crimson Moth. But what if he'd been wasting his time? What if, all along, it was Cressida who was the true threat and walking amongst them? At the thought, bile rose, burning in his throat. He swallowed thickly.

"Seems like your raid was unsuccessful," said Harrow, frowning, as they returned to the entrance of the print shop.

"They must have heard us enter the building."

Up ahead, the three soldiers he'd sent into the alley were returning empty-handed. Leaving Harrow and Gideon, Laila went to grill the soldiers on what they'd seen. Gideon should send one of them to arrest the print shop owner and bring him to headquarters for questioning. Before the man fled.

Gideon stared through the windows of the print shop ahead. The lights were on, and he saw soldiers searching the premises. There might not be witches within, but there could be some clue as to what they'd been meeting about.

When Laila was out of earshot, Harrow reached for Gideon's arm, stopping him from entering the shop. "How did things go with Rune? Did you get what you needed from her?"

Gideon winced. This was not a conversation he wanted to have right now.

"I changed my mind."

Harrow slit her eyes. "What?"

"About Rune. It makes no sense. If she was secretly saving witches, why would Cressida have tried to kill her the other night? The simplest explanation is that we were wrong. She isn't a witch."

And I can't sleep with the girl my brother is in love with.

"Maybe," she said. "Or maybe not."

"Harrow—"

"Hear me out." She held up a slim hand. "The Crimson Moth doesn't kill witches; she saves them, right?"

He crossed his arms, waiting for her point.

"The other night, the Good Commander gave her no choice but to kill Seraphine when he called Rune to the platform and handed her a purging knife. If Rune is the Moth, she would never purge another witch, and it was a matter of seconds before everyone watching realized. Cressida's spell could have just as easily been a diversion. It interrupted the purging, preventing Rune from revealing herself while also making her look like a target. The two are just as likely to be in league with each other."

Gideon frowned, not liking how much sense this made.

"Or," he argued, "Rune isn't a witch, and Cressida interceded to stop her from killing Seraphine."

"But you can't know for certain which it is, can you? Not until you sleep with Rune and find her scars."

The words planted a seed of doubt inside Gideon. He didn't want it there. He wanted to dig it up and stomp on it.

"Catching the Crimson Moth is no longer the priority," he told her. "We need to find Cressida and put a stop to whatever she's planning."

"Why are you suddenly so reluctant to see this through?" said Harrow, her gaze searching him. "If Rune is the Moth, and the Moth is in league with Cressida, catching the former will help you put a stop to the latter."

That seed of doubt sprouted into a full-fledged weed, spreading through him, choking out his defenses. Harrow's logic was sound, and it worried Gideon that he'd considered none of this.

Suddenly, Harrow barked a laugh.

"Oh, Comrade. Tell me you didn't." Gideon glanced over and found her eyes crinkling. "*This* is a twist I didn't expect!"

"What are you on about?" He turned back toward the print shop, heading for the door.

"You went and fell in love with that pretty little socialite."

Gideon flinched, halting at the shop entrance.

Harrow stepped lightly around him, smirking as she entered the shop. "Why else would you give up so easily?"

Gideon's hands fisted.

What if she was right? What if this game he'd been playing with Rune—and the feelings she evoked in him—had compromised his ability to think? He begrudgingly followed Harrow inside, stepping around the soldiers ransacking the print shop, searching boxes and cabinets and closets.

"It's equally possible that we suspect the wrong girl," said Gideon, keeping his voice down. "Rune might not be a witch."

A mocking smile twisted her mouth. "If she's not a witch, how did she melt your frozen heart?"

"Who has a frozen heart?" Laila asked, polishing her pistol as she rejoined them.

"No one," said Gideon, moving up the stairs.

Harrow smirked harder.

Both Laila and Harrow followed him into the back room, where the ring of candles burned and Cressida's signature still glimmered in the air.

"Who are we talking about?" he heard Laila ask.

"*Focus,*" snapped Gideon. "Cressida Roseblood is alive and hatching some plot. We need to know how many witches she's gathering at these meetings and what, exactly, they're about."

He stepped into the circle, crouching down to study the spellmarks drawn in blood on the floorboards, wishing he could decipher them. It was times like this where he wondered if they'd been too hasty, burning all the spell books. It would be useful to have them as a reference.

Gideon could trace these marks and bring them to Seraphine Oakes, who was still in custody. She would know what they were, but was unlikely to be cooperative.

"If I were a vengeful witch planning retribution," said Harrow, crouching down next to him, touching the marks with her fingers, "I would make my move on Liberty Day."

"I second that," said Laila, walking around the room, looking for anything they might have missed the first time. "We should at least—"

Beside Gideon, Harrow's head snapped up. "Do you smell that?"

"Smell what?" asked Laila.

Gideon sniffed the air. *Blood and roses.*

"It smells like . . ."

"Magic," said Gideon, rising to his feet. Fear snaked through his insides. "They're still here."

He looked to the rafters, but the beams were empty. Harrow rose to her feet beside him. The smell was growing stronger by the second, making Gideon queasy.

"We need to find the source," said Harrow, moving for the door.

Gideon's spine tingled. That bad feeling was back. Something was wrong. The fog. The empty room. The freshly lit candles, as if the meeting hadn't even started yet when they'd burst through the door.

As if they'd been set up.

We were expected.

"Harrow, wait."

She'd reached the door. Gideon stepped out of the circle, intending to stop her. But before he could grab her arm and pull her back into the room, a loud BOOM! shook the walls and floors. The red-hot force of an explosion threw him backward, slamming his body into solid brick.

Fire flared across his vision seconds before the world went black.

FORTY-SIX

RUNE

*F*OR THE PAST TWO years, ever since Nan's death, Rune spent most nights tossing and turning in bed, her mind spinning with anxious thoughts as she went over plans, pieced together information, and mentally punished herself for the witches she hadn't saved.

Tonight, she slept worse than ever. Nightmares about Nan kept her trapped, and when Rune finally woke from them, thrashing in her covers, a sheen of feverish sweat coated her skin.

It was still dark, but Rune rose anyway, afraid to shut her eyes again. Dressing warmly, she saddled Lady and rode down to the shore, trying to clear her head while the sun rose, scattering the mist off the sea.

When she returned to Wintersea House, Lizbeth was walking toward her through the gardens, her hands coiled around a rolled-up newspaper.

Rune dismounted Lady. "What is it?"

Lizbeth handed the paper to her. "You should read it yourself."

Rune unrolled the *New Herald*, the regime's official newspaper, and glanced down at the front page. In bold black letters, the first headline read: WITCH ATTACK. DOZENS DEAD.

320

Her heart stumbled.

A witch attack?

With one hand squeezing the leather strips of Lady's lead, Rune quickly scanned the report.

Late last night, Blood Guard soldiers led by Captain Gideon Sharpe raided a print shop believed to be harboring witches. The soldiers were lured into a trap set by the witches they'd come to arrest. A dozen men and women were inside the building when it exploded. As help rushed to the scene, a second explosion tore through Blood Guard headquarters. As of this morning, the fires are still raging. Twenty-seven are confirmed dead and many more are injured.

Rune's ears rang as she stared at Gideon's name. Two explosions. Twenty-seven dead. She scanned down to the bottom of the page, but there was no other information.

The *New Herald* hadn't printed the names of the deceased.

Is he one of them?

Choking down her fear, Rune tossed the newspaper on the ground and swiftly remounted. Grabbing Lady's reins, she sent them sailing toward town.

Rune could see two pillars of billowing smoke long before she reached the capital. She headed straight for the print shop, where Gideon's raid had taken place. It was past noon when she neared the smoking ruin. Ash filled the air, stinging her lungs.

As she arrived at the building's scorched shell, the horrible thoughts Rune had tried to suppress broke through and an image of Gideon's charred body appeared in her mind, unmooring her.

It felt like the air had been sucked from the world.

She couldn't breathe.

Rune reached for her old hatred of the Blood Guard captain like she would for a weapon, to defend herself against the surge of overwhelming feelings. But her hatred was nowhere to be found.

She swung herself down from the saddle and pushed her way into the crowd of gawking bystanders.

"Is there anyone still in there?" she asked, feeling dizzy. "Does anyone know the names of the dead?"

But the bystanders were all asking the same questions. As she shoved her way to the front, people with buckets of water rushed inside or emerged with empty ones, telling the crowd to get back.

"You can't come in here, miss," said one of them. "It's still smoldering."

"Have you seen Gideon Sharpe?"

No one had.

Rune raced Lady to Blood Guard headquarters, the site of the second attack. The former Royal Library looked like a giant skull, blackened and burnt, with fires still raging in its hollow eyes. The explosion had shattered the glass walls, and the shards lay scattered in the street, shining like a sea.

TWENTY-SEVEN DEAD blared in her mind.

Rune's stomach clenched.

Did Cressida do this?

Instead of going home to Wintersea to wait for news, or riding to Thornwood Hall in case Alex had more information, she turned Lady and rode for Old Town. Tying the horse to a nearby hitching post, she approached Gideon's tenement.

Rune knocked on his door, listening for footsteps within.

When no one came, she knocked again. Louder this time.

I hate you, Gideon Sharpe. I hate you so much, it hurts. And if you don't open this door, I'll go on hating you forever . . .

There was still no answer.

She banged on the wood. Pounding and pounding until her hands hurt. Trying to pound away the image of his scorched corpse stuck behind her eyelids.

Rune was going to be sick.

When it became clear no one was coming, she collapsed against the door, pressing her forehead to the wood, wondering where this tempest of emotions had come from. A whirlwind of sadness and longing and something else. Something she didn't want to acknowledge. Turning her back to the door, she sank to the ground.

Drawing her knees to her chest, she remembered him stepping into the black flames that had come to devour her. While everyone else ran away, he had run toward her.

A sob surged up her throat.

Rune felt people walking past, trying not to stare at the silly little aristo weeping on the ground in the wrong part of town. Rune didn't care. A tempest was crashing through her, threatening to shatter her apart, and it was everything she could do to hold herself together.

As she wept on his doorstep, a concerned passerby approached. Through her tears, Rune saw their blurred boots.

Leave me alone, she thought, pulling her knees tighter to her chest.

"Rune?"

She glanced up to find a young man in a Blood Guard uniform. His red wool jacket was missing, and blood stained the collared white shirt he wore. A gash in his forehead had been recently stitched, and there was a vicious bruise on his cheek.

The breath froze in her lungs.

Rune pushed herself to her feet.

"What are you doing here?" said Gideon, staring at her like she was a puzzle he couldn't figure out.

At the sight of him, *alive*, Rune burst into tears all over again. She tried to wipe them away. Tried to catch her breath between great heaving gasps. But it was impossible.

"Hey. *Hey.* It's all right . . ." He was suddenly right in front of her, his hands solid and warm on her shoulders. "Everything is all right."

"I thought you were dead!" she managed between sobs.

She reached for his shirt, clenching it in her fists, and pressed her forehead into the hollow of his throat as she trembled all over.

His hands found her waist, holding her lightly. "And that . . . upsets you this much? The thought of me dead?"

She pulled back, staring at him. Was he joking? His expression was unreadable.

"Gideon, the thought of you inside that building . . . it felt like being held underwater." She lowered her gaze to the pulse at the base of his throat. "Like being starved of air."

His hand touched her chin, bringing her eyes back to his. Studying her for a long time.

"That might be the nicest thing anyone's ever said to me."

The reflection in his eyes portrayed a girl whose face was splotchy from crying, her hair a wild tangle from riding so hard. She was a mess. Still dressed in nothing but riding leathers. Not at all the girl she went to great pains to portray.

Alarmed, she drew back against the door behind her. "*Merciful Ancients*, I look frightful. I should get home . . ." Before anyone else saw her, and her reputation was damaged further.

Rune moved to step around him.

Gideon held out his hand. She walked into it, halting. Keeping his palm pressed to her stomach, he urged her gently back against the door. She glanced up and found him staring at her like she was out of her mind. "You have never been more beautiful than this moment."

The words made her pulse kick. *What?*

He stepped closer. Lifting his hand to her hair, he tangled his fingers in it. "You're exquisite, Rune."

She swallowed. *I am?*

Suddenly, all concern for her reputation vanished.

"Where were you?" she said. "I asked everywhere, but no one knew what happened to you."

"I was at the hospital, with my friend. She was hurt in the explosion."

He smelled like smoke and gunpowder. And beneath that, *Gideon.*

With her back to the door, Rune tilted her face to his. "Will she be all right?"

He nodded.

The haunted shadows in his eyes were gone, leaving something raw and yearning. His tender fingers traced along her jaw, making her ache.

He was unraveling her.

You're vulnerable, she told herself. *Get Lady and ride straight back to Wintersea. Before you do something you'll regret.*

But not two minutes ago, Rune had thought she'd never see him again. And though it shouldn't have mattered, though none of this should matter, she couldn't tear her gaze away from him.

She was like a deer making eyes at the wolf that wanted to eat her for lunch.

Stupid deer.

But she knew the fear of not having him now, and she suddenly wanted all of him. Body and soul. It was a dangerous feeling. One that could cost her everything.

Gideon lowered his mouth to hers. Her heart hammered harder. She wondered how she'd ever thought it a cruel-looking mouth. It was a very nice mouth. Reverent and devoted, wanting to please her. Rune trembled beneath it.

She was drowning, and he was air. She hadn't even realized how much she needed him until he was gone.

"Do you want to come in?" he breathed against her lips.

The question sparked a fire inside her.

No, said her brain. But her mouth defied her.

"More than anything."

Gideon reached for the knob beside her hip. Still kissing her, he turned it and pushed the door open, guiding her backward.

He kicked the door shut behind them.

FORTY-SEVEN

GIDEON

*I*T WAS UNNATURAL, THE way he wanted her. Like nothing else in the world mattered more than bringing her upstairs, peeling her out of those riding leathers, and guiding her down to the bed. Like nothing mattered more than *her*. Maybe it was the brush with death, but even his little brother's feelings were suddenly of no consequence.

Rune was everything he hadn't believed could exist in a girl.

He wanted her, and she clearly wanted him. She told him as much when she coiled her arms around his shoulders and lifted herself onto his hips. The breath shuddered out of him. His hands tightened on her thighs, pulling her closer.

Her mouth was soft and warm. Fierce and hungry. Undoing all of his restraint.

Harrow thought his desire for Rune was nothing more than witchcraft. That it prevented him from seeing the truth.

There's one way to find out for sure, he thought, cupping her neck. Kissing her harder.

Did you look between her thighs? Because if I were a witch hiding in plain sight, that's definitely where I'd keep mine.

Gideon needed to get Harrow's voice out of his head, because the thought of being between Rune's thighs made him stop halfway up the stairs, overcome. He pinned her against the wall, breathing hard as he debated unhooking her legs from around his waist, dropping to his knees, and going down on her right here in the stairwell.

No, he thought as Rune nipped his throat, struggling to regain his senses. *You don't even know what she likes.*

She might not even know what she likes.

Gideon still didn't know if she'd ever done what they were about to do.

Start in the bed, he told himself, bringing her the rest of the way to the second floor, where he opened the door to his apartment and carried her inside. He would start there, and if he proved himself worthy of her, maybe this could be more than a game. Not just flirting and kissing and courting, but a life shared. Maybe Gideon could have all of her.

But would she want all of him?

He was terrified to even hope for it.

Start in the bed.

FORTY-EIGHT

RUNE

*R*UNE HAD WORKED IT all out in her head on the way up the stairs.

She was the Crimson Moth. The girl who secretly saved witches from the purge. To keep saving them, she needed a permanent source of intel. And Gideon Sharpe was that source.

She *needed* him.

It had nothing to do with the way he growled her name against her throat. Or the way he worshipped her with every stroke of his hands. Or the fact that he thought she was most beautiful when she was a huge mess.

Rune needed to give in to this deadly attraction because it was the best way to make her worst enemy believe, with no more doubts, that she wasn't a witch. That she had nothing to hide.

Tonight, she would put Gideon's suspicions to death forever.

Tonight, she would win this game once and for all.

These are the things she told herself as Gideon carried her into his apartment. She had to. Because if she didn't, a deeper truth would come roaring to the surface. A truth that asked: *What if?*

What if she wasn't a witch and he wasn't a witch hunter?

What if this didn't have to be pretend?

Inside, he set her down and shut the door behind them. In the momentary absence of him, Rune took in her surroundings. Pale light from the streetlamps spilled through the windows, silhouetting the spare furnishings. Rune had the strangest urge to turn on the lights and commit every shelf, floorboard, and piece of furniture to memory. As if every object might tell her a secret about him. Rune wanted to know them all.

Gideon's hand found hers. He tugged her through a door and into the room beyond. When Rune sighted the dark outline of a bed and realized where they were, her stomach tightened. She felt like she always did before a heist: equal parts nervous and excited.

He kissed down her throat, his fingers working the clasp at the top of her riding jacket. "Promise you'll tell me if you change your mind . . ."

Arching her throat, she buried her hands in his hair. "I won't change my mind."

"But if you do . . ."

"Gideon." Close to his ear, Rune whispered: "Less talking."

He smiled against her skin.

His hands made quick work of her buttons, and her jacket loosened. Peeling it off her, he dropped it on the floor. Rune wore only a bralette underneath, the white lace illuminated by the pale light from the street.

At the sight of it, Gideon made a rough sound in his throat. Her whole body shivered in response. Rune tugged the hem of his shirt out from where it tucked into his trousers and slid her palms underneath, skidding up his warm, solid chest.

He worked at the button of her leather riding leggings as he kissed the hollow of her throat, the line of her collarbone, the skin through the lace of her bralette. Pulling her deeper under his spell.

When her leggings were loose enough, his hand dipped beneath the line of her underwear, sliding warm fingers between her thighs.

A tiny sound escaped Rune, who trembled beneath his caresses.

Gideon didn't stop. Her fingers curled into her palms at the pleasure he was stoking. Her breathing turned uneven. She looped her arms around his neck and pressed her face against his shirt, unable to think. No longer caring how dangerous he was. How bad for her.

"Take off your shirt," she said. "I want to see you."

He immediately obliged, eager to please.

"Anything else you'd like me to . . ."

Grabbing the bottom hem of her bralette, Rune tugged it over her head and dropped it on the floor.

He sucked in a breath. *"Rune."*

She took his hands and pressed them to her skin, guiding him to the places she most wanted to be touched. His palms moved over her, exploring every inch of her. Cupping her soft curves. Stroking her bare skin.

She relished the roughness and warmth of his hands.

Rune pushed down her leggings next, and her underwear with them, kicking herself free. At the sight of her, Gideon's breath shuddered out of him. She dragged the tip of her nose carefully across his jaw as she undid the buttons of his uniform trousers. A moment later, they too dropped to the floor.

"Can we move to the bed?" she asked.

"We can do anything you want."

Cupping her neck, Gideon kissed her, walking her backward. Rune sighed against his lips, letting him lead her there.

Her bare calves hit the wood of the bed frame behind her.

Drawing back the covers, she sat down and drew him in after her. He straddled her legs as he bent to kiss her. Rune lost herself in the sensation of his mouth on the bare skin of her stomach, the scrape of his teeth on her hip bone, the roughness of his cheeks as he kissed between her thighs.

Rune had never known this kind of hunger. He was drowning her in it. Drowning her with his mouth and his hands and the growl of her name deep in his throat. Bringing her to the cusp of a world she'd never dreamed existed.

Before thrusting her over the edge, Gideon came back up.

"Wait, no," said Rune, breathless. "Why are you stopping?"

"Oh, I'm not stopping." He lowered himself gently on top of her, nuzzling her cheek. "I was just warming you up."

Oh.

He moved against her.

Oh.

Her legs tightened around him like a snare.

"Unless you'd prefer me down there . . ."

"No," she breathed, as his hands moved over her again, fingers stroking, warming. She liked him up here. The heat of his skin on hers. The delicious, heavy weight of him.

"Are you all right?" He sounded almost breathless.

She nodded, feeling her temperature rise. Her skin flushed as sweat gathered on her hairline. "Yes," she breathed out.

He kept going.

"Your heart is racing . . ."

She nodded. She knew. Looping her arms around his neck, she pulled him closer. She pressed her mouth to the scar on his chest, tasting him.

He spoke her name like an incantation. It made the warm ache between her legs sharpen and grow until she was more ache than girl.

Gideon continued, moving against her. Deeper, harder, insistent.

She was losing control.

"Gideon . . ."

"Do you want to stop?"

"No. *No.*" A laugh escaped her. "Please don't stop."

Her arms tightened. The hand cupping her breast fell away as his arm curled around her waist, pulling her into him, focusing completely on this task. When she arched against him one last time, something broke. The blood roared in her ears. The world beyond them disappeared.

Lost in the shattering, she called out his name.

He sighed.

"Rune."

She clung to him, waiting for the world to settle back into place. Wondering if it would forever be off its orbit now.

He kissed her shoulder, her throat.

"I didn't know," she whispered when they stopped, staring up at him.

"Didn't know . . . ?"

"That it would be like that."

He pushed himself onto his forearms, brow furrowing as he searched her face. As if she'd just told him he hadn't satisfied her.

"Like what?"

Rune smiled, tenderly cupping his face.

"Powerful," she whispered, kissing the crease between his brows away. "Like two souls fusing into one."

Like a kind of magic.

"Oh," he said, and grinned.

Grinned.

Rune had never seen Gideon Sharpe grin in her whole life. Were there other ways to make him light up like that?

She wanted to find out.

❦

IT WAS ONLY LATER, after Gideon fell asleep with Rune cocooned in his arms, that she lay awake, her whole body buzzing with a frightening realization.

I'm in love with him.

Instead of getting Gideon Sharpe out of her system tonight, Rune had gone and gotten herself addicted.

The hunted had fallen for the hunter.

FORTY-NINE

GIDEON

GIDEON WOKE TO THE sound of the floorboards creaking. He opened his eyes, letting his sight adjust to the darkness, and saw Rune's silhouette picking up her underclothes from the floor.

He sat up, watching her pull them on, thinking of her only hours before. The way she arched against his hand, his mouth. The soft sounds she made when he did something she liked.

His body tightened with desire.

Gideon had been exceptionally thorough tonight. He could therefore say, without a doubt, that Rune Winters had no casting scars anywhere on her body.

He could also say, without a doubt, that he wanted to do what they'd done again.

And again.

And again.

His chest knotted. This feeling she stirred in him—not desire, but something deeper—scared him a little. It felt like a tethering. Like he'd given her a piece of himself tonight, maybe long before tonight, and in doing so, handed her power over him.

The last time he'd done that with someone . . .

Gideon smothered the thought.

"Had your fill of me?" he asked while she gathered the rest of her clothes.

Rune froze like a mouse sighted by a hawk.

"What? No, I . . ." Her voice sounded strange. Unsteady.

Gideon moved to the edge of the bed. "What's wrong?"

"N-nothing," she said, hugging the bundle of leathers. Gideon lit the lamp on the bedside table and got out of bed. "It's just that I should go home. The servants will worry."

But Gideon knew that Rune regularly attended the parties of other aristocrats. Parties that often ended at dawn. The servants of Wintersea House would be used to their mistress coming home at all hours of the night.

In the lamplight, he saw the shine of tears in her eyes.

Standing now, Gideon stayed where he was, wondering if he'd caused this. Had he misunderstood, somehow? Maybe she'd wanted none of it.

"You're afraid of something," he said. "Tell me what it is."

She bit down on her lip.

Gideon wanted to close the gap between them, take her face in his hands, and tell her he'd protect her. But he held himself still.

"*You*," she whispered. "I'm afraid of *you*."

His heart sank like a stone.

"Me?"

She backed up a step. "The way you make me feel is . . ." She hugged the bundle of clothes tighter. "I'm afraid it's something I could get used to. Something I could *need*." She shook her head. "I'm afraid you'll be the end of me, Gideon." And then, much more quietly: "Maybe you already are."

She seemed to truly believe this—that he had some strange power to crush her.

Did she think he was using her?

Aren't I using her? he thought, remembering his conversation with Harrow.

Hadn't he brought her into his bed to prove she wasn't a witch?

No, he thought. That was merely his justification for taking what he wanted and not caring if it hurt his brother.

The sudden thought of it—of what he'd done with the girl Alex loved—felt like a punch.

Gideon clenched and unclenched his fists. He stood at a crossroads here. One with two clear paths forking before him.

The first road was the one he'd meant to take all along: pretending to court Rune in order to catch the Crimson Moth. That road was always going to end with Gideon letting her go—to the purge, if she was a witch; to Alex, if she wasn't. It was the higher road. The road that allowed Gideon to keep his conscience intact. To stay on it, all Gideon had to do was end this charade.

But now there was another road open to him. This one had Rune standing on it, telling him that she was falling in love with him. That this wasn't pretend for her.

The right thing to do, the *noble* thing, was to choose the first road. To end this tonight. All Gideon had to do was lie and say he didn't feel the same way.

But Gideon wasn't noble. And he didn't do the right thing.

Because he wanted this.

"I'm scared, too."

She glanced sharply up at him.

Gideon had kept to himself these past few years for good reason. He'd made himself vulnerable with Cressida, and she'd taken that vulnerability and used it as a weapon against him. He needed to be careful. He couldn't let just anyone in.

"What if I asked you to trust me?"

Rune looked like she might burst into tears at the question. "You want me to trust you?"

"We could trust each other," he said, stepping toward her.

From the look on her face, she thought this a difficult, if not impossible, task.

"Do you trust this?" He leaned in to kiss her temple. Her pulse responded, beating out a frenzied rhythm. "Or this?" Pushing back her hair, he brushed his lips against the sensitive skin behind her ear, making her quiver. "What about this?" He pressed his hand between her hip bones, moving slowly downward.

Her breathing changed, becoming shallow and rapid. She softened beneath him, melting fast. Like she was ice and he was fire.

Why did it feel this good to please her?

"I want all of you, Rune." Gideon kissed her brow. "Not just tonight, but every moment from now on."

"I want that, too," she breathed, tilting her head back. "But how would it work? Help me imagine it."

Gideon smiled as he thought about it.

"Every day, after my shift ends, I'll come home to you, and we'll cook dinner together."

"I have servants for that."

He nipped the tip of her nose. "You're ruining this fantasy already."

"Sorry," she whispered. "Go on."

He continued, trailing kisses across her bare shoulder. "Every night after dinner, we'll take a long walk through Wintersea, and I'll pick you a bouquet of wildflowers, and we'll talk . . . or be silent. I don't really care, as long as you're next to me."

He could feel her softening.

"Would you attend some of my parties?"

His hands palmed up her bare back. "All of them."

She pulled away a little, glancing at him. "But you hate parties. I don't think you're fond of my friends, either."

"I can learn to like them." His arms locked around her waist and dragged her back to him. "I can be civil."

She raised an eyebrow, as if to say, *Can you?*

For you, yes.

She bit down on her lip again, thinking. "And you'll dance with me?"

"That's a given."

"What if we fight all the time?"

"I'd rather fight with you than do most other things."

Her forehead pinched in surprise. "You would?"

"Yes." He dragged the bridge of his nose across her cheekbone, breathing in her soapy scent. "And after we're done fighting, I'll take you to bed, and we'll reconcile. In fact, I think we should fight every day just so we can make up every night."

Gideon felt her breath quicken. She liked the sound of that.

He was wearing her down.

"You won't come to resent me?" she whispered.

"For what?" His breath tangled with hers.

"For being shallow and silly."

"You aren't those things, Rune."

She wrinkled her nose. "Sometimes I will be."

"Sometimes I'll be a brute. Can you handle that?"

Rune cocked her head. "I think so." A small smile tugged at her mouth. "Yes." She ran her hands up his chest and over his shoulders, sliding her fingers into his hair.

"Do you need more persuading?"

"Mmm, yes please," she murmured, tugging his mouth down to hers. "Try using fewer words this time."

Gideon laughed against her lips, then hiked her onto his hips and carried her back to the bed.

⁘

THE NEXT MORNING, GIDEON woke to a sleeping Rune tucked against his chest. Right where she was supposed to be. Her rose-gold hair spilled across the white pillows, and from this close, he could count every freckle speckling her shoulders.

He'd half expected to wake in an empty bed, every trace of her gone. Or, worse, discover he'd dreamt it.

But she was still here. And it felt *right*. Like she belonged in his bed, curled up against him.

Touching his lips to her shoulder, Gideon breathed her in.

Rune didn't wear the artificial perfumes so popular among the New Republic's elite. She didn't smell like lilacs or jasmine or roses; she smelled like herself. Like standing at the edge of the bluffs after a storm. Like a gulp of fresh sea air.

Gideon wanted to inhale her.

Rune stirred, her grip tightening on the sheets between them. Gideon froze, watching her forehead crease in a frown. Like she was having an unpleasant dream. He wanted to touch his thumb to that crease. Gently rub it away.

Rune tried to cuddle closer. She slid her leg between both of his and bent her knee, hooking them tighter together. Satisfied, she fell still again, drifting deeper.

I'm afraid you'll be the end of me.

Gideon wanted to convince her that she couldn't be more wrong.

He waited until she was fast asleep again before gently untangling their legs and carefully removing himself from the bed. After dressing, he finally tore his eyes away from her to brew himself a cup of coffee. Then he strode downstairs and into his parents' old studio.

With Rune's words still clanging through his head, he opened the door to a shallow closet he hadn't opened in years. He flicked the wall switch and the light inside sputtered to life, illuminating a space full of dusty boxes.

Gideon glanced to the uppermost shelf, where an odd assortment of books was stacked. It was his mother's collection, books she'd used for inspiration. When he found the one he wanted—an encyclopedia of wildflowers—he pulled it down, blew the dust off, then cracked it open.

He skimmed the pages until he found the entry he was looking for. Opening the book wider, he studied the botanical drawing before him.

Perhaps there was a way to prove his intentions were genuine.

Gideon had started toward the fabrics when someone knocked on the shop door. Wondering who would visit at this hour, he left the encyclopedia on the table and went to answer it.

Harrow stood on the other side. Half of her face was battered, and a curve of black stitches arced down her cheek. One of her arms was in a splint.

"Shouldn't you still be in the hospital?" he asked.

Beside Harrow stood Laila, out of uniform, her dark brown hair pulled back in an elegant bun.

"He talked."

Both girls pushed past him into the room.

"Who talked?" asked Gideon, shutting the door behind them.

"The print shop owner," Laila answered. "We arrested him early this morning and brought him into custody."

Harrow turned a chair at the worktable backward and plunked herself onto it.

"A student at the university paid him for the use of his store-room, alleging to need it for a school project. The owner says he didn't know what it was being used for."

Gideon crossed his arms. "He didn't find it suspicious that a *student* required the use of a storeroom?"

Laila's shoulders lifted. "The money must have been enough to stifle his curiosity."

"Did you get the student's name?"

Laila shook her head. "Only a description. Based on his ac-count, the sketch artist drafted this likeness." She slid her hand into the pocket of her trousers and pulled out a folded piece of paper, holding it out to Gideon.

Uncrossing his arms, he took the paper, unfolding it to study the sketch. A girl stared back at him. Her dark, shoulder-length curls matched her dark sunken eyes, which were partially hid-den behind spectacles.

"Looks remarkably like Rune's friend, don't you think?" said Harrow.

Verity de Wilde, she meant.

Sure, there was a slight resemblance. But this sketch could easily be some other nearsighted scholar. He handed it back to Laila. "We'll need more than a sketch to prove it."

"You could start by asking your sweetheart where her friend was the night of the attack," said Harrow, her arms crossed over the back of the chair, her tone sharp.

Gideon ran a hand through his hair, not liking where this was going.

"I disagree," said Laila, leaning against his worktable. "If the suspect *is* Verity de Wilde, Rune was likely in on the scheme. Asking her will send her running to warn her friend."

"Hold on," said Gideon. "We can't know *this*"—he held up the vague sketch—"is Verity de Wilde. Even if it resembles her somewhat, the print shop owner might have given a false description."

Harrow started to say something, but Gideon held up his hand, locking eyes with her. "More importantly: Rune wasn't in on the scheme."

Harrow slit her eyes. "You're certain of that?"

Gideon remembered Rune sitting outside his front door, weeping. Believing him dead.

He thought of everything they'd done last night.

"She's not a witch."

"Do you have proof this time?" Harrow's voice dripped with suspicion.

Aware of Laila's gaze, Gideon shifted uncomfortably. But if this was a standoff, he wouldn't be intimidated. Rune deserved to be exonerated.

"The proof is currently sleeping in my bed."

"You *slept* with Rune Winters?" Laila's eyes widened. "Are you out of your mind?"

Gideon glanced at his hunting partner, wanting to defend Rune. But Harrow already suspected he was bewitched by her. If he proved that suspicion true, she would accuse him of being compromised. If he was compromised, Laila would have to report him.

So he said, "It was the only way to know for sure."

"He means it was the best way to search her for casting scars," Harrow clarified, her honeyed eyes still fixed on Gideon. Like a cat waiting for a mouse to show itself. "And? How was it, Comrade? Was she everything you hoped she'd be?"

His whole body prickled, not liking her tone—or the question. But he needed to be careful here, for Rune's sake as much as his own. He needed to make Harrow and Laila believe he felt nothing for her. That what he'd done with Rune was pure business.

He forced the words out.

"I've had better," he said, staring Harrow down. "You were right; it was no chore. But I'm not about to repeat the endeavor anytime soon." The lie sank inside him like poison. "She's a pretty face, nothing more."

Harrow looked like she was about to respond when a floorboard creaked outside the room. As if someone stood listening on the other side of the door.

All three of them looked to the closed door.

In three strides, Gideon crossed the room and swung it open.

Rune stood in the frame, her face pale, her hair a tangle. The look of shock and hurt in her eyes was like an axe splitting open his chest.

"Rune . . ."

Visibly trembling, she stammered, "I-I have to go."

Before he could stop her, she turned on her heel and stumbled out into the street.

FIFTY

RUNE

RUNE DIDN'T KNOW WHAT hurt more: that Gideon would stoop so low in his quest to unmask the Crimson Moth, or that she'd fallen for his ruse.

I've had better. The words haunted her as she stepped into the street, lurching toward Lady, who waited dutifully at her hitching post. *She's a pretty face, nothing more.*

As if sleeping with her was a task to accomplish. Something to get over with.

If she hadn't walked in on that conversation, she would still believe it was the real thing. That he truly liked her. Maybe even *loved* her.

She wanted to cry.

This is over. No more courtship games. No more playing pretend. *I am done with Gideon Sharpe.*

He'd done her a favor. Cured her of what might have been the start of a pathetic, one-sided, *deadly* infatuation.

And yet . . .

Gideon caught up to her.

"Rune, wait."

As he grabbed her wrist, Rune wrenched herself free and spun to face him.

"Don't."

He stumbled back, raising both hands in surrender. His breath puffed in the brisk morning air. "I . . . I didn't mean any of that."

Right. *Sure.*

Afraid she might burst into tears, not wanting him anywhere near her when she did, she ran the rest of the way to Lady's side.

Around them, people stopped what they were doing to stare.

"Please give me a chance to explain. What you heard—"

"What I heard was sickening!" she said, stepping into Lady's stirrup and pushing herself up and into the saddle. Because she was furious, she added: "Even for someone like *you*."

Gideon stepped back. "Someone like me."

She shook her head. "I was right about you from the beginning. Verity and Alex were right about you. You're a selfish, horrible brute. You don't care who you hurt, as long as you get what you want. You *repulse* me."

He recoiled at those words. But Rune wasn't sorry for saying them.

Unable to look at him a moment longer, she gathered Lady's reins and turned away from the Blood Guard captain. "You and I are done, Gideon. I never want to see you again."

Rune urged the horse into a canter.

She couldn't put him behind her fast enough.

FIFTY-ONE

GIDEON

GIDEON SLOWED HIS STEPS, watching her flee.

She didn't look back. Not once.

He was that forgettable.

Did you really expect this would end happily?

Suspicion had tainted his relationship with Rune from the beginning. Gideon had only agreed to this farce of a courtship because he'd believed her to be the Crimson Moth, a belief proven false last night.

He'd been wrong.

So wrong.

And now that he trusted her fully, now that he knew what it felt like to wake up beside her, to believe a life with her was within reach, he'd gone and ruined everything.

Letting his head fall back, Gideon let out a shuddering breath. He deserved every bit of her wrath. After agreeing to Harrow's asinine plan, Gideon was all that Rune accused him of and more.

Sickening.

A *stupid brute.*

He deserved to lose her.

FIFTY-TWO

RUNE

*T*HE NORTH WIND WHIPPED Rune's hair across her cheeks. Lady's hooves kicked the dirt of the country laneways. Fields and bogs and forests blurred at the edges of her vision.

I want all of you, Rune. Not just tonight, but every moment from now on.

She felt feverish. Possessed. Unable to stop thinking about what she and Gideon had done. About the possibilities she'd let herself want.

I am such a fool!

Rune couldn't shake off the memory of his mouth trailing reverently down her body, or the tenderness in his voice as he whispered sweet things in the dark.

I'm scared, too, he'd told her.

We could trust each other, he'd said. As if he'd meant every word.

She let the tears fall as she rode, letting the wind dry them. She pushed Lady harder, wanting to kill the thing inside her that bloomed at Gideon's touch. Wanting to put him behind her forever.

Rune had known all along that he was hunting her. That he wanted her dead. Gideon was nothing more than a cruel boy who liked to kill witches.

Sweet Mercy, why does this hurt so much?

Suddenly, Lady slowed. Rune palmed the tears from her eyes and looked up. She hadn't even realized the destination she'd been riding toward until it loomed before her.

Thornwood Hall.

One of the stable hands saw her arrive and met her at the entrance to the house. Rune dismounted and handed him Lady's reins, quickly taking the steps past the two marble lions and through the doors.

Alex was in the hallway, speaking with a servant. The moment she appeared, he paused and turned toward her.

"Rune?"

At the sight of her tearstained face, his own darkened. Dismissing the servant, he moved toward her and took her shoulders in his hands. "What's happened?"

She closed her eyes. Alexander Sharpe. The boy she didn't have to hide from. Gentle Alex who would never hurt or betray her. The person she could tell anything to.

"You were right about Gideon. I'm done with him."

A series of contradictory emotions chased each other across his face. Shock. Relief. And . . . something else. Something Rune couldn't put her finger on.

"Did he hurt you?"

"What? *No.*" Not physically. "He . . ." She glanced toward the servant still lingering in this hall. Not wanting to be overheard, Rune took one of Alex's hands and led him into the conservatory, shutting the door behind them.

"Your brother has suspected me this whole time." Pressing both hands to her temples, she shook her head. She walked past the piano and toward Alex's writing desk, pivoted and walked back again. "He was only pretending to court me because he thought I was the Moth."

"Does he still think you're the Moth?"

Rune thought back to the snippet of conversation she'd overheard. After waking in an empty bed and realizing it was midmorning, she'd dressed and followed the sound of Gideon's voice downstairs. She'd only heard the end of his upsetting conversation with Laila and Harrow, but Gideon had seemed adamant: he didn't think she was a witch.

"I don't think so."

"But you don't know for sure."

"I . . ."

"Rune." Alex's voice sounded strange. Rune, still pacing, had reached the writing desk again. "Please don't make me leave you here."

She turned to face him. "What do you mean?"

"Here. On this island." He started toward her. "If I have to leave you behind, it will kill me. Please come with me."

She shook her head. "You know I can't leave."

Rune watched Alex reach into his breast pocket and pull something out. Stopping in front of her, he reached for her hand.

"I didn't think I'd have the courage to ever do this . . ."

She looked down to see him push a silver ring onto her second smallest finger. It was thin and cool against her skin.

"I have stood by for years and watched you strategically pick out suitors. I look at the men you choose, notice the ways they don't deserve you, and wonder why you don't see what's right in front of you. But you can't, can you?"

Rune pulled her hand from his, cradling it in the space between them, running her fingertips over the thin band.

What is he saying?

"It's why you're so afraid to look at me sometimes. Because I know what you are, and I know what you've done, and I *love* you."

Rune's heart fluttered in her chest.

What?

His face was inches from hers now, his breath warm on her lips. "I love you, Rune Winters. I have since the day I met you."

Her eyes burned.

"I love you," he repeated, taking her face in his hands. "Do you believe me?"

He loved her. Not like a friend, or a sister. But like a . . .

"Be my wife, Rune. Come with me to Caelis. Let me give you the life you should have had."

One by one, the tears fell. Rune pressed her hands to her eyes to hide them. *His wife.*

Alex was her safe harbor. He was everything she didn't deserve.

But do I love him?

As a friend, yes. Like a brother, definitely.

Could he be more than that?

Rune didn't know. Maybe.

But there was a problem. He was leaving soon. Leaving for good. And she couldn't go with him.

She stepped back, shaking her head. "If I went with you to Caelis, I would spend every day eaten up by guilt and self-loathing."

"You do that now," he pointed out.

She glanced away. "Maybe so, but at least here I can do something about it. I can't leave helpless witches to be murdered while I live out some fantasy far away."

"Rune."

His hands settled on her hips.

"Look at me."

She dragged her eyes back to his.

"Do you think this is what Kestrel wanted for you? A life

spent atoning for an impossible choice—a choice she *wanted* you to make? Do you think she wanted you to risk yourself again and again until the day they finally kill you? It's time for you to forgive yourself."

Her eyes burned.

It wasn't as simple as that.

"I—"

"Cressida is alive and she's more powerful than you'll ever be. Let her take up your cause." Before she realized what was happening, Alex leaned in. "She can finish what you started."

And then: he kissed her.

Kissing Alex wasn't at all like kissing his brother. Gideon was dangerous. Deadly. Literally hunting her. She could never be with Gideon unless she wanted to be dead.

When Alex kissed her, there was no hungry fire burning through her. No desperate yearning. No warm ache.

But there was gentleness, and comfort, and safety.

There was love.

Maybe I could . . .

Alex's hands trailed down her arms and settled around her waist, pulling her closer. When his kisses turned hungry, she leaned in, open to the possibility of him. He backed her toward the desk and lifted her onto it. When he stepped between her legs, pulling her flush against him, Rune felt the tiniest spark flicker somewhere inside her.

One day, maybe, that spark could catch and burn into a steady flame.

"Come with me, Rune. Your grandmother would want you to be happy."

Rune had no defense against his arguments this time. Nan had loved her more than anything; she *did* want Rune to be happy. And Alex was right about Cressida—there wasn't a more powerful witch alive. It was silly to insist she could do more than the youngest witch queen could.

"You *deserve* to be happy," he murmured against her lips. "Let me try to make you happy."

Rune couldn't remember the last time she'd cried so much in one day.

"Okay," she whispered.

He pulled back, lips parting in surprise. "Really?"

She nodded. "I'll go with you to Caelis. I'll be your wife."

Alex wasn't the strategic choice; he was the safe one. The boy she could be herself with. The boy she could *actually* share a life with—because he didn't want her dead.

FIFTY-THREE

RUNE

*R*UNE SPENT THE FOLLOWING day packing suitcases and making a list of things to send for once she and Alex were settled on the Continent. They had decided Rune would leave on the same ship as Alex the morning after Seraphine's rescue.

Which was in two days.

An electric feeling zipped down her spine.

"There's a pile of suitcases sitting on your front doorstep," came a sudden voice. "Do you have visitors?"

Rune looked up from her packing list to find Verity sweeping into the casting room, her heeled boots clicking on the floorboards as she pulled her gloves off her hands.

Rune had sent a carriage to fetch her friend early, before Alex arrived for their last meeting about tomorrow's heist. Rising from the desk, Rune bit her lip and turned toward her friend, who scanned the room, her attention homing in on the stacks of wooden crates crammed full of spell books, and the empty shelves beyond them. Verity's brows knit.

"That's what I wanted to tell you about." Rune's stomach knotted. She wasn't looking forward to this conversation—or to leaving Verity behind. Taking a deep breath, she said, "I'm leaving the New Republic."

Verity's gaze shot to hers.

"I'm going with Alex to Caelis." Rune touched the thin chain around her neck, lifting it out of her bodice so Verity could see the ring hanging from it. "He asked me to marry him."

Verity blinked. "And you accepted him."

"I know you wanted me to choose someone more *useful* . . ." Rune wrinkled her nose, not liking the insinuation that Alex wasn't valuable. "But I—"

"No," Verity interrupted, shaking her head. "No, I'm glad you didn't take my advice." She stepped toward Rune and reached for her hands, gripping them tightly. Her dark eyes glittered as she said, "I never should have made that stupid list. I wasn't thinking about you. I was thinking about the mission." She shook her head harder, as if angry with herself. "I've been a rotten friend."

Rune let out a breath. "I thought you'd be more upset."

"I *am* upset. You're like a sister to me." She looked stern, suddenly. "I don't want you to leave, but I also want you to be happy. And safe. In Caelis, you can be both. Besides, Alex adores you. He'll spoil you for sure."

Rune smiled. "You'll visit us?"

Verity squeezed her hands. "Of course."

Rune pulled her into a hug, not even minding her perfume. "Thank you for understanding."

"I'll always understand," Verity whispered.

❦

SHORTLY AFTER ALEX ARRIVED, the three of them gathered in Rune's casting room one last time to discuss tomorrow's plan. As the sun dipped below the horizon, Verity pulled out two stolen Blood Guard uniforms from her rucksack.

"It might be a little big," she said, handing one over to Rune. "But it should do the trick."

The red wool coat, cotton shirt, breeches, boots, and hat were all stolen from the student in her dormitory. Hopefully, the girl wouldn't notice before Verity returned them.

Rune took the stack of clothes. "Why are there two?"

"This one is for me," said Verity, taking off her spectacles to rub her fingers against her tired eyes.

"But why do you need one?"

"I'm coming with you."

Rune frowned at her friend. "Absolutely not. It's too dangerous, Verity."

Verity ignored her, picking up the black soldier's hat and placing it on her head. "Everyone knows that witch hunters work in pairs, if not packs. It might look suspicious if you're alone."

"I agree," said Alex. He sat cross-legged beside Rune, one hand planted on the floorboards behind her, his shoulder touching hers. With his closeness came the comforting warmth of him, along with his leather and oak smell. "You'll be safer with Verity at your side."

Rune slit her eyes at them both. "And if something goes wrong?"

Verity tilted her chin back so the brim of the soldier's hat stopped obscuring her view. "Then you won't be alone when they throw you in a cell."

From the firm press of her lips, she wouldn't take no for an answer.

Admittedly, Rune felt calmer knowing Verity would be there. "Fine," she sighed. "*Thank you.*"

She set her stack of clothes on the carpet in front of her, next to Gideon's access coin and her last remaining vial of blood. It was mostly full. She'd been trying to save as much of it for tomorrow's heist as possible, in case something went wrong and she needed to cast a spell—or several—to get them out.

It would have been nice to replenish at least some of her blood stores before tomorrow, but her monthly cycle hadn't started yet.

"It would make me feel better if we went through the plan one last time," said Alex.

So they did.

At three o'clock in the afternoon, Rune would meet Verity at her dormitory, and together they would don their Blood Guard uniforms. While crowds of people filled the streets for the Liberty Day festivities, they would travel to the palace and enter the prison. The earlier, the better, since they didn't know when the Good Commander was planning to purge Seraphine.

Alex would wait with the horses a block away.

Once inside, Rune and Verity would use Gideon's access coin to get past the seventh gate, telling the guards they had orders to bring Seraphine to her purging. They would retrieve Seraphine, usher her out of the palace prison, and bring her to Alex and the waiting horses.

From there, Rune and Alex would hide Seraphine at Thornwood Hall. The next day, they would board the ship to Caelis with Seraphine concealed in their cargo, bound for freedom.

Rune's heart stuttered at the thought. In two days, she'd be sailing across the Barrow Strait, toward a new life.

As if hearing her thoughts, Alex reached for her hand, lacing their fingers together.

Verity yawned.

"We should all try to get some sleep tonight," said Rune, worried about her exhausted friend. She pushed up from the casting room floor. "Come on. I'll walk you both out."

AFTER SEEING BOTH VERITY and Alex off, Rune returned to her bedroom and changed into her nightgown. Just before climbing into her bedsheets, she saw a box tied with a ribbon at the foot of her bed.

Rune had been so busy packing for Caelis all day, Lizbeth must not have wanted to bother her with it.

Sitting down on the bed, she pulled the box toward her and tugged the folded piece of paper out from under the ribbon. Unfolding it, she recognized the handwriting and immediately stopped reading.

It was from Gideon.

The conversation she'd overheard between him and the girl called Harrow flared anew inside her, burning like a hot iron. Anger and hurt blazed in her chest.

She wanted to throw his letter onto the fire, unread.

Except . . . was it fair to hate him so much for pretending? Rune had pretended right along with him. She'd used him the same way he'd used her.

It was Rune who'd invited him to her bedroom the night of their first kiss. *She* had considered crossing that uncrossable line in her attempt to extract what she needed from him. She'd practically begged him to take her into his bed the other night—to trick him, once and for all. To make him believe the lie she'd built in order to dupe him into marrying her, so she could use him in the future.

At least, that was part of it. The smallest part of it, but still.

Rune had been holding Gideon Sharpe to a different standard, despite playing the same game. Really, she was no different than him.

The thought made her squirm uncomfortably.

Taking a deep breath, she lifted the letter and started to read:

Rune—

The things you overheard yesterday morning—as despicable as they were—I said to protect us both. If I'd told Harrow the truth, she would declare me compromised. I needed her and Laila to believe in your innocence, and the best way to do that was to make them think I felt nothing for you.

It doesn't absolve my actions—it's true that I started courting you to try and uncover the Moth. I don't expect your forgiveness. But I need you to know that what we did the other night wasn't a lie. Not for me. Everything I said that night, I meant.

Gideon

Rune felt like someone had dropped an anchor inside of her, pulling her down to the bottom of the sea.

She wanted to believe him.

She'd be a fool to believe him.

And that was exactly the point, wasn't it? No matter what he said or did, Rune couldn't trust him. He thought her innocent—that's why he was apologizing. That's why he fancied himself in love with her. But if he knew the truth . . .

He'd arrest me right now and hand me over to be purged.

The thought steadied her. Gideon was her enemy.

And I'm marrying his brother.

Rune worried her lip in her teeth. She wasn't only marrying Alex; she was leaving with him. At the very least, Gideon deserved to hear that from her.

She needed to tell him. And say goodbye.

Glancing down to the box, Rune freed the ribbon, lifted the lid, and pushed back the brown paper inside.

A bouquet of silk buttercups sprung from the packaging.

Her pulse hummed in her throat as she reached to pick them up. The flowers were simpler than the rose he'd given her at her after-party, but ten times as plentiful. Rune held the bouquet in her hands, stroking the tiny petals made of buttery silk, tracing the fine stitches.

He made these.

Rune had told Gideon that buttercups were her favorite flower, and instead of picking some, he *sewed* them for her. Had he stayed up all night doing so?

The humming in her throat turned to pounding.

Why did it have to be *Gideon* who knew how to speak to her soul?

It made her eyes prickle.

I can't accept these.

She needed to give the flowers back.

Tomorrow, she thought. *I'll return them before I meet Verity.* Because after tomorrow, who knew when she'd see him again?

Before rescuing Seraphine, she would put Gideon behind her for good, and with him, her role as Rune Winters. She'd play the shallow socialite no longer. The path she'd started on when Nan died was ending; the days of risking her life as the Crimson Moth were almost over.

Rune was headed down a new path. One that led to Caelis,

and to Alex. To safety and joy. Rune was going to live the life Nan wanted for her. The one that was stolen from them both the day the Blood Guard dragged her away.

So, she laid the bouquet of silk flowers back in the box and closed the lid.

Tomorrow she would say goodbye to Gideon Sharpe— forever.

FIFTY-FOUR

RUNE

ARCANA: (n) the deadliest category of spell.

Arcana Spells require blood taken from someone against their will in a quantity that often results in the donor's death. Arcanas are not only deadly for the donor, they are corrosive to the soul of the witch who uses them. For this reason, they were outlawed by Queen Raine the Innocent. Types of Arcana Spells range from complex illusions sustained over long periods to forbidden acts like raising the dead back to life.

> —From Rules of Magic *by Queen Callidora the Valiant*

*T*HE NEXT MORNING, RUNE could barely open her eyes as the sun beamed in through her window.

Get up, she thought, feeling more tired than she had in years. Like her limbs had turned to sand. Like her eyelids were made of stone.

Was this how Verity felt all the time?

You need to save Seraphine today.

And from the position of the sun, it was nearly midday.

Remembering the flowers Gideon made for her, and how she'd resolved to return them, Rune groaned and dragged herself from her bed. She dictated a quick telegram message to Lizbeth, asking Gideon if they could meet this afternoon.

His answer arrived an hour later, short and to the point.

```
MISS RUNE WINTERS
WINTERSEA HOUSE


   MEET ME AT THE STUDIO. 2 O'CLOCK.


                         GIDEON
```

Two o'clock gave Rune plenty of time before convening with Verity an hour later.

After quickly putting food in her stomach, Rune went to collect what she needed for tonight: the stolen uniform, Gideon's access coin, and her last vial of blood. During her meeting with Alex and Verity, she'd put the coin and the vial inside the pocket of the uniform, and left the uniform folded on her casting table.

But when she went to retrieve them, only the uniform was there.

The pockets were empty.

Rune dropped to her knees, looking under the desk to see if the items had fallen onto the carpet. But there was no sign of either the coin or the vial. She checked the uniform's pockets again. Empty. She checked every inch of the casting room, then her bedroom. Nothing.

Rune ground her palms into her eyes, trying to think. Was she so tired, she misremembered where she'd put them?

Without that vial, and the start of her monthly cycle nowhere in sight, Rune had no blood to cast with. And without an access coin, she'd never get past the gates of the prison.

Verity must have taken the wrong uniform by accident.

If Rune left Wintersea now, she'd be able to stop at the university before meeting Gideon and collect the vial and coin from Verity. She quickly donned her riding clothes and tucked Alex's ring—still on a chain around her neck—under the collar of her shirt.

As the silver band settled between her breasts, images of the future flashed in her mind: Standing with Alex on the prow of the boat as the mainland came into view. Walking together through the elegant streets of Caelis. Finding a group of friends they didn't need to hide their true selves from. Reading by the fire while he played the piano late into the evening.

Soon, she told herself, throwing a cloak over her shoulders and fastening it at her throat. *Soon.*

After packing the Blood Guard uniform in one of Lady's saddlebags, and the box of silk flowers from Gideon in another, Rune mentally checked that she had everything she needed—minus her vial and coin—then headed for the university. Leaving Lady in the school's stable, she took the familiar paths across the campus and arrived at Summer Hall. After pulling open the double doors and nodding to the staff behind the front desk, she turned down the dormitory halls, which were quiet at this time of day, since most students were in class.

When she arrived at Verity's door, Rune knocked once.

"Verity?"

No one answered. She knocked louder, and when there was still no answer, she tried the knob, which was unlocked. Turning it, she pushed the door open and stepped inside.

"Verity, did I . . ."

Rune froze. The room was tinier than she remembered. More like a closet. And instead of Verity's bed in the corner, there were a mop and bucket. There were no bookshelves overflowing with books or glass jars full of research projects, only shelves full of cleaning supplies. A ceramic sink stood along the wall, with dirty rags drying over its side.

"Can I help you?" said a gruff voice behind her.

Rune turned to find a rosy-cheeked woman with hands on her hips, staring down at Rune like *she* was the oddity here.

"Oh. Um." She must have turned down the wrong hall. "I'm looking for my friend. Verity de Wilde."

"Unless your friend is a broom, you won't find her in here."

"Right." Rune swallowed. "My mistake."

The woman muttered something under her breath as Rune stepped around her. Out in the hall, she glanced back over her shoulder, certain that was the door to Verity's room.

But it can't be, she thought, continuing on, trying to orient herself. *It belongs to a broom closet.*

She circled the main floor, looking for Verity's actual room, but kept coming back to the closet, where the woman was filling a bucket of soapy water.

Could Rune be so tired she'd forgotten where her best friend's room was?

This didn't bode well for this afternoon.

Giving up, she returned to the front desk and smiled politely, approaching the young woman behind it. "Hello. This is embarrassing, but I'm looking for my friend. Verity de Wilde. Can you point me toward her room?"

The girl gave her a funny look. "What was the last name?"

". . . de Wilde."

The girl took out a clipboard and ran her finger down a list of names and room numbers. She did it twice before glancing back to Rune. "I think you're in the wrong building. No one here has that name."

Rune blinked. "What?"

The girl repeated the words, much more slowly this time. As if that would help Rune understand.

"Verity de Wilde doesn't live here."

Rune glanced at the familiar purple dahlias on the wallpaper. Then the grass-green tiles beneath her feet.

"This is Summer Hall."

The girl behind the desk nodded. "That's right. Which hall are you looking for?"

This one, thought Rune.

A bad feeling cramped her stomach. But she was already running late. If she didn't leave soon, she wouldn't make it to Gideon's by two o'clock.

"Thank you," she said, backing out the double doors.

Outside, the air had grown colder, the sun hung low in the sky, and thunderous storm clouds were rolling in from over the sea.

Am I losing my mind?

First, the missing blood vial and access coin. Now, a missing Verity?

As Rune ran for the stables, her cloak billowing out behind her, she tried to think.

She'd been to Summer Hall hundreds of times. She could easily picture Verity's room in her mind. The white roses on the wallpaper. Verity's perpetually unmade bed. The towering stacks of used books on the floor, threatening to spill over at any moment.

It couldn't not exist.

Unless it was an illusion.

That thought stopped Rune in her tracks.

She thought of the way Verity was always poring over Rune's spell books, her fingers tracing the symbols.

Was she memorizing them?

She thought of the perfume Verity doused herself in, the scent so strong, it often gave Rune a headache.

What if she douses herself intentionally to cover another scent?

The scent of her magic.

But that would make Verity a witch. And if it was true, why hide herself from Rune, who was *also* a witch?

The sky darkened overhead, and Rune looked up. Storm clouds were rolling in fast.

Her head spun, unable to make sense of it. But Rune was running out of time; she was late to meet Gideon. Once she did, she would head for the palace, where, she hoped, Verity would be waiting with an explanation.

As the rain started to fall, she fetched Lady from the stables, and together they raced toward Old Town.

FIFTY-FIVE

RUNE

GIDEON WAITED FOR HER in the doorway.

Leaving Lady in the rain, which was coming down in sheets, Rune withdrew the boxed flowers from the saddlebag and made a run for it, keeping the hood of her cloak pulled over her hair.

She was grateful for the storm. It would help cover her tracks once she'd gotten Seraphine out of the palace.

As Gideon held open the door for her, Rune stepped, dripping, into the foyer.

"Come in," he said, heading into his parents' shop, where the lights were already on.

His gunpowder smell filled the entryway, bringing a rush of memories swirling through Rune. Memories she did *not* want to relive right now. She pushed them aside and followed him in, letting the door fall shut behind her.

"I can't stay long."

"Somewhere important to be?"

His voice sounded strange. Like someone had wrung out all the emotion, leaving it empty and cold.

"N-no, I . . ."

Where to start? So much had happened since three nights ago. *First: the flowers.*

She held out the box containing the silk flowers he'd made for her. "I came here to return this."

Gideon turned to face her. Stubble shadowed his cheeks, and there were dark circles under his eyes, as if he hadn't slept all night. He stood at the long worktable, and when he didn't reach to take the box, Rune approached and set it down on the wooden surface. She immediately stepped back, putting space between them.

Now: the engagement.

Rune had been dreading this part. She'd gone over the words in her head, trying to find the right way to tell him about her and Alex, but none of them seemed right.

"Can I ask you something, Miss Winters?"

"Of course," said Rune, happy for the interruption, but wondering why he was being so formal.

"Was any of it real?"

"Real?" She frowned. "What do you mean?"

"You. Me. *Us.*" Gideon shoved his hands in his pockets. "What we did three nights ago. Did you mean any of it? Or were you toying with me the whole time?"

Her stomach dipped. What was he talking about?

He withdrew his hands and held out both fists, turning them over. When his hands unfurled, Rune saw what lay on each of his palms.

A vial of blood and an access coin.

How . . . ?

"This is how you manage it," said Gideon, lifting the vial to study it. "It's why you don't have any casting scars."

Rune froze.

He knows what I am.

"Crimson Moth," he breathed as his gaze met hers. "I've finally caught you."

She backed away from him. *Stupid, stupid girl.* This was a trap. She'd not only walked straight into it, *she* set it up!

Turning on her heel, Rune launched herself back through the shop's entrance, into the foyer. As she grabbed the handle of the door leading out onto the street, where Lady waited for her, someone pulled it open from the other side.

Laila Creed stood in the frame. Behind her were half a dozen Blood Guard soldiers, their pistols drawn.

Rune stumbled back. She glanced at the stairs, knowing where they led. If she could get to the top and barricade herself inside Gideon's apartment, she might escape through a window . . .

"Not so fast, *witch.*"

Laila grabbed a fistful of her hair, yanking her backward. Pain pierced Rune's scalp as she hit the floor. Tears stung her eyes as she tried to get up, but every movement only made Laila pull harder. Forcing her to fall still.

Strong hands seized her arms, dragging her inside the shop. The door slammed shut behind them.

The brute whose meaty fingers dug into Rune's arms shoved her forward. She tripped, stumbling to her knees before Gideon—who didn't move to help her.

"I d-don't understand." The cement floor was cold beneath her palms. "H-how did you—"

"I came to Wintersea last night," said Gideon. "Wanting to apologize in person and set the record straight."

Of course. The flowers. It wasn't Lizbeth who left them on her bed. It was Gideon.

"When I arrived, the house was dark, and no servant greeted me. I almost turned around and left, but the sound of voices stopped me. My first thought was that Cressida had come for you. Fearing the worst, I followed the voices."

He heard us plotting to rescue Seraphine, she realized.

"You can imagine my surprise when your bedroom wall opened up before my eyes. I hid myself while you, Verity, and my little brother walked out of your casting room."

That's how he found the vial of blood. While Rune was showing Alex and Verity out, he must have snuck inside the casting room. He would have seen everything: the spell books, the blood vials, the symbols on the floor.

"I'm not sure what disgusts me more," said Gideon. "What you *are*, or that I fell for your act."

Those words stung like a slap.

"Want us to strip her down, Captain?" said the brute behind her.

"He's already looked," said Rune, rising to her knees, her voice quaking with anger. "Haven't you, Gideon? You searched every inch of me three nights ago."

Gideon's face darkened. "There's no need to strip her. I have all the proof I need."

"We should search her at least," said Laila. "She might be armed."

"Fine. Search her." He nodded to a soldier in the foyer. "Her horse is outside. Check the saddlebags."

Rune quailed. The stolen Blood Guard uniform was in her saddlebag.

This is the end, she realized. The evidence mounting against her was too damning.

Laila hauled Rune to her feet, then unclasped her cloak and handed it off. As the meaty one held Rune's arms, Laila crouched down, feeling inside Rune's riding boots with one hand while the other kept her pistol aimed at Rune's face. "No sudden movements."

As Laila's hand moved up one leg, then the other, Rune stared at Gideon. Remembering all over again what he was. A formidable enemy. A boy who wanted girls like her strung up and killed.

He'd been gathering evidence against her from the beginning, waiting for the right moment to bring her down. The gifts. The kisses. The words whispered in the dark between his bedsheets . . .

None of it had meant a thing.

"You are everything I thought you were," she told him.

Laila found the knife strapped to Rune's thigh, pulled it out, and tossed it aside. Gideon watched it go skittering across the floor.

"And you," said Gideon, voice quiet, "are nothing at all like I imagined you'd be."

For someone who'd been hunting her so relentlessly for two years, she would have thought he'd be more triumphant. Gloating and preening. Instead, he looked . . . destroyed.

Laila continued patting Rune's body, never once meeting her gaze. Like Rune was no better than a dog.

"There's nothing else," Rune told her, face burning. "Just the knife."

"I'll be the judge of that," said Laila.

The soldier who'd searched her saddlebags came back inside, approaching Gideon with the stolen Blood Guard uniform in hand. He set the clothes down on the table.

Rune swallowed, watching Gideon's eyes narrow on the uniform, clearly wondering how she'd acquired it.

"What's this?" Laila pressed the cold barrel of her pistol to Rune's chest, tugging at the silver chain hanging there, the bottom of which was hidden below her shirt.

Rune watched as Laila used her gun to lift the ring Alex gave her out from beneath her collar. It dangled in the air, catching the light.

Rune tried to seize it, but her arms were pinned, and Laila

beat her to it. The girl's fist closed around the silver band. She yanked hard, breaking the chain, and handed it over to Gideon.

From the way his jaw clenched, she knew he recognized it immediately.

Rune felt like the world was falling apart around her. This wasn't how she'd wanted him to find out.

"You're *engaged* to him?"

He looked like he'd been punched in the stomach.

"I was going to tell you." Rune pulled one arm free and stepped toward him, her fingers brushing his sleeve. "Gideon . . ."

He flinched away from her, as if she'd burned him. His eyes blackened as they met hers.

"Never touch me again."

Rune shrank back, feeling something wither inside her.

But why should she cower? He was the one who'd tricked her into falling in love with him. He was the one consumed by hate. He was the one handing her over to be slaughtered.

Rune straightened. "That's right. I *am* engaged to him. Your brother is twice the man you'll ever be."

The hurt in his eyes was unmistakable.

"You know what?" Stepping close, he took her hand and shoved the ring back onto her finger. "Keep it."

For some strange reason, the gesture made Rune want to burst into tears.

"We're done here," he said, brushing past her. "Arrest the Crimson Moth."

She watched him walk away, the soldiers parting before him. Watched the door slam as he trod outside, leaving her at the mercy of witch hunters.

As if he couldn't bear to breathe the same air as her for another second.

FIFTY-SIX

GIDEON

GIDEON SMASHED RUNE'S VIAL on the cobbles, watching the rain wash the blood away.

He couldn't stop thinking about his mother's ring on that chain around her neck. A ring he'd given Alex for safekeeping.

Alex had proposed to Rune. And Rune had accepted him.

You are a fucking fool, he told himself as he mounted his horse.

Of course none of it had meant anything. Of course *he* didn't mean anything. Not to her. It was all a game, and though he supposed he'd won in the end, somehow, he'd still come out with nothing.

She'd chosen Alex.

And who wouldn't?

Alex is twice the man you'll ever be.

The words turned Gideon's heart to stone.

Why did it even matter? She was the Crimson Moth—a perpetual thorn in his side for two years now. A fucking *witch*.

He'd been deceived a second time. He'd opened himself up only to be skewered *again*. He'd believed in the girl Rune pretended to be. He'd allowed himself to hope. To think that maybe they could have something beautiful together. Something *good*.

Was there some flaw in Gideon that made him so naive? So susceptible to deception?

He ran a hand across his face, swiping off rain droplets. When Laila had finally secured the witch in restraints, shoving her out of his parents' old shop and dragging her onto a horse, Gideon couldn't bring himself to look at Rune. He stared straight ahead as he led them through the storm to the center of town, toward the purging platform standing in the main square, where Seraphine's execution was soon to take place.

Now, a second witch would join her.

Lightning flashed as they arrived, illuminating the beams of the platform. A crowd had already gathered, waiting for the purgings to start.

Gideon tried to harden his pathetic heart against what came next. He should be celebrating his capture of a notorious criminal. This witch had been his obsession for two years. Hunting her down, putting her to death, seeing justice finally done.

She was the reason he got out of bed every morning.

But now that he had her, and justice was at hand, all he felt was hollow.

"Gideon!"

His brother's voice made his head turn sharply, searching the crowd. He spotted Alex in the distance. Rain plastered his blond hair to his head as he pushed through the bodies.

Gideon swung down from his horse.

"What the hell are you doing?" Alex shouted, drenched with rain.

"What am *I* doing?"

Alex pushed past Gideon, moving for Rune, who was still mounted on Laila's horse. "Let her go."

Gideon grabbed his brother's lapel and swung him back. "Watch yourself, brother. You're on dangerous ground."

Alex glared at him, his normally gentle eyes full of fury. He jabbed his finger in Rune's direction while the crowd hissed and spat at her. "You're perfectly fine with this?"

Keeping himself between his brother and the Crimson Moth, Gideon repeated something Bart Wentholt once said: "Someone has to do the dirty work of protecting you from dangerous witches."

"She's not a dangerous witch!" Alex shouted in his face. "She's an innocent girl!"

"*Innocent?*" Gideon almost laughed. "She's bewitched you, Alex."

She's bewitched us both.

"Would you look at yourself, for once!" Rain ran in rivulets down Alex's face. "This warped sense of justice is destroying you!" He shook his head, sending droplets flying. "You're about to murder the girl I *love*. Don't you see how messed up that is?"

Gideon's hands fisted.

"She's a witch, Alex." His voice was as cold as the gray sky overhead. "Sympathizing with them is an offense punishable by death."

Alex lifted his chin, defiant. "Arrest me, then."

The words landed like a blow. After all these years spent trying to protect Alex, his little brother was throwing Gideon's sacrifices back in his face.

"Don't be a fool," Gideon said. He had an overwhelming urge to grab his little brother and drag him away. Lock him inside some closet until this was all over. Possibly never let him out. For Alex's own sake.

His brother's eyes were bright fire. Staring Gideon down, he shouted loud enough for the entire crowd to hear: "I knew she was the Crimson Moth and I didn't tell you!"

"Alex," Rune interrupted from behind them both. "Don't do this."

Gideon's heart twisted as he watched their eyes meet. Heard the tremble in Rune's voice as she said, "Please, *please* walk away."

"Heed her," said Gideon.

Alex stared at her. "I'm sorry, Rune, if you think I'm going to stand here quietly and watch you die, you're an idiot." Turning his back on both his fiancée and his brother, he addressed the bloodthirsty crowd. "I helped her steal witches from my brother's prison cells! I helped smuggle criminals off this godforsaken island! *I'm guilty!*"

His eyes flashed as he turned back to Gideon. "Now arrest me."

Gideon's jaw clenched. Alex had declared in no uncertain terms that he was an enemy of the Republic. A witch sympathizer.

He knew what he had to do.

But Alex was his little brother, and it was Gideon's job to keep him safe at all costs.

"Captain," Laila said softly. "If you don't, I will."

She held out a set of iron shackles, the chains clinking in the wind. Alex held out his fists, waiting. Daring Gideon to do the unthinkable.

But Gideon had a sworn duty: to root out witches and their sympathizers. To prevent them from ever rising again to wreak their tyranny on the innocent. It was his purpose. His *calling*.

So, with his heart breaking in his chest, Gideon took the cold chains from Laila and locked them around his little brother's wrists.

FIFTY-SEVEN

RUNE

*T*HE WITCH MANACLES RESTED heavily in Rune's lap, the cold iron enclosing her hands from wrist to fingertip, ensuring she couldn't cut herself or draw a spellmark.

Thunder rumbled overhead as she looked out over the crowd. Many of those spitting on her, cursing her, demanding she pay for her crimes with her life, were the same people who'd once sat around her table and danced in her ballroom.

It didn't surprise Rune.

These people had never been her friends.

In one sense, it was a relief. Rune didn't have to pretend anymore. They finally knew what she was. She cared about Alex, though, who now faced certain death. Whose own brother would deliver him to it.

Their gazes caught across the heads of the Blood Guard soldiers between them.

"You should have renounced me," she told him as Laila grabbed her arms and dragged her down from the horse. "You could have saved yourself."

"You can't renounce your own heart," said Alex, stepping toward her, eyes brimming with emotion. He lowered his head, pressing his cheek to her temple.

Before he could do more, Gideon separated them. "Enough."

Rune's gaze skimmed the front of the Blood Guard captain's jacket. The scarlet wool was so soaked with rain, it looked almost black.

Gideon seemed made of stone. Cold and immovable as a mountain.

"It's time," he said, turning her toward the purging platform.

There were two sets of steps, one on each side. As he steered Rune toward the closest ones, she saw someone being led up the other set. A birdlike woman with a cloud of black curls. *Seraphine.* The same iron restraints enclosed her hands.

Rune tried to swallow her fear.

This was always where it was going to end. You sent Nan to the purge, and now you'll follow her.

Thinking she could escape with Alex had been a mistake. Only fools believed in happy endings.

As Gideon guided her to her death, Rune thought of how fitting it was that he should be the one to hand her over. She'd spent two years hating this boy. It seemed appropriate that she should go on hating him until her last drawn breath.

Except even here, at the end, her hate failed her.

Rune knew what witches had done to his family. She knew the horrors he'd suffered at a witch queen's hands. Rune, like a certain witch before her, had toyed with Gideon. Deceived and betrayed him. He had every reason to believe that all witches were the same: horribly cruel and unspeakably evil.

So how could she hate him?

Especially with his hand pressed to the small of her back. Even in his anger, he was tender with her. Stoic Gideon—so firm in his conviction, so diligent in his duty—was reluctant. *Conflicted.* She felt it in the gentle press of his palm.

Rune remembered the last words Nan had spoken before

the knife slashed her throat. *I love you,* she'd whispered, while staring at Rune in the crowd below.

Rune swallowed the lump in her throat and glanced up at the boy beside her.

I forgive you, she thought. Perhaps that made her a fool, but what did that matter, if this was the end?

In forgiving him, a strange thing happened: Rune found forgiveness for herself, too. For what she'd done to Nan.

The thing she'd needed all this time was right there inside her.

Gideon didn't look at her as he handed her to the four Blood Guard soldiers waiting to secure her ankles in chains. Chains that would raise her upside down to be slaughtered. The steady warmth of his palm disappeared from her back as he turned to walk away.

"Gideon."

He flinched and stopped, but didn't look back.

"I'm sorry," she said. "I'm so sorry for all of it."

Finally, he glanced at her, and the wounded look on his face pierced like a knife.

Above the heavy plink of the rain, she heard him say, "So am I."

He strode off as the cold iron bit her bare ankles, and the locks clicked into place.

FIFTY-EIGHT

RUNE

SERAPHINE AND RUNE STOOD side by side now. The crank tightened their chains, preparing to lift them feet-first toward the sky, baring their throats to the purging knife.

Seraphine's dark eyes narrowed on Rune. But instead of being surprised that Rune was a witch, she said: "Why did you inform on Kestrel?"

Tears fell as the inevitability of it all sank in. "Someone betrayed us. The Blood Guard would have killed us both: Nan, for being a witch; me, for not handing her in. She told me if I loved her, I had to betray her. So she wouldn't have to watch me die."

Seraphine's forehead creased, almost delicately.

Lightning flashed, and the charge in the air raised the hair on Rune's skin.

"Nan told me to find you. I came to your house the night they arrested you. I spent two years tracking you down and got there too late."

What would have happened if she'd arrived an hour earlier? Would either of them be here, awaiting the knife?

"I failed both of you."

Seraphine's gaze sharpened.

"No," she said, her irises flaring strangely as something in the distance caught her attention. "I don't think you have."

Light flickered at the edge of Rune's vision. When she looked up, four black fiery comets hit the platform like cannonballs, aimed directly at the guards on either side of her and Seraphine. Rune heard the thud of their bodies hitting the wood.

All around them, the platform burned. Despite the rain, heat sizzled in the air. More fireballs hit, striking the wooden beam overhead. Rune covered her head with her manacled hands, but knew it was of little use. She and Seraphine were completely exposed.

Something *cracked* and Rune looked up to see the beam directly overhead start to split.

Then fall.

As the heavy timber descended on them, Seraphine dived at Rune, knocking her out of the way. The beam crashed through the platform floor right where they'd both been standing.

Seraphine pushed herself up. "Are you all right?"

Rune nodded.

It smelled like burning flesh and . . . something else.

Blood and roses, she thought.

Magic.

Rune had smelled this same scent once before, on the night of the Luminaries Dinner. It rolled over her like a wave.

Someone in the crowd screamed.

As more screams joined the first, Seraphine flew to the wooden rail at the edge of the platform, leaning as far as the chains around her ankles would let her. Rune was about to push herself to her feet, when her stomach cramped. Like a warm, achy swell in her lower belly.

That ache. She spent the better part of every month waiting for it.

As something warm and wet pooled between her thighs, a rush of relief came over Rune.

Her monthly cycle had started.

Fresh blood to cast with . . .

Except she had no way to use it. Her hands were trapped in iron. Wondering why no soldiers were coming to simply kill them and get it over with, Rune pushed to her feet, joining Seraphine at the wooden rail, scanning the platform.

"Merciful Ancients," murmured Seraphine.

Dozens of figures cloaked in gray were sweeping across the city square, heading for the platform. The scarlet uniforms of the Blood Guard were cutting toward them, while the crowd in between swelled. Chaos erupted. Citizens tried to scatter, screaming and pushing, trying to get out of the way.

Beneath the dark sky, thunder rumbled dangerously as gunfire rang through the air.

Rune squinted, trying to see the faces beneath the gray hoods. "Who are they?"

"Witches," said Seraphine.

Rune's heart skipped at that word. She squinted harder, realizing she recognized some of the girls beneath the hoods. Witches she'd rescued from Gideon's clutches. Most she didn't know at all. But leading them was a girl she knew by heart.

Verity de Wilde.

Her spectacles flashed when the lightning flickered, and her brown ringlets were loose around her shoulders. In her hand was a knife Rune had never seen before. One shaped like a crescent.

"Cressida Roseblood is alive . . ." Seraphine's eyes narrowed. ". . . and has somehow gained a witch army."

"That's not Cressida." Rune corrected her. "That's my friend Verity."

Rune had met Cressida. Verity and the youngest witch queen looked nothing alike.

"I assure you," said Seraphine, "that girl is a Roseblood. She's simply altered her appearance."

Rune frowned, forced to recall Verity's missing dorm room. Her endless exhaustion. Her heavily perfumed scent.

Was it all one elaborate illusion?

The magnitude of it—endlessly pretending to be someone else for two years straight—would require a lot of power.

And a lot of fresh blood.

A terrible feeling was taking hold of Rune.

Verity had reacted almost defensively when questioned about the Roseblood sisters using Arcana spells. And Verity had been at the Luminaries Dinner the night Cressida Roseblood was also in attendance. What if Verity was responsible for the spellfire?

What if Verity de Wilde *was* Cressida Roseblood in disguise?

"I'm sorry," said Seraphine. "But your friend Verity doesn't exist. Or if she did, she doesn't anymore."

"Are you saying Cressida *killed* Verity and stole her identity?"

"It's very likely, yes."

"But that means . . ."

Cressida Roseblood, not Verity de Wilde, had been Rune's closest confidant for two years—without her knowing.

This whole time, Rune had trusted and confided in a *murderer*. In the girl who'd tortured Gideon and killed his little sister.

She rested her restrained hands on the wood railing to steady herself.

It can't be true.

Verity was her friend.

But Rune had only become friends with Verity in the months

after the revolution. By then, Cressida was dethroned and on the run. That left plenty of time to kill the girl and subsume her identity *before* befriending Rune.

The thought of Verity—the real Verity, a girl Rune was forced to concede she didn't know at all—being cornered by the witch queen made Rune feel like she was going to throw up.

How could I have missed the signs?

Rune watched the girl cutting through the crowd with a small army of witches in her wake. Despite her horror and loathing, that girl was the closest thing she and Seraphine had to an ally right now.

Everyone else in that crowd wanted them dead.

Rune remembered the countless times Verity—*no, Cressida*—had absently traced the spellmarks on the open pages of her spell books. If she'd been memorizing all of Rune's spells, then she likely knew the one that would set Rune and Seraphine's hands free.

Picklock.

Leaning as far as she could over the railing, Rune's voice battled with the thunder as she shouted: "My Queen!"

The girl who'd stolen Verity's identity glanced up, her gaze swooping like a hawk to Rune.

As smoke filled the air, Rune raised her ironclad hands.

"A little help?"

The witch queen smiled, and Rune shivered at the sight. Holding out her pale forearm, which was covered in bloody spellmarks, she smudged the symbols with her hand.

The illusion fell away.

She was Verity no longer.

That curly brown hair straightened, lightening to moon-white. Her dark eyes turned crystalline blue. And the curves of her body fell away, flattening and lengthening into the wispy queen Rune remembered.

Snatching a young woman from the crowd, Cressida pulled back the girl's hair. As her victim screamed and fought, trying to get away, Cressida bared the girl's pale throat to her knife's crescent edge, and slit it.

Rune glanced away too late to unsee the red blood, running like rivulets down her neck. The girl dropped to the stones, choking on it. Cressida dipped her fingers in the blood and drew a new symbol.

The spell flared to life. The locks of Rune and Seraphine's manacles clicked. The heavy iron blocks imprisoning their hands opened, along with the chains around their ankles. Both fell, hitting the burning platform with a clattering thud.

Rune and Seraphine were free.

FIFTY-NINE

GIDEON

*T*HE CROWD ERUPTED AROUND Gideon. Everywhere he looked, people screamed and pushed, trying to get out of the square and away from the witches descending on them. Gideon leaned into the jostle and crush, drawing his pistol.

Witches outnumbered his soldiers. The spellfire had killed the Blood Guard soldiers on the platform, leaving only those on the ground. There were enough left to handle a purging, but not a full-on attack. And the furious sound of gunfire cracking across the square meant the witches were armed.

His soldiers were outnumbered *and* outgunned.

Gideon had known Cressida was planning something. He should have prepared for this. He should have been ready for anything.

The crowd scattered and thinned, leaving only the witches—dozens of them, cloaked in gray. They advanced, moving like a synchronized unit. Those in front fired and fell back to reload, while those behind stepped forward to cover them.

Crack crack crack!

Bullets whizzed past Gideon. He returned their fire, calling for the Blood Guard to fall back to the purging platform, whose wooden frame—now going up in flames—could be used to take cover.

Gideon kept firing as they followed his commands. All except Laila, who stood shooting alongside him.

"Go," he told her.

She ignored him, her pistol smoking. "Some of those girls are the witches we captured."

Gideon nodded. The very ones Rune set free, with the help of his brother.

"And the witch leading them . . ."

Gideon shuddered. *Cressida.* The girl from his nightmares was here, in the flesh. He didn't want to think about what that would mean. If they lost this fight . . .

Suddenly, the witches halted. Their firing stopped and silence rang out through the square.

"Gideon Sharpe!" Cressida shouted. "Tell your dogs to stand down!"

Her voice sent a lightning-like jolt down Gideon's legs, unbalancing him.

He and Laila both stopped firing. But they kept their guns raised. When the Blood Guard behind them did the same, Cressida stepped forward, out of the formation, with another witch at her side.

The second witch dragged someone along by the collar. Her captive stumbled. His face was so bloodied and bruised that Gideon didn't recognize him at first.

"Papa!" Laila cried out.

Gideon looked closer. It *was* Nicolas Creed. The man who'd picked him up from the alley stones behind the boxing ring; the man who'd taught Gideon how to fight back.

How did she capture him?

The Good Commander was heavily guarded at all times.

But if Cress could disguise herself as Verity, she could disguise herself as anyone. One of Nicolas's most devoted soldiers, perhaps. His wife, or one of his children. He wouldn't have stood a chance.

The witch threw the Good Commander to the ground at Cressida's feet.

Laila lowered her gun and stepped forward. Gideon's arm shot out to stop her.

"Keep your head," he said. "It's the only way to help him now."

Laila swallowed, nodding, and fell back beside Gideon, her eyes trained on her father.

Cressida sheathed her cutting knife—a crescent-shaped blade Gideon knew too well—and drew out a pistol. Stepping forward, she pressed the barrel to Nicolas's temple. Bright red blood stained her fingers, and all down one scarred arm were faded spellmarks.

Her sharp gaze focused on Gideon. "Tell your soldiers to disarm themselves and pile their weapons here." She nodded to a spot several feet in front of her. "Then bring me Rune Winters and Seraphine Oakes. Do it now, or I'll kill him."

Nicolas knelt on the ground, his hands bound behind his back. The Commander raised his eyes to them, one of which was swollen shut.

Laila's grip tightened on her pistol.

Nicolas's gaze held Gideon's. "Do not obey her. Do not stand down."

Cressida pressed the barrel harder into his temple. Her dark eyes flashed. "Bring me the weapons, Gideon."

"Remember what it was like when we lived at their mercy."

Cressida looked sharply down, staring at her quarry. "Nicolas," she crooned softly. *Deceptively.* Gideon knew that voice. His senses heightened, morphing into fear. "Stop talking."

"Commander," he warned. "Respectfully, I think you should do as she says."

Nicolas glanced from Gideon to Laila and back. They may have beaten his body, but his spirit was fully intact. He looked not resigned, but resolved. "Think of what she will do to the ones you love. Think of what she will do to *you*. Do you want to live like that again? Or do you—"

A shot rang out.

Gideon flinched.

Laila sucked in a breath.

Silence bled through the square as the Commander's body tipped slowly forward, collapsing in a heap. His eyes were blank as they stared at Gideon.

A cold numbness spread through Gideon's chest. He stared at his mentor—a man who'd been like a father to him—now dead on the stones.

"That's enough of that," said Cressida.

"Papa . . ."

Laila moved, forcing Gideon to move, too. Sheathing his pistol, he grabbed her hard around the middle, stopping her from going anywhere near the witch.

"I'll kill you. I'll kill you!" Laila bucked against him. "Let me go, Gideon!!"

Gideon wrestled the gun out of her hand and threw it on the ground in front of Cressida. His arms pinned Laila against his chest, immobilizing her.

"Let me go let me go let me go . . ."

She was weeping now. Begging. Gideon held on tighter. This wasn't the Laila he knew. Laila was tough. Resilient. Indestructible.

He couldn't let Cressida break her, too.

"Keep your head," he said again, fury bunching his chest. He wasn't sure if he was speaking the words to Laila, or himself. "It's what your father would want you to do."

This was why the revolution had needed to happen. It was why Gideon became a witch hunter. To never again be at their mercy. To ensure none of them returned to power.

"Gideon?"

Gideon looked to find Alex standing next to him. His brother's wrists were free of shackles, and his hands held out the coat of a Blood Guard officer, swooped like a basket. Inside were the guns of Gideon's soldiers. Alex was collecting them for the witch queen.

Rune and Seraphine stood beside him.

There was an unspoken apology in Alex's eyes as he held out the coat, waiting for Gideon to add his pistol to the pile. Gideon wanted to spit on his apology. Alex had clearly lied about killing the youngest Roseblood sister on the night of the revolution. It made him wonder how far back his brother's involvement in this conspiracy went.

Alex was as complicit as Rune.

Gideon released Laila, who fell to her knees weeping, then dropped his gun in with the rest.

"You don't know what you've done."

Alex said nothing. Only turned to deliver the guns, followed by Rune and Seraphine. Gideon watched his brother lay the weapons at Cressida's feet. Watched the smile spread across her lips. It was the smile from his nightmares. The smile of someone who knew the power they wielded over you, and wanted you to know it, too.

The smile of a monster back from the dead.

Cressida lifted her pistol, this time pointing it directly at *him*.

"One more thing," she said. "You're coming with us, Gideon."

He almost laughed. "No, thank you. I'd rather be dead."

That smile slid away.

"Would you rather *her* be dead?" She pointed the gun at Laila, who was still on her knees.

Gideon stepped in front of Laila, shielding her from the bullet. "You'll find there are a lot of us who'd choose death over cowering before you again, Cress."

Her eyes narrowed.

"Fair enough," she said, aiming her pistol at his chest.

Gideon waited for the bullet. Welcoming it. He hoped death would come swiftly.

Except the bullet never came.

When the gun went off, his brother stepped in front of it.

SIXTY

GIDEON

"𝒩O!"

Alex staggered back at the impact. Gideon heard Rune scream. Alex swayed and turned to look at his brother.

Their eyes met.

The blood was already blooming across his chest.

"No no no . . ."

The entire square disappeared as Alex came into sharp focus. His chin tipped downward to look at the red stain soaking quickly through his white shirt. He touched it with his fingers, realization dawning.

Gideon started toward his little brother. Needing to catch him before he fell. Before his eyes went as blank as Nicolas's.

Please, no. You're all I have left . . .

SIXTY-ONE

RUNE

A SCREAM TORE OUT OF Rune's throat as she watched Cressida raise the gun and pull the trigger. She'd been so consumed by Gideon in the line of fire that she hadn't seen Alex step forward until it was too late.

"ALEX!" Gideon bellowed.

Rune felt her heart fall out of her chest.

This was a living nightmare.

Gideon was already moving toward his brother. But Rune was much closer. When Alex's legs buckled beneath him, it was Rune who was there to catch him.

Her arms clasped around his waist, sinking beneath his weight. His eyes fixed on her face as the blood seeped through his shirt, the stain growing wider by the second.

"Rune," he whispered as she lowered him to the ground. "Do me a favor? Tell my brother I love him."

Her eyes burned. She shook her head, cradling him against her. "You can tell him yourself."

The sudden sound of guns going off, of bullets whizzing overhead, made Rune look up. She heard shouting and boots thudding in unison. Saw a sea of red uniforms flood the square.

The Blood Guard army had arrived. Alongside trained soldiers marched average citizens, advancing toward the witches.

There had to be thousands of them. Merchants and dockwork-ers. Mothers and sons. Patriots who would rather risk their lives than see the Reign of Witches resurrected.

They were swarming the square. Surrounding the witches.

We're done for.

Rune glanced at Cressida, whose face had gone white, her mouth a grim line.

"What's happening?" asked Alex.

"This is the end," said Rune. "It's all over."

Alex lifted his hand to her face, bringing her attention back to him.

"I want you to do one last thing for me."

Rune pulled him tighter, closer. As if her embrace alone could stem Death's tide. "Hush. Don't tax yourself." She would hold on to him until they killed her and pried him out of her cold, lifeless arms.

He lifted his other hand toward her, cradling her face now as warm blood seeped out of his chest wound, soaking Rune's clothes and pooling onto the stones. "I don't have long. But you . . . you have a whole life ahead of you. *Rune.* I want you to live it."

She closed her eyes. "It doesn't matter now." She lowered her lips to his hair. Even if they could survive this, she'd lost every-thing. Everyone knew what she was. Gideon wanted her dead. And now Alex . . .

"I'm begging you, Rune. Save yourself."

She shook her head. The acrid smell of gunpowder burned in the air once more. Any moment, the Blood Guard would start picking them off one by one. Cressida was powerful, but she couldn't single-handedly stop an army aided by thousands of determined patriots.

With her eyes still closed, Alex took her hand in his and

pressed her palm to his chest, where the bullet had gone in. His blood was warm and wet beneath her skin.

"I'm giving you permission."

Her eyes fluttered open. *What?*

"You've only ever cast small spells and illusions because you've never had enough fresh blood to do more."

Her brows knit. "What are you saying?"

"Use *my* blood. I won't require it much longer." He smiled, a little sadly. "Take as much of it as you need."

"I . . . I can't." But she could, and they both knew it. Magic only corrupted a witch if blood was taken against someone's will. "Even if I could, what would be the point?"

His eyes dimmed.

"The point is to live," he said, tucking a strand of her hair behind her ear. "The point is to let me give you this one small thing, because I couldn't give you the rest."

Rune touched her forehead to his, her chin quivering.

"Promise me my death isn't for nothing, Rune. Tell me you'll use it to save yourself."

She shook her head no.

"Please."

Rune squeezed her eyes shut, knowing it was selfish to refuse him. If their positions were reversed, she'd be begging him to do the same.

If she was going to lose him, she could give him this one last thing. Couldn't she?

"All right." Her voice shook. Tears dripped. *"I promise."*

With his hand in her hair, Alex pulled her mouth down to his, kissing her one last time.

Rune kissed back, that small spark flickering inside her. A spark that would never get the chance to grow into a steady flame.

She kissed him until his chest fell and didn't rise again beneath her palm. Until his last breath died on her lips.

When she pulled away, his golden eyes were calm as a glassy sea. Reflecting the stormy sky overhead.

Alex was gone.

A sob surged from her depths. She wanted to stay weeping over him. To lie down beside him until death came for her, too.

It was the promise she'd made him that stopped her. She couldn't break it.

The world spun like she'd stepped into the eye of a hurricane. The air smelled of blood and smoke, magic and gunshots. As Rune recalled the pages of her grandmother's spell books, the shouting soldiers and cracking pistols seemed to go quiet and still.

She'd skimmed through so many spells over the years, most of which she couldn't cast because she didn't have the blood required.

Now she did.

She needed to make the most of it.

Save yourself, Alex's voice echoed in her mind.

As his body grew cold beneath her hand, Rune let his words guide her. She recalled the last spell book she'd opened, remembering a spell too powerful for a witch like her to cast.

Earth Sunderer.

The seven golden marks flared to life inside her mind.

With Alex still in her arms, she lifted her hand from his blood and started to draw on the stone slabs around them. It shouldn't have been possible to remember them so clearly, but she did. She traced each mark into the ground, her hand guided by something nameless. Ancient. That familiar roar crashed in her ears. Brine bloomed on her tongue. That powerful wave was swelling, only this time, Rune was swelling with it. Her fingers moved as if possessed, the magic itself guiding her.

It seemed impossible that she could recall all seven marks perfectly. And yet, the moment she finished one, she started on the next.

Is this what being a witch is supposed to feel like?

Good. Easy. *Right.*

With an immense amount of fresh blood, nothing held her back. That ocean inside Rune wasn't happening *to* her; it *was* her. She and the magic were one.

When she finished the last line of the final mark, encasing both her and Alex in a circle of glowing white symbols, her bloody fingers lifted from the earth. As they did, that thunderous wave crashed, shuddering through her, bursting out of her as the ground shook and an earsplitting roar tore the world in two.

SIXTY-TWO

GIDEON

GIDEON WATCHED HIS BROTHER collapse. Watched Rune catch him and sink to the ground beneath his weight. Watched Alex cradle Rune's face in his hands, and Rune lean down to kiss him.

And that's when Gideon's steps faltered.

Because Alex didn't want Gideon at his side. He wanted *her* there.

When he heard Rune's heart-shattering sob, he knew his brother was gone.

His throat constricted. *No . . .*

Alex was dead. Killed by a bullet meant for Gideon.

All the color seemed to drain from the world.

I didn't get to say goodbye.

He fell to his knees, hands fisting in the stones. He pressed his forehead to his fists, his whole body shaking at the loss of the last person he had left. A ragged cry ripped through him, tearing out of his throat.

Is this my lot? To fail everyone I love?

A sudden BOOM! resounded through the square. Gideon lifted his head to find the world gone dark. As if someone had swallowed the sun. He heard the cracking before he felt it: the earth quaking. Rising and falling beneath his feet. Like an unruly sea.

The metallic tang of blood magic spread through the air, mingling with another scent. Salt. Like the sea.

Gideon tried to rise, but kept losing his balance.

When the sunlight returned, he found a black chasm widening in front of him, separating him from his brother's body, and into the void poured the ocean. Protecting the witches from those coming to kill them. Tearing the town square in half.

The ground continued to shake, forcing Gideon to step away from the edge, lest the shuddering earth thrust him over. As white waves churned, rushing to fill the gap, the dust from the earthquake rose into the air, turning it gray. His brother disappeared behind it.

Gideon turned to the surrounding chaos. Looking for Laila or Harrow—whose voice he now heard, barking orders. Hoping neither of them were near that widening chasm. If they were, they'd be swallowed.

When he glanced back, he found Cressida staring at him from the other side. Through the gray. Seraphine stood at her left. Rune, at her right.

Cressida's pale eyes narrowed on Gideon, and he knew this was far from over.

The witch queen retreated. Her movement caused the dust to swirl, concealing her behind it. Seraphine followed, leaving only Rune, whose sorrowful gaze locked with Gideon's until the dust cloud swallowed her, too.

His hands curled into fists.

"I will never stop hunting you, Rune Winters. No matter where you go, I will come for you."

In her absence, Gideon saw something flutter in the air above the chasm. Small and red and delicate, its wings shimmering in the gloom.

A crimson moth.

Gideon's heart hardened at the sight of it.

ENTR'ACTE

RUNE

*R*UNE STARED OUT OVER the sparkling sea, watching the broken island in the distance grow smaller and smaller. She felt like a stranger in her own body. Everything that made her *Rune Winters* was on that island—or had been—and she was sailing away from it.

As the gulls cawed overhead and the sails snapped in the wind, she listed off all the things she'd lost:

Wintersea, her home.

Lady, her loyal horse.

Alex, her beloved friend.

Rune swallowed, remembering him in those last moments. Gazing up at her, full of love and trust.

He would never finish his studies now, nor write another song. His music would no longer fill any halls, luring Rune to him. She would never again step into his arms and know she was safe. Never sit beside him at the opera, or the symphony. Never stroll the streets of Caelis at his side.

He was gone.

Rune felt broken beneath the weight of his absence. Their dreams of a new life were scattered to the corners of the earth, never to be put back together.

A sound from behind made her glance away from the porthole.

Across the cabin of Rune's cargo ship, Cressida sat at a table with several other witches, planning their next move. Rune watched Cressida stand up and lean over the map spread across the table, pressing her fingertip to some point Rune couldn't see. As she moved, the botanical scars snaking down her arms shimmered silver in the candlelight.

It was painful to look at her.

For two years, Rune had trusted the girl across the cabin with her life, believing she was Verity de Wilde. It made her dizzy to think that the entire time, her best friend hadn't been a scholarship student, but a murderess.

What are we to each other now?

And what would Cressida expect from Rune when they landed on the Continent?

This whole time, Rune had been unwittingly saving witches for Cressida's army. And now that they knew the heir to the Roseblood line was alive, more witches were flocking to her. Rune's cargo ship was sailing to Caelis, where the witch queen would bolster her army and prepare to take back what was stolen from them all—ushering in a new Reign of Witches.

Rune was no fan of the New Republic, where her life was now forfeit. But neither did she want to return to what had come before the regime. She knew what Cressida was capable of and had no interest in swapping one evil for another.

But she had nowhere else to go. She couldn't return home, where the Blood Guard waited to kill her. And with Alex gone, there was nothing waiting for her ahead.

Someone cleared their throat beside Rune, yanking her out of her thoughts. She turned away from the porthole and found Seraphine, her thin hands cupped around a mug of steaming tea.

"If you can tear a city in half," said Seraphine, "she'll want to know what else you're capable of. In case you can be of use to her."

Rune recoiled at the thought. "I have no intention of being useful to her."

Seraphine shot her a look. "It's better to be useful than to be dead."

Rune considered the young woman beside her, sipping her tea. Peeking up from Seraphine's lace collar was the hint of a silver casting scar carved into her umber skin. But Rune couldn't make out the pattern. Feathers, maybe.

A bird?

Nan's voice suddenly appeared in Rune's mind: *Darling, find Seraphine Oakes.*

Rune had been so busy trying to accomplish the first part of Nan's request, she'd never given thought to the second.

She'll tell you everything I couldn't.

"She wanted you to train me," said Rune. If she had any hope of surviving what came next, she would need as much help as she could get.

"Who?"

"My grandmother."

Seraphine's thin brows shot toward her forehead. "Did she, now?"

"I think it's why she asked me to find you. I think, somehow, she knew I was a witch."

Beside her, Seraphine's chest rose and fell with a sigh as she lowered her mug.

"You have a lot of catching up to do," she said, looking Rune up and down.

Rune was about to say she wasn't afraid to work hard, that she was determined to learn as much as she could, when Cressida glanced up, catching her gaze.

A chill dug into the base of her spine.

There was something insatiable in the witch queen's expression.

It was the look of a predator. Someone capable of killing innocent Verity de Wilde and subsuming her identity so perfectly, no one noticed. Someone capable of ensnaring brave Gideon Sharpe, then breaking his spirit into a million fractured pieces.

Gideon.

Rune had been desperately trying not to think of him.

She tore her gaze away from Cressida, unable to deny the Gideon-shaped hole in her chest—like a bullet wound.

He walked in her dreams every night. Those dark eyes filling with hate, penetrating straight to her heart. His stern mouth cursing her name, swearing to hunt her down. When she woke, her cheeks were wet from weeping in her sleep. Crying out for him and the life—the *partnership*—she'd been deluded into thinking he wanted with her.

Rune had to remind herself, every time, that they were mortal enemies. That their hatred for each other was what wove them together—not love or affection. And *this* was why it felt so wrong to have an ocean between them: the Blood Guard captain had been hunting the Crimson Moth for so long, she felt lost without him trailing her.

Gideon was her perfect rival; a deadly enemy to outwit. Without him, Rune could only be half of her full potential. It was why, deep down, she *wanted* him to come for her. She ached for the challenge of him. She needed to finish what lay unfinished between them.

Turning back to the porthole, Rune stared out at the cold sea. She didn't know what lay on the horizon; the future was shrouded in mist.

Only one thing was certain.

Gideon would come for her, and when he did, Rune would be ready.

ACKNOWLEDGMENTS

First of all: thank you to Baroness Orczy for giving us *The Scarlet Pimpernel,* a story that has lived in my imagination since childhood and (loosely) inspired this one.

Special thanks to Danielle Burby, for believing in this story *so hard* and always setting the bar so high.

Thanks to Vicki Lame for taking a chance on this when it was just an idea and helping me turn it into a Real Book. And to the team at Wednesday Books for being so darn amazing: Vanessa Aguirre, Sara Goodman, Eileen Rothschild, Kerri Resnick, Alexis Neuville, Austin Adams, Brant Janeway, Alyssa Gammello, Chris Leonowicz, Eric Meyer, Cassie Gutman, and Martha Cipolla.

Thanks to Taryn Fagerness, for giving this witch and her hunter wings to fly across the world.

Thanks, Elizabeth Vaziri and Ajebowale Roberts, for championing this book, and the entire team at Magpie for bringing it to UK readers.

Tanaz, Jo, Rosaria, and Eloise: for reading early drafts and giving me razor-sharp feedback. Thanks also to Emily and Whitney for speedy proofreading!

Canada Council for the Arts: thank you for funding this project. It's easy to talk the talk, but you folks truly walk the walk when it comes to supporting women artists and working mothers. My endless thanks to all of you.

Extra-special thanks to Jolene, Dad, Mum, Art, and Myrna for watching the baby while I wrote this book. I could not be both a mother and a writer without your tremendous help.

Sibyl, thanks for changing my life for the better.

Last (and best) of all, Joe: for doing the laundry, making the meals, reading the drafts, building me a writing shed, and doing this wild and precious thing called life alongside me. I love you, comrade.